CUSTOMER SERVICE EXCELLENCE

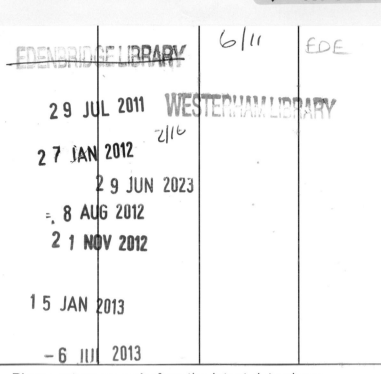

Libraries & Archives

00884\DTP\RN\07.07   LIB 7

Lisa Gardner sold her first novel when she was twenty years old and has since been published in over a dozen countries. She graduated magna cum laude from the University of Pennsylvania with a degree in international relations. Now living in New England with her family, she spends her time writing, travelling and hiking.

Her previous novels, include, *Gone, Hide, Say Goodbye* and *The Neighbour*.

Visit her website at www.lisagardner.com

LIVE TO TELL

In Boston, four members of a family have been brutally murdered. The father is now in intensive care — a possible suspect. Murder-suicide? Or something worse? Police detective D.D. Warren knows there's more to this case. Danielle Burton is a dedicated children's nurse in a locked-down paediatric psych ward. But she's haunted by the family tragedy that shattered her life twenty-five years ago. The dark anniversary is approaching, and when D.D. Warren and her partner show up at the facility, Danielle realizes: it has started again. A devoted mother, Victoria Oliver will do anything to ensure that her troubled son has some semblance of a childhood. She will love him no matter what — keep him safe — even when the threat comes from within her own house.

Books by Lisa Gardner
Published by The House of Ulverscroft:

THE NEXT ACCIDENT
THE SURVIVORS CLUB
THE KILLING HOUR
ALONE
GONE
HIDE
SAY GOODBYE
THE NEIGHBOUR

LISA GARDNER

LIVE TO TELL

Complete and Unabridged

CHARNWOOD
Leicester

First published in Great Britain in 2010 by
Orion Books, an imprint of
The Orion Publishing Group Ltd., London

First Charnwood Edition
published 2011
by arrangement with
The Orion Publishing Group Ltd.
An Hachette UK Company, London

British Library CIP Data

Gardner, Lisa.
 Live to tell.
 1. Warren, D. D. (Fictitious character)- -Fiction.
 2. Police- -Massachusetts- -Boston- -Fiction.
 3. Family violence- -Fiction. 4. Suspense fiction.
 5. Large type books.
 I. Title
 813.6–dc22

 ISBN 978–1–4448–0722–6

Published by
A. Thorpe (Publishing)
Anstey, Leicestershire

Set by Words & Graphics Ltd.
Anstey, Leicestershire
Printed and bound in Great Britain by
T. J. International Ltd., Padstow, Cornwall

This book is printed on acid-free paper

Prologue

DANIELLE

I don't remember that night much anymore. In the beginning, it seems like you'll never forget. But time is a nebulous thing, especially for a child. And year by year, bit by bit, details started to fade from my memory. Coping skills, Dr. Frank assured me. The natural evolution of my psyche starting to heal. Nothing to feel guilty about.

But of course, I do.

I remember waking up to a scream. Maybe my mother's, but according to the police report, most likely my sister's. It was dark in my room. I was disoriented, couldn't see. And there was a smell in the air. That's what I remember most clearly after all these years. A smoky odor I thought might be from a fire, but was actually cordite, drifting down the hall.

More noises. Things I could hear but not see: pounding footsteps, the thud of a body falling down the stairs. Then my father's voice, booming from outside my bedroom door.

'Oh Danny girl. My pretty, pretty Danny girl.'

My door opened. A bright glowing rectangle amidst a field of black. My father's shadow, looming in the doorway.

'Danny girl,' he sang more brightly. 'My pretty, pretty Danny girl.'

1

Then he tapped the gun against his forehead and pulled the trigger.

* * *

I'm not sure what happened immediately after that. Did I get out of bed? Did I dial 911? Did I try to revive my mother, or maybe stop the blood pouring from my sister's shattered head or my brother's broken body?

I remember another man walking into my room. He spoke in a soothing voice, told me everything was okay now, I was safe. He picked me up in his arms, though I was nine years old and too big to be treated like a baby. He told me to close my eyes. He told me not to look.

I nodded against his shoulder, but of course I kept my eyes open.

I had to see. I had to record. I had to remember. It is the duty of the lone survivor.

* * *

According to the police report, my father was drunk that night. He'd consumed at least a fifth of whiskey before loading his service revolver. He'd lost his job with the sheriff's department the week before — after being reprimanded twice for showing up for work in a less-than-sober state. Sheriff Wayne, the man who carried me out of the house, had hoped the termination would force my father to clean up his act, maybe join AA. I guess my father had other ideas.

He started in the bedroom, catching my mother next to her bed. Then he moved on to my thirteen-year-old sister, who'd stuck her head out of her room, probably to see what was going on. My eleven-year-old brother also appeared in the hallway. He tried to run for it. My father shot him in the back, and Johnny fell down the stairs. It wasn't a clean shot and it took Johnny a while to die.

I don't remember this, of course. But I read the official report on my eighteenth birthday.

I was looking for an answer that I've never found.

My father killed my entire family except me. Did that mean he loved me the most, or hated me the most?

'What do you think?' Dr. Frank always replied.

I think this is the story of my life.

★ ★ ★

I wish I could tell you the color of my mother's eyes. I know logically they were blue, because after my family died, I went to live with Aunt Helen, my mother's sister. Aunt Helen's are blue, and judging by the photos I have left, she and my mother were spitting images of each other.

Except that's the problem. Aunt Helen looks so much like my mother that over the years, she's become my mother. I see Aunt Helen's eyes in my mind. I hear her voice, feel her hands tucking me in at night. And I ache because I want my mother back. But she's gone from me, my traitorous memory killing her more effectively than my father did, so that I was driven to look up police reports and crime-scene photos, and now the only image I have of my mom is a curiously slack face staring up at the camera with a hole in the middle of her forehead.

I have photos of Natalie and Johnny and me sitting on a porch, our arms around one another. We look very happy, but I can't remember anymore if my siblings teased me or tolerated me. Did they ever guess that one night they would die, while I would get to live? Did they ever imagine, on that sunny afternoon, that none of their dreams would come true?

'Survivor's guilt,' Dr. Frank would remind me gently. 'None of this is your fault.'

The story of my life.

⋆ ⋆ ⋆

Aunt Helen did right by me. She was over forty and childless, a corporate lawyer married to her job, when I came to live with her. She had a one-bedroom condo in downtown Boston, so for the first year, I slept on the couch. That was okay, because for the first year, I didn't sleep anyway, so she and I would stay up all night, watching reruns of *I Love Lucy*, and trying not to think of what had happened one week ago, then one month ago, then one year ago.

It's a kind of countdown, except you never get any closer to a destination. Each day sucks as much as the one before. You simply start to accept the general suckiness.

Aunt Helen found Dr. Frank for me. She enrolled me in a private school where the small class size meant I got constant supervision and lots of one-on-one care. I couldn't read the first two years. I couldn't process letters, couldn't remember how to count. I got out of bed each day, and that took so much energy, I couldn't do much else. I didn't make friends. I didn't look teachers in the eye.

I sat, day after day, trying so hard to remember each detail, my mother's eyes, my sister's scream, my brother's goofy grin, I had no room in my head for anything else.

Then one day when I was walking down the street, I saw a man lean over and kiss his little girl on top of the head. A random moment of fatherly tenderness. His daughter looked up at him, and her round little face lit into a million-watt smile.

And my heart broke, just like that.

I started to cry, sobbing incoherently through the streets of Boston as I stumbled my way back to my aunt's condo. When she came home four hours later, I was still weeping on the leather sofa. So she joined me. We spent an entire week crying together on the couch, with *Gilligan's Island* playing in the backdrop.

'The rat bastard,' she said when we'd finally finished weeping. 'That fucking, fucking rat bastard.'

And I wondered if she hated my father for

slaughtering her sister, or for saddling her with an unwanted child.

The story of my life.

★ ★ ★

I survived. And even if I don't always remember, I do live, the survivor's ultimate responsibility.

I grew up. I went to college. I became a pediatric psych nurse. Now I spend my days at a locked-down pediatric psych ward in Boston, working with the six-year-old boy who's already hearing voices, the eight-year-old girl who self-mutilates, the twelve-year-old big brother who absolutely, positively can't be left alone with his younger siblings.

We're an acute care facility. We don't *fix* these kids. We stabilize them, using proper medications, a nurturing environment, and whatever other tricks we can pull out of our sleeves. Then we observe. We try to figure out what makes each child tick, and we write up recommendations for the next set of experts who will ultimately deal with these kids, either at a residential program, or a long-term-care institution, or a supervised return to the home environment.

Some of our kids make progress. They become the best person they can be, a triumph by anyone's definition. Some of our children commit suicide. Others commit murder. They become that headline you've read in the paper: 'Troubled Youth Opens Fire'; 'Older Brother Slaughters Entire Family.' And people die, whether they had anything to do with it or not.

I know what you're thinking. You're thinking I took this job to save lost children like me. Or perhaps, even more heroically, I took this job to avert tragedies like the one that happened to my family.

I understand what you're thinking.

But you don't know me yet.

THURSDAY

1

Thursday night, Sergeant Detective D. D. Warren was out on a date. It wasn't the worst date she'd ever been on. It wasn't the best date she'd ever been on. It was, however, the only date she'd been on in quite some time, so unless Chip the accountant turned out to be a total loser, she planned on taking him home for a rigorous session of balance-the-ledger.

So far, they'd made it through half a loaf of bread soaked in olive oil, and half a cow seared medium rare. Chip had managed not to talk about the prime rib bleeding all over her plate or her need to sop up juices with yet another slice of bread. Most men were taken aback by her appetite. They needed to joke uncomfortably about her ability to tuck away plate after plate of food. Then they felt the need to joke even more uncomfortably that, of course, none of it showed on her girlish figure.

Yeah, yeah, she had the appetite of a sumo wrestler but the build of a cover girl. She was nearly forty, for God's sake, and well aware by now of her freakish metabolism. She certainly didn't need any soft-middled desk jockey pointing it out. Food was her passion. Mostly because her job with Boston PD's homicide unit didn't leave much time for sex.

She polished off the prime rib, went to work on the twice-baked potato. Chip was a forensic accountant. They'd been set up by the wife of a friend of a guy in the unit. Yep, it made that much sense to D.D. as well. But here she was, sitting in a coveted booth at the Hilltop Steakhouse, and really, Chip was all right. Little doughy in the middle, little bald on top, but funny. D.D. liked funny. When he smiled, the corners of his deep brown eyes crinkled and that was good enough for her.

She was having meat and potatoes for dinner and, if all went as planned, Chip for dessert.

So, of course, her pager went off.

She scowled, shoved it to the back of her waistband, as if that would make a difference.

'What's that?' Chip asked, catching the chime.

'Birth control,' she muttered.

Chip blushed to the roots of his receding brown hair, then in the next minute grinned with such self-deprecating power she nearly went weak in the knees.

Better be good, D.D. thought. *Better be a fucking massacre, or I'll be damned if I'm giving up my night*.

But then she read the call and was sorry she'd ever thought such a thing.

Chip the funny accountant got a kiss on the cheek.

Then Sergeant Detective D. D. Warren hit the road.

*　*　*

D.D. had been a Boston PD detective for nearly twelve years now. She'd started out investigating

12

traffic fatalities and drug-related homicides before graduating to such major media events as the discovery of six mummified corpses in an underground chamber; then, more recently, the disappearance of a beautiful young schoolteacher from South Boston. Her bosses liked to put her in front of the camera. Nothing like a pretty blonde detective to mix things up.

She didn't mind. D.D. thrived on stress. Enjoyed a good pressurecooker case even more than an all-you-can-eat buffet. Only drawback was the toll on her personal life. As a sergeant in the homicide unit, D.D. was the leader of a three-person squad. It wasn't uncommon for them to spend all day tracking down leads, interviewing informants, or revisiting crime scenes. Then they spent most of the night writing up the resulting interviews, affidavits, and/or warrant requests. Each squad also had to take turns being 'on deck,' meaning they caught the next case called in, keeping them stuck in a permanent vortex of top-priority active cases, still-unsolved old cases, and at least one or two fresh call-outs per week.

D.D. didn't sleep much. Or date much. Or really do anything much. Which had been fine until last year, when she'd turned thirty-eight and watched her ex-lover get married and start a family. Suddenly, the tough, brash sergeant who considered herself wed to her job found herself studying *Good Housekeeping* magazine and, even worse, *Modern Bride*. One day, she picked up *Parenting*. There was nothing more depressing than a nearly forty-year-old single, childless homicide detective reading *Parenting* magazine alone in her North End condo.

Especially when she realized some of the articles on dealing with toddlers applied to managing her squad as well.

She recycled the magazines, then vowed to go on a date. Which had led to Chip — poor, almost-got-his-brains-screwed-out Chip — and now had her on her way to Dorchester. Wasn't even her squad's turn on deck, but the notification had been 'red ball,' meaning something big and bad enough had happened to warrant all hands on deck.

D.D. turned off I-93, then made her way through the maze of streets to the largely working-class neighborhood. Among local officers, Dorchester was known for its drugs, shootings, and raucous neighborhood parties that led to more drugs and shootings. BPD's local field district, C-11, had set up a noise reduction hotline as well as a designated 'Party Car' to patrol on weekends. Five hundred phone tips and numerous preventive arrests later, Dorchester was finally seeing a decline in homicides, rapes, and aggravated assaults. On the other hand, burglaries were way up. Go figure.

Under the guidance of her vehicle's navigational system, D.D. ended up on a fairly nice street, double lanes dotted with modest stamps of green lawn and flanked with a long row of tightly nestled three-story homes, many sporting large front porches and an occasional turret.

Most of these dwellings had been carved into

14

multiple-living units over the years, with as many as six to eight in a single house. It was still a nice-looking area, the lawns neatly mowed, the front-porch banisters freshly painted. The softer side of Dorchester, she decided, more and more curious.

D.D. spotted a pileup of Crown Vics, and slowed to park. It was eight-thirty on a Thursday night, August sun just starting to fade on the horizon. She could make out the white ME's vehicle straight ahead, as well as the traveling crime lab. The vans were bookended by the usual cluster of media trucks and neighborhood gawkers.

When D.D. had first read the location of the call, she'd assumed drugs. Probably a gangland shooting. A bad one, given that the deputy superintendent wanted all eighteen detectives in attendance, so most likely involving collateral damage. Maybe a grandmother caught sitting on her front porch, maybe kids playing on the sidewalk. These things happened, and no, they didn't get any easier to take. But you handled it, because this was Boston, and that's what a Boston detective did.

Now, however, as D.D. climbed out of her car, clipped her credentials to the waistband of her skinny black jeans, and retrieved a plain white shirt to button up over her date cleavage, she was thinking, *Not drugs*. She was thinking this was something worse. She slung a light jacket over her sidearm, and headed up the sidewalk toward the lion's den.

D.D. pushed her way through the first wave of

jostling adults and curious children. She did her best to keep focused, but still caught phrases such as 'shots fired . . . ' 'heard squealing like a stuck pig . . . ' 'Why, I just saw her unloading groceries not four hours before . . . '

'Excuse me, excuse me, pardon me. Police sergeant. Buddy, out of the way.' She broke through, ducking under the yellow tape roping off portions of the sidewalk, and finally arrived at the epicenter of crime-scene chaos.

The house before her was a gray-painted triple-decker boasting a broad-columned front porch and large American flag. Both front doors were wide open, enabling better traffic flow of investigative personnel, as well as the ME's metal gurney.

D.D. noted delicate lace curtains framed in bay windows on either side of the front door. In addition to the American flag, the porch contained four cheerful pots of red geraniums, half a dozen blue folding chairs, and a hanging piece of slate that had been painted with more red geraniums and the bright yellow declaration: *Welcome*.

Yep, definitely something worse than gun-toting, tennis-shoe-tossing drug dealers.

D.D. sighed, put on her game face, and approached the uniformed officer stationed at the base of the front steps. She rattled off her name and badge number. In turn, the officer dutifully recorded the info in the murder book, then jerked his head down to the bin at his feet.

D.D. obediently fished out booties and a hair covering. So it was that kind of crime scene.

She climbed the steps slowly, keeping to one side. They appeared recently stained, a light Cape Cod gray that suited the rest of the house. The porch was homey, well kept. Clean enough that she suspected it had been recently broom swept. Perhaps after unloading groceries, a household member had tidied up?

It would've been better if the porch had been dirty, covered in dust. That might have yielded shoe treads. That might have helped catch whoever did the bad thing D.D. was about to find inside.

She took another breath right outside the door, inhaled the scent of sawdust and drying blood. She heard a reporter calling for a statement. She heard the snap of a camera, the roar of a media chopper, and white noise all around. Gawkers behind, detectives ahead, reporters above.

Chaos: loud, smelly, overwhelming.

Her job now was to make it right.

She got to it.

2

VICTORIA

'I'm thirsty,' he says.

'What would you like?' I offer.

'Woman, bring me a drink, or I'll break your fucking face.'

He doesn't sound angry. That's how these things often go. Sometimes, the storm arrives quickly. One moment he's watching TV, the next he's tearing apart the living room. Other times, he lingers on the precipice. Say or do the right thing, and calm will be restored. Say or do the wrong thing, on the other hand . . .

I get off the couch. It's Thursday evening, an ungodly hot and humid August night in Boston. The kind of night best spent at a beach or at a giant swimming pool. Of course, neither one is an option for us. We've spent the afternoon inside, watching the History Channel while basking in air-conditioning. I'd hoped a quiet evening might be soothing for him. Now I don't know.

Inside the kitchen, I debate my options. A drink order involves a vast array of land mines: First, guess the proper beverage. Then select the right glass/mug/cup. Not to mention ice or no ice, straw or no straw, cocktail napkin or coaster.

Once, I wouldnt've refused such a belligerent demand. I would've demanded nice words, nice

18

voice. *I'm not your servant,* I would've reminded him. *You will treat me with respect.*

These things happen, though. Not all at once. But bit by bit, moment by moment, choice by choice. There are pieces of yourself that, once you give away, you can never get back again.

I go with the blue mug, a recent favorite, and tap water — less mess when he inevitably tosses the contents into my face. My hands are already shaking. I take several calming breaths. *He hasn't gone over the edge yet. Remember, he hasn't gone over the edge. Not yet.*

I carry the mug into the living room, where I set it on the glass coffee table while watching him beneath my lowered eyelids. If his feet remain flat on the floor, I will continue with appeasement. If he's already twitching, perhaps tapping a foot, or rolling his shoulder in the way that often precedes a sudden, hard-thrown punch, then I will bolt. Get down the hall, grab the Ativan, and dope him up.

I'm telling you, there are pieces of yourself that, once you give away, you can never get back again.

He picks up the mug, feet stable, shoulders loose. He takes an experimental sip, pauses . . .

Sets it down again.

I have just resumed breathing, when he grabs the plastic mug and slams it against the side of my head.

I reel back, not so much from the force of the plastic cup as from the shock of the blow.

'What the fuck is this?' he screams, two inches

19

from my water-drenched face. 'What the fuck is this?'

'Water,' I reply, stupidly.

He tries to club me again, more water spraying the couch, then we're off and running, me dashing for the medicine cabinet in the downstairs lavette, him determined to wrestle me to the ground so he can beat my head against the hardwood floor, or wrap his fingers around my throat.

He catches my ankle at the edge of the family room. I go down hard on my right knee. Reflexively, I kick back. I hear him roar in frustration as I break free and bolt four more steps.

He catches me in the side, crashing me against the wainscoting. The chair rail slams into my ribs with bruising force.

'BITCH! Bitch, bitch, bitch.'

'Please,' I whisper. No good reason. Maybe because you have to say something. 'Please, please, please.'

He grabs my wrist, squeezing so hard I can feel small bones grinding together.

'Please, sweetheart,' I whisper again, desperately trying to sound soothing. 'Please let go, honey. You're hurting me.'

But he doesn't let go. I've read him wrong, missed the signs, and now he's gone to the dark place. I can say anything, do anything — it doesn't matter. He's a feral animal, needing someone to hurt.

And I think, as I often think during these times, that I still love him. Love him so much my heart breaks more than any bones, and now, even now, I have to be careful. I don't want to hurt him.

Then, in the next instant, I lash out with my foot, connecting behind his kneecap. He goes down just as I wrench my hand free. I race for the bathroom, crashing open the medicine cabinet and scrambling for the orange prescription bottle.

'I'm going to kill you!' he roars in the hallway. 'I'm going to stab you a million times. I'm gonna fucking rip off your head. I'll eat your heart, I'll drain your blood. I'll kill you, I'll kill you, I'll kill you.'

Then the sound I don't want to hear — the *whap whap* of his bare feet slapping down the hall as he wheels around and runs for the kitchen.

Ativan, Ativan, Ativan. Dammit, where's the Ativan?

I hit the bottle with the side of my hand. It falls to the floor, rolls across the tiles.

I hear another scream, pure unadulterated rage, and know he's just discovered that I locked up the kitchen knives. I did it two weeks ago, in the middle of the night, when he was sleeping. You have to keep one step ahead. You have to.

The Ativan has rolled behind the toilet. My fingers are shaking too hard. I can't reach it, can't roll it out. I hear crashing now. Cherry cabinet doors being flung open, cups, plates, serving platters being tossed onto imported Italian tile. I changed everything over to Melamine and plastic years ago, which only pisses him off more. He has to trash the kitchen, does it every time, even as the lack of shattering damage drives him further over the edge.

Another loud crash, then silence. I find myself holding my breath, then bend over the toilet, scrabbling for the damn prescription bottle. The quiet stretches on, unnerving me more than the destruction.

What's he doing? What has he discovered? What have I missed?

Dammit, I need the Ativan *now*.

I force myself to breathe, to steady my strung-out nerves. Towel, that's the trick. Roll up the towel, poke it behind the toilet, push the prescription bottle out the other side. Got it.

Tranquilizer tablets firmly in hand, I creep into the hallway of my now silent home, already terrified of what I might find.

One step. Two, three, four . . .

I approach the end of the hallway. Expansive family room on the left, followed by formal dining room, leading to the gourmet kitchen to the right, then circling around into the vaulted foyer. I peer behind the dying ficus tree in the corner, then tiptoe into the family room, mindful of the ambush spots behind the L-shaped sofa, beside the battered entertainment unit, and underneath the tattered silk drapes.

What have I missed? What have I failed to consider and what will it cost me?

Other images crowd my brain. The time he bolted out of the pantry with a wooden meat tenderizer and cracked two of my ribs before I managed to get away. Or the first time he picked

22

up a meat cleaver, going after my arm, but in his enraged state slicing open his own thigh. I was afraid he'd severed an artery and would bleed out if I ran away, so I stood my ground, eventually wrestling the knife from his grasp. Then I comforted him while he sobbed in pain, and the blood from both of our wounds soaked into the Persian rug in our beautiful vaulted entryway.

Can't think of these things now. Must remain focused. Find him. Calm him. Drug him.

I creep through the family room, approaching the dining room, taking in all shadowed corners, trying to listen for sounds from behind. The kitchen opens back into the foyer. That makes it easy for him to circle around, attack from the rear.

One foot in front of the other. Inch by inch, prescription bottle clutched like pepper spray in my fist.

I discover him in the kitchen. He has pulled down his jeans and is now defecating on the rug. He looks up as I approach, an expression of malevolent triumph crossing his face.

'What do you think of your precious rug now?' he sneers. 'What's so fucking *special* about it now?'

I approach him steadily, holding out the bottle of Ativan. 'Please, baby. You know I love you. Please.'

For his response, he scoops up a pile of excrement and smears it across his bare belly.

'I'm gonna kill you,' he says, calmer now, conversational.

I don't say a word, just hold out the bottle of tablets.

'I'm gonna do it in the middle of the night. But I'll wake you up first. I want you to *know*.'

I hold out the tablets.

'You locked up the knives,' he chants. 'You locked up the knives. But did you lock up *all* the knives? Did you, did you, did you?'

He smiles, gleefully, and my gaze goes instinctively to the drying rack, contents now strewn across the kitchen floor. Had there been a knife in that rack? Had I washed one just this morning? I can't remember, and that's going to cost me. Something is always going to cost me.

I twist off the lid of the prescription bottle. 'It's time to rest, sweetheart. You know you'll feel better after you've had a little rest.'

I pour a couple of tablets into the palm of my hand, stepping close enough that the heat and stench of his body flood my nostrils. Slowly, I open his mouth with one finger and poke the first quick-dissolving tablet into the pouch of his cheek.

In turn, he cups his stained fingers around my neck and, almost tenderly, rubs the hollow of my neck.

'I will kill you quickly,' he promises me. 'With a knife. I'll slide the blade in. Right here.'

His thumb brushes over the pulse beating wildly in my throat, as if he's mentally rehearsing the death blow.

Then I can see his facial muscles start to relax as the drug takes effect. His hand falls away, and he smiles again. Sweetly now. A ray of sunshine through the storm, and I want to cry but I don't. I don't.

There are pieces of yourself, so many pieces of yourself, that, once you give away, you cannot get back again.

Ten minutes later, I have him in bed. I strip off what remains of his clothes. Wipe down his body with a soapy washcloth, though I know from previous experience that the smell of excrement will linger on his skin. Later, he will ask me questions about that, and I will lie to him with my answers, because that's what I've learned to do.

I clean him up. I clean me up. The dishes will go through the dishwasher, then be replaced in the cupboards. The rug will be left on the curb on trash day. But all that can wait.

Now, in the silence of the aftermath, I return to his bedroom. In the lamplight, I admire the quiet, still lines of his face. The way his hair curves into one golden cowlick right above his left temple, the way his lips always purse slightly in his sleep, like a baby's. I stroke my fingers across the softness of his cheek. I take his hand, lax now, not hurting, not destroying, and hold it in my own.

And I wonder if tonight will be the night he will finally kill me.

Meet Evan, my son.

He is eight years old.

3

'Started in the dining room,' Detective Phil LeBlanc was explaining to Detective D. D. Warren. Phil wore a pair of chinos and a white-collared golf shirt with a ketchup stain above the embroidered emblem. Apparently, he'd been at a family barbecue when he'd received the call. Now he pointed to the rectangular table, currently set for six. The plates held traces of a recently consumed dinner, with several empty serving platters in the middle. D.D. counted three empty cans of Bud Light, two at one end of the table, one at the other.

The table was old-looking, a warm-hued oak. A nice table, she was willing to bet, maybe an antique. The chairs, on the other hand, were more blue folding chairs, companions to the ones on the front porch. So the residents could afford a solid wood table, but not yet the chairs. That fit with the overall feel of the space. Freshly painted, but conspicuously empty.

The dishes were thin white Melamine. Simple, but set off against bright red place mats and blue linen napkins. Red, white, and blue again. A theme to the household.

'Maybe they started to argue,' Phil theorized. 'They were eating together, had a few beers, then started to get into it. Maybe she tried to walk away, and that set him off.'

D.D. nodded absently, still walking around the

26

table. The hardwood floors appeared recently refinished, buffed to a high gloss that glimmered with hints of her own reflection as she walked across. They'd been working on this space. Sweat equity would be her guess. A working-class family building a future together, trying to get ahead during tough economic times, until . . .

'Where's Neil?' D.D. asked, referring to the third member of their homicide squad.

'Upstairs. Top two floors are midrenovation. We think the activity was confined to this level, but then again, lots of power tools and sharp objects to account for.'

D.D. nodded. Given the red ball call-out, she'd expected to find the scene crawling with investigators. Instead, it was pretty quiet. But three floors to search, secure, then process, that explained a lot. Plus guys would already be out, canvassing neighbors, tracking down known associates. Crime scenes like this were best worked fresh. Throw a lot of bodies at it, get in, get out, get it done.

'What do we know about the residents?' she asked.

'Single family. Mom, dad, three kids. Second marriage for both, so not sure yet whose kids were whose. Patrick Harrington would be head of household. Date of birth nineteen sixty-eight. Recently unemployed. Had been working for a local hardware store, but it went out of business.'

'When?' D.D. squatted to study the area rug under the table. Neutral beige; it appeared recently vacuumed. Freshly swept porch, newly vacuumed rug. She added *clean freak* next to

27

patriotic on her mental list of household traits.

'Couple of weeks or so. Neighbor said the couple bought the whole place at a foreclosure auction eight months ago. They planned on fixing it up, using his skills and employee discount, no doubt, then they'd live in part, rent part. They just got the downstairs completed, however, when, *boom*, he lost his job. Goodbye, hourly wage. Goodbye, employee discount.'

'Hello giant mortgage with no rental income,' D.D. finished for him.

'Yep. Had to suck.'

'So couple's stressed.' D.D. straightened up. 'What did she do?'

'Denise Harrington worked as a receptionist at a dentist's office. Mrs. Nancy Seers, lives across the street, said Denise got off work by three each day so she could meet the kids' bus. That was a priority.'

'Ages?'

'Ummm . . . ' Phil flipped through his notes. 'Nine, twelve, and fourteen. Boy, girl, boy.'

D.D. nodded, turned away from the table, and headed back into the kitchen. A frying pan remained on the stove. Smelled like olive oil and chicken grease. Next to it was a giant pot, like the kind used for corn on the cob or pounds of pasta. More signs of meal prep on the counters: a half-used head of lettuce, bag of carrots, partly sliced cucumber.

She looked for additional beer cans, finding three more in the trash. She opened the refrigerator, found it fairly loaded — proof of recent grocery shopping? — with the usual assortment of bread, eggs, lunch meat, produce, and mystery meals in Tupperware. The refrigerator door yielded two dozen condiments and a half-consumed bottle of Cavit pinot grigio. No more beer. So, assuming that a six-pack had been purchased, then all six beers had been consumed.

But six cans of Bud split between two grown adults? Or even mostly consumed by one? Not enough for a drunken rampage. She didn't buy it.

Jack McCabe from the ID unit had entered. He looked at the food-covered counters, sighed heavily. 'It's been photographed?' he asked.

'It's been photographed,' Phil assured him.

Jack sighed again. D.D. didn't blame him. Processing this scene would be painstaking and, most likely, unproductive. But you had to do what you had to do.

'Start with the knife,' she told him.

'There isn't a knife,' Jack said, staring at the counter.

'There has to be some kind of knife,' D.D. said, gesturing at the sliced cucumber.

'Oh, there's a knife,' Phil said.

'Ah fuck,' D.D. said, and followed Phil into the hallway.

★ ★ ★

Halfway down the hall, they encountered the first sign of blood spatter. It started midway on the high-gloss floor, then continued toward the back of the house, presumably toward the

29

bedrooms, in a mix of spots and streaks.

A man in a brown suit was standing farther down the hall, next to the blood trail. He appeared to be sketching the marks and the corresponding evidence placards.

'You should see this,' he said, so D.D. and Phil walked over. 'Note that the droplets actually radiate in two different directions, plus the smear marks, here and here?'

D.D. crouched down, obediently peered at the spatter. True enough, half the droplets seemed to spray forward, the other half sprayed back, and yes, there were two distinct smear tracks, as if two items had been dragged through the bloody mess.

'He caught her first in the bedroom,' the man was saying conversationally. 'Struck the first blow. She got around him, though, and ran this way. Unfortunately, she didn't make it.'

'He stabbed her again?' D.D. asked, frowning.

'No. That'd give us spray arcing across the wall as well as castoff, most likely on the ceiling, depending on the direction of the blow. He just grabbed her. By the hair maybe. Then dragged her to the back of the house, with the others, where he finished her off. See, first pattern of droplets are from her running toward the door. Second set is from her traveling the opposite direction. While the smears — '

'Heels of her feet,' D.D. murmured.

'Yep. Helluva thing to do to your own stepdaughter.' The man finished up his sketch, stuck out his hand. 'You must be Sergeant

Warren. Alex Wilson. I'm Phil's shadow for a month.'

D.D. glanced at Phil; he shrugged. 'True, just heard it myself about thirty minutes ago. You know how it is: We're always the last to know.'

D.D. took the man's hand, but she was frowning. 'And your affiliation is . . . ?'

'Detective, back in the day. 'Bout eight years ago, I traded in field-work for teaching at the Academy. Been feeling a little rusty, however, so I asked permission to shadow a detective off and on for a month. Eight years is a long time in the biz. Between all the advancements in digital photography and digital fingerprinting, I'm starting to feel like a walking, talking dinosaur.'

'You worked for the BPD eight years ago?'

'Nope. Worked out of Amherst. Why?'

'Just making conversation.' D.D. continued to study the man. She pegged his age for early forties, which was uncomfortably close to her own, given that he'd just referred to himself as a dinosaur. He wasn't too tall, maybe five eleven, still relatively trim. His short dark hair was liberally sprinkled with silver, and his blue eyes crinkled at the corners when he frowned. A working man's George Clooney. She could appreciate that.

So, Alex Wilson from Amherst. She'd have to ask around.

'All right, Professor. What else do you have to show us?'

'I think it started with the wife.' Alex led them down the hallway, keeping to one side in order to avoid the blood trail. 'Maybe they started arguing at dinner, dunno. But he followed her into the bedroom, got her from behind. This one was quick. One hard blow, severing the spinal column at the base of the skull. Even if she lived long enough to scream, the blow would've paralyzed her. She went down on her knees, her heart stopping before she bled out.'

Alex passed through a doorway on the right. D.D. found herself in a fairly large bedroom furnished with a king-size mattress and two mismatched dressers that looked as if they'd been picked up at a rummage sale. The bed was topped with an old flowered quilt. Two pink-colored sheets served as curtains over the windows.

On top of the largest dresser sat an assortment of framed photos, including an eight-by-ten of a smiling sandy-haired bride and grinning dark-haired groom. On the floor in front of the dresser was a conspicuously large dark stain covering at least a dozen floorboards. What was left of the sandy-haired bride, presumably.

'Where's the body?'

'You'll see,' Alex said. He led them back into the hall, stepped gingerly over the blood spatter and into the next bedroom. This one was smaller and painted a rich blue. Posters of Tom Brady peppered one wall, while rows of shelving containing signed footballs and various sports trophies covered the others.

To the right, a twin mattress bore a Patriots-themed comforter. Directly ahead stood a card table that appeared to serve as a desk, with a metal chair half pushed back. Beside the chair, on the floor, loomed another dark stain.

'Oldest son,' Alex supplied. 'Maybe he heard the disturbance in his parents' room. Stood up to take a look. To judge from the trophies, the kid's athletic and he's a decent size for his age. After the mom, the next logical threat. So the subject entered the room quickly and decisively. Kid's probably still thinking, *What the hell?* when the subject catches him in the side, slicing between the ribs, straight into the heart.'

'Single blow again?' D.D. asked sharply.

'These two, yes.'

'First in the back of the neck, then between the ribs. I'm thinking the subject has had some training,' she said.

'I'm guessing special forces. Stabbing's messy business, but this guy has it down to a science.'

'All right,' D.D. said briskly. 'Mom's down. Oldest son is down. Now what?'

'Got two left. Twelve-year-old girl, nine-year-old boy. Probably hoped to take them one at a time, but turns out both of them are in her room.'

Alex vacated the blue room and they proceeded single file down the hallway again. This time the blood spatter turned, leading them through a doorway into a bright pink room bearing purple window valances and half a dozen posters of Hannah Montana and the Jonas Brothers.

'Now things are a little more complicated here, as you can see.' Alex gestured to the floor, which was a dizzying array of spray droplets, blood pools, and yellow evidence placards. 'I'm guessing, purely to judge by the condition of the bodies, that he got the boy first.'

'Why the boy?'

'Single mortal wound. Look at the bed.'

D.D. belatedly realized the purple comforter wasn't really purple. It used to be a dark pink, the original color now skewed by another sizable pool of blood, with a matching spray pattern arcing across the opposite wall.

'The kids knew,' Alex said, more softly now, less academic. 'No closets in the room. So they huddled in the corner. Brother and sister together, taking a last stand. The subject came in. He must've been a sight by then. Covered in back spray from hammering down the first death blow, let alone the second. Kids stood shoulder to shoulder, next to the bed.

'Boy broke first, that's my guess,' Alex continued. 'Tried to get around the subject by springing up onto the bed. Didn't work. Subject sliced open the kid's throat as the boy attempted to bolt past. Game over. Girl's probably screaming by then. But she doesn't freeze, which is interesting. Most people facing such a scene . . .'

Alex's voice faded, then he cleared his throat, continued on: 'The girl runs. Takes advantage of her own brother's death to sprint for the front door. Of all of them, she's the only one who gets a chance. He wounds her. Right here.' Alex pointed with his pencil to a round smeared spot. 'Maybe the subject was aiming for her neck, but got her shoulder instead. The blow knocked her

34

off balance, hence smudge here and smudge there, probably made by her feet, but she keeps on trucking, God bless her.

'Gets halfway down that hallway, running the race of her life. And then — '

'He catches her,' D.D. fills in, then pauses. 'But doesn't kill her? Drags her away?'

Alex shrugged. 'Who knows? She's the last one left and he has her incapacitated. Maybe he realized he didn't have to rush. Or maybe he just wanted her to suffer a little more. She got away. That pissed him off.'

'Sexual assault?' D.D. asked.

'Ask the ME. Clothing is intact. Nothing obvious.'

'You think she's the stepdaughter?'

'Spitting image of the mom, doesn't look a thing like the dad.'

'So maybe his goal was sexual in nature. Was attracted to her, wanted her for himself . . . '

Alex looked at her.

'Come on, I'll show you the rest.'

★   ★   ★

The back of the house opened onto a screened-in porch. Kind of place to hang out during the mosquito-filled summer evenings. This area obviously hadn't been included in the renovations; several screens were ripped, the linoleum floor peeled back at the seams. But that was okay. The ripped floor was now covered in blood, while the lone piece of furniture, a broken-down futon, had, according to Alex,

35

become the resting place of an entire family.

'He laid them out side by side. First the mom, then the oldest son, then the daughter, then the youngest son.'

Alex pointed toward the blood-soaked mattress, currently buzzing with flies drawn to the scent of fresh kill.

'ME has the bodies?' D.D. asked.

'Yeah. Given the heat and fly activity, body removal was a priority.'

'You're saying the daughter was killed back here, though?'

'On the futon, I think. ME will have to analyze, but it looks like he brought her back here, then strangled her — manual asphyxiation. Patrick's a big guy. It wouldn't have taken him that long.'

'Then he moved all the other bodies?'

'I'm guessing in that order. He'd want her taken care of first, then he'd tend to housekeeping.'

D.D. frowned, not liking it. 'You're saying the subject carried three bodies through the house to this one room. Why don't we see more blood? Seems like we should see trails of it everywhere.'

Alex shrugged. 'ME can tell you more, but I'm guessing the bodies had already bled out. Kept the process clean.'

D.D. frowned. 'I don't get it. We're talking the dad, right? First he slaughters his family person by person, then he brings them together for one last family reunion?'

'I think he was apologizing.'

'*Excuse me?*'

36

'If we assume the father did it, then he's a family annihilator,' Alex stated. 'Now, maybe the event started impulsively — got in a fight with the wife and it went too far. Or maybe it didn't. Maybe this is what he'd planned all along. But think of the nature of a family annihilator: Why do these guys kill?'

D.D. looked at him. 'I don't know. Why do these guys kill?'

'Because they think they're doing their family a favor.'

'Yet another reason I'm single, now that you mention it.'

Alex smiled wryly. 'Times were hard. I bet when we dig deeper, we'll find the financial picture even bleaker. Maybe they were facing foreclosure, about to be kicked to the curb. The pressure mounts. The father starts thinking he'd be better off dead, but he doesn't want to hurt his family. That gets him thinking that *they'd* be better off dead. It's too cruel to just kill himself. So he'll do right by them — he'll kill them all.'

'Shit,' D.D. said, staring down at the blood-churned floor, swatting away another buzzing fly.

'He takes them out one by one. Then he carries each one of them back here and lays them down side by side. Maybe he prays over them then. Or says absolution, or gives them some little speech he's already prepared in his head. *I love you, I only want what's best for you, I'll see you soon.* Then he picks up the twenty-two and taps one to the forehead.'

'He shot himself?' Phil spoke up. 'Pussy.'

37

'True. Especially given that he didn't get the job done.'

D.D. did a double take: 'Are you saying — '

'Yep. Father's undergoing surgery now at Mass General. With any luck, they'll save him. Then we can nail his ass.'

'The father's still alive,' D.D. murmured, looking at the blood, waving away the hungry flies. She finally smiled. It was a distinctively wolfish expression on her face. 'I think we're gonna have some fun with this after all.'

★　★　★

They were walking back toward the front of the house, past the dining room, when it came to her. She drew up short. Belatedly, Phil and his shadow followed suit.

'Hey, Professor,' she said. 'I got a question for you.'

Alex arched a brow, but waited.

'Okay, so father kills the mother, the fourteen-year-old boy, the nine-year-old boy, and the twelve-year-old daughter, then shoots himself in the forehead.'

'Current theory, yes.'

'Based upon blood evidence.'

'Based upon preliminary exam of the blood evidence, yes.'

'It's an impressive analysis,' she told him. 'Very well done. I can tell that you're hell on wheels in the classroom.'

Alex didn't say a word, which confirmed that he was as smart as he looked.

'But there's another major piece of evidence.'
'Which is?'
'The dining room.'
Alex and Phil turned toward the dining room.

Phil asked the question first: 'What about the dining room?'

Alex, on the other hand, got it. 'Crap,' he said.

'Yeah, it's always slightly more complicated than we'd like it to be,' D.D. agreed. She looked at Phil. 'We got five bodies, right? Four dead, one in critical condition. Five bodies for five family members.'

Phil nodded.

D.D. shrugged. 'Then why is the table set for six?'

4

DANIELLE

You want to know what it means to be a pediatric psych nurse? Welcome to the Pediatric Evaluation Clinic of Boston, otherwise known as PECB. Our unit occupies the top floor of the larger Kirkland Medical Center. We like to believe we have some of the best views in Boston, which is only fair as we serve the toughest citizens.

Thursday night, I sat in the hallway of the pediatric ward observing our newest charge. Her name was Lucy and she'd been admitted this afternoon. We'd had only twenty-four hours to prepare for her arrival, which hadn't been enough, but we did our best. Most of our kids shared a double room; Lucy had her own. Most of the rooms included two twin beds, bedside tables, and matching wardrobes. Lucy's room had a mattress and a single blanket, that was it.

We'd learned the hard way that the shatter-proof glass on our eighth-story windows didn't always hold up to an enraged child armed with a twenty-pound nightstand.

Lucy was a primal child. That meant she'd been so severely and continuously abused that her humanity had been stripped from her.

She didn't wear clothes, use silverware, or tend to basic hygiene. She didn't speak and had never

40

been potty-trained. According to her file, she had spent most of her life in a disconnected freezer unit with bullet holes for ventilation. Her time out of the freezer had been worse than her time in. The result was a nine-year-old girl who existed like a wild animal. And if we weren't careful, she'd train us to treat her like one.

First hour she was admitted, Lucy greeted our nurse manager by defecating into her own hand, then eating the feces. Twenty minutes later, a milieu counselor — MC — observed her ripping out the insides of her pillow and stuffing it into various orifices. The pillow was removed; Lucy wouldn't allow us to tend to the stuffing. An hour after that, she scratched open her arm with a fingernail, then drew patterns on the wall with her blood.

First observation of our new charge: Any form of attention seemed to trigger a need to debase herself. If Lucy had an audience, she had to hurt.

By four in the afternoon, we agreed to confine Lucy to her room and assign one staff member to monitor her. Rather than the five-minute check system, where an MC accounts for every child's whereabouts every five minutes, one staff member would observe Lucy as discreetly as possible, noting every twenty minutes.

Tonight, that was lucky me.

It took until eleven for the kids to settle down. Some were sleeping on mattresses in the well-lit hall; these were the kids who were terrified of the dark. Others could only sleep alone in a pitch-black room. Others still required music or

41

white noise or, for one child, a ticking clock simulating his lost mother's heartbeat. We set up everyone accordingly.

For Lucy's first night, I did nothing special. Just sat with my back to her doorway and read stories to the other children. From time to time, I'd catch Lucy's reflection in the silver half dome mounted in the ceiling above me. The mirrored half domes dotted the broad hallway at strategic intervals — our version of a security system, as they reflected back activities from inside each patient room.

Lucy seemed to be listening to the story. She'd curled up on the floor, waving one hand through the air, the way a cat might study its own paw. If I read faster, her hand moved faster. If I read slower, her rhythm adjusted accordingly.

Then, twenty minutes later, she'd disappeared. In the dome's distorted reflection, I'd finally spotted her foot sticking out from beneath the mattress. When she didn't move, I turned around to study her room directly. It appeared that she'd pulled the mattress over her body and had finally gone to sleep. From time to time, her foot would twitch, as if from a dream.

I settled in myself, sitting on the floor with my back against the wall. There were over half a dozen other staff members scattered down the hall. Nighttime in the unit was paperwork time. Gotta catch up while you had the chance.

None of the kids would sleep for long. Some of the more manic ones required food every three hours, though you'd never know it to judge by their skeletal frames. Others just couldn't sleep.

Nighttime meant old terrors and fresh fears. A subconscious buffet of every evil thing ever done to them. Kids woke up crying. Kids woke up screaming. And some woke up primed for battle. Fight or flight. Not everyone was born to run.

I flipped open the first patient chart, and felt my eyelids already getting heavy. I'd been working a lot lately. More and more shifts. Less and less sleep. I needed to keep busy, especially this time of year.

Four days and counting. Then it would be twenty-five years down, and one more to go. Keep on trucking, the duty of the lone survivor.

I wondered what Lucy would think, if she knew that for years I'd slept tucked beneath a mattress myself.

★ ★ ★

On my eighteenth birthday, I seduced Sheriff-Wayne. I hadn't started out with a plan. I'd run into him in Boston, three days prior. He'd brought his wife, grown daughter, and two grandkids to the Public Garden to see the Swan Boats. The sun was out, a beautiful spring day where tulips waved and children shrieked as they chased ducks and squirrels across the sprawling green grounds.

SheriffWayne didn't recognize me. I suppose I'd changed in the past nine years. My dark hair was long, cut in a sleek line with overgrown bangs. I wore low-slung jeans and a yellow-striped top from Urban Outfitters. My Aunt Helen had turned her white-trash niece into Boston hip. At least we both liked to think so.

I recognized Sheriff Wayne from the back. It wasn't how he looked; it was how he moved. The solid roll of his legs across the pathway as he corralled bouncing grandkids, herding them steadily back to the family fold.

Sheriff Wayne noticed me standing a ways off, staring at him. He turned back to the women on either side of him, then it must've hit him. The nagging sense of familiarity clicked and he whirled around, taking me in squarely.

'Danielle,' he said, and the sound of his voice again, after all these years of living in my dreams, the lone whisper of safety amidst so many images of blood and violence, finally released me. I took a step forward. Then another.

His wife and daughter had noticed by then. His daughter was confused by my approach. His wife — Sheila was her name — must have remembered me. She held very still, and I could see the quiet sympathy in her eyes.

Sheriff Wayne took over. Shook my hand, made the introductions between myself, his wife, daughter, and grandkids. He smoothed it over, in the way a man who broke up bar fights would know how to do. I might have been the daughter of an old friend, reacquainted after all these years. We made small talk of the sunny day and the beautiful park. He told me of his other child, a grown son who lived in New York. We marveled over his granddaughter, who hid behind her

44

mother's legs, and his grandson, who loved chasing squirrels.

I mentioned I would be starting college in the fall. Sheriff Wayne shook my hand again, all quiet approval. Look at me and how I had turned out.

Look at me, the lone survivor.

They continued with their day, following the curving path down to the Swan Boats. I studied the empty space where they used to stand.

And I knew, in that instant, I had to see Sheriff Wayne again. I had to have him.

* * *

I called the next day. It had been nice to see him in the park. His daughter was lovely, his grandkids adorable. Listen, I had some questions. I didn't want to put him on the spot, but maybe we could get together. Have dinner. Just once.

I could hear his reluctance. But he was a decent man, so his decency won out, brought him to me.

I gave him the address of the studio apartment I had moved into that fall, a baby step in my preparations for college. I implied he would pick me up and we'd go out to dinner. I already knew otherwise.

I folded up my futon bed. Pulled out the card table and topped it with my favorite floral print. I set a nice table, coordinating red and yellow stoneware plates set against a rich backdrop. A shock of purple flowers in the middle. Two long white tapered candles in the crystal candlestick holders my mother had once received as a wedding gift and probably opened with a sense of joy and optimism.

She couldn't have known. I told myself that all the time. She couldn't have known.

I wore low-rider jeans and a white buttoned top. I left my dark hair down. I liked how it looked, a jolt of dark against the light.

Beneath, I wore the world's tiniest champagne-colored demi-bra and a lace thong. I'm not the world's biggest-built girl, but I know how to use what I have.

When Sheriff Wayne arrived, I could tell he was dismayed by the scene. The pretty table in the middle of a very small apartment. The scent of bubbling spaghetti sauce and cooking pasta.

I didn't give him a chance to think about things.

Come in, come in, I said at once, all bright smiles and youthful exuberance. Sorry for the small space. It's different living in the city. I took his coat before he had a chance to blink, hung it on the coatrack as I prattled away. I know we'd talked about going out, but I was a little nervous about having our conversation in public, so if he didn't mind, I'd decided to throw together a little pasta and gravy. Not the best cook, still learning, yada yada yada.

What could the poor man say? What could the poor man do?

He assured me my apartment was very nice. The sauce smelled good. Of course we could eat in. Whatever made me more comfortable.

I sat him at the table, poured him a liberal

46

glass of red wine. Nothing for myself; that would've been inappropriate. I added some music. He didn't strike me as a Nine Inch Nails kind of guy, so I went with light jazz.

We started with dinner salad. He sat stiffly, not touching his wine, keeping his eyes on his plate. He had aged well. Squarely built, solid but not fat. Gray hair on top of a broad, mustached face. He moved concisely, with an economy of motion that appealed to me.

He asked about my aunt, my schooling, my plans for the future. I painted for him a light overview of my new and improved life. It was what he needed to hear; once, he'd carried me through my father's house, his arms tight around my bony shoulders, his voice a warm whisper in my ear. '*Don't look honey. You're safe now, you're safe.*'

I dished up penne pasta. Covered it in red sauce.

Then I got serious.

I didn't ask about my father. Instead, I dredged from Sheriff Wayne's memory all the bright, shining moments of my mother's laugh and Johnny's mischievous ways and Natalie's compassion for animals. Turns out, my sister had once adopted a wild bunny she'd found struck by a car and nursed it back to health. She wanted to work with animals. I learned that from Sheriff Wayne. And my brother liked to climb to the tops of trees, then call for my mother to come see, so she could raise her hands and shriek in mock horror.

The memories got to him, of course. Hurt him

even more than me, because these people remained real in his mind, whereas they'd long ago become ghosts to me.

The wine went quickly. Who could blame him?

He offered to clear the dishes. I watched him move around in my tiny kitchenette, gestures less steady after two hours of intense emotions, plus a full bottle of Chianti. He stacked the dishes in the sink. Rinsed each one. Placed them in a pile to soak. Then the pans. Then his wineglass. Then my water glass. Two forks. Two spoons. Two knives.

When he returned to the table, I could see the effects of the evening in the haggard lines of his face. He tried to speak, but I wouldn't let him.

'Shhh,' I said. 'Shhh . . . '

As I undid the first button of my top, then the second, then the third, exposing, inch by inch, long lines of bare, bronzed skin, a lacy wisp of lingerie.

'Don't,' he said. 'You shouldn't . . . not right — '

'Shhh . . . '

I straddled his lap. I let my shirt fall open, rocking my hips gently against his groin. He tried to protest again, his mouth forming faint words that I pretended not to hear. I feathered my hands through his buzz-cut hair. I touched the solid lines of his shoulders. And I felt his body start to respond as my white shirt drifted down to the floor, as I arched my back and offered myself to him.

'Danielle . . . ' A last desperate plea.

'Shhh . . . '

I led his mouth to my breast. When I felt his lips finally close over my lace-covered nipple, the need that swept over me, the pure need, cut deeper than any grief ever had.

I took him, the man who'd once saved me, and for a brief moment, he was mine.

★　★　★

It was only years later, after completing my studies and embarking on a career in the psychiatric field, that I finally understood the damage I'd done to Sheriff Wayne that night. I'd hurt, and I'd branded him with that pain, forcing him to carry the scar of my wounds, a decent man who had to live out his days with his wife, his children, his grandchildren, knowing there was one night he didn't measure up to his standards as a husband, father, protector of the community.

Afterward, when I slept at night, I could no longer hear his voice. I was alone with the blood and the cordite. No one carried me out of my father's house anymore.

I suppose it was the least I deserved.

5

They wrapped the scene at 11:53 p.m. Not that they were done with it, but they were done for now. The detectives returned to HQ for a case conference. An entire unit can start a case, but an entire unit can't end one. For that, they needed the point person, the one detective's head that would rest in the noose if the job didn't get done.

D.D. won the honors; it wasn't a big surprise, but she still felt compelled to offer a small acceptance speech:

'On behalf of myself and my entire squad, I graciously accept your faith in our efforts — '

Some hooting from the back of the room, a few tossed pieces of balled-up paper. She picked up the ammo that landed closest and lobbed it back.

'Of course, we fully expect to have this wrapped by morning — '

A fresh round of catcalls, then one wiseass's observation that morning would be six minutes from now. D.D. retrieved a fresh ball of crumpled paper, and nailed that detective between the eyes.

'So you all can go back to protecting the fine citizens of Boston,' she concluded over the growing din. 'We got this one covered.'

The deputy superintendent rolled his eyes when she sat down, but didn't say a word. It had been a long night in a bad scene; the detectives were entitled to blow off some steam.

'Gotta do a press conference,' was all the boss had to say.

'First thing in the morning,' D.D. assured him. 'What's the party line?'

'Don't know.' She grabbed her jacket from the back of her chair, then gestured to her squadmate, Phil, that it was time to motor. 'Ask me when we get back from the hospital.'

★ ★ ★

Patrick Harrington, former father of three, had been recovering from brain surgery for the past three hours when D.D. and Phil arrived at the hospital. According to the charge nurse, he was in no condition to talk.

'Let us be the judge of that,' D.D. informed the nurse as she and Phil flashed their credentials.

The nurse wasn't impressed. 'Sweetheart, the man is in a drug-induced coma with a manometer attached to his skull to measure intracranial pressure. I don't care if you're packing a pass to the Pearly Gates; man can't talk yet, because the man *can't* talk.'

That stole some of D.D.'s thunder. 'When do you think he'll come around?'

The nurse looked D.D. up and down. D.D. returned the scrutiny. Hospitals had policies concerning a patient's right to privacy. For that matter, the legal system had scribbled a line or two on the subject. But take it from a detective

— at the end of the day, the world remained a human system. Some head nurses were bulldogs when it came to protecting their patients. Others were willing to consider the big picture, if things were presented in the right manner.

The charge nurse picked up a chart, glanced at the notes. 'In my professional opinion,' she offered up, 'hell if I know.'

'How did the surgery go?' Phil interjected. The nurse glanced at him, noted the ketchup stain on his white shirt, and smiled a little.

'Surgeon removed the foreign body. That should help matters.'

D.D. leaned against the nurses' station. Now that the nurse's body language had relaxed slightly, it was time to press the advantage. She glanced at the woman's name tag. 'So, Terri, did you hear what Patrick did to his family?'

'Some kind of domestic incident.' Nurse Terri regarded them seriously. 'Maybe he didn't like his wife's cooking. If you ask me, we see too much of that around here. More men need to start liking burnt food.'

'Ah, but there was a bit more to it than a spat with the missus. Kids were involved. Three kids. He got 'em all.'

Nurse Terri hesitated, showed the first glimmer of interest. 'He killed his own kids?'

'Nine, twelve, and fourteen. All dead.'

'Oh Blessed Mary . . . '

'That's what we think happened. It would be a good thing to *know*, however. I mean, there's a little difference between four people slaughtered by a family member than, say, by a deranged

52

maniac who's possibly still wandering free. Really, it would be good to dot our 'i's and cross our 't's here. As Patrick's the lone survivor . . . '

Nurse Terri sighed heavily, seemed to finally relent. 'Look, I can't make the unconscious conscious, not even for Boston's finest. I can see, however, if Dr. Poor is still around. He was the admitting doc in the ER. He might have something to offer.'

'Perfect.'

'Might as well make yourselves comfortable. Doctors answer only to God, not charge nurses, so this could take a while.'

'Somehow, I bet you have your ways of making a doctor hustle.'

'Honey, don't I wish.'

*   *   *

D.D. and Phil grabbed coffee from the basement cafeteria and made themselves at home. The waiting room chairs were low slung, the kind that were tempting to position three across as a makeshift bed. D.D. focused on her coffee. She'd slept well last night. Apparently, that would be it for a while.

She thought briefly of Chip, felt a pang of longing for the great sex she still wasn't going to have, then returned to the matters at hand.

'What did you think of Professor Alex?' she asked Phil.

'You mean my new shadow?' Phil shrugged. 'Seems all right. Smart, keeps out of the way, speaks mostly when he has something useful to say. So far, that puts him ahead of half our unit.'

D.D. smiled. 'Have you looked him up?'

'I'll make some calls in the morning.'

'Okay.'

They lapsed into silence, Phil blowing experimentally on his coffee, D.D. already sipping hers.

'And your plans tonight?' Phil finally asked.

'Don't ask.'

He grinned. 'Hey, wasn't tonight the big date with Charlie's wife's friend?'

'I'm telling you, don't go there.'

'You went to dinner first, didn't you? Come on, D.D., you should know better by now. You get a night off, you can't be wasting time on fine dining. Cut straight to the chase before the pager finds you.'

'What? Drag a stranger through my door and bang his brains out? Hi, hello, the bedroom is down the hall.'

'Trust me, guys won't complain.'

'Men are pigs.'

'Exactly.'

D.D. rolled her eyes. 'You and Betsy have been married, what, ninety years now? What would you know of twenty-first-century dating?'

'Oh, but I hear things.'

D.D. was spared further heckling as a harried-looking doctor blasted through the double doors. His hair stood up in brown tufts, and he had both hands shoved deep in the pockets of his white lab coat.

'Detectives,' he called out.

'Dr. Poor.' D.D. and Phil stood up.

He waved at them to follow, so they fell in step as he dashed across the waiting room, through another set of double doors, then made his way through the maze of sterile hallways. 'Gotta get some coffee. You need any more? It's pretty good here. For a hospital and all.'

'We're all set, thanks,' D.D. replied. She and Phil had to work to keep up with the doctor's rapid strides. 'So, Doctor, we have some questions regarding a patient who was admitted to the ER early this evening, a Patrick Harrington — '

'Injury?'

'What?'

'Injury. What was he admitted for? I don't have time for names, just wounds.'

'Uh, small-caliber gunshot wound to the head.'

'Ah.' The doctor nodded vigorously, taking a left, then a right, then bursting down a flight of steps to the lower-level cafeteria. 'GSW to the left temple, yes? No exit wound, so I'm guessing a twenty-two. Bullet mushroomed upon impact, lost too much velocity to blow out the back of the skull. You know, I saw two separate gunshot wounds last week caused by forty-fours. Blows the skull to smithereens. I think the drug dealers are watching too much *Dirty Harry*.'

They'd arrived at the basement cafeteria. Dr. Poor beelined for the java station. D.D. thought he might have had quite a bit of coffee already.

'We're interested in Harrington,' she prodded.

The doctor nodded, poured heavy cream and

55

four packets of sugar into his cup, stirred, then found a lid.

'Okay. Single GSW to the head. Upon admittance, we debrided the wound, examined the damage to the scalp, and evaluated the head injury. Patient had only limited responsiveness and scored poorly on the Glasgow coma test. I sent the patient for an urgent CT scan, then referred him to surgery for removal of the projectile lodged in the left posterior frontal area of the brain. I believe the neurosurgeon on call this evening was Dr. Badger. He does good work, if that helps you.'

'Prognosis?' Phil spoke up.

Dr. Poor made a waffling gesture with his hand. 'Three issues with head injuries. First, the bleeding. Second, the direct trauma. Third, the resulting swelling. So far, the patient has survived the bleeding and direct trauma. Swelling, however, remains a concern, as is risk of infection. And, for that matter, further bleeding. Even the best neurosurgeon can do only so much to repair the damage inflicted by a bullet to the brain. It's like throwing a butter knife into a bowl of pudding. The pudding doesn't stand a chance.'

'When will he regain consciousness?' D.D. asked.

'Haven't a clue. I'd have to look at his chart. I'm guessing he's heavily sedated, which is probably for the best.'

'But we need to ask him some questions,' she persisted impatiently.

Dr. Poor arched a brow. 'Half the man's brain

has been turned into the Panama Canal. What do you think he could tell you at the moment?'

D.D. and Phil exchanged glances. It was hardly surprising news, but disappointing.

'Can you describe the entry wound?' Phil asked.

D.D. chewed her bottom lip. She knew what Phil was going for. From a detective's perspective, it would've been better if their suspected shooter had died at the scene. In which case, the ME's office would've bagged the man's hands and preserved the contact wound on the left temple. Back in the morgue, the ME would then test the shooter's hands for gunpowder residue while conducting a forensic examination of the entry wound. In twenty-four hours or less, they'd have scientific evidence that Patrick Harrington had died from a self-inflicted gunshot wound to the head.

Furthermore, Harrington's clothes would have been carefully preserved, then analyzed for blood spatter and other evidence related to the homicidal rampage. Bada bing, bada boom, the blood spots on Subject's A's clothing tied to the wounds inflicted on Victims B, C, D, and E, meaning Patrick Harrington stabbed his entire family before shooting himself in the head.

Case closed, detectives move on.

Instead, their suspected family annihilator had been rushed to the hospital by the EMTs. Where his bloody clothing had been cut off and tossed aside. Where his hands and wounds had been washed and scrubbed. Where countless opportunities to collect evidence had been sacrificed in an attempt to save the sorry bastard's life.

Now they were left with an ER doc's first impressions of the subject and his injuries. D.D. would've preferred dealing with the ME.

Dr. Poor pried the lid off his coffee, blew on the sugared brew, seemed to be searching his memory. 'I'd have to check the notes, but the entry wound was several centimeters in diameter, burn marks around the edges — '

'Close contact,' Phil interrupted.

The doctor nodded. 'I'd say a close contact-entry wound.'

Phil made a note.

But then the doctor shook his head. 'You want to know if this guy shot himself? That's what you're thinking, right? A self-inflected gunshot wound?'

'That's what we're trying to determine,' Phil stated carefully.

'To judge from the CT scan, I'd say that's unlikely.'

'What do you mean?' D.D. said.

'It's a matter of trajectory. Think about it. The entry wound was to the left temple, and the bullet came to rest in the left posterior region. That's a pretty straight line. If you think about trying to replicate that shot . . . ' The doctor set down his coffee, cocking his right fingers into a makeshift gun and trying to bend his right wrist enough to form a straight shot into his left temple. 'It's not that it can't be done, but it's awkward. Especially given that the person is probably on an adrenaline rush, has endorphins dumping everywhere from trauma, stress, anticipation . . . Most self-inflicted gunshot wounds we see are angled. Maybe the person flinches at the last second in anticipation, jerks the barrel slightly down or sideways. But a clean, direct hit . . .'

He appeared skeptical, picking back up his coffee cup, taking another sip. 'Then again, it's not the easiest thing to determine the pathway of a bullet through the brain.'

'What do you mean?' D.D. asked.

'I mean, after the initial trauma, the increased intracranial pressure collapses the path the bullet took through the brain. So we can see where the bullet started, the entry wound, and where it ended, the resting place, but it's possible it bounced around in between. Maybe not *probable*,' he hedged. 'But possible.'

'You see a fair amount of self-inflicted gunshot wounds?' D.D. asked him.

'Enough, I think.'

'How does this compare? Gut reaction, doesn't have to be scientific. It's just us three standing here.'

The doctor waffled again. 'Can't really say there's a quintessential self-inflicted wound. Other than it's almost always a male. But gun type, location of wound . . . Too many variables to make that call.'

D.D. scowled, wanting a more definitive answer, but again, not terribly surprised. Doctors hated to be nailed down. 'Did you notice his hands?'

'Nope, too busy looking at his head.'

59

'Did he say anything, have any moments of consciousness?'

'Not when I was around.' The doctor had his coffee between both his hands and seemed ready to motor again. He headed toward the cafeteria exit. They followed, more slowly this time.

At the last moment, he turned. 'Might want to check with the charge nurse, though,' he called back. 'Find out who admitted him. That person might know more.'

The doctor disappeared up the stairs.

They went in search of Nurse Terri.

* * *

Turned out, Rebecca Moore, currently working a double, had been the ER nurse who'd admitted Patrick Harrington. She pulled herself away from a vomiting three-year-old to answer their questions.

D.D. recoiled at the smell. Phil remained steadfast. He had four kids at home, and liked to joke that he worked homicide to escape the gore.

'You admitted a gunshot victim earlier this evening: Patrick Harrington,' D.D. prodded. 'We were wondering if you could tell us anything about him.'

'GSW to the head?' Rebecca wanted to know.

'That's our man.'

'EMTs brought him in. I noted his vitals, then paged Dr. Poor, given the head injury. He referred the patient to Dr. Badger for surgery.'

'Was the patient conscious when he first came in?'

60

'No, ma'am.'

'Did he ever regain consciousness while in the ER?'

'No, ma'am — Oh wait, when they were wheeling him out for the CT scan. He opened his eyes then.'

'What did he do?'

'He was moving his lips, looked like he was trying to speak.'

'Did you hear what he said?' Phil asked sharply.

The nurse shrugged. 'I can't be certain. Sounded like 'hussie.''

6

VICTORIA

A knife is missing. It's four a.m., and I've crept out of bed to take inventory. Evan woke up at eleven, midnight, two a.m., and three. Now he will probably make it until five. At least I hope so.

I haven't slept, but that's nothing unusual. The first few weeks of sleep deprivation are the hardest. Now it's been so long since I've had more than three consecutive hours of rest that it's the nights I do sleep that mess me up. I find myself foggy, barely able to pull it together. It's as if, having finally gotten sleep, my body realizes what it's been missing and rebels.

I don't have time for rebellions, so I've given myself middle-of-the-night chores. Several times a week, this includes inventory of the kitchen utensils.

He must have gotten the knife from the drying rack. I try to be diligent, but I'm rarely functioning at one hundred percent. My fine motor skills have eroded to the point that I drop small objects half a dozen times a day. When people speak to me, I have moments when I see their mouths moving, but I can't process English.

Evan once watched a show describing how Navy SEALs must survive more than ninety-six hours without sleep as part of Hell Week. I wanted to scream at the TV, *Ninety-six hours, my ass. Try eight years!*

I might have started laughing hysterically. These things happen.

Now I try to marshal my limited coping skills. Assuming Evan got the knife from the drying rack, he had roughly three to five minutes alone with it before I discovered him in the kitchen. He would've hidden it; he's clever that way. But somewhere close; he wouldn't have time to make it downstairs and back, nor could he go down the hallway because I would hear him. So the knife is close, stashed somewhere in the kitchen, dining room, entryway, or family room. I should be able to find it — I just have to think.

I drag myself off the kitchen floor. The kitchen is cast in shadow, illuminated solely by the undercabinet lights. I've come to yearn for the dark solitude of these early-morning hours, when my son finally sleeps and I have thirty, forty, fifty precious minutes to myself.

I find a flashlight, then creep into the foyer, where I pause to listen for sounds from upstairs. I can see the glow in the upstairs hall, from Evan's room. He demands an overhead light for nighttime, as well as a radio playing at daytime volume. He can't stand the dark; he's terrified of the phantom he believes lives in the gloom.

Sometimes the phantom tells him things. For example, sometimes the phantom tells him to kill me.

I love my son. I still remember the first moment I was finally allowed to hold him. I remember the endless days and nights of rocking him, feeling his greedy little lips suckle at my breast, the weight of his impossibly tiny body as he finally grew sated and drifted off. I remember the scent of talcum powder. The silky feel of his fine hair. The way he'd sigh as he nestled against me.

Evan was born ten weeks premature. I'd like to say it was just one of those things, but according to the doctor, it was all my fault.

Back in those days, Michael and I lived a marvelously shallow life. We owned a giant old Colonial in Cambridge, which we'd painstakingly remodeled to fit in with the other historic homes in the neighborhood. Michael worked long hours as a vice president with a major finance company in Boston, while I networked with our upscale neighbors as a much-sought-after interior decorator. I designed kitchens for doctors, window treatments for lawyers, and custom-made sofas for various professional athletes.

Michael and I had both grown up poor. Now we merrily evaluated our days by what designer clothes we'd purchased, or what up-and-coming Boston power player we'd met. I interspersed two-hundred-dollar facials with rare-antiques shopping, just as Michael filled his calendar with strategic lunches and box seats at various sporting events. Weekends meant the Cape in the summer, or our 'lodge' in the White Mountains during the winter.

When I became pregnant, it was one more exercise in conspicuous consumption. I ordered cashmere sweaters from Pea in the Pod, layette sets from Burberry, and, of course, an English pram. I overhauled the nursery while taking up yoga and switching from my morning coffee to decaffeinated green tea. Nothing would be too good for our child. Nothing.

Michael gifted me with a diamond necklace, a two-carat eternity circle to brand me as his elegant, knocked-up wife. He also started a tradition of taking me to a fresh Boston hotspot every Saturday night, where we would savor four-course dinners and joke about how, soon, these kinds of evenings would be a thing of the past. He would drink gin and tonics. I would sip cranberry juice. We would stay out until two in the morning just because we could, but also because deep inside, we weren't that sad life was about to change.

We loved each other. We really did. And like so many young married couples, we believed there was nothing we couldn't handle, no challenge we couldn't face, no hurdle we couldn't jump, as long as we had each other.

Then, unbeknownst to me, a bacterial infection reached my womb. On the outside, I looked healthy, vibrant, glowing. On the inside, I'd started to poison my unborn child.

I don't remember much of the ambulance ride. I'd started to bleed. A lot. My neighbor Tracey had the good sense to dial 911. She sat with me in the back. Held my hand while EMTs cut off my suede maternity pants and barked out commands that frightened me. Where were the words of reassurance, the assertions that this was a minor mishap, *Your baby is fine, nothing to worry about, ma'am.*

I lost consciousness at the hospital. Michael arrived moments after the ambulance. According to my neighbor, he had such a tight grip on my hand, the doctors had to pry his fingers from mine to wheel me in for the emergency C-section.

Then, ready or not, Evan Michael Oliver was born into the world.

Evan weighed three pounds four ounces. When I first met him, he was the size of a kitten, lying in the middle of the isolette with half a dozen wires and tubes dangling from his tiny, wrinkled body. He was covered with fine hair, and so translucent he appeared blue, but that was really the color of his veins, spun out like fine lace beneath the surface of his skin.

He needed the incubator for warmth, a ventilator attached to a blender to help him breathe, and a feeding tube to deliver essential nutrients. He required a blood pressure monitor and a cardiorespiratory monitor. Then there was the drainage pump, the IV, and various other lines that came and went as Evan struggled to fight off infection while still developing properly working internal organs.

He lived in the enclosed isolette like a china doll in a display case. We could look, but not touch. So we stood for brief moments, shoulder to shoulder, filled with that terrible sensation you get when things aren't just wrong, they are WRONG, and you keep waiting for the situation to end, even as specialists yap at you.

The grief counselor kindly offered to call our parents. 'You don't have to go through this alone. Reach out to your community, lean on your families and friends.'

Michael, stone-faced, never replied. Finally, the counselor took the hint and disappeared. It wasn't her fault we didn't have families and friends — at least, not in the sense she meant. My mother had never forgiven me for becoming more beautiful than her, while Michael's siblings spent more time in than out of jail. We'd given up on everyone years ago. We had each other, and that, we constantly reminded ourselves, was enough.

I wanted to scream that first day. I was only allowed to visit Evan for minutes at a time in the NICU, then it was back to my own hospital room, where I would lie on my side, my traitorous stomach pooled beside me. Nurses brought me medications. The lactation consultant taught me how to operate the breast pump. I was supposed to sleep, focus on recuperating. Mostly I lay in the dark and reviewed the past thirty weeks in my mind over and over again. Was it the sip of champagne I'd had at New Year's? Maybe the fumes from the paint I'd selected for the nursery? Where had I failed? If I could just identify the moment, then go back in time . . .

Michael journeyed between the NICU and my room, an ashen-faced man uncertain of who needed him most, his fresh-out-of-surgery wife or his barely breathing son. He didn't speak. He didn't weep. He just moved, ten minutes in this room, ten minutes in that room, as if movement would keep the situation under control. His dark hair started to gray overnight. His strong shoulders seemed to stoop. But he kept walking, room to room, ward to ward, a man on a mission.

I thought Evan would sleep round the clock. All energy conserved for growing, but inevitably, as nurses adjusted his IV or feeding tube, Evan would wake up, staring at us wide-eyed, as if trying to absorb everything about this strange new world.

'He's a fighter,' the nurses would say, chuckling over his waving fists even as he blocked their movements. 'That's a good sign, honey. He's a tough one.'

And he would kick his thin little legs, as if in agreement.

Eventually, I was allowed to touch his cheek. Then one day I finally got to cradle him against my chest, Michael standing beside me, his hand gripping my shoulder so tight it hurt.

Evan opened his eyes again. He stared at both of us, eyes so round in his tiny, wizened head.

And we did what parents do in the NICU.

We promised everything — our grand house, our designer clothes, our self-absorbed careers. We promised it all. Our very lives. We would give up every single piece of ourselves. We would do whatever had to be done, we would lose whatever had to be lost.

If only our son would live.

★ ★ ★

I can't find the knife. I've searched around the ficus tree, along the floorboards, between the folds of the shredded curtains. I take up sofa cushions, peer into every nook and cranny of the entertainment system. I beam my flashlight under furniture and over cabinets. I know Evan's favorite places. The knife's not in any of them.

He has it. I know he has it.

He's outsmarted me.

The sun will be up soon. I can see the edge of the night sky beginning to lighten, and for a moment, I'm so tired, I want to cry.

'Mommy.'

I whirl around. Evan's standing behind me. He wears his favorite *Star Wars* pajamas, his hands clasped behind his back.

I'm breathing too hard. I have the flashlight in my hands, so I beam it into his pale face. I don't want him to see how badly he's scared me.

'Evan. Show me your hands.'

'I want to see Chelsea.'

'Not right now.'

'Is it morning, Mommy?'

'No, honey, it's still nighttime. What's behind your back, darling?'

'Can we see Chelsea?' he asks again.

'Not right now,' I repeat steadily, still eyeing his hands, still waiting to see what he'll do next.

'I want to go to the park,' he says.

'In the morning, honey.'

'I want to make a new friend today.'

'Evan, turn around now. It's time for bed.'

Evan abruptly sticks out his hands. He turns them palm up, so I can see that they're empty, that he hasn't been holding anything. The expression on his face is guileless, but then, as I watch, I can see it. A shadow moving in the back of his eyes. A faint smile curving one corner of his mouth.

He knows what I am looking for.

He knows he has it, and that I don't know what to do.

The shadow in his eyes moves again, and I fight the chill creeping up my spine. Evan isn't the only one in this house who's afraid of the phantom.

I take a deep breath, snapping off the flashlight and putting my hand on my son's shoulder. His body is relaxed beneath my touch. He lets me lead him to the foyer, up the stairs. We follow the bright glow to his bedroom, where I tuck him back into bed. He's already half-asleep, his eyes heavy-lidded as I brush a few blonde wisps from his forehead.

'I love you to the moon and the stars and back again,' he murmurs, a line from our favorite book.

I caress his cheek. 'I love you, too.'

'I don't want to hurt you,' he says dreamily, already drifting off. His blue eyes open. 'But I do.'

70

FRIDAY

7

D.D. slept until seven the next morning, an unusual luxury when working a high-burn case. She needed the two extra hours of shut-eye, given the late-night trip to the hospital. More to the point, today would be about interviewing friends and family, and they generally didn't care for detectives knocking on their doors before nine.

She showered, downed two shots of espresso, and considered the morning. Neil had agreed to spend the day with the ME, attending the autopsies. That left her and Phil to follow up on the initial canvass of the Harringtons' neighbors.

D.D. swung by HQ long enough to skim the pile of reports on her desk, including the transcripts from interviews conducted last night with available neighbors. Two individuals stood out: a Mrs. Patricia Bruni and a Mr. Dexter Harding. Both claimed to know the Harringtons well: Mrs. Bruni attended the same church; Mr. Dexter hosted poker night with the father.

As good a starting point as any, D.D. decided. She took the transcripts with her, then headed into Dorchester, where Phil had promised to meet her outside of the Harringtons' sealed-off home.

Neighborhood was quiet this morning, maybe even somber, but that could've been D.D.'s imagination. She always found it eerie to visit a scene the day after. The blood was no longer fresh, the sounds and smells had faded into memory. The house became a shell of what used to be. Once a family had lived here. Maybe they'd laughed and loved and been happy. Maybe not. But one way or another, they'd been carving out a life. And now they weren't. Just like that.

D.D. pulled in behind a Chevy Tahoe. She spotted Phil up ahead, standing in the middle of the sidewalk. Beside him was his new shadow, Police Academy professor Alex Wilson.

D.D. frowned, already aggravated, though she couldn't say why. She opened her car door, felt the ripe August heat slap against her face, and scowled harder. She clipped her creds to the waistband of her jeans, wished she could've been wearing a tank top instead of a short-sleeved blue cotton shirt, and got on with it.

Phil and Alex stood head-to-head in dark suits, apparently becoming fast friends. Both men looked up when she approached. Phil wiped a smile from his face; that already had her suspicious.

'Hey,' she tossed out to Phil, then turned her attention to Alex. 'Back for more?'

'Glutton for punishment,' he assured her.

'We're interviewing today, building profiles of the vics. Not exactly crime-scene material.'

The professor shrugged. 'Never know when you might learn something useful.'

She remained skeptical. Alex wore a charcoal-colored jacket over a blue dress shirt, dark slacks. He should be sweating, she thought, given the

74

heat. It bothered her that he didn't sweat, especially when she could already feel the first bead trickling down her spine to pool at the small of her back.

'Okay,' she said crisply, unfolding her paperwork. 'We have two primary targets this morning. Mrs. Patricia Bruni and Mr. Dexter Harding. In the interest of time, I'll take Bruni. You two can take Harding.'

Phil looked her. Alex looked at Phil.

'What?' she demanded.

'It would be better if we did them together,' Phil told her. 'Multiple impressions of what the individual has to say.'

'Three on one? We'll intimidate them before they say the first word.'

'Then you take the lead,' Phil replied easily. 'We'll hang back, blend into the backdrop.'

'Ride my coattails?'

'Exactly.' Phil took the first sheet from her. 'Patricia Bruni. Lives four houses up. Let's go.'

He started walking before she could say another word. Alex paused a beat, then fell in step beside her. 'Heard you had an interesting night at the hospital,' he commented.

'Not really.'

'I caught the Red Sox game myself.'

'Never follow baseball.'

'More of a Patriots fan?'

'More of a homicide fan. In case you forgot, fieldwork doesn't keep regular hours.'

She sounded prickly even to herself. Alex just grinned. That was it. He and Phil were up to something.

'What are your thoughts on Italian food?' Alex asked.

'Food is good,' D.D. allowed.

'Great. We'll have to get some later.'

They arrived at Patricia Bruni's house, another triple-decker with a broad front porch. D.D. was distracted.

'When? Do you mean for lunch?'

'Something like that,' Alex said, and with that enigmatic grin still on his face he followed her up the front steps.

* * *

Patricia Bruni turned out to be a wizened old black lady who went by Miss Patsy and believed in serving her guests, even cops, megaglasses of iced tea. D.D. had a good feeling about Miss Patsy, and not just for the cold iced tea; in D.D.'s experience, wizened old ladies always knew the most about what was going on in the neighborhood.

Miss Patsy invited them inside, 'out of the heat,' she said, and they gratefully followed her into her lower-level unit, where window air conditioners chugged away at full throttle. Her home was modest, boasting six rooms, lots of furniture, and an impressive collection of Hummel figurines. From what D.D. could tell, if it was small and breakable, Miss Patsy collected it.

D.D. took up the antique wooden chair across from Patsy. It was fun to watch Phil and Alex stand awkwardly in front of the camel-backed love seat, trying to figure out how to sit on its broken-down form. Alex finally perched gingerly on the edge. Older and heavier, Phil reluctantly followed suit. The love seat groaned, but held.

'You're here about the Harringtons,' Miss Patsy said straight off, patting her tightly coiled hair. 'I tried to tell that officer last night, don't you be thinking this was drugs or any of that other nonsense. Patrick and Denise were nice folks. Good Christian couple. We're lucky to have them on the block.'

'They live here long?' D.D. asked, sipping her iced tea. Sweet and cold. She loved Miss Patsy already.

'Bought the house last fall,' Patsy provided, confirming the timeline D.D. already had in her head. 'Duffys lived in it before that. Kept a lot of late hours, the Duffys did. Seemed to entertain on a regular basis, if you know what I mean.'

'Drug dealers?' D.D. ventured.

'Didn't hear it from me,' Patsy said, while nodding with her entire upper body.

'So the Duffys moved out, the Harringtons moved in. Get to see the new family very often?'

'Yes, ma'am. Denise came by the very first week with some pumpkin bread. She introduced herself and the kids, had 'em all lined up proper like. Said they were real excited to be living in the neighborhood and wondered if I could recommend a family-friendly church for them.'

'Did you?'

'First Congregational Church. Good community church and you can walk from here to there.' Patsy leaned forward again. 'I'm not supposed to drive, you know. Had a little problem hitting the wrong pedal last year. But it's okay, they've repaired that wall of the pharmacy now. Good as new.'

Alex made a sputtering noise from the love seat; iced tea down the wrong pipe. Phil obligingly whacked him on the back.

D.D. ignored them both. 'How often did you see the family?'

'Oh, least once a week at church. More during the summer. This is a nice neighborhood. Lots of kids play outside during the day. I like to take my tea on the front porch and watch the little ones riding their bikes and whatnot. Does a body good.'

'And the Harrington kids? What did they like to do?'

'Football, the boys. You'd see the older one and younger one playing catch. The girl, she was getting to that age where she just wanted to hang out with her friends. Denise commented that Molly was always pestering her for a ride to the mall. But sometimes, on the cooler evenings, you'd see a whole group out playing capture the flag or maybe hide-and-seek through everyone's yards. Not a bad place to live, our neighborhood.'

D.D. made a note. 'What were the kids doing this summer? Once school was out?'

'Summer camp at the Y,' Miss Patsy answered. ''Course, their father was home during the day, working on the house. Sometimes you'd see them hanging out with him. They liked to take breaks on the front porch. Renovation this time of year had to be pretty hot work.' Miss Patsy fanned herself.

'Family entertain much? Socialize with the rest of the block?'

'Yes, ma'am. They were happy to live here, wanted to get to know everyone. I had the impression their previous home wasn't in a very safe neighborhood — not a good place for kids, Denise would say. Like I said, they were real happy to move here.'

'You ever hear them fighting?' D.D. asked bluntly. 'Patrick and Denise?'

'You mean screaming at each other in the middle of the night?'

'Yeah, that sort of thing.'

'No, ma'am.' Miss Patsy said it primly.

'We heard Patrick lost his job. Money must've been tight.'

'Tough times all over,' Miss Patsy observed. 'I still saw them putting a dollar or two in the tithe plate when it passed; they weren't destitute yet.'

'Never heard them argue about it? Or taking an extra cocktail or two to help them unwind?'

'Never saw them drinking anything stronger than wine and beer. They were responsible people.'

'Drugs?'

'I already told you — no need to go down that road. Not with the Harringtons.' Miss Patsy gave a little sniff, as if maybe the same could not be said for some of the other neighbors.

'What about Denise and the kids? Did they have a tendency toward large bruises, broken bones? Report a lot of strange accidents?'

'Like falling down the stairs or running into doorknobs?' Miss Patsy asked.

'Exactly.'

'No, ma'am. Patrick didn't beat his family. Maybe he should've with the younger one. Lord knows I watched that kid provoke his father time and time again. But Patrick held his temper. He was a good man. In church, he would pray for patience. He knew what he was up against.'

D.D. exchanged glances with Phil and Alex. 'What do you mean, 'what he was up against'?'

'The younger son, the adopted child, he was trouble. Face of an angel, soul of the Devil, if you ask me.'

'The youngest child was adopted? The boy?' D.D. flipped through her notes. 'Oswald?'

'Ozzie's mother died when he was three years old. Guess folks didn't find her until months later. All that time, he lived in the apartment with her body, eating every last piece of food in the cupboards, including flour, cardboard, powdered lemonade. Denise told me when the social workers tried to take him away, the poor child broke down and started screaming uncontrollably. He spent some time in a psychiatric unit for little kids. I never knew they even had such a thing.'

This was news. D.D. could feel both Alex and Phil leaning forward. She kept her eyes on Miss Patsy. 'Know the name of the hospital where they admitted the child?'

'Someplace in Boston. He was there until last year. They brought him home once they moved here.'

'Sounds like you and Denise spoke quite a bit,' D.D. probed. 'She come over often? Maybe join you for iced tea on the porch?'

Miss Patsy nodded easily. 'Sure. This summer she came by couple of times a week. Sometimes she brought me cookies, maybe a pie. She's a very gracious woman, Denise. And yes, she was probably looking for a little time away from the family.' Miss Patsy held up a hand. 'Not saying that she and her husband were fighting. But she worked all day, then came home to three kids, one of them right demanding. Can't blame the woman for seeking out a little iced tea and adult company, can you?'

'Probably not. Denise ever mention any . . . extracurricular activities? Maybe she and Patrick weren't fighting. But maybe she'd met someone who'd caught her eye, or he'd found someone who caught his eye. These things happen. Maybe Denise was looking for a little womanly advice?'

'Never mentioned it,' Miss Patsy said, folding her hands on her lap. There was a moment of silence, then Miss Patsy regarded D.D. straight in the eye. 'Did Ozzie do it? Rumor mill is the whole family was slaughtered like chickens. Always thought that boy would do something terrible one day. Though maybe,' she sighed, 'not as terrible as this.'

'Miss Patsy, what makes you think Ozzie might be capable of doing something like murder?'

Miss Patsy sniffed a little. 'Heavens, what to mention? Boy was up and down, up and down the street all day, sunup to sundown if they'd let him. At church, he still had to attend the toddler room, 'cause he couldn't make it through the service. Had the worst case of fidget you ever did see. Rolling up his pant legs, rolling down his pants legs. Sitting up, sitting down, shifting right, shifting left. Never saw a child so ready to burst out of his own skin.

'And no sense of boundaries. Child would walk through your front door without knocking if you left it unlocked. Several of the neighbors kept finding him in their yards, sitting on their patio furniture as if he owned the place. Then there was the incident with him and Mr. Harding's barbecue. Boy said the grill turned over by 'accident,' but I gotta say, I wouldn't put it past him to dump hot coals on a wooden deck. When he felt slighted, he could be cruel. Did I mention the squirrels?'

'You haven't mentioned the squirrels.'

'He liked to throw stones at them. I yelled at him more times than I could count to leave the poor squirrels alone. Then you know what he did? I caught him one day in my own backyard, yanking a squirrel off the bird feeder. Guess he'd crept up on it while it was eating. Why, he grabbed it by its tail, whipped it around two or three times, then slammed its head into the feeder post. Terrible, terrible thing. Blood everywhere. He just stood over the poor creature, and smiled.

'Normal boys don't smile like that, Mrs. Detective Sergeant. Normal boys don't lick the blood off their hands.'

D.D. couldn't think of anything to say to that. Apparently, neither could Phil or Alex. 'When . . . when did this happen?' she ventured finally.

'May, or maybe June. Beginning of summer, we'll say. Ozzie wasn't allowed out of the house alone after that. Mostly, his older brother, Jacob, came out to keep tabs on him. Now, Jacob's a good boy. Strong and fast. Good arm, I'm told. Makings of a first-rate quarterback, to hear his father speak. Jacob seemed to be able to keep Ozzie in line.'

Miss Patsy paused, seemed to realize she had just spoken of Jacob in the present tense, and caught her breath in a small hiccup. 'Oh,' she said, and that one sad word spoke volumes of a family that did not exist anymore.

D.D. gave the woman a moment. She took another sip of her iced tea. She was almost done with her glass; Alex and Phil were as well.

Alex leaned forward, seemed to have something to say. D.D. nodded slightly and he cleared his throat.

'Miss Patsy?' he asked gently.

The old woman turned her gaze to him.

'Were you home last night?'

'Yes, sir.'

'What exactly did you hear?'

'Nothing out of the ordinary. But I was inside, had the air conditioners running. Can't hear much of anything over that hum.'

'Did you talk to any of the family members earlier in the day?'

'No, sir. Just saw Denise out, sweeping the front porch, when I went on my evening shuffle.

I gave her a little wave and she waved back.'

'Did she mention having company?'

'Not to me, sir.'

'Notice any strange cars in the neighborhood?'

'Oh, there were several. Always is this time of year, with all the summer barbecues.' She smiled faintly. 'We folks in Dorchester like to have fun.'

'Do you know of anyone who might bear a grudge against Patrick or Denise?' D.D. spoke up. 'Did either of them mention getting in a fight with anyone? How was their relationship with their ex-spouses?'

'Patrick was a widower; Denise never spoke of her former husband. I got the impression he was out of the picture. Maybe not so interested in domestic life. I certainly never saw anyone coming by to take the kids every other weekend.'

D.D. made a note. 'Times are hard,' she said softly, looking at Miss Patsy. 'Sounds like Patrick and Denise had a lot on their plate. Three kids to manage — one with some challenges. Plus, they had an entire triple-decker to remodel, then Patrick lost his job. That's a lot of stress for one family. Things happen when people are under that kind of stress.'

'The Harringtons are good people,' Miss Patsy repeated firmly.

'And the last time you spoke to either Denise or Patrick . . . ?'

'Two days ago. Denise came by around nine o'clock and we had a little wine on the front porch. Jacob was starting up football practice and had just been picked for the first string. She was gonna take Molly back-to-school shopping this weekend.' Miss Patsy shrugged. 'We talked of normal things, everyday things. Denise seemed happy enough to me.'

D.D. nodded, made another note — *Money??* — then rose off the chair, digging out her card. 'Thank you for your time, Miss Patsy. If you think of anything else, please give me a call. Oh, and, of course, thanks for the excellent iced tea.'

Miss Patsy nodded, shuffled to her feet. Phil offered to carry their glasses and iced tea pitcher back to the kitchen. Miss Patsy let him.

'It's true they're all dead?' Miss Patsy asked as she escorted them to her front door. 'Patrick, Denise, Jacob, Molly, and Ozzie?'

'Patrick's hospitalized. Critical condition.'

'Poor, poor man,' Miss Patsy murmured. 'I don't know what's worse: for him to join his family in Heaven, or for him to recover all alone. Sad choices for a good man. I guess you just never know what's really going on with your neighbors, do you?'

'Nope,' agreed D.D. 'You never do.'

8

By the time they were done with Mr. Dexter
Harding, it was after twelve and D.D. was
starving. Alex proposed that they break for
lunch. He knew a great little Italian bistro not far
from here. He said this more to D.D. than to
Phil, and Phil took the hint, ducking out with
some mumbled excuse about stacks of paperwork waiting for him on his desk.

D.D. was suspicious of her partner's abrupt
departure, but it was Italian food, so she didn't
press the matter.

She and Alex caravanned to the corner
restaurant, which featured green awnings and
the smell of garlic and fresh baked bread. D.D.
inhaled twice and decided she'd found a new
home.

Alex ordered lasagna. She went with chicken
parm. The waitress brought fresh bread to dip in
olive oil. D.D. tore her way through the steaming
loaf while checking phone messages. Patrick
Harrington remained in a drug-induced coma.
Neil, D.D.'s other squadmate, had made it
through the autopsy of the wife with no
surprises. The ME would start in on the girl after
lunch.

Finally, she had a message from Chip, the
almost-got-laid accountant, wondering if D.D.
wanted to try dinner a second time around.

She did, but given the way the morning was

going, Chip was going to have to be a very patient man.

'Okay,' D.D. declared half a loaf later, trying to check surreptitiously for olive oil dripping down her chin. 'We spent last night with one crime scene and the morning with two neighbors. You're the professor — what d'ya think?'

'Will there be a quiz later?' Alex asked mildly; he'd also been checking messages. Now he put away his phone and reached for the bread basket.

'Please. This case was supposed to be wrapped up five hours ago. You're gonna have to start detecting a lot quicker if you wanna roll with my squad.'

He arched a brow, seemed amused. He was a good-looking guy, D.D. decided. The charcoal-colored suit worked with his dark blue eyes and salt-and-pepper hair. A good-looking guy with good taste in restaurants. Hmm.

'Let's review the basics,' he said now, his deep baritone sounding very much like the teacher he purported to be. 'We have a crime scene with four stabbed and one shot, close contact to the head. Blood evidence tells us the victims were taken out one by one. The pattern would at first blush appear to be a murder-suicide, with the head of the household, Patrick Harrington, stabbing his entire family before shooting himself in the head.'

'At first blush,' D.D. agreed.

'Now, we'd love Patrick's take on this, but so far he's one step above a vegetable in the ICU, so that's not going to happen yet.'

'Darn convenient for him,' D.D. groused, then went for more bread.

'Which brings us to impressions of the family by friends and neighbors. We have the lovely Miss Patsy — '

'Very lovely,' D.D. interjected.

'Fabulous iced tea,' Alex agreed. 'Though a little heavy on the breakable figurines.'

'Don't sneeze in that house; it'll cost you.'

'Miss Patsy likes Denise and Patrick very much. Considers them stand-up parents, good Christians, and all-around nice neighbors, who did have a lot on their plate but were holding up well enough. On the other hand, she is not a fan of their adopted son, Ozzie, who has a history of creepiness.'

'Licking the blood off his hand . . . ' D.D. shivered.

'Now, the second neighbor, Dexter Harding, had a bit to add to that puzzle. Economic situation was a bit more dire than Miss Patsy understood from Denise. According to Dexter, Patrick considered them down to their last two months of operating income. Not a good place to be.'

'Ah, but according to Dexter, Patrick had a plan,' D.D. countered. 'Patrick believed he was just two weeks from finishing the second floor. Say he gave himself six weeks to get it rented, asking for first and last month's rent, plus deposit. That would be a significant cash injection due in the next two to eight weeks.'

'So we have a family in a tense economic condition, but not hopeless. Few things go according to plan, they could pull out of it.'

'Which suggests,' D.D. commented, 'that Patrick has reason to be stressed, but perhaps is not yet suicidal. I mean, why go postal now? You'd think if he's gonna lose it, it'll be eight weeks from now when he can't find a renter, doesn't get the money, etc., etc.'

'Logically speaking, yes,' Alex agreed. 'But he's still stressed, the wife's still stressed. Maybe someone said something last night at dinner. The daughter charged too much at the mall, the expenses for the older son's football uniform were higher than expected. All you need is a trigger. Things unfold from there.'

'Patrick can't stand the thought of his family ending up homeless, his kids becoming wards of the state . . . ' D.D. filled in. 'All of a sudden, Patrick convinces himself that killing his own family is the right thing to do. And our solid Christian neighbor turns into a family annihilator.'

The waitress appeared, sliding oval plates smothered in red sauce in front of each of them. The smell alone made D.D.'s mouth water. She loaded her chicken parm with grated cheese and went to town.

'Brings us back to the kid,' she managed after the third bite.

'Ah, but which one?' Alex asked with an arched brow. He was taking more time with his lasagna. A patient man, she observed. Probably had to be for working crime scenes. She wondered what had taken him from the field to the classroom, and what now made him want to be out in the field again.

'I mean Ozzie,' she prompted. 'You know, the one that kills squirrels for sport. Why? You're not suspecting the oldest, are you?'

The neighbor Dexter Harding had had some news: The Harringtons were not a family of five after all. They were a family of six. Patrick had an oldest son from a previous marriage who was currently in Iraq. In honor of Private William Edward Harrington, aka Billy, Denise often set a sixth plate at the table. The Harrington version of tie a yellow ribbon 'round the old oak tree.

It appeared they didn't have to worry about a mystery guest anymore. Unfortunately, Billy Harrington was about to get some very bad news from home.

'We should at least confirm the kid's in Iraq,' Alex said.

'Well, duh.'

He grinned at her. 'How's the chicken parm?'

'Love it.'

'I can tell.'

'How's the lasagna?'

'Almost as good as my grandmother's.'

D.D. eyed him suspiciously. 'With a last name like Wilson, you want me to believe you know about red sauce?'

'Ah, but my mother's a Capozzoli.'

'I stand corrected. With a name like Capozzoli, your grandmother can probably make some gravy.'

'She taught me everything I know,' Alex commented.

D.D. paused, fork midair. 'You can cook?'

'It's my passion. Nothing like a Sunday afternoon rolling out pasta while simmering a nice sauce Bolognese.'

D.D. couldn't swallow.

'You should come over for dinner sometime,' Alex said.

D.D. finally got it: the whispers, the exchanged glances ... 'Phil sold me out. Told you the quickest way inside my pants is through my stomach.'

'Didn't even cost me thirty pieces of silver,' Alex confirmed cheerfully. 'You should still come over for dinner.'

'I don't date fellow detectives.'

'I'm not a detective.' He smiled at her. 'For the next month, I'm just playing the part on TV.'

'Problem with dating another detective,' she continued as if she hadn't heard him, 'is that all you end up doing is talking shop.'

'We can talk food. What I enjoy cooking, what you enjoy eating.'

'I enjoy eating everything.'

'Works for me.'

She eyed him skeptically. 'Don't let my current good mood fool you; I'm a bitch most of the time.'

'Don't let my current charm fool you; I get as pissed off as the next guy.'

'Why the classroom?' she asked. 'Why leave the field for the classroom?'

'Had a wife. Wanted kids. More traditional hours seemed a good idea at the time.'

'What happened? She change her mind about Bolognese sauce?'

'Couldn't get pregnant. When my wife couldn't become a mother, she decided she didn't want to be a wife either. We split amicably two years back.'

'You're still teaching.'

'I like it.'

'But you're here now.'

'I like this, too.'

'That's awfully likable,' D.D. said with a scowl.

'Which is why you should come over for dinner.'

'I don't do kids,' she warned. 'I'm too old, too cranky.'

'Perfect, because I was just hoping for lots of sex.'

D.D. laughed, surprised and a little charmed. Laughter felt good after eighteen hours of working a crime scene. So did lunch. 'I'll think about it,' she said finally. She took a bite, chewed, swallowed. 'Now, back to the matters at hand: What do we make of nine-year-old Ozzie Harrington?'

'Kid's tricky,' Alex said at last.

'Kid's dead.'

'We've already had allegations of animal cruelty and petty arson. I'm guessing there's bed-wetting in there somewhere, which makes him a textbook serial killer.'

'Dexter thought the barbecue accident was really an accident,' D.D. countered.

'Dexter fidgeted uncontrollably every time we mentioned Ozzie's name. Kid gave him the heebie-jeebies. He was just trying to be polite about it.'

92

'He said Patrick and Denise could control Ozzie. Also, that Ozzie worshipped his older brother Jacob. Seems unlikely, then, that Ozzie would turn on them, especially one by one like that.'

'That's the problem,' Alex said. 'A nine-year-old boy with a history of severe psychiatric problems could absolutely take out an entire family. In the middle of the night, armed with a shotgun or baseball bat, going from bedroom to bedroom . . . If that were our crime scene, I'd say the freaky son did it and Patrick was lucky to get out alive.'

'But it's dinnertime with a kitchen knife,' D.D. said quietly. 'Patrick's not a small guy. Then you have fourteen-year-old Jacob, also athletic. Seems like the two of them would be able to wrestle a scrawny nine-year-old to the ground.'

'And you'd see more defensive wounds,' Alex said. 'From the girl, everyone. Ozzie's the smallest member of the household. They'd absolutely put up a struggle. For that matter, I'm not sure a nine-year-old would have the strength to strike the mortal blow to Mrs. Harrington. We'll get a report back soon enough, but I'm already guessing the angle of the blow suggests someone taller than Denise, not shorter.'

'Methodology makes it tricky,' D.D. commented. 'Assuming Ozzie is the perpetrator, that means he, what? Shot his father with a gun. Then grabbed a kitchen knife and killed his mother with a single blow, killed his older brother with a single blow, then chased his sister through the house before ultimately catching her and strangling her. Then, after all that, he slit his own throat? Tough way to commit hari-kari.'

'Actually, I've seen it done.'

'Really?'

'Case back in ninety-seven. Depressed ad executive slit his own throat. We had our doubts, given the injury, but the ME could prove it from the angle of incision. Don't ask me. There are times forensics seems like pure voodoo.'

'All right. So Ozzie slit his own throat. Then he carried the bodies through the house to a single location? It just doesn't make sense. Blood tells us Ozzie's throat was slit in the sister's bedroom. Physical size tells us there was no way Ozzie would've had the strength to drag his mother or father through the house.'

'Which brings us back to Patrick,' Alex agreed. 'Only logical explanation.'

D.D. pushed back her plate. 'So why don't I feel good about it?'

'Because sometimes, we never understand our neighbors, not even after the fact.'

D.D. sighed, thought he had a point. 'We dig into the financials, bet we're going to find some consumer debt, some past-due bills. We'll see just how on edge the Harringtons were living. Then we'll pay a visit to the kids' school, Denise's work, Patrick's former employer, round out our victim profiles.'

'We should also pay a visit to the psychiatric unit where Ozzie stayed. Remember, Miss Patsy said he was hospitalized for a bit.'

'I thought we just ruled out Ozzie.'

Alex shrugged. 'There's still something we don't know. Or, for that matter, someone.'

9

DANIELLE

Lucy escaped shortly before three.

I should've seen it coming. She'd started the day remarkably calm. By eight a.m., she'd eaten dry Cheerios without throwing the cup at anyone passing by. At eight-thirty, she crept out of her room long enough to swipe a toy car Benny had left in the hall. She'd tucked it under her chin as she scampered on all fours to a corner of her room. Then she'd set the Hot Wheel on the floor and proceeded to bat it around like a cat toy.

Benny cried when he discovered the car gone, then stopped crying when he saw the crazy naked girl smiling over it. She caught him watching her, too, and simply went back to playing, versus throwing feces at him.

I was so pleased by this progress, I decided to make an attempt at basic hygiene.

We don't force our kids to shower. We don't force them to eat, brush their teeth, or even get dressed. We understand that some of these kids, because of sensory issues, feel the spray of a shower as a thousand needles stinging their skin. We understand some of these kids, because of various compulsions, can only eat frozen food, or mashed-up food, or yellow food, or prepackaged food. We understand that some of these kids, because of limited social skills, can't walk down

96

the hallway without picking a fight.

Hygiene's complicated. Mealtimes are complicated. Just getting up each morning is complicated.

So we take a broad approach. This is our schedule. We'd like you to follow it, but we're willing to work with you. Tell us what you need. Together, we can make this happen.

Some parents hate us. They view our ward as nothing but summer camp, kowtowing to their problem child's every whim.

Of course, half of these parents are as traumatized as the kids. They've spent years being kicked, hit, bit, screamed at, and otherwise verbally abused by their own child. Maybe on Mother's Day, their ten-year-old drew a picture of Mommy being stabbed to death, and signed it *Die Bitch Die*. Now a part of them wants to see their son finally be held accountable for his actions, or feel that their daughter is being ground to dust. We're the professionals. We should force each child to color within the lines. But we don't. We let the kids watch TV. We bring them Game Boys, we engage them in board games, we let them rollerblade down the hall.

We're acute care. Our goal is to reduce agitation so a kid can finally get through the day without exploding. Then, once the child is 'workable,' we hope to gain insight into that kid's behavior that will be valuable for long-term care.

There are two questions we're trying to answer with each child:

What's going on in this child's head that I wish *weren't* (e.g., cognitive distortions)? What *isn't* going on in this child's head that I wish were (e.g., cognitive deficiencies)? You answer these two questions, you can learn a lot about a kid.

Twenty-four hours later, I needed to learn a lot more about Lucy.

First, I filled a giant bucket with water, then carried it to her room. I didn't look at her when I entered, didn't acknowledge her in any way. I set down the bucket, then gave her my back.

I counted to ten.

When she didn't attack, I moved to phase two: I pulled a small sponge out of my pocket, dipped it into the water, and starting scrubbing the nearest wall. I still didn't look at her. If attention is one of her triggers, then my job's not to give her any attention.

After another minute, I started to hum. Something low and melodic. Some children respond positively to rhythmic music; I was curious about Lucy.

She still didn't react, so I grew more serious. I scrubbed feces and blood off all four walls. Then I picked up my bucket and disappeared.

Now the moment of judgment: Will Lucy leave the space as is, or will she feel a need to trash her room again, to violate her personal space as she seems to feel a need to violate herself?

When twenty minutes passed without any drama, I brought her lunch. Cut-up vegetables, a cheese stick, some fresh bread, a cup of water. I stood in the hallway where I could monitor her reflection in the silver ceiling globe without being seen.

Lucy went after the bread first. She picked it up between her hands and squished it into a ball, then placed it on the floor and watched it slowly expand. Then she resquished it, until the bread was balled tight enough to bat around on the carpet.

She played with her food for a bit, content in her catlike alter ego. I wondered why a cat. What was it about felines that she thought would keep her safe?

After a bit, she picked up the bread ball between her cupped hands and ate it. She licked her hands afterward, then lapped up some water from the cup. The cheese suffered the same fate as the bread. She didn't eat the vegetables but hid them under her mattress. I wasn't surprised. Lots of kids hoarded food, maybe due to compulsion, or from a long history of going hungry. I left the vegetables for now, if only to see what she'd do with them later.

Thirty minutes later, I entered Lucy's room to fetch her plate and cup. I kept my back to her. No displays, so we were making progress.

Back in the kitchen, I filled a smaller bowl with warm water and found a clean sponge. This time when I entered Lucy's room, I sat sideways to her. She was by the window, studying a giant square of light on her floor, formed by the sun. She splayed her fingers in the sunbeam, watching the shadow made by her fingers. Then she turned toward the window, closing her eyes and letting the sun fall upon her face.

For an instant, she wore an expression that could almost be called happiness.

I gave her a bit. When she finally seemed to be tiring of sun and shadows, I picked up the sponge, dipped it in the bowl of water, and held it over my bare forearm. I squeezed out droplets, letting the water trickle down. I wanted her to notice this new, intriguing game.

I played for a bit. I dropped water here and there, making dark patterns on my clothes, the flooring, wherever I felt like it. When working with kids, it's always helpful to be childish.

After a while, I could tell Lucy was watching me. She wouldn't draw closer, but she was curious. So I stretched it out five more minutes. I splashed water on my face, trickled it in my hair. Then I got up and walked out of the room, leaving the water and sponge behind.

It was tempting to stop and watch. But she was a child, not an exhibit at the zoo. So I kept marching. One of our recent charges, Jorge, ran up to me. I agreed to play dominoes with him. Then it was craft time with Aimee, a twelve-year-old girl admitted for attempted suicide. She sat with her body collapsed on itself, drawing a black sky with black rain. I suggested she add color, so she dotted red on top of the black. Now the sky was bleeding.

I hugged her before I headed back down the hall.

I found Lucy, sitting back in the sunbeam. She had the water bowl beside her, the sponge in her hand.

Her face was finally clean. She'd wiped off

streaks of feces, used the water to smooth back her matted hair. She sat now, with her clean face held up to the sun, and the small curve of her lips almost made my heart break.

★ ★ ★

The next time I checked in, she was gone. The empty water bowl and sponge were stacked neatly in the sunbeam. Otherwise, the room was empty. Lucy had flown the coop.

★ ★ ★

I didn't worry at first. We're a lockdown ward, meaning Lucy was here somewhere. I just had to find her.

I contacted the milieu counselor in charge of 'checks' — accounting for every child's position every five minutes. Greg had the duty, meaning he'd been roaming the unit for the past hour. He hadn't seen Lucy — she was the exception to our five-minute check rule; her assigned staff member, namely me, was supposed to write down her location every twenty minutes. Greg passed the word along, and soon we were all on a Lucy hunt.

Kids joined us. This was hide-and-seek on a grand scale, and the kids who'd been with us for a while knew the drill and were happy to help. Since our unit didn't have video cameras, we took advantage of the silver globes in the ceiling, searching for Lucy's reflection. According to the globes, she wasn't in the main hallway, the dorm rooms, or the family room. Now we got serious.

We went through cupboards, wardrobes, nightstands, bathrooms, and closets. The kitchen area was locked, but we checked anyway, just in case. The Admin space was locked; we tossed the warren of small rooms as well.

By three-fifteen, when we still hadn't found Lucy, the staff, not to mention some of the kids, started to grow agitated.

Greg took charge of the kids. Time for afternoon snack. The staff peeled off, returning to the business of running the unit. Karen, the nurse manager, pulled me aside.

'When did you last see her?'

'Two-fifteen,' I reported.

'What was she doing?'

'Sitting in a sunbeam, making shadows with her fingers.'

Karen arched one brow, intrigued. 'When did you notice she was missing?'

I hesitated. 'Two forty-five.'

Karen looked at me. 'That's thirty minutes, Danielle, not twenty. We agreed someone would check her every twenty minutes.'

I had no good excuse, so I simply nodded.

Karen regarded me for a moment. She'd been working most of her adult life with troubled kids and her gaze was penetrating. I could tell she'd finally noted the month and day and made the connection I thought she'd make at least a week ago.

That's the life of the sole survivor: You never escaped the anniversary date.

'Is Lucy too much for you?' Karen asked abruptly.

'No.'

'We've always been willing to work with you, Danielle,' she stated crisply. 'But you have to be willing to work with us. Understand?'

'Lucy's not too much,' I said, voice stronger.

But Karen remained uncertain. She finally sighed, moved along. 'Is Lucy still naked?'

'Last I saw.'

'Then she couldn't have gotten far.'

Karen made the decision to contact the medical center's security. The full hospital went to lockdown, and I felt about three inches tall. I'd lost my charge. I'd breached protocol in a place where protocol breaches were unacceptable. And while my personal life wasn't anything to write home about, I took my job seriously. I was a dedicated nurse. Some days, I was even a great nurse.

Apparently, today wasn't one of those days. We had an emergency staff meeting, with Karen briskly assigning hospital floors to each of us to search. Security was also making a sweep.

I had the first and second floors. I headed out, feeling sick in my stomach.

Where would Lucy go? What would she do?

Then I had an idea.

I bolted for the hospital solarium.

★ ★ ★

Ten minutes later, I'd found Lucy. She was behind a potted palm, in a full-blaze sun, curled

103

up like a cat and sound asleep with her head on her joined hands. Somewhere during her adventures, she'd found a green surgical scrub top and was now wearing it like a gown. She nearly blended into the floor, her dark hair obscuring her freshly scrubbed face.

I radioed upstairs that I'd found her.

Then, because this was the best rest I'd seen her get, I took a seat on the floor and waited.

Greg eventually came down, sat beside me. 'Tough day,' he said, after a moment.

'She's okay. That's what matters.'

'Bad luck, getting out. Must have snuck through the doors when an outsider was coming or going.'

He said it casually, but we both knew there would be an investigation. It was extremely bad luck Lucy made it through two sets of locked doors. Such bad luck, it'd never happened in all the years I'd worked here, and I still couldn't imagine how a naked nine-year-old girl had done it now.

Heads would roll over this. Maybe mine.

I felt anxious. I couldn't lose this job. I loved this job, especially this time of year, when — Karen was right — I wasn't altogether sane and they kept me anyway.

Greg touched my cheek. For a change, I didn't flinch. Greg and I had been coworkers for years. He was a good-looking guy. Tall, fit, a natural jungle gym for small boys bursting out of their own skin. He dressed like a football coach, and spoke with the best baritone on the unit. Even the worst kids shut up just to catch the timbre of his speech.

He'd asked me out for the first time two years ago. I'd never said yes. He'd never stopped asking. I didn't know how one guy could take so much rejection and still come back for more, but maybe that went with the job.

Now I found myself thinking of Sheriff Wayne again. But I refused to cry, because that would be stupid.

Lucy finally stirred. She raised her head, blinked her eyes, regarded us owlishly.

Quickly, before she was awake enough to fight, Greg and I tucked her between us and hustled her to the elevators.

I was still thinking of too many things. That it was three days away. That it shouldn't matter anymore. A date on a calendar, a day that rolled by once a year. And I knew Karen had finally figured out my schedule, why I'd been logging so many hours. Because the date did matter, somehow it always mattered, and in another twenty-four hours or so, I'd have to disappear. I wouldn't be fit for the kids. I wouldn't be fit for adults.

And I certainly wouldn't be fit for a decent guy like Greg, who'd want to hold me and make it all better.

Once a year, I didn't want it to be all better.

Once a year, I liked honing my rage.

Because I am the lone survivor, and I'm still pissed off about that.

The elevator took us up to the eighth floor. I waved my ID to enter the lobby. Karen was waiting for us, but not alone. A blonde woman with curly hair and a salt-and-pepper-haired man in a charcoal-colored suit stood beside her. Both were holding out police shields.

'Danielle,' Karen began.

And I knew, right at that moment, that it had started again.

10

VICTORIA

What does it feel like for a father to leave his child? Does he wake up in the morning remembering his son's first smile? Maybe the way his baby used to fit in the curve of his arm, solemn blue eyes peering up, rosebud lips pursed thoughtfully?

Does he remember the first time his boy said 'Daddy'? Or the way Evan used to run to the door and throw his arms around his father's legs?

Does he torture himself with the what-ifs, the might-have-beens? The vision he had of one day coaching his son's soccer team? The dream of attending their first Patriots game together, or maybe cheering for the Celtics at the Garden? Does he consider the gaping hole in his future where the driving lessons, man-to-man talks, and first shave should've been?

Does he know that in the days and weeks afterward, Evan fell asleep still crying for the father who never came?

When Michael and I finally brought Evan home from the NICU, we were convinced the worst was behind us. He sat up at three months. Crawled at ten months. The pediatrician was impressed.

He cried, sometimes for hours at a stretch.

Sleep was difficult, naptimes nearly nonexistent. I read books on various sleep techniques while reporting the challenges to the doctor. Babies cried, he assured me. Evan wasn't exhibiting any signs of colic and was steadily gaining weight, always a concern with a preemie. As far as the medical experts were concerned, Evan was fussy but fabulous. Michael and I took that to heart. This was our son, our parenting experience, fussy but fabulous.

Michael was hands-on in those days. When he came home from work, he'd take his turn pacing the house with Evan crying against his shoulder. He'd encourage me to take some time for myself. Read a book, indulge in a bubble bath, take a nap. Together we could handle this.

At fourteen months, Evan made the transition from crawling to running. Suddenly, he slept much better at night, maybe because he raced around like a rocket all day. I went from endlessly soothing a baby to frantically chasing a toddler. Evan didn't seem to have a sense of his own space. He ran into walls, fell off chairs, and walked in front of moving swings. At the playground, he was a threat to himself and others.

He didn't fear strangers. He didn't believe other kids ever wanted to play alone. He ran into groups, elbowed his way into other children's sandboxes. He had this hundred-watt smile and these brilliant blue eyes. At fourteen months, it was as if the world already wasn't big enough for him. He had so much to do, so much to see, and so much to say.

An older woman once sat beside me on a park bench just to listen to the magic of Evan's laughter as he rolled in a pile of fall leaves.

'He is an old soul,' she told me before leaving. 'A very old soul. Watch him. Listen to him. He will teach you what you need to know.'

Around this time Evan stopped wearing clothes. He'd always cried if we dressed him in anything other than cotton. Now he refused even that. I found shirts, socks, pants, diapers strewn down the hallway, and sometimes across swing sets. I put the clothes back on. He took them back off.

We stayed home more often; naked eighteen-month-olds weren't always welcome at a public park.

Evan also started some new and alarming habits. For example, he took to climbing onto the kitchen counter so he could play with the knives. He liked to hold them by the blade, as if he needed to slice open his palms in order to understand how sharp the edges were. The same went with the stove. I gave up cooking unless Michael was home. Evan was obsessed with the burners. The more we told him they were hot, the more he *needed* to place his fingers across the glowing red coils.

It was like living with a bull in a china shop. One day he broke all the eggs in the kitchen in order to hear how they would sound (I was on the phone). The next afternoon, he smashed every bottle of perfume I owned against the tile floor, to see how far the glass would shatter (I was in the downstairs lavette). I caught him climbing the china cabinet one afternoon, and wisely padlocked the doors (I'd been in the shower, but realized I couldn't hear Evan and went bolting through the house in nothing but a towel).

We saw our first expert, a child development specialist. We received our first diagnosis. Evan suffered from global Sensory Integration Disorder; his brain was properly receiving input from his five senses, but could not prioritize the sensations. Meaning he existed in an overstimulated state — a full cup, the specialist explained to us, where each new sound, scent, touch, smell, and taste was another drip, drip, drip into an overflowing vessel. Some things he could not tolerate at all: the rasp of a zipper, the feel of denim. Other sensations he fixated on, trying to get them to penetrate the clutter of his brain — what is sharp, what is hot, what is pain. He was like a moth, drawn to the flame.

Evan started to receive occupational therapy. Michael agreed that I needed help, so we hired our first in a string of what would become fourteen part-time nannies.

I went on walks to clear my head and refresh my body. Then I came home to my crazy, exuberant wild child. He would bowl me over with his hugs. Light up the world with the exuberance of his laughter. We would wrestle, tickle, and play endless games of hide-and-seek.

Then he would scream over having to brush his teeth. Or fly into a rage over having been served pasta on the wrong-colored plate. He threw one of Michael's golf balls through our family room window when we asked him to put on shoes. He slapped me across the face when I told him it was time for bed.

Our first nanny quit, then the second, the third.

When Evan was happy, he was so happy. But when he was angry, he was so angry, and when he was sad . . . he was so, so sad.

We received our second diagnosis: Mood Disorder NOS (Not Otherwise Specified). At four, we put him on clonidine, a drug generally used with ADHD to help moderate impulsive and oppositional behavior. We hoped the clonidine would take off the edge, allowing Evan to find some measure of self-control.

He improved in the short term. Slept better at night. Less manic during the day. Between the clonidine and a one-to-one aide, it appeared he might survive preschool.

Time, Michael and I told ourselves. Evan just needed time. Time for the occupational therapy to assist with the hypersensitivity. Time to better develop his own coping skills. We had challenges, but all parents had challenges. Right?

Evan started kindergarten. He interrupted the teacher. He laughed at inappropriate times. He screamed if told to stop doing an activity he wanted to do, and refused to engage in an activity he didn't want to do.

In the first eight weeks, Michael and I were summoned to the school nearly a dozen times. We sat there self-consciously. Well-groomed, professional parents who had no idea why our child was a five-year-old hoodlum. We loved

Evan. We set boundaries for him. We fought for him.

Still, Evan wanted to do what Evan wanted to do and he was willing to employ any means necessary to get his way.

Third and fourth diagnoses: ADHD and Anxiety Disorder NOS. At the school's insistence, we put him on the antidepressant Lexapro. Lexapro affects the serotonin levels in the brain. We were told it would calm Evan, help him focus.

Your son's brain is a busy, busy place, the specialist told us. *Imagine standing in the middle of a parade and trying to remain still while hearing the horns blow in your ear and feeling the marchers sweep by. Evan loves you. Evan wants to do well. But Evan can't exit from the parade long enough to be Evan.*

We dutifully filled the prescription. It's the American way, right? Your child is disruptive, misbehaving, nonconforming. Drug him.

Two weeks later, while quietly sketching a picture of a race car, Evan sat up and drove his pencil through the eardrum of the five-year-old girl sitting beside him.

That was the end of kindergarten for Evan.

Later, we learned Evan suffered from a paradoxical reaction to the Lexapro. A paradoxical reaction is when a drug has the opposite effect than intended. For example, a pain reliever causes pain. Or a sedative causes hyperactivity. Lexapro was supposed to calm our son. Instead, it sent him into a new orbit of agitation, and he acted accordingly.

We found a new doctor for Evan. Best Ph.D. in Boston, we were told. I hired nanny number nine and settled in to home-school Evan.

Michael started working longer hours. Gotta pay for the specialists, he would say, as if I couldn't smell the perfume that lingered on his coat, or see how many times he checked his cell phone for text messages.

I wondered if she was young and beautiful, maybe with frosted blonde hair that didn't suffer from neglected roots. Maybe her womb had never filled with poison. Maybe she could take her son to the grocery store without him hurling produce at the other shoppers. Maybe she went to restaurants without her child dumping pasta on the floor and making handprints out of red sauce.

Maybe she slept through the night and read the newspaper each morning and could converse wittily on a variety of adult topics.

Or maybe she just giggled, and told Michael he was perfect.

You try as a parent. You love beyond reason. You fight beyond endurance. You hope beyond despair.

You never think, until the very last moment, that it still might not be enough.

★　★　★

It's four in the afternoon on Friday, and the sky is dark with thunder-clouds. Given the intense August heat, most people are grateful for the upcoming relief. I don't care. I left the house five minutes late and now I'm driving too fast, trying to make up for lost time.

I have only two hours. I get them twice a week. It's not like I can leave my eight-year-old with the teenager down the street. But Michael pays child support, and I use that money for respite care, so that twice weekly a specially trained person comes to watch Evan. One of those days, I go to the grocery store, pharmacy, bank, doing all the things I can't do with Evan in tow. That was last night. Tonight, my second night off for the week, I drive to Friendly's.

My daughter is waiting for me there.

Chelsea sits in a back booth; Michael's across from her. He's wearing a light summer suit over the top of a striking blue Johnston & Murphy shirt. The suit drapes his muscled frame nicely. Obviously, he's been keeping up with his weekly boxing habit. You can take the boy out of the neighborhood, but not the neighborhood out of the boy.

When Michael spots me weaving my way through the crowded dining room, he puts away his BlackBerry and slides to standing.

'Victoria,' Michael says.

'Michael,' I answer.

Same exchange, every week. We never deviate.

'I'll be back at six-thirty.' He says this more to Chelsea than to me, bending down, giving her a kiss on the cheek.

Then he's gone and I'm alone with my daughter.

Chelsea's six. She has Michael's dark hair, my fine features. She holds herself tight, tall for her

114

age, mature for her years. Living with an older brother like Evan can do that to a girl.

'Have you ordered?' I ask, sliding into Michael's seat, placing my purse beside me on the red vinyl.

She shakes her head.

'What looks good?' I sound forced. It's like this every week. I have one evening to try to prove to my daughter I love her. She has six evenings that tell her otherwise.

Chelsea closes her menu, doesn't say anything. A balloon pops across the room, and she flinches. By the terms of our divorce decree, Michael's supposed to provide counseling for Chelsea, but I don't know if he's doing it. After all the experts we saw for Evan, he's soured on that sort of thing.

But Chelsea isn't Evan. She's a lovely little girl who spent her first five years never knowing if her brother would hug her with affection or attack her in a psychotic rage. She learned by age two when to run and lock herself in the nearest bathroom. By three, she could dial 911. And she was there, eleven months ago, when Evan found the crowbar in the garage and went after every window in the house.

Michael and Chelsea left the next day. It's been me and Evan ever since.

'How's school?' I ask.

She shrugs. I have to honor the mood, so I reach across the table for the cup filled with crayons. I flip over my place mat and start drawing a picture. After a moment, Chelsea does the same. We color a bit in silence, and I tell myself it's enough.

The waitress comes. I order a garden salad. Chelsea goes with chicken fingers.

We color some more.

'I get to be the flower girl,' Chelsea says abruptly.

I pause, force myself to find yellow, add to my gardenscape. *Wedding?* The divorce was only finalized six months ago. I knew Michael was seeing someone, but this . . . It seems undignified somehow. A gross display in the middle of a funeral.

'You get to be a flower girl?' I ask.

'In Daddy and Melinda's wedding. It will be during Christmas. I get to wear green velvet.'

'You'll . . . you'll look beautiful.'

'Daddy says Melinda will be my new Mommy.' Chelsea's not coloring anymore. She's staring at me.

'She'll become your stepmom. You'll have a stepmom and a mom after the wedding.'

'Do stepmoms like to eat at Friendly's?'

I can't do it. I put down the crayon, stare hard at the tabletop. 'I love you, Chelsea.'

She picks up her crayon and returns to coloring. 'I'm mad,' she says, almost conversationally. 'I don't want a new mom. Sarah has one, and she says stepmoms are no fun. And I don't like green velvet. It's hot. The dress is ugly.'

I say nothing.

'I want to rip the dress,' she continues. 'I want to get scissors and cut it up. Cut, cut, cut. Or maybe I could drip paint all over it. Drip, drip,

116

drip. Then I wouldn't have to wear it.' She looks up again. 'Mommy, am I turning into Evan?'

My heart twists. I take her hand. There are so many things I'd like to say to her. That she's special, unique, beautiful. That I have loved her since the moment she was born. That none of this is her fault, not her brother's illness and certainly not the Sophie's Choice made by her mother every day.

'You're *not* your brother, Chelsea. Evan . . . Evan has things in his head no one else has. His brain works differently. That's why he gets so mad he can't control himself. You're not like that. Your brain isn't his brain. You are you. And it's okay if you get mad. Sometimes, we all get mad.'

'I don't like Melinda,' Chelsea says, more plaintive now. 'Daddy's always at work. He's no fun anymore.'

'I'm sorry.'

'Weddings are stupid. Stepmoms are stupid. Stupid, stupid, stupid.'

'I'm sorry.'

'Why can't Evan go away? Daddy says that if Evan would just go away . . . '

I don't answer. This is where Michael and I diverge. He wants his children to be fixable, whereas I've come to accept that our son has an illness no doctor can currently cure. Evan's still our child, however, and just because he's troubled is no reason to throw him away.

The waitress arrives with our food. She slides two oval plates onto the table. I rearrange my salad. Chelsea pokes at her french fries.

'Evan misses you,' I say after a moment. 'He wishes you could both go to the park.'

Chelsea nods. There were times she and Evan were close. When he was calmer, in his sweet, charming mode. He would play dress-up with Chelsea, even let her do his hair. They'd play hide-and-seek, or form a rock band using all the kitchen pans. Those times, he was amazing and I imagine she misses that big brother. I also imagine there are plenty of other incidents she wishes to forget.

Chelsea is why Michael left me. He claimed my inability to institutionalize Evan was putting our daughter's life at risk. Is he right? Am I right? How will we ever know? The world doesn't give us perfect choices, and I couldn't figure out how to sacrifice my son, not even for my daughter.

So here I am and here she is, and I love her so much my chest hurts and I can't swallow my food. I just sit here, across from this quiet little girl, and I try to will my love into her. If I force my love across the table, form it in a tight little ball, and hit her with it again and again, maybe she will feel it. Maybe, for one instant, she will know I love her more than Evan, which is why I had to let her go.

She'll be okay. Evan, however, needs me.

We draw some more. I ignore my salad. She eats french fries. She tells me she got to try the violin at music camp. And Sarah and her got into a fight, because Sarah said Hannah Montana was better than The Cheetah Girls, but then they both agreed that *High School*

Musical is the best ever and now they're friends again. Dance starts in two weeks. She is nervous for the first day at school. She wants to know if we can go shopping together for school clothes. I tell her I will try. I can tell from the look on her face she already knows it won't happen.

The waitress clears our plates. Chelsea perks up at the thought of ice cream. She goes with the junior sundae. I decline, though ice cream would be good for me. I could use some weight on my frame. Maybe I should go on an ice cream diet. I will eat a gallon a day and balloon out to three hundred pounds. It's not like anyone would care.

Self-pity gets me nowhere, so I reach across the table and hold my daughter's hand again. Tonight, she lets me. Next week, I'll have to wait and see.

She's going to have a second mother. Some woman I've never met. I try to picture her, and my brain locks on some twenty-something blonde. Younger, prettier, perkier than me. She'll help Chelsea pick out clothes for school, maybe braid her hair. She'll be the first to hear of Chelsea's school dramas, perhaps give her advice for handling her equally dramatic friends. They will bond. Maybe there'll come a week when Chelsea won't want to come to Friendly's anymore.

I want to be bitter, but what would be the point? Chelsea's job is to grow up, move forward. My job is to let her go. I just didn't think it would be happening at the age of six.

Michael appears in the dining room. He

doesn't say anything, just stands there. Chelsea and I take the hint. I place money on the table for the check, then gather my things. By the time I slide out of the booth, Michael is already at the front doors, Chelsea lagging somewhere in between, trying to split the difference between her father ahead, her mother behind.

I catch up with her and we push out through the glass doors, where the storm has finally broken and cooling rain comes down in sheets. We hesitate under the awning, gathering ourselves for the sprint to the cars. Michael uses the moment to say, 'I'm sure Chelsea mentioned the wedding to you.'

'Congratulations,' I say. Then ruin the moment by adding, 'When would you like Evan to get fitted for a tux?'

The look he shoots me would've killed a lesser woman. I deliver it right back. I dare him to deny our firstborn child, who still asks when his father will be coming home.

'I didn't leave you,' Michael states crisply, voice low, so Chelsea won't hear. 'You left me. You left me the second you decided his needs mattered more than anyone else's.'

'He's a child — '

'Who needs professional full-time care.'

'An institution, you mean.'

'There are other ways to help him. You refused to consider any of them. You decided you knew best. You and only you could help him. After that, Chelsea and I didn't matter anymore. You can't blame us for getting on with our lives.'

But I do, I want to tell him, *I do.*

He motions to Chelsea that it's time to go. Her head is down, her body language subdued. Even if she can't hear the words, she knows we're fighting and it's hurt her.

I put my arms around my daughter. I feel the silk of her hair, the lightness of her slender body. I inhale the scent of coconut shampoo and Crayola markers. I hug her, hard, for this hug has to last me an entire week. Then I let her go.

She and her father bolt across the rain-swept parking lot, hands over their heads to protect themselves from the deluge. Minutes later, they're both in Michael's BMW and it's pulling away, rear lights glowing red in the gloom.

* * *

I don't know how it feels for a father to leave his son. I only know how it feels for a mother to leave her daughter, my heart driving away from me and leaving a gaping hole in the middle of my chest.

I step out in the storm, unhurried now. I let the rain soak my hair, batter my white blouse. I let the deluge pound against my face.

Friday night. *Three more days*, I think.

I drive home to Evan.

11

D.D. had never been to a locked-down pediatric psych ward, and she wasn't sure she wanted to start. But of all members of the Harrington family, Ozzie remained the most intriguing. Patrick's former employer had nothing but positive things to say. Denise's boss was so choked up over her murder he could barely speak. They got bursts of 'great woman,' 'devoted mom,' 'heart as big as the sky,' in between fresh bouts of muffled sobbing.

Phil phoned in with the credit report; it was about what they'd expected. The Harringtons were down to their last eight hundred in the bank. They had a substantial mortgage payment due, not to mention ten grand in credit cards. Up until this point, the family had never missed a payment. Chances were, that had been about to change.

In the plus column, the Harringtons received a check every month from the state for Ozzie; also, Denise had just gotten a modest raise at her receptionist job. Judging by the going rate in Dorchester, the family could hang on if they got the upper two floors rented. Phil and Professor Alex were going to walk through the space this evening to estimate just how close Patrick might have been to that goal.

And if the Harringtons did lose the house? Patrick's first wife was dead; Denise's first husband, out of the picture. Did Patrick or Denise have other family that could take them in? Was there a possibility of them receiving assistance from the church?

D.D. wanted answers to those questions. Better yet, she wanted to find out if Denise or Patrick had made the same inquiries. From their perspective, how deep was the chasm that loomed in front of them? Was it a matter of *Oh well, we can always move in with brother Joe?* Or was it *Dammit, we're facing three kids in a homeless shelter with no hope of getting out?*

Eighteen hours after the initial call, D.D. had four dead, and one in critical condition. For suspects she got to choose between a middle-aged family man and his nine-year-old psychotic son. The father had more physical capability. The son had more mental inclination.

Which brought her and her new shadow, Professor Alex, to the Pediatric Evaluation Clinic of Boston, part of the Kirkland Medical Center.

First steps into the locked-down psych unit weren't what D.D. expected. The ceiling yawned nine feet above. Natural light poured in massive windows to illuminate pale green carpeting and soft blue walls. Built-in benches featured fabrics dotted with small yellow ducks, while a cluster of wooden tables bore buckets of Legos. Place reminded her of a waiting room in an upscale pediatrician's office. Except the kids checked in for a much longer stay.

D.D. was just turning toward Alex when a black girl with twin braids flapping underneath her red helmet whizzed by on Rollerblades. A second later, a smaller boy in sagging blue sweatpants followed in hot pursuit, not as well balanced, but churning forward for all he was worth.

D.D. jumped back. Alex, too.

'Becca, Arnie, not beyond the orange cone!' a man's voice boomed. The girl and boy each turned — her gracefully, him awkwardly — then raced back the other direction, barely missing D.D. and Alex a second time.

'Sorry,' the man called out, sounding more amused than annoyed. A younger guy with buzz-cut brown hair, he stood next to an orange cone in the middle of the hall. He looked like a gym coach, wearing blue sweatpants and a white T-shirt that defined a well-developed set of pecs. In his hand, he carried a clipboard, while a lanyard bearing ID and a set of keys jangled around his neck.

His charges zipped straight toward the large window at the opposite end of the long hallway. He turned to follow. 'Slow down, Arnie. Easy, buddy; you don't have to win the race your first time out.'

D.D. decided it was safer to stand with her back against the wall. So did Alex. They'd made it through the locked front doors into the lobby, then through the next set of locked doors connecting the reception area to the unit. Now they were waiting for their designated nurse, Danielle Burton, to join them; she'd needed to fetch Ozzie Harrington's file, and had left them standing next to a common area.

The left half of the space was set up with half

124

a dozen oak tables — the dining/craft/games space. The right half contained several comfy-looking couches lined up in front of a screen — the TV/movie lounge.

As D.D. watched, one dark head popped up from behind the first sofa, followed quickly by two more. The kids' gazes zoomed in on D.D. and Alex, then the three boys scrambled over the furniture.

'*Hola. ¿Cómo está?*' the smallest boy said, running up, then stopping in front of them, his bare toes touching D.D.'s pointed black shoes, his face all earnest interest. His two friends lined up behind him. D.D. pegged the leader's age at seven or eight. He had his jeans rolled up all the way to his thighs. As he stood there, he started folding and unfolding his right pants leg.

'*Bueno,*' D.D. ventured. '*¿Y tú?*'

'*Que bueno.* Did you find Lucy? *¿Dónde está?*'

D.D. didn't know who Lucy was. She looked at Alex; he shrugged.

The door next to them opened, and Danielle Burton reappeared. All three boys turned to her, the first tugging on the hem of her T-shirt.

'*¿Dónde está, Lucy? ¿Dónde, dónde?*'

'*Está bien, está bien,*' the nurse soothed. She ruffled the boy's inky black hair. '*Lucy está aquí. Tranquilo,* okay?'

'Okay,' the boy agreed.

'This is Jimmy.' Danielle introduced the lead boy to Alex and D.D. 'And here are his partners in crime, Benny and Jorge. If you ever want a dynamite game of Matchbox cars, these are your boys.'

Alex took the bait. He squatted until he was eye level with Jimmy and asked, 'What's your favorite car?'

'Monster car!' Jimmy whooped. He stuck out his arms and took off in a wide-arcing run, looking more like an airplane than a car to D.D. But Benny and Jorge apparently thought this was good enough, and they took off running around the tables in the common room as well.

'*Walking* feet,' Danielle called out.

The boys slowed to a trot. The nurse seemed to feel that was close enough. She gestured with her hand and D.D. and Alex followed her to the left, where a smaller corridor led to a bank of classrooms.

Danielle found an empty room, gesturing for them to enter. D.D. and Alex had started their inquiry with the nurse manager, Karen Rober. She wasn't as hands-on, however, recommending they speak to Danielle, who, conveniently enough, walked through the front doors a moment later. The look that had passed over Danielle's features when she'd spotted D.D.'s police creds had been interesting. A mix of horror and anger. And, immediately after, shuttered tightness.

Karen had assigned Danielle to the detectives. Otherwise, D.D. wasn't sure the young nurse would've agreed to walk down the hall with them, let alone answer any questions. Now Danielle pulled out a chair at the wooden table, set down her files, sat, fidgeted, and got back up again.

'I'm gonna grab some water,' she announced. 'Need anything?'

D.D. and Alex shook their heads. The nurse popped out; they took their seats.

'First impressions?' D.D. murmured.

'Twitchy,' Alex said.

'She *should* be twitchy. She's being questioned by the police.'

'Twitchier,' he amended.

'Yeah, that's what I think, too.'

Danielle reappeared, bearing a cup with a lid and a straw. She took a seat across from Alex and D.D., not as close as she could be, but not too far away. The nurse was younger than D.D. would've thought. Athletic build, dark hair swept back in a ponytail. Pretty, under normal circumstances. Tense, given these circumstances.

'Sure you don't need anything?' the nurse asked, plucking at the manila folder in front of her.

'We're good,' D.D. replied. 'Busy afternoon?'

'We've had busier.'

'How many kids are out there?' D.D. asked, easing into things. She wanted to take her time with Danielle. She was curious what made the nurse tick — or fidget, as the case might be.

'Fifteen. More crowded than we'd like, but not acute.'

'Acute?'

Danielle had to think about it. 'A psych ward is acute when we have more than we can handle. It's not a specific number of kids; it's the dynamics of the kids. Eight kids can send us over the top if they're involved cases that didn't mix well. On the other hand, we've effectively handled up to eighteen.' She paused. 'Not that I'd like to do that again.'

'How long have you been here?' D.D. asked.

'Eight years.'

'Sounds like a long time, given the field of work.'

The nurse shrugged. 'We're a progressive unit, which makes us a better place to work than most pediatric psych wards. Some of our MCs have been here twenty years or more.'

'MCs?' Alex spoke up.

'Milieu counselors. Did you notice the guy in the hallway? The one with the great baritone?'

'The gym coach,' D.D. filled in.

'That's Greg. He's a milieu counselor. We refer to the environment within our unit as the milieu. Greg's job is to help sustain that environment — safe, nurturing, dynamic. Mine, too, but I'm an RN. MCs don't need to have a degree, just a lot of energy and creativity to work with the kids.'

'What makes this a progressive unit?'

'We don't snow kids — '

' 'Snow'?' D.D. interrupted.

'Drug them senseless. Most of our kids are on multiple prescriptions. Plus we use PRNs — medications given as needed, say Benadryl — to help soothe a child having a bad day. But we medicate to a functional, not nonfunctional, state.'

Danielle fiddled with the straw in her cup.

When D.D. didn't immediately ask another question, letting the silence draw out, the nurse volunteered on her own:

'We also refuse to physically restrain the kids. During an outburst, most psych units will resort to tying a kid to a bed. They tell the kid it's for his own good, but it's still a shitty thing to do. Let me put it this way: Once we had a five-year-old girl whose shoulders wouldn't stay in their sockets because her parents' idea of babysitting was to hog-tie her so they could go drinking. When the girl was finally admitted to the ER for severe dehydration, an intern ordered physical restraints because the girl kept freaking out. Can you imagine how that must've felt to her? She finally gets away from her parents, and she's still being trussed up like cattle. Eighty percent of our kids have already suffered a severe trauma. We don't need to add to that.'

D.D. was impressed. 'So,' she summarized, 'no snowing, no tying. When the kids go all *Lord of the Flies*, what d'you do?'

'CPS — collaborative problem-solving. CPS was developed by Dr. Ross Greene, an expert in explosive children. Dr. Greene's primary assumption is that a child will do well if a child *can* do well. Meaning, if we have children who won't do well, it's because they don't know how — maybe they have issues with frustration tolerance, or rigid thinking, or cognitive deficiencies. Our goal then is to teach the child the skills he or she is lacking, through CPS.'

D.D. considered this. Tried it on a couple of times, actually. She didn't buy it. She glanced over at Alex, who appeared equally skeptical.

This time, he took the lead: 'You're saying a child goes psycho and you . . . talk her out of it? *Hey, honey, please stop throwing a chair out that window. Now, now, Georgie, no more strangling baby Jane.*'

Danielle finally cracked a smile. 'Interestingly enough, most of our parents sound just as convinced as you. Example?'

'Example,' he agreed.

'Ten-year-old girl. Admitted with a history of explosive rages and petty arson. Within two hours of arrival, she walked up to Greg — the gym coach — and decked him. Didn't say a word. Hit first, thought later.'

'What did Greg do?' D.D. asked.

'Nothing. Guy's a good two hundred and twenty pounds and the girl barely topped seventy. Blow glanced off his stomach. Then she tried to kick him in the balls. That got him moving faster.'

Alex's eyes widened. 'But no snowing, no tying?'

'Two male counselors intervened, trying to guide the girl back to her room. She lashed out again, screaming at the top of her lungs. Other kids started getting wiggy, so our nurse manager ordered the male MCs to disappear. Second they were out of sight, the girl calmed down and returned peacefully to her room on her own.'

'It was the men who set her off,' D.D. filled in. 'The girl had an issue with men.'

'Exactly. Large men with dark hair, who may or may not bear a resemblance to the girl's stepdad, as a matter of fact. That's what triggered her outburst. Observing that gave us something to work with. Something we would not have learned if we'd restrained her or medicated her.'

'All right,' Alex granted. 'No snowing, no tying. But where's the talking?'

'Once the girl calmed down, I reviewed the incident with her. We discussed what she did. I talked to her about other options for approaching boys that didn't involve trying to kill them. It was an ongoing process, obviously, but that's what we're here for — to help kids understand what's going on inside their heads, and what they can do to manage their jumbled emotions. Kids want to do well. They want to feel in control. And they're willing to work, if you're willing to guide.'

'Did the girl get better?' Alex asked.

'By the end of her stay, she and Greg were best buds. You'd never know.'

'And Ozzie Harrington?' D.D. said. 'Was he another success story — one day roaring like a lion, next day gentle as a lamb?'

Danielle shuttered up. She sat back, stroking the top of the manila file with her thumb. When she met D.D.'s gaze again, her blue eyes were wary, but also hard. A woman who'd been there, and done that. Curious and more curious, D.D. thought.

'Tell me what happened,' the nurse said, avoiding D.D.'s question.

'Been watching the news?' D.D. asked.

'No. Been working the unit.'

'Why do you assume an unhappy ending?' D.D. pressed.

'Ozzie's dead,' Danielle stated.

'Again, why assume the negative?'

'Because Karen told me to talk to you, and if Ozzie were still alive, answering your questions would violate his rights.'

D.D. considered the matter. 'Yeah, he's dead.'

'Just him, or did he hurt others?'

'Why don't you tell us what you think?'

'Fuck it.' Danielle broke open the case file and began.

* * *

'Oswald was admitted in the spring of last year. He'd spent six months with his foster family before suffering a 'psychotic break.' The parents had gone out for the evening, leaving him and their two other children alone with a babysitter. Halfway through dinner, both their cell phones started ringing. The babysitter and two kids were now locked in the bathroom. Ozzie was on the other side of the door, armed with a hammer and screaming he was going to kill them.

'The parents ordered the babysitter to call nine-one-one, then headed home. They arrived around the same time two officers were wrestling Ozzie to the ground. The EMTs sedated the boy and brought him to the ER, which referred him to us.

'Upon admittance, he was nearly catatonic. We see this often in a child who's just experienced a significant traumatic event. We kept him on

Ativan for the first forty-eight hours, while we caught up on his patient history. Ozzie's file revealed multiple diagnoses, including severe ADHD, attachment disorder, Nonverbal Learning Disorder, Mood Disorder NOS, and other nonspecific development delays. The psychiatrist expressed concern that, due to the death of Ozzie's birth mother, not enough was known about the first three years of his life.'

'Meaning?' D.D. prodded.

'Ozzie's speech and social skills were delayed. At eight, he showed some traits that were autistic in nature — he wouldn't make eye contact, he sat and rocked for hours, while mumbling sounds only he understood.'

'You're talking Rain Man?' D.D. clarified, making a note.

'That would be one example of an individual on the Autism Spectrum Disorder,' the nurse answered dryly. 'Bear in mind, it is a spectrum, and you shouldn't count on Hollywood for information. In Ozzie's case, we determined the traits weren't due to ASD, but were more consistent with the kind of self-soothing techniques learned by severely neglected children. Ozzie was a feral child.'

'So not Rain Man, but Tarzan?' Alex spoke up.

Danielle shot him a look.

'With a feral child,' she continued pointedly, 'there's no caretaker present to meet the child's needs, disrupting the normal development cycle. The child cries. Nothing happens. The child stops crying. And talking, and bonding, and having any sense of belonging to a larger world.

Mentally, the child atrophies, leading to delayed speech and socialization in Ozzie's case.'

D.D. frowned. 'I thought Ozzie's mom died when he was three. He was home alone with the body, but surely a couple of weeks of abandonment doesn't cause everything you just described.'

'According to the ME, Ozzie's mother had died eight to ten weeks prior to discovery. During that time, it appears Ozzie survived by eating dry cereal, uncooked pasta, and anything else he could forage from the cupboards. He was also a good climber, which helped him get water from the sink, etc. In fact, social services thought his survival skills were particularly well developed for a three-year-old — meaning maybe Ozzie's mother was sick for a bit before she died. Maybe, in fact, Ozzie had been taking care of himself for a long while, which would explain his feral traits.'

'So Ozzie got off to a rough start,' D.D. summarized. 'But eventually, the proper authorities got involved and . . . '

'And he ping-ponged through seven or eight foster families before landing with the Harringtons.'

'Why the Harringtons?'

'Have to ask the state. Though,' Danielle corrected herself, 'the parents, Denise and Patrick, both seemed very committed to him. Some foster families request special-needs kids. They have a background with special needs — either grew up with a special-needs sibling, or have occupational training. Some believe they can make a difference and want to try.'

'And Denise and Patrick?' D.D. prodded.

'I don't think they had any idea what they were getting into,' the nurse answered bluntly. 'But they appeared committed to helping Ozzie. They struck me as the religious type — doing God's will here on earth.'

D.D. made a note. That sounded consistent with other things they'd learned about the happy couple.

'So Ozzie had this psychotic break. What does that mean?'

'He stripped off his clothes, then went around the house with a hammer, trashing the furniture while screaming death threats.'

'So he had a particularly violent temper tantrum?'

'Oh, if he'd caught someone, he would've hurt them,' Danielle said seriously. 'A kid in such an elevated rage-state is having an out-of-body experience. You can't reach them with words, with love, with logic. They're gone, in orbit. Afterward, they'll remember almost nothing of what they said or did, including that they bashed the brains out of the family dog, or tore apart their own favorite teddy bear. Hiding is the best policy. And in the aftermath, the entire family needs post-traumatic stress counseling, especially the siblings.'

D.D. made a note of that, too. *Therapist for the Harrington family?* Things can come out in therapy . . .

'After Ozzie's admitted here, then what happens?'

Danielle shrugged. 'We started him on aripiprazole, often used for the treatment of schizophrenia and bipolar disorder. That seemed to pull him together for about eight weeks, then he began to suffer from akathisia and we had to take him off.'

'Akathisia?'

'Ozzie complained that it felt like little people were inside his skin, crunching his bones. That's akathisia. He also started suffering from perseverative thoughts.'

'Perseverative thoughts?' D.D.

'It's like OCD, except with thinking. He'd get a notion in his head, *I want a red car*, and then he couldn't get it back out. He'd spend six, seven hours saying over and over again, *I want a red car, I want a red car, I want a red car*. Now substitute *red rum* for *red car*, and you can see the danger of perseverative thoughts.'

D.D.'s eyes widened. 'He's going through all this, and he's what, seven, eight years old?'

'He's going through all this, and yes, he's eight. And we're seeing more kids like him all the time. Parents think the worst thing that can happen to their five-year-old is cancer. They're wrong; the worst thing that can happen to their five-year-old is mental illness. Cancer, the docs have tools available. Mental illness in prepubescents . . . There are so few drugs we can use, then the kids develop a tolerance, and by age eight we're out of options. They require a lifetime regimen of antipsychotic medication, except we don't have anything left. One week we get them stabilized. The next they plunge back into the abyss.'

'Is that what happened to Ozzie?' D.D. asked.

Danielle picked up the case file, read briskly. 'We took Ozzie off the aripiprazole. At which time he claimed ghosts were appearing in the windows of his room and ordering him to kill people. So we put him back on a very low dosage of aripiprazole, trying to minimize the side effects while still making some attempt at regulating his brain chemistry. In the short term, we noticed a positive change in behavior.'

'In the short term,' D.D. repeated. 'Meaning in the long term . . . ?'

'We don't know.'

'You don't know?'

The nurse shook her head. 'His parents discharged him. Against our advice. They had moved, gotten a new place. Denise said it was time to bring him home.'

Alex held up a hand. 'Whoa, whoa, whoa. Ozzie reports ghosts are telling him to murder people, and they take him home?'

'It happens.'

D.D. leaned forward. 'Tell me, Danielle. Forget the file for a second. It's you and me, trying to understand what happened to one boy. What made you think Ozzie had hurt someone? Why were you so certain this story had an unhappy ending? Why did he leave?'

Danielle didn't answer right away. Her jaw worked. Then, just as D.D. was starting to lose hope . . .

'Denise found a spiritual healer,' the nurse

expelled curtly. 'A shaman who promised to make Ozzie all better. No chemicals. No crazy drugs. He was going to heal Ozzie by bringing him into the light.'

'Say what?'

'Exactly. This is a boy with severe psychoses. And she's gonna cure him by bringing him to 'an expert in negative and positive energies'? We tried to get her to reconsider, but her mind was set. We hadn't helped her son, so she'd found someone who could.'

'I don't think it took,' Alex said.

'Why? Your turn. What happened?'

'We don't know. But the family's dead.'

'The family? The *whole* family?' Danielle's face paled. The nurse blinked, looking shaky, then almost panic-stricken. In the next instant, she blinked again, and her features smoothed to glass. 'The news,' she murmured. 'The family from Dorchester. I caught a snippet, just on the radio. That was Ozzie?'

'That was someone,' D.D. corrected.

'I thought the father did it. That's what the reporter implied.'

'That's what we're trying to find out.'

Danielle looked down at the table, shaking her head. 'Goddammit. We told them. We warned Denise . . . You have to . . . Andrew Lightfoot. That's who you need to see. You want to know what happened to Ozzie Harrington, go ask Andrew Lightfoot. That arrogant son of a bitch.'

12

At 10:37 p.m., Patrick Harrington died. The news pissed D.D. off. It probably didn't do wonders for him either.

She was at her desk. Not returning Chip's phone call. Not exploring fine dining with Alex. It was Friday night, and she was doing what she inevitably did with her evenings, working her way through a stack of reports, trying to make sense of what had happened one evening in Dorchester that had now left five dead.

Physical evidence aside, D.D. liked the kid for it. She didn't know why. The troubled history, the psychotic episodes, his penchant for beating squirrels to death, then licking their blood off his hands. If she got to pick her perp, she was going with Ozzie Harrington. In fact, she'd had a brilliant flash of insight regarding Patrick Harrington's last word. What if he hadn't been saying 'hussy,' as the ER nurse had assumed? What if he'd been saying 'Ozzie' instead?

Not an accusation against his wife, but a last-gasp effort to name the guilty party.

It all sounded good to her, until she went over the crime scene again. Fact: Whoever delivered the killing blows was most likely taller than five six. Fact: Ozzie could hardly slash his own throat in his sister's bedroom, then carry himself to the screened-in porch. Fact: According to psychiatric nurse Danielle Burton, Ozzie's first psychotic break had involved overall destruction. The Harrington crime scene, on the other hand, was methodical in nature. This wasn't a kid going berserk. This was someone systematically hunting down individual members of an entire family.

Which brought her back to Patrick Harrington. He was a do-gooder. Trying to move his family to a better neighborhood. Trying to save a troubled kid. Trying to succeed at a second marriage with a blended family. Then he lost his job. Then he got behind in his renovations. Then his adopted son started taking out neighborhood rodents. Maybe the pressure mounted, the growing chasm between what life was supposed to be and what it was actually becoming.

Can't save the world? Then he'll leave it — and take his innocent darlings with him.

D.D. could buy that logic. A grand jury could buy that logic. Except Phil and Alex had swept through the upper two floors of the Harringtons' home, and as far as they were concerned, Patrick was only days away from completion. Following that revelation, they'd searched the *Boston Globe*, and sure enough, Patrick had placed a rental ad, which had started running just this morning. So the guy finally makes arrangements to rent out the top two floors of his triple-decker, then decides,

Fuck it, I won't even give it one weekend for a potential renter to materialize, I'll just kill everyone tonight.

Impulsive crime, Alex kept telling her. Impulsive crime.

D.D. wasn't sure about that. She'd just worked her way through eight different character testimonies, and each and every one of them agreed Patrick was a stand-up sort of guy. How did a man leap from steady father figure to impulsive family annihilator in five minutes or less?

Dammit, she wanted a pepperoni pizza.

Actually, she wanted sex. On her desk would do nicely. Just sweep the papers aside. Toss the files on the floor. Strip off her jeans, rip off Alex's starched blue shirt, and go to town. He struck her as the kind of guy who would be both patient and intense. She'd like patient and intense. She'd like strong male fingers gripping her ass. She'd like the sensation of a hard-muscled body pounding into hers.

She'd like one moment when she was not Sergeant D.D. Warren, Supercop, but a woman instead.

Is this what a biological clock did to a female? Fried her brain cells, ruined her work ethic, made her stupid?

She was not getting married. She was not having children. She was not going to have sex in her office. So she might as well read the fucking case reports, because this was her life. This was what she had left. Five dead in Dorchester and no one alive to tell the tale.

She made it ten more minutes, then said *Screw it* and headed home. Time for a cold shower, reheated Chinese food, and a good night's sleep.

D.D. was just pulling onto I-93 when her cell phone rang.

She grabbed it impatiently, barked out a greeting.

It was Phil; he didn't sound good. 'We got another one.'

'Another what?'

'Family. Dead. The male with a bullet between his eyes. Get over here, D.D. And bring your Vicks.'

★ ★ ★

D.D. was not a fan of vapor rub or scented cotton balls when working a crime scene. Some of the guys rubbed lemon juice on their hands, then cupped their palms over their noses. Others chewed half a pack of spearmint gum — swore that overwhelming their taste buds limited their olfactory senses.

D.D. was old-fashioned. She believed to effectively work a scene, you needed all your senses, including smell.

She regretted her high standards the second she walked through the door.

'What the fuck is that?' she snapped, one hand immediately covering her nose and mouth, the other swatting at a fly.

Alex Wilson was standing in the cramped family room. Rather heroically, he held out his

142

handkerchief. Her eyes were watering, but she waved him off.

'Jesus Christ,' she muttered. She remained standing in the doorway, trying to get her bearings while controlling her gag reflex.

Place looked like a dump. The floor at her feet swam in garbage. She saw grease-stained cheeseburger wrappers, empty containers of McDonald's fries, wads of tissues, and — heaven help her — a soiled diaper. Then the diaper moved and the world's fattest cockroach streaked across the dirt-brown carpet before disappearing beneath an open pizza box dotted with green-colored pepperoni.

'Son of a bitch.' D.D. was back out the door, off the front steps, and over the edge of the property, where she willed herself not to puke in front of the crime-scene team or, heaven help her, the local news. Her eyes swam with tears. It took several gulping breaths of rain-swept August air to calm her stomach.

She had just straightened, turning toward the house to debate round two, when she spotted Bobby Dodge ducking beneath the yellow crime-scene tape at the end of the drive. Given a choice between tap-dancing with a cockroach or tangling with a Massachusetts State Police detective, she headed straight for the state cop. Who also happened to be her former lover. Who also now happened to be a happily married man.

'My crime scene,' D.D. stated by way of greeting.

'My apologies,' Bobby replied easily. They went too far back for him to ever be seriously insulted. D.D. found that annoying. The rain three hours ago had finally brought the August heat down into the eighties. It was still muggy, and Bobby had his sports jacket slung over his right arm, revealing a dark blue short-sleeved shirt embroidered with the gold insignia of the state police.

'Why are you here?' D.D. demanded.

'I was in the neighborhood?' He grinned at her. He was cute when he grinned and he knew it.

'Don't you have a baby to tend to, or something like that?'

'Carina Lillian,' he said immediately, already fishing into his back pocket for the photo. 'Nine pounds thirteen ounces. Isn't she beautiful?'

He moved closer to one of the outdoor floodlights, holding the wallet-sized photo beneath the glow. D.D. registered fat red cheeks, narrow little eyes, and a distinctly pointed head.

'She looks just like you,' D.D. assured him.

'Vaginal birth,' he said proudly.

And thanks to those two words, D.D. thought, she would never have sex again. 'Annabelle?' she asked, referring to Bobby's wife.

'Doing great. Breast-feeding like a champ and getting Carina settled onto a nice schedule. Whole family's great. And you?'

'I'm not breast-feeding like a champ.'

'Someone's loss,' Bobby told her.

'Why are you at my crime scene?'

'We have an interest.'

'Ah, but I have jurisdiction.'

'Which is why I thought we could walk

144

through it together.'

'Please — you were hoping I wasn't here yet, and you could wander through at your leisure.'

'From plan A to plan B,' Bobby agreed.

'Tell me about your interest.'

'Marijuana,' he said.

'Dealing?'

'And importing, we believe.'

She frowned, studying him. 'You think this is some kind of gangland hit?'

He shrugged. 'I was hoping to walk through the scene to see if it feels like some kind of gangland hit.'

'Whole family, you know.'

'That's what I was told.'

'Lot of bodies for marijuana wars,' D.D. said. 'Meth, okay. Heroin, sure. But the dope dealers . . .'

'Don't like to get so bonged up, I know.' Inside joke. Cops. They had to have something to laugh about.

'All right,' D.D. conceded. 'You can join the party. But I still think this is my scene.'

'Then you still have my apologies.'

★ ★ ★

D.D. made it all the way into the family room this time. Alex was no longer there, but had left an array of yellow evidence placards in his wake. D.D. held her hand over her nose and breathed shallowly through her mouth. Her gag reflex started to kick in, so she pinched her forearm as hard as she could. The pain overrode the smell. Lucky her.

Beside her, Bobby had gone quiet. He used to be a police sniper, and his ability to retreat, to be both in the moment and outside of the moment, had always appealed to D.D. Now she could feel the coiled tension in him. He was appalled but, like any good cop, focusing his rage.

In the middle of the cockroach-infested family room sat a brown-and-gold plaid couch. And in the middle of the brown-and-gold plaid couch sprawled a dead white male, duded up as a wannabe Rastafarian, complete with a rainbow knit hat. D.D. put his age in the late twenties, early thirties. He sported a dozen tremendously long dreadlocks, two large sightless brown eyes, and one small bullet hole, center of his forehead. His right arm was flung off the sofa, toward the floor. Beneath his dangling fingers, on top of a paper bag filled with God knows what, rested a snub-nosed handgun. Looked like a twenty-two to D.D.

'Not much blood,' Bobby commented.

'Probably soaked into the sofa,' D.D. muttered.

She noticed that a wadded-up tissue about three feet away was starting to move. She wondered how many rules of Crime Scene 101 she'd violate if she pulled out her Glock and went after whatever was under the tissue.

A cockroach crawled out, stopped for a second — she swore to God it was studying them — then went about its cockroach business, disappearing beneath another foul pile of refuse.

'I'm showering with bleach when I get home,'

D.D. gritted out between clenched teeth.

'Eucalyptus oil,' Bobby informed her. 'Pour it straight in the bath. Works every time.' He added primly, 'And it makes for very soft skin.'

D.D. shook her head. She turned away from Mr. Dreadlocks and, feeling a bit hopeless about the whole damn thing, headed deeper into the house.

The woman had gone down in the kitchenette just off the family room. The knife, bearing a black curved handle that matched the set in the wooden block on the counter, was still lodged in her back. This hadn't been a clean kill. The grime-covered floor was further soiled with red streak marks from the woman trying to crawl forward on her elbows. She'd made it about four inches before succumbing to her injury.

The kitchen stank worse than the family room. D.D. noted rotting food in the sink, sour milk on the table, and mold growing up one corner wall. She'd seen some things in her time. She'd heard some things in her time. She still didn't know how anyone could live like this.

Off the kitchen was the lone bathroom. Garbage overflowed the shower stall, including gallon jugs filled with yellow liquid. The toilet was clogged and didn't appear to be working. That made D.D. eye the gallon jugs all over again, wishing she didn't know what she now knew.

Leaving the kitchen area, they made it to the hallway. A kid, looked sixteen, seventeen, was spread-eagled outside the first bedroom door. He appeared to have been shot twice. First time in

147

the upper leg. Second time was the money shot
— a neat round hole one inch above his left eye.

Inside the bedroom, Alex was bent over the
body of an adolescent girl. She was wearing
shorts and a tank top. It appeared she'd been
sleeping on the twin-sized bed. She'd tossed
back the cover sheet, maybe hearing a noise in
the hall. She'd just made it to sitting when the
bullet caught her above her right eye. She'd
fallen to the side, one of her hands still fisting the
stained pink sheet.

This room was cleaner, D.D. noted. Impossibly small and cramped, but neater. The girl had
painted the walls pink with swirls of green and
blue. Her sanctuary, D.D. thought, and noted a
pile of paperback novels stacked in the corner.

'Third child's behind me,' Alex spoke up.

'Third child?'

'On the floor.'

D.D. and Bobby sidestepped their way to the
foot of the bed. Sure enough, in the three feet
between the twin bed and the outside wall was a
small cushion, and on top of the cushion was a
much younger child, probably three or four. She
had a tattered blanket clenched in her fingers
and one thumb still popped in her mouth. She
could've been sleeping, except for the blood on
her left temple.

'Never woke up,' Alex said, his voice subdued,
tense.

'So it would seem,' D.D. murmured. 'Is that a
dog bed? Is she sleeping on a *dog* bed?'

'Looks it,' Bobby said, his voice flat.

'And what the hell is going on with her arms

148

and legs?' D.D. had managed to inch closer, noting a myriad of fresh red cuts and faded silvery scars crisscrossing the girl's limbs. D.D. counted a dozen marks on one dirty leg alone. It looked as if someone had taken a razor to the child, and not just once.

'Please tell me someone had called child services,' she muttered. Then realized it didn't matter. At least not anymore.

She and Bobby slid back out of this bedroom, made it around the teenage boy, and headed for the last room. It was only slightly larger than the first. A double bed was wedged against the wall. An old wooden cradle sat beside the bed.

Bobby stopped moving.

'I got it,' D.D. said. 'I got it.'

She left him in the doorway, walked straight to the cradle, and looked in. She forced herself to take her time, to spend a good two to three minutes on it. She considered this a service to the dead. Don't rush their last moments. Study them. Remember them. Honor them.

Then nail the son of a bitch who did it.

She returned to the doorway, her voice low, steadier than she would've thought. 'Infant. Dead. Not shot. I'm guessing suffocated. There's a pillow on its stomach.'

'Boy or girl?' Bobby asked.

'Does it matter?'

'Boy or girl?' he snarled.

'Girl. Come on, Bobby. Out of the house.'

He followed her, because in a residence this small, there wasn't much choice. Every step they took risked trampling a piece of evidence or,

149

worse, one of the bodies. Better to get out, into the humid summer night.

By mutual consent, they paused outside the front door. Took a second to breathe in deep gulps of heavy, moist air. The noise had built at the end of the drive. Neighbors, reporters, busybodies. Nothing like an August crime scene to bring out a block party.

D.D. was disgusted. Enraged. Disheartened.

Some nights, this job was too hard.

'Male first, then the mother and kids?' Bobby asked.

She shook her head. 'No assumptions. Wait for the crime-scene geeks to sort it out. Did you recognize Alex Wilson inside?'

Bobby shook his head.

'He teaches crime-scene management at the Academy and is shadowing our unit for the month. Smart guy. By morning, he'll have something to report.'

'Is he single?' Bobby asked her.

'Bite me.'

'You started it.'

She gave him a look. 'How?'

'You called him smart. And you never think men are smart.'

'Well, I once thought you were smart, so obviously my batting average isn't perfect.'

'I miss you, too,' he assured her.

They both fell silent, once more contemplating the scene.

'So you think the male did it?' Bobby asked.

'We didn't see any drugs.'

'Not in the house,' Bobby agreed. 'What do

you say we check around back?'

They checked around back, found a small wooden shack that looked a bit like an outhouse. Inside, bales of marijuana were stacked floor to ceiling.

'Hello, drug dealer,' Bobby murmured.

'Goodbye, gangland hit,' D.D. corrected.

'How do you figure?'

'When was the last time one dealer offed another dealer, only to leave behind the first dealer's stash? If this was about drugs, no way these bales would still be sitting here.'

'Maybe the rival couldn't find them.'

She shot him a look, then glanced pointedly at her watch. 'We found them — in less than sixty seconds, I might add.'

Bobby pursed his lips. 'If not a gangland hit, then what?'

D.D. was troubled. 'I don't know,' she acknowledged.

They both fell silent. 'Your crime scene,' Bobby said finally. 'My apologies.'

She looked at him, his steady gray eyes, the solid shoulders she had once let herself cry on. 'My regret,' she said.

They walked back around the house.

Bobby exited down the drive.

D.D. returned to the scene.

13

DANIELLE

Lucy started screaming shortly after midnight. The desperate, high-pitched shriek sent four of us bolting down the hall. We made the mistake of pouring into her room as one unit, and the sight of so many adults sent her into a fresh paroxysm of terror.

She attacked the window, beating it with her fists. When the shatterproof glass held, she whirled around and slammed herself into the neighboring wall. Her head whipped back. She cried out again, before careening across the room and pounding into the next wall. She still wore the oversized top, and it flapped around her bony knees like a giant green cape.

I put up a hand, gesturing for everyone to hold still. Technically, I wasn't even on the clock. I'd logged out hours ago, but had never made it home. I'd debriefed with Karen, visited with Greg, caught up on some paperwork. I'd worked for thirty-six of the past forty-eight hours. Now I was tired, frazzled from Lucy's escape, and wrung out from the detectives' visit. After they'd left, I'd made the mistake of looking up the Dorchester murders on the Internet. I could picture Ozzie inside that white-trimmed triple-decker. Patrick, Denise, Ozzie's older brother and sister.

And that put my father's voice back in my head. '*Oh Danny girl. My pretty, pretty Danny girl.*'

Two and half days now. Sixty hours and counting.

'She's disassociating,' Cecille, an MC, murmured beside me.

She was right. Lucy's dark eyes held a glassy sheen and she was striking out at things only she could see. Her nightmare had carried her to the wasteland between sleeping and waking. She was reacting to our presence, but not really processing. Kids like this were nearly impossible to wake, and it almost always ended badly.

Now Lucy flung herself against another wall and started pounding her head.

'Ativan,' Ed stated across the room. He was an older MC, heavyset, balding. He liked to cook and the kids loved him for it.

'No shit,' I muttered back.

'I can get her.' Ed was already on the balls of his feet, preparing his heft for action. He was going to rush her, try to grab her in a bear hug. The feeling of being enveloped soothed some kids, helped bring them down. I knew immediately Lucy wasn't that kind of kid.

'No!' I grabbed his arm, stalling him. 'Touch her and she'll go nuts.'

'She's already nuts. We gotta get her sedated before she takes everyone with her. It's nighttime, Danielle. You know what it's like at night.'

I knew, but forcefully grabbing a child as damaged as Lucy . . . I couldn't stomach it.

153

'Everyone out,' I ordered. 'Just out. We're not doing any good.'

Lucy was back at the window, banging futilely against the glass. There was a hopelessness to her actions that hurt to watch. As if she knew the glass wouldn't break, as if she knew she couldn't escape, but she had to try.

How long had she banged on the freezer door? How many hours and days had she spent, forced into a fetal position, feeling her arms and legs burn from the cramping muscles?

These kids were tougher than us. These kids were braver than us. That's why we loved them so.

We backed out slowly, easing into the lit hallway, where the domino effects of Lucy's outburst were already in motion. Kids were off their mattresses, looking wild-eyed as Lucy launched into a fresh series of shrieks. Jimmy raced by, arms outstretched as he reacted to the stress by making like an airplane and taking flight. Jorge and Benny were hot on his heels.

Verbal kids were chattering away. Nonverbal kids were curling into balls. Suicidal Aimee stood in the doorway, looking as if the world were ending, but then, she'd known it would. She disappeared, shuffling back into the darkness of her room, and Cecille swiftly followed her.

Lucy began to wail. A thin, anguished sound that built, then fell off, then rose to a crescendo all over again.

'Make it stop, make it stop, make it stop!' Jimmy yelled, roaring down the hallway, arms straight out, bathrobe flapping.

Lucy wailed louder.

'*Stop, stop, stop!*' Benny and Jorge took up the chant.

'Midnight matinee,' Ed boomed over the growing uproar. 'To the movie room. Popcorn for all.'

He started to herd dazed and distraught children away from Lucy's room, toward the common area. I joined suit, gathering as many kids as possible as I worked my way to the medicine dispensary. I tried to appear as if I were merely walking fast when, really, I wanted to bolt.

The wails continued, a long heartbreaking ladder that made the adults pale, even as we pasted reassuring smiles upon our faces.

I found myself picturing my father. He was standing in my doorway, framed by a halo of hallway light. '*Oh Danny girl. My pretty, pretty Danny girl.*'

The pitch of his last words matched Lucy's wail perfectly. Songs for the dying.

I wanted Lucy to shut up. I needed her voice out of my head.

I finally reached the dispensary and grabbed the Ativan. Two more kids went racing by. I snagged the first, then the second, got them to the movie room, where the MCs were getting it together now. A movie was on, audio blasting almost loud enough to drown out the ruckus down the hall.

Lucy screamed more frantically, and I bolted for the rest of my supplies. Having the proper sedative was only half the battle. The real problem would be administering it. Most kids, we talked through the process or even bribed. Lucy, however, didn't have language skills.

She was a mystery to us, and she was a mystery now screaming so shrilly my head hurt. The windows should shatter. The building should implode from so much anguish.

'*Oh Danny girl. My pretty, pretty Danny girl.*'

I grabbed three pieces of cheese and a boombox and raced down the hall.

★ ★ ★

I walked straight into the room. Lucy was so beside herself, I figured it hardly mattered. She must've spotted me out of the corner of her eye, however, for she launched herself at me immediately, fingers curled into claws, gouging at my eyes.

She caught me in the shoulder. I staggered back, surprised, making a low, involuntary *oomph* under my breath.

I had an image of tangled brown hair, and dark, desperate eyes too big in her pale face. She launched herself again. Instinctively, I brought up the boombox and used it to block. She whacked it with her hand, hard enough to hurt. Her arm recoiled. She held her right hand against her chest and whimpered.

I hit Play, filling the room with a light piano mix. Music soothes the savage beast.

Not Lucy. She kicked at my shins.

I pedaled backwards, trying to put distance between us. She stalked me, up on the balls of her feet, gaze never leaving my face.

She wanted to gouge out my eyes, dig her fingers into my sockets and squeeze. I could see it on her face. Something had gone off inside of her. A switch thrown. A link with humanity further breaking. She wanted blood. She needed it.

I kept moving, careful to stay out of corners and remain within line of sight of the doorway.

I was stronger.

She was faster, a swirling blur of green shirt and pale, flashing limbs.

She lashed out with her foot again, catching me in the side of my knee. I stumbled and the boombox fell to the floor. She snatched it up and hurled it at the window. It bounced off the shatterproof glass, landing on the floor, where George Winston resiliently carried on.

Lucy didn't seem to notice. I was already up, moving quickly toward the open doorway. She seemed to register the angle, instantly understanding my intent. She dashed left, cutting me off from the doorway, herding me deeper into the room. I got the mattress between us, thinking that might help. Then I started circling back around, always mindful of the doorway.

Lucy gave up on stalking, leaping across the mattress instead.

The direct attack caught me off guard. I barely got my hands up before she head-butted me in the stomach. The force of her attack carried us both back, slamming me into the window. She was wild now, clawing with her fingers, jabbing with her knees. I tried to catch her hands, make some attempt to subdue her.

She grabbed my arm with both of her hands and yanked, hard. The sudden force bent me forward, and she immediately leaped upon my back, grabbing fistfuls of my hair. Then she got one hand around my neck and squeezed.

I careened over to the next wall, backing into it solidly. She held, so I performed Greg's favorite maneuver — I bent forward and flipped her over my head.

She landed on the floor hard, the wind knocked from her small chest. I saw her eyes widen, her mouth forming a soundless *oh*. She was stalled, but probably not for long. Quickly, before she could get back on her feet, I jammed a tablet of Ativan into the first piece of cheese and formed it into a messy ball. I rolled it to her, then stumbled toward the open doorway.

Ed was standing there, looking horrified.

'What the — '

'Shut up! She's not done yet.'

True to my words, Lucy was already lurching to her feet. She swayed more now, her eyes gone flat, glassy. She staggered forward one step, then another. Her toe hit the cheese ball, sent it rolling across the carpet.

The motion caught her eye. She stilled, staring at it.

I held my breath, taking out the other two pieces of cheese and busily rolling them up. Think *cat*. That's what soothes Lucy. Get her into a feline state of mind.

I rolled the second piece of cheese across the

floor, shooting it like a marble into her line of sight. Lucy tracked that one, then jerked back to the first. I could see her body rearranging itself, instinctively taking on a more feline pose. I tossed the third piece toward her feet: That did the trick. She pounced, catching it in her now pawlike hands and batting it into the air.

'Where is the Ativan?' Ed was asking. 'For heaven's sake, Danielle — '

'*Shut up!*'

I didn't want him distracting her. I needed her focused on the cheese. *Play with the cute little cheese balls. Bat them around. Then gobble them up.*

She made me work for it. Five minutes going on six, seven, eight. One ball started to disintegrate. I held my breath, waiting for the tablet to be revealed. But that ball contained only cheese. Lucy finally stopped, lapping little bits of cheddar off the carpet, then making her way to the next ball, then the next. One . . . two . . . three.

The cheese was consumed, the tablet downed. I finally sagged with relief, realizing for the first time that my legs were unsteady, and my arms felt like they were on fire. I had blood on the backs of my hands. More running down my cheek.

'Did you . . . ? How did . . . ?' Ed started again.

'It was in the cheese,' I murmured, tugging him back, trying to get him out of the doorway. 'She just needs a few minutes. It's over now, she'll be out soon.'

159

'Jesus, Danielle, your face, your neck . . . You need medical attention.'

'Then it's a good thing we work at a hospital!' I didn't mean to snap at him, but couldn't help myself. I was still wired, nerves all jangled. I wished Greg were here. I wished . . . I needed . . .

Then I thought of George Winston, still plugging away on the floor of Lucy's room, and I wanted to laugh, then I wanted to cry, and I knew it was all too much.

I retreated to the bathroom, where I splashed water on my face and told myself I absolutely, positively did not still hear my father singing in my head.

* * *

When I returned to Lucy's room fifteen minutes later, she was curled up in a corner, one arm extended above her head. She was moving her hand this way and that, watching the shadows her fingers made upon the wall. Her movements were lethargic; the sedative was bringing her down.

She'd sleep soon. I wondered what she'd see when she closed her eyes. I wondered how she found the strength to get up again.

I eased into her room this time, making my body small. I halted not far from her and sat cross-legged. Her head turned. Her jaw was slack, her cheeks had lost their angry flush.

She looked like what she was — a nine-year-old girl who'd been through too much.

I wanted to brush back the tangle of her hair, but I kept my hands at my side.

'It's okay now,' I whispered. Probably more for my benefit than hers. 'Rough night, but these things happen.'

She cocked her head as if listening to my words, then resumed studying the flow of her fingers, held high above her head.

'You're safe here,' I told her. 'We're not going to hurt you. All we ask is the same consideration. No more attacks, okay, Lucy? We don't hit here. We don't bite, kick, or pull hair. It's one of the only things we'll ask of you. To treat us nicely. We'll treat you nicely, too.'

'Bad man,' she chimed, her voice so soft, so girlish, it took me a second to register that she'd spoken.

'Lucy?'

'Bad man,' she said again.

I didn't know what to say. Lucy was speaking. She had language skills.

'It's okay,' I whispered. 'No bad men. You're safe here.'

Lucy turned her head. Her eyes were heavy-lidded, the Ativan taking effect. She reached across and grabbed my hand. Her fingers were strong, her grip tighter than I would've thought, given the sedative.

'*Bad man,*' she said again, fierce this time, urgent, her eyes blazing into mine.

'It's okay — ' I tried again.

'No,' she said mournfully. 'No.' She released my hand, curled up, and went to sleep.

161

I stayed beside her, watching over her thin, pale form.

'Bad men die. Life gets better,' I said, to both of us. Then I shivered.

SATURDAY

14

D.D. knew she was in trouble when she woke up to a commercial for a sexual lubricant. According to the ad, the man used one lubricant for a cool tingle, the woman used another for a warming thrill, and then, when they got together . . .

D.D. wanted to know. Hell, she *needed* to know.

She spent several minutes, standing half-naked in her family room, staring at the TV screen as if it would repeat the commercial. Except this time, it would be her and, say, Alex Wilson in that rumpled bed. She'd be wearing one of his silk ties. He'd be wearing nothing at all.

Ah dammit.

Life sucked.

D.D. climbed aboard her treadmill, banged out three seven-minute miles, then downed two shots of espresso and went to work.

She pulled into HQ by eight-thirty, bearing a dozen donuts. Most of her squad were too health-conscious to eat donuts. That was okay. In her current mood, she'd be good for half the batch. She started with a Boston crème, poured a fresh cup of coffee, à la homicide unit, and got serious.

By nine a.m. Saturday morning, she had her squad plus Alex in her tiny office. They had approximately thirty minutes to hash out the past forty-eight hours, then she needed to report to the deputy superintendent. Given last night's crime scene, did they have two independent incidents of mass murder? Or did they have one much larger, more horrifying crime? Option A meant two cases handled by two squads. Option B would involve the formal creation of a task-force.

D.D. handed out large coffees, gestured to the half-empty box of pastries, then assumed the position beside the blank dry-erase board. Alex sat in front of her. Given that it was Saturday, he wore khaki pants and a rich blue golf shirt. The shirt emphasized the deep color of his eyes. The pants draped fit, athletic legs.

Then there were his hands, with those long, callused fingers resting upon his knees . . .

'What happened to all the donuts?' Phil spoke up.

'Bite me,' D.D. said. She returned to the whiteboard. 'Victimology,' she announced. 'We got the Harringtons in Dorchester . . .'

'White, working-class Christians,' Phil summarized. He'd found a maple frosted, and was chewing contentedly.

'School, employment, church, social clubs, prior address?'

Phil rattled off a geographic profile of the Harringtons' known activities and organizations. D.D. dutifully wrote down each answer, then drew a line down the middle of the whiteboard to create a second column. 'Okay, now we have the Laraquette-Solis clan.'

'White, low-income drug dealers,' Phil provided.

Alex spoke up. 'Four children, four different fathers.'

'Long history with child services.' Phil again.

'Long history with immigration,' Neil, their third squadmate, countered from the back. Neil's skin held the ghostly pallor of someone who spent too much time under fluorescent bulbs. Given that he'd spent the past two days at the ME's office, overseeing the Harrington autopsies, and there were now six more dead . . . Neil used to be an EMT. Made him the best man for the job.

'Turns out that Hermes Laraquette was from Barbados,' Neil continued now. He glanced at his notes. 'Hermes was a Redleg — some small white underclass that descended from indentured servants, criminals, etc. INS has been looking for him, which is one case file they can now close.'

'School, employment, church, social clubs, prior address?' D.D. prompted.

This list was thin. The Laraquette-Solis clan lived across Boston, in Jamaica Plains. They were not known for their community involvement or their social consciousness. The family had moved into the neighborhood six months ago, and while Hermes liked to saunter around in his rainbow knit hat, the woman and kids were rarely seen outside.

D.D. couldn't imagine it. How could anyone stay inside with that smell?

She studied the list under the Harrington

name, then the list under the Laraquette name. Nothing leapt out at her.

'Enemies?' she prodded.

No one could think of any enemies for the Harringtons. The Laraquettes, on the other hand . . . They'd need days to research that list, given Hermes's drug dealings. D.D. filled in TBD, for 'to be determined.'

'So,' she declared briskly, 'according to our lists, there's no obvious overlap between the Harringtons' world and the Laraquettes'. From a logical perspective, how could these two families know each other?'

'Mission work, maybe,' Alex spoke up, 'if the Harringtons' church does anything with low-income families. Or their own volunteer efforts.'

'Worth checking,' D.D. agreed. 'The Harringtons are do-gooders and the Laraquettes could use some good done. Other connections?'

'The kids,' Neil suggested. 'Teenage boys are close in age. Maybe knew each other from sporting activities, summer camps, that kind of thing.'

D.D. wrote it down.

'Foster families, troubled kids,' Phil continued, brainstorming. 'Harringtons adopted Ozzie, who we know passed through a variety of households before reaching them.'

'You're thinking the Laraquettes once fostered Ozzie?' D.D. was dubious. 'I'd think it would be the other way around — child services looking to place the Laraquette children to get them the hell out of that house.'

'That, too,' Phil agreed. 'Again, we know the

Harringtons had an interest in at-risk kids, and we know the Laraquette kids were at risk.'

'All right, from that perspective, I can buy it. We'll call social services. They always love to hear from us. Other possibilities?'

The group was quiet, so D.D. made a few notes, then cleared the whiteboard and set them up for discussion number two: crime scenes.

Neil, the autopsy guru, led the way. 'ME confirmed that the mother, Denise Harrington; the older son, Jacob; and the younger son, Oswald, all died of a single knife wound. Of note, there are no hesitation marks on any of the wounds.'

'Christ,' Phil muttered, the lone family man in the room.

'The girl, Molly, suffered a knife wound to the upper left arm. Cause of death, however, was manual asphyxiation. Fractured hyoid bone, which indicates a perpetrator of considerable manual strength.'

'Like a nine-year-old boy?' D.D. spoke up.

Neil gave her a look. 'Not likely.' He glanced back down at his notes. 'As for the father, Patrick Harrington, ME hasn't gotten to him yet. According to the doctor's report, however, he died due to complications from a gunshot wound — swelling of the brain.'

'Okay. So three stabbed, one strangled, one shot. Kind of original right there. Most family annihilators have a singular approach, don't they?' D.D. looked to Alex for an answer.

He nodded. 'Traditional approaches include shooting, drugging, and/or carbon monoxide poisoning. Sometimes, you see a case where the father figure drugs the family first, presumably to limit their suffering, then shoots them. If we look at teenage family annihilators — the abused son seeking retribution — methodology expands to bludgeoning and/or arson. I haven't heard of a case where a single attacker switches weapons as he/she goes along.'

'Single attacker,' D.D. picked up. 'Let's talk about the number of perpetrators for a second. What about cases where the adolescent child has a partner in crime, like the daughter and her boyfriend who kill her family so they can be together. Or wasn't there a case where a daughter and her lesbian lover murdered her grandparents so they could be together? Stuff like that.'

'When a teenager is the instigator of family annihilation,' Alex said, 'there are instances of partner involvement. In those cases, however, both partners murder the offending family members, then escape together. Not kill the family, plus the adolescent instigator, and then the partner gets away.'

'Coconspirator turned on the instigator?'

'Why?' Alex asked.

'Hell if I know.'

'Not probable,' Alex said. 'Furthermore, the Harrington scene is methodical. Two teenagers on a killing spree are never gonna get through a house that clean. We're looking for a perpetrator of above-average strength and intelligence. Patient, calculating, and skilled. Find me that teenager, and we'll talk.'

'Fair enough,' D.D. said. 'What do we know about the knife?'

'The knife used in the Harrington attack matched a set found in the kitchen.' Phil had finished his donut and was brushing crumbs off his rounded belly. 'Handle too smeared to yield prints.'

'And the handgun?'

'Registered to Patrick Harrington. His prints on the handle.'

'So murder weapons came from inside the home?'

Phil nodded.

'All right. The Laraquette-Solis scene?'

Alex took the lead this time, picking up his notes. 'Mixed methodology. Four shot — the adult male in the family room, the teenage boy in the hallway, and two girls in their bedroom. Adult female, Audi Solis, was fatally stabbed in the kitchen. Baby was suffocated in her crib, presumably with a pillow. Order unknown at this time. Could be father did family, then lay down on the sofa and shot himself. Could be he was taken out first, then the family, with the handgun returned to the father to implicate him in the crime.'

'Knife?' D.D. asked.

'Matches the set found in the kitchen,' Phil repeated. 'Handle didn't yield prints.'

'Gun?'

'Unregistered, serial number filed off.'

'Stolen,' D.D. said. 'Black market.'

'Most likely. Given Hermes's lifestyle . . . '

'Hot gun for the dope dealer,' D.D. concluded.

171

She paused for a minute, considering their list. 'Interesting that both scenes yield the same three methodologies for murder: shooting, stabbing, asphyxiation. And that in both scenes, the murder weapons originated from inside the home.'

'Not conclusive,' Alex cautioned.

'Not. But interesting. In your words, this type of crime generally has a singular approach. We now have two scenes where an entire family was eliminated using three separate methodologies, and the murder weapons were found inside the home. What are the odds of that?'

'Copycat?' Neil asked from the back.

D.D. shook her head. 'Can't be. We haven't released cause of death to the media yet. They know Patrick Harrington was admitted to the hospital for a gunshot wound. But we didn't release stabbing, and we definitely never revealed that Molly Harrington was strangled.'

More silence, which was answer enough.

D.D. set down the blue dry-erase marker.

'Houston,' she declared, 'I think we have a problem.'

★   ★   ★

D.D.'s boss didn't want to go nuts yet. Sure, there were some disturbing coincidences between the Harrington scene and the Laraquette case. But coincidence could be just coincidence, while the formation of an official taskforce was bound to attract media attention. Next thing you knew, some Nancy Grace wannabe would announce the two cases were conclusively linked, with a madman running around Boston murdering entire families. Phones would ring nonstop. The mayor would demand a statement. Things would get messy.

It was August. People were hot and short-tempered. The less said the better.

Instead, the deputy superintendent came up with the bright idea that D.D.'s squad could handle both investigations. Thus, if any more *coincidences* were discovered, they'd be quick to put the pieces together.

D.D. pointed out that assigning three detectives to cover two mass murders was asking a bit much.

D.D.'s boss countered that she was essentially working with a four-man squad: She had Academy professor Alex Wilson to assist with prepping reports on the crime scenes.

She demanded two more detectives, bare minimum.

He granted her Boston's drug squad to assist with background info on Hermes.

It was more than D.D. normally got from her stressed-out, budget-bound boss, so she considered it a victory.

Her squad accepted the news without blinking. So they'd be eating at their desks and neglecting their families. That went without saying in this day and age of reduced government funding and escalating rates of homicide. You didn't become a detective for the lifestyle.

Given that their weekend appeared grim, D.D.

173

decided the first thing they should do was break for lunch. Half a dozen donuts doesn't last a girl as long as you'd think. Fortunately, the BPD cafeteria was not only located conveniently downstairs but was known for its food.

D.D. went with rare roast beef on rye, fully loaded, plus a giant slice of lemon cake. Phil, who she would swear was half woman, ordered a chef's salad. Neil requested egg salad, a questionable choice, D.D. thought, for a man due back at the morgue. The lanky redhead downed his sandwich in four bites, then was out the door, whistling cheerfully. D.D. suspected he'd taken an interest in the ME. God knows they were spending a lot of quality time together.

Alex settled in beside D.D. with grilled chicken and penne pasta. She gave him grudging respect for eating hot food on a day when it was over ninety.

He loaded up on salt, red-pepper flakes, then Parmesan. After a bit of experimenting, he seemed to decide his lunch was good to go. High maintenance when it came to food.

Naked. In her bed. Cold chills. Warm thrills.

D.D. took a giant bite of sandwich.

'You can't really believe the two cases are linked,' Alex asked after a minute. Phil was sorting his way through his salad, avoiding tomatoes, loading up on ranch dressing. He looked up at this, eyeing D.D. with equal skepticism.

She took another bite, chewed, swallowed. 'Can't decide,' she said at last.

'Well, you gotta think something,' Phil

countered, 'since you just bought us both cases.'

'Victims have nothing in common,' Alex said. 'Given the difference between the two families' geography, occupations, and lifestyle, what are the odds they knew the same homicidal maniac?'

'Could be a stranger crime,' D.D. said with a shrug.

Alex arched a brow. 'Even lower probability, given that you're talking about an attack on an entire family, which, at least in the Harrington case, occurred while still daylight. A disorganized killer might have the impulsiveness for such an attack, but not the methodical approach. Organized killers generally take the time to scout out risky targets.'

'One of BTK's first crimes was an attack on a family right after breakfast,' D.D. said, referring to the notorious Bind Torture Kill murderer who operated for decades in Kansas. 'He talked himself through the front door, then held a gun on the kids until the parents agreed to be tied up. Once he subdued the parents, he proceeded according to plan.'

'No evidence of bondage at our scenes,' Phil pointed out.

'And BTK stalked his targets first,' Alex said firmly. 'He spent months on reconnaissance before he made his move. We're talking two crimes that occurred within thirty-six hours of each other. Where's the time for stalking, for identifying each family member, formulating a strategy for attack, and, here's a thought, for knowing that each household happened to have a twenty-two handgun on-site, let alone get possession of it?'

'Perpetrator got lucky?'

Alex gave her a look. 'If it's a serial case,' he continued relentlessly, 'where's the downtime? Most of these guys take a moment between victims, revel in a job well done.'

'That's sick,' D.D. said crossly, mostly annoyed that Alex was right, which meant she was wrong. Being horny was hard enough, but being horny and stupid would be too much to bear.

'That's the point,' Alex was saying. 'One killer for two entire families in a span of less than thirty-six hours is a long shot. That kind of bloodlust, combined with such high-level control . . . ' His voice trailed off. 'I can't picture it. It doesn't fit.'

'But two fathers independently deciding to kill their wife and kids, using the same three methods, within a day of each other — *that* makes sense?'

'Coincidences happen.'

'It's not a *coincidence*!'

'Then, what?'

'We need more information. I know: We'll investigate. What a great idea!'

Alex rolled his eyes at her. D.D. moved on to her lemon cake.

'I think we should have our auras cleansed,' she announced.

'Hey,' said Phil. 'I'm a family man . . . '

'Then you can call child services and get everything you can on Oswald Harrington and the Laraquettes. Alex, you're with me.'

'But I showered just this morning.'

'Not that kind of cleansing. We're going to tend to our inner beauty.'

'You mean a spa?'

'No, it's time we call upon Denise Harrington's favorite shaman, Andrew Lightfoot.'

15

VICTORIA

Evan walked into my room at 4:14 a.m. and demanded to go to the park. He asked again at 4:33, 4:39, 4:43, 4:58, 5:05, and 5:12.

It's 5:26 now, and we're walking to the park.

The morning's beautiful. The rain the night before has washed away the worst of the humidity. The air is warm, but pleasant, like a kiss against our cheeks. We walk the half a dozen blocks, breakfast in hand, and watch the sun paint the horizon. Being at the easternmost edge of the time zone, Massachusetts has one of the first sunrises in the country. I like to think of the early daybreaks as an exclusive treat for people who will spend their lives dropping their 'r's.' Other states have better enunciation. We get this.

'I see purple,' Evan says excitedly, pointing to the horizon and running circles around me. 'There's yellow and orange and fuchsia!'

'Fuchsia' is one of his favorite words. I don't know why.

The park comes into view. I expected the playground to be empty at this hour. Instead, a small boy waddles around the two swing sets and impressive climbing structure, his mother watching from a nearby bench.

I hesitate. Evan dashes ahead. 'A friend! Mommy, Mommy, a new friend!'

By the time I make it to the playground, Evan has already run half a dozen exuberant circles around the toddler. The small boy doesn't appear overwhelmed, but is grinning at Evan as if meeting a clown for the first time. Encouraged, Evan zips figure 8s all over the playground. The boy toddles after him.

I feel my usual sense of parenting pessimism. Maybe Evan will play nicely with the boy. Maybe they'll enjoy each other's company. Evan misses other children so much. Maybe that will give him the incentive to be gentle. Maybe.

I sit down on the bench next to the other mom. It seems the hospitable thing to do.

'Good morning,' she says brightly, a young girl, maybe twenty-two, twenty-three, with long brown hair held back in a ponytail. 'I didn't expect to see anyone else in the park this time of morning.'

'Neither did I,' I agree, trying to summon a smile energetic enough to match her own. Belatedly, I stick out a hand. 'I'm Victoria. That's my son, Evan.'

'Becki,' she says. 'That's Ronald. He's three.'

'Evan's eight.'

'Wow, he's a morning person,' she laughs, watching Evan race up and down the slide. He's already ditched his flip-flops and is in bare feet. I wonder how long before his dark blue gym shorts and red T-shirt follow suit.

'We just moved here,' Becki offers. 'As in, the moving van unloaded yesterday afternoon. We still don't have all the beds set up, nor the window air conditioners in. By five this morning,

179

it seemed better to get outside. Ronald can run around while it's still cool out, then maybe I can get him to nap through the heat.'

Next to the playground is a soccer field. Around the soccer field is a wooded fringe that separates the park from the neighboring houses. Evan has veered away from the little boy and is racing up and down the white lines of the soccer field. I allow myself to relax a fraction, take a sip of coffee.

'Where did you move from?' I ask Becki.

'North Carolina.'

'That explains the lovely accent,' I murmur without thinking, and Becki beams at the compliment. It occurs to me that Evan isn't the only one who misses his friends. I don't belong to any social groups anymore. I don't have clients, or coworkers, or close neighbors. I don't attend playgroups, or hang out with the other moms after school. I see a respite worker twice a week and talk to my six-year-old daughter once a week. That's the extent of my social life.

I'm pleased I can still make small talk. 'What brought you to Massachusetts,' I ask now, warming to the moment. I hold out a ziplock bag containing banana muffins. Becki hesitates, then accepts one.

'My husband's job. He's a project engineer. They move him around every few years.'

'You're lucky to land in Cambridge,' I tell her. 'This is a great family area. You'll love it here.'

'Thanks!' she says brightly. 'In all honesty, I picked the town because of the universities. I'm kind of hoping that now Ronnie's three, I can take some night courses.'

I check on Evan again. He's made it to the far soccer goal and is climbing in the black netting. Ronald has spotted him and is working his way down the field on his shorter legs.

Becki calls him back and the toddler obediently swings around and returns to the jungle gym. 'Sorry,' she says self-consciously. 'Nervous mother. Sometimes he bolts on me, so I don't like for him to get too far away. I know he's only three but, wow, can he run!'

'I know what you mean,' I assure her. 'I haven't been able to keep up with Evan since he was two. Kids are all muscle and speed. We can't compete.'

She nods, working on her muffin. 'Evan's an only child?' she asks at last.

'He has a sister,' I reply. 'She's with her father.'

Becki glances at me, but doesn't pry. I put away the muffins. Get out a container of fresh strawberries.

'Will you have a second child?' I ask.

'I hope so. Once I finish up my degree at least. Ronnie was a bit of an oops. A happy oops,' Becki corrects hastily, coloring slightly. 'But I'd hoped to finish college first.'

'Of course.' Evan's still working the soccer field; Ronald's back at the jungle gym. I get the lid off the strawberries, hold them out.

'That reminds me — I gotta get to the grocery store,' Becki comments, selecting a strawberry and taking a bite. 'Actually, where *is* the grocery store?'

I give her directions, and that leads her to digging through her diaper bag for a notepad, and that leads me to sketching out several rough maps with the best local restaurants, a great bookstore, this absolutely wonderful bakery over on Huron Avenue. I feel like I'm drawing a map to the life I used to live. Here are places where you should shop, eat, and play. Here are things you, your husband, and your children would enjoy doing.

Cambridge is such a nice town, filled with historic grandeur mixed with the hip Harvard scene. Maybe I could bring Evan to the park more often. Maybe I could attempt the special-needs playgroup again. Or perhaps the local pool. Evan's pretty good at pools. The swimming tires him out, keeps him distracted. I could bring a book, relax in the sun. I could mix us both fun, fruity drinks. Strawberry smoothies, virgin piña coladas. Michael and I went to Baja once, where we drank the best piña coladas, made with fresh fruit juice and rum. We'd drink them starting at sunrise, while lounging on the beach, digging our toes into the warm, white sand . . .

'Victoria?'

I'm lost in my fantasy, making the mistake of remembering better days, of wanting a life beyond the cage in which I live. The high-pitched note in Becki's voice brings me back. I stop drawing a map to the best coffee shop. I look at the playground. It takes me only a second to understand Becki's shrill tone.

Evan and the little boy are gone.

182

★ ★ ★

I start with the usual platitudes. They couldn't have gone far, we'd only glanced away for a minute. Why doesn't she check by the street? I'll start with the woods.

Becki obediently rushes toward the empty sidewalk. I make a beeline for the woods, calling Evan's and Ronnie's names. Nothing.

My heart's beating too hard, my breath growing shallow. Maybe the boys are playing hide-and-seek. Maybe Evan saw Ronnie toddle off, and set out to rescue him. Maybe they'd just gotten curious. Boys do that. Some boys at least.

I trot down the impossibly long wooded perimeter, calling, calling, calling. Nothing. Nothing. Nothing.

Then I start to think about things a mother shouldn't have to think about. Those two young boys in the United Kingdom who'd lured the toddler away from the mall and killed him down by the railroad tracks. Then an incident much closer to home, where two teenagers had murdered a seven-year-old boy by shoving gravel down his throat — they hadn't wanted him to tell his parents they'd stolen his bike. Or maybe the case of the six-year-old who'd lit the three-year-old on fire. Or the child who'd murdered his neighbor with a wrestling move, then stuffed her body under his mattress.

I make it down one side of the field, across the end, then work my way along the other, calling the boys' names. The woods aren't that deep. I can see the rooftops of neighboring homes

183

through the boughs of green trees. The morning's quiet; the sounds of traffic, muted. The boys should be able to hear me. Ronnie, at the very least, should call back.

Unless Evan won't let him.

My pulse spikes, lights dancing in front of my eyes. I'm going to pass out. *Can't pass out. Have to think, have to think, have to think.*

Evan's not responding. Why isn't he responding? Because he doesn't want me to find him. Because he's Evan and he's playing some game and he doesn't want to bother with me just yet. He wants to do what Evan wants to do, whatever that might be.

Incentive. That's what it comes down to when you are a parent. Evan isn't responding, because reducing my fear/panic/insanity isn't enough incentive for him. He needs something better.

'Snack time,' I call out, as if this is an everyday morning. Becki and I just happen to both be racing up and down the soccer field without our children in sight. 'Banana muffins and strawberries! Come on, who's hungry?'

Evan loves banana muffins. It's some of the only baking he lets me do.

Becki takes up the chant. We both work the wooded edges. 'Snack time. Muffins and strawberries. Come on, boys, it's getting late.'

I can tell by the rising pitch of Becki's voice that as minute passes into minute, she's starting to panic. It's one thing to lose your toddler for thirty seconds. Quite another to still not be able to find him after a couple of minutes of hard searching.

184

It's not working. Evan isn't budging for banana muffins. I need something better.

I return to Becki, turning her so our backs are to the neighboring woods. 'Evan sometimes plays this game,' I begin, wondering if my voice sounds as thin and strained to her as it does to me. 'He hides and won't come out unless there's good reason.'

'What?' she says, clearly preoccupied.

'Do you have a cell phone?'

'Yes.' She digs it out of her pocket and I take it from her, punching in my number.

'I'm going to run to the other end of the field,' I say. 'Then I want you to press Send. Don't look at your phone. Don't look as if you're making the call. Once I answer, you can hang up.'

Becki seems confused, but she nods, obedient in her fear, wanting something — anything — to return her world to right. She heads down one end of the field, still calling Ronnie's name, while I reach the other side. I try not to fidget with my phone or appear like I'm expecting a call. Evan can be very clever.

Thirty seconds later, my phone rings. I don't grab it right away. I give it a moment or two. Then I make a big show of taking it out of my pocket, glancing at the screen. I put my phone to my ear. 'Hello, darling,' My voice still doesn't sound natural. Maybe that's okay. I'm looking for my missing son, so of course I'm still a little stressed.

'You want to talk to Evan? I . . . I don't know where he is, honey. Ummm, ummm, let me see.' I hold the phone away from my ear, then call

185

out, 'Evan, Chelsea's on the phone. Evan. Your sister's calling for you.'

I cross to the other side of the field. Repeat the show, alternating between having a fictional conversation with a dead phone and calling for Evan to take his sister's call. Becki has stopped searching. She's standing by the playground, just staring at me.

She's starting to figure it out. That her new 'friends' aren't as normal as they appeared. That something's wrong with us, and that something could hurt her.

'Chelsea has to go,' I call out now. 'Come on, Evan. Now or never. It's your sister.'

At the last minute, just as I'm starting to give up, a bush rustles toward the end of the soccer field. Evan appears. He stands right in front of the bush, his hand on Ronnie's shoulder. The little boy is crying soundlessly, the way kids do when they're utterly terrified. Ronnie doesn't try to step away from Evan, but remains in place, his shirt torn, face smeared with dirt, hair tangled with twigs.

'Chelsea?' Evan asks.

I look my son in the eye. Hold out the phone without hesitation. 'Chelsea,' I say firmly.

Evan lets Ronnie go. The little boy bolts for his mother, who scoops him up immediately into her protective embrace. Evan walks to my side and takes the phone. He holds it to his ear only a second, then hands it back.

'You lied to me.'

'Why did you take Ronnie away?'

'You tricked me.'

'Why did you take Ronnie away?'

My angelic son smiles at me. 'I'll never tell.'

I slap my son across the face. Vaguely, I'm aware of screaming. Becki, I think. Only later do I realize that it's me.

* * *

Becki doesn't call the cops. Maybe she should. But with Ronnie still clutched against her chest, she grabs the diaper bag and bolts out of the park. My hand-drawn maps never made it into her bag. The haste of her departure scatters them across the playground. I watch them flutter about.

Directions to the life I used to live.

Beside me, Evan's sobbing, holding his red-stained cheek. My unexpected act of violence has shocked him, transforming him into a confused eight-year-old, attacked by his own mother.

I should hate myself for what I've done. I should feel remorseful, guilt-stricken. But I can't feel anything. Nothing at all.

After another moment, I cross to the park bench. I pack up the muffins, the strawberries, my travel mug of coffee. I tuck each item into my flowered bag, arranging them just so. I cross to the slide. Pick up Evan's shoes, lay them carefully on top of the containers. Evan has stopped crying. He stands, shoulders hunched, hands cupping his thin face, hiccuping miserably.

I could leave him. I could throw the bag over my shoulder, start walking, and never look back.

Someone would find him. The authorities, unable to contact me, would call his father. Michael could have him back. Evan would be happy about that.

Maybe I could walk to Mexico. Drink a piña colada. Dip my toes into the sand. I wonder how warm the water would feel this time of year.

'Mommy,' Evan whimpers. 'Mommy, I want to go home.'

So we go home, where I give us both Ativan and we go to sleep.

★ ★ ★

Later, three hours, four, six? It's hard to say. Evan sits on the couch watching *SpongeBob*. I hide in the kitchen, dialing a number I'm not supposed to dial anymore. We're on a break. He needed some time. Things had grown strange in the past month. Once, he'd even scared me.

Now none of that seems to matter. Not that last episode, and the way his eyes had turned into black pools and I'd felt the hair stand up on the back of my neck. Not the strange, guttural way his voice had sounded when he said he needed to go away. Had some business to tend to. But he'd call me on Monday. He'd have a surprise for me on Monday.

It's Saturday afternoon. Monday is forty-eight hours. I can't make it that long. I need him. Dear God, I need someone.

Ringing. Once. Twice. Three times.

I almost hang up. Then:

'Hello?'

188

The second I hear his deep baritone, it hits me. The stress, the terror, the unrelenting fear. Not that my son will kill me, but that despite my best efforts, he will hurt someone else. He's growing older, getting bigger, stronger, smarter. How long can I keep this up? How much longer before he wins at his own game?

The deep freeze gives way. I start to cry, and once I start, I can't stop.

'I can't do it,' I sob into the phone. 'I just can't do it anymore. I'm not strong enough.'

'Shhh, shhh, shhh,' he soothes. 'I'll help you, Victoria. Of course I'll help you. Now take a deep breath and tell me everything.'

16

Andrew Lightfoot lived in Rockport, about thirty minutes north of Boston. The quaint little town was perched on the edge of the Atlantic coast and offered all the requisite tourist amenities, including hand-scooped ice cream, saltwater taffy, and pounds of homemade fudge. D.D. would love to live in Rockport, assuming she ever won the lottery.

The GPS system obediently directed them to Lightfoot's DMV address. D.D. followed the long narrow driveway until a house suddenly burst out of the windswept landscape in front of her. Beside her, Alex whistled. She simply stared, craning her head to see better through the front windshield.

Andrew Lightfoot owned a mansion. A staggeringly tall, modernistic structure that rose straight up from the rocky coastline and featured towers of glass oriented toward the vast gray-green sea.

'Three to four million, easy,' Alex price-tagged the home. 'How many auras do you have to cleanse to earn this kind of real estate?'

'Don't know, but next major hurricane, whole house is a do-over.'

'I think they use a special glass now,' Alex commented.

D.D. remained dubious. 'I think builders have forgotten how major the hurricanes we can get up here are.'

She parked the car next to a gurgling waterfall that flowed down a pile of decorative rocks. Next to the waterfall stood discreet piles of smaller stones, granite pavers engraved with Japanese symbols and a sparse collection of dainty flowers and ornamental grasses. Very Zen, she supposed. It put her immediately on edge.

D.D. and Alex made their way up the sinuous walkway. An oversized front door, fashioned from glass framed in maple, enabled them to see all the way through the house to the ocean on the other side. Seven-foot-high windowpanes on both sides of the door expanded the view. A small brown dog sat in the right-hand window. It spotted their approach and started yapping.

'Nice guard dog,' Alex remarked.

'Small dogs bite more people than the large breeds do. Toy dogs just have better PR.'

'It's the pink bow in the hair.'

'Ignore the accessories, watch the teeth,' D.D. advised.

Alex slanted her a look. 'Funny. I was told the same thing about you.'

She flashed her canines at him, then knocked on the door. The little dog spun in a circle, reaching new pitches of hysteria. Then, from somewhere deep inside the house, D.D. heard a male voice calling, 'Thank you, Tibbie. I'm coming. Easy, sweetheart. Easy.'

A man appeared in the entryway, his frame eclipsed by the light from the windows behind him. D.D. had an impression of height, then the door swung open and he stood before them. She nearly fell back a step, catching herself at the last second and forcing herself to hold steady.

'Can I help you?' the man asked politely. He wore a thin green T-shirt stretched across rippling pecs and washboard abs. His cream linen trousers emphasized long toned legs, while a simple leather cord drew attention to his tanned neck and the shaggy ends of his sun-streaked hair.

Expensive house. Impressive man. And the smell of fresh baked bread.

'Andrew Lightfoot?' D.D. asked, her voice slightly breathless.

'Boston PD,' Alex supplied, after the man nodded. Alex shot D.D. a curious glance when she remained speechless. 'Sergeant D. D. Warren, Detective Alex Wilson,' he provided. 'May we come in?'

'Absolutely.' Lightfoot stepped back, gesturing for them to enter. Their presence didn't seem to surprise him. The Harrington murders were currently front-page news. Given Lightfoot's work with the family, maybe he'd already connected the dots and anticipated a visit from Boston's finest.

Tibbie the dog had stopped barking, and was now running in circles around them. She stopped to sniff Alex's ankle, then growled at D.D., then returned to Alex once more.

'Tibbie,' Lightfoot chided, not too harshly. 'Forgive her. She's a Tibetan spaniel. The breed goes back two thousand years, once serving as guard dogs for the Tibetan monasteries. Naturally, Tibbie has deeply held opinions regarding strangers.'

192

Lightfoot smiled at D.D., leaning forward to whisper: 'She's also a little spoiled and doesn't care for competition from other beautiful women.' He winked, straightened, stepped away from the entranceway. 'Please, make yourselves comfortable. I have just baked some croissants. I will put together a tray for us. Coffee or tea?'

'Coffee,' Alex said politely.

D.D. nodded her agreement.

Lightfoot disappeared. Tibbie stayed behind, flirting with Alex. The detective bent down, holding out his hand to the pint-sized spaniel. She sniffed his fingers carefully, then leapt into his arms and made herself at home.

'Nice doggy,' Alex said, obviously impressed with himself. He walked into the vast living space, new friend cradled in his arms. D.D. followed in his wake.

The inside of Lightfoot's home was as impressive as the outside. The floor was covered in a gray-green slate. Lush plants softened load-bearing columns. Pale sofas and low-backed chairs formed distinct sitting areas. Mostly, however, one admired a wall of four yawning windows that overlooked the Atlantic Ocean.

The windows were open this morning, overhead fans circulating tangy ocean air and rustling the palm fronds. D.D. could hear seagulls in the distance and smell the salt of the sea. Nice life if you could get it, she thought. She wondered just how exactly a spiritual healer could get it.

Lightfoot reappeared, carrying a bamboo tray piled high with croissants, three mugs, and a

French press filled to the brim. He placed the tray on the coffee table closest to the grand piano so D.D. and Alex moved over there. Lightfoot spotted his dog in Alex's arms and smiled ruefully.

'You know, I'm still in the room,' he told his fickle pet. She raised her head at the sound of his voice and yawned. He chuckled. 'Tibbie is an excellent judge of character,' he informed Alex. 'I find canines to be much more open and perceptive of energy fields. Hence, their effectiveness as therapy dogs. If we would only open up our minds as much as they do, we would all be better helpers in the world.'

D.D. accepted a cup of coffee and a warm croissant. She took a seat next to Alex. Lightfoot positioned himself on the chair directly across from them, one leg crossed casually over the other. He still appeared relaxed, the congenial host warmly showing off his home. Interesting demeanor for a man whose client had just been brutally murdered.

'Do you know why we're here?' D.D. asked.

Lightfoot steepled his fingers, shook his head. 'I have faith, however, you will tell me when you are ready.'

This surprised D.D. She shot a glance at Alex, who appeared equally startled. Quickly, they schooled their features.

'Watch much TV?' D.D. fished.

'Don't own a single set,' Lightfoot replied easily.

'You're not interested in the news? Too earthly for you?'

Lightfoot smiled. 'I'm afraid I'm addicted to the Internet as a source of information. And, yes, I read plenty of news. But the past few days I have been 'off the grid,' as they say. I just wrapped up a particularly demanding case and needed some time with just the sound of the wind and the waves.'

'Case?' Alex asked, still petting the dog.

'Ever hear of Jo Rhodes?' Lightfoot queried.

D.D. and Alex shook their heads.

'She was a famous burlesque dancer who was brutally murdered in the twenties. Her body was found mutilated and hanged in a hotel room, the killer never caught. I happened to encounter her soul on the spiritual interplanes. Angry, angry presence. No tolerance for men, as you might imagine. Originally, I blocked her out. But then I began to wonder. It seemed such a tragedy, first murdered, now trapped by her own hate. I decided to offer my help.'

'You interviewed a ghost to identify her killer?' D.D. asked in confusion.

Lightfoot smiled at her. 'No, I helped Jo let go of her rage. Her killer died twenty years ago. It was her own negativity that was holding her back. It took a few sessions, but she rediscovered the light inside of herself. Then she journeyed on. A satisfying experience, but a very draining one.'

D.D. didn't know what to say. She set down her coffee. 'Mr. Lightfoot — '

'Andrew.'

'Mr. Lightfoot,' she repeated. 'What exactly do you do?'

'In colloquial terms, I am an expert in woo-woo.'

' 'Woo-woo'?'

'Woo-woo. You know, sixth sense, spiritual powers, other planes of being. It's been my experience that cops are also adept at woo-woo — you just don't call it such. Detective's instinct, gut feel. It's that little extra that helps get the job done.'

D.D. regarded him skeptically. 'So you sell . . . woo-woo, and' — she gestured around the airy living room — 'that earns you all this?'

'Before woo-woo,' Lightfoot provided easily, 'I was an investment banker. A very good investment banker. I drove a Porsche, fucked women based on their cup size, and screwed over my rivals. I amassed tens of millions of dollars in materialistic wealth. And achieved total spiritual depletion. Money is not happiness, though I'll be the first to say it was fun trying for a bit.'

'So you just walked away?'

'One day on my way to work, I passed a fortune-teller. She grabbed my arm and demanded to know why I was wasting my talents. I should be healing lost souls, not working Wall Street, she said. Naturally, I shook her off. Crazy old bat. But a week later, I had dinner with a college buddy who'd just been diagnosed with skin cancer. On a lark, I reached across the table and grabbed his hand. I felt searing heat. Like my hand was on fire, then my arm, my chest, my face, my hair. By the time I managed to let go, I couldn't breathe, couldn't think. I staggered out of the restaurant, drank eight glasses of water, and went to bed.

'Next day, my friend called. He'd gone to his doctor to discuss treatment options, and the growth on his back was gone. They tested four other places on his body. No cancer cells. All gone. I quit my job the next day.'

D.D. arched a brow. 'So you traded in your crass, materialistic life in order to selflessly share your gift with mankind. All right. How does mankind find you?'

'Word of mouth. The Internet.'

'You have a website?'

He smiled. 'AndrewLightfoot.com. You might enjoy signing up for the online meditation. I link together thousands of consciousnesses via the Internet and channel all of their energies toward a common goal. Powerful, powerful stuff.'

'What's the common goal?'

'Enhancing the light. Defeating the dark.'

' 'The dark'?'

'Energies work both ways. For every positive, there is a negative. Common sense can agree on that much.' He paused, eyed them expectantly.

'I'll grant that much,' D.D. concurred. Beside her, Alex nodded. He was munching his second croissant with the dog still nestled on his lap.

'Can you also agree that each of us radiates our own energy, some more strongly than others? Perhaps you think of it as force of personality, or natural charisma. We choose friends because their mere presence makes us joyful or relaxed. We avoid others because being around them is hurtful to us or 'brings us down.' We consider them negative — whether angry, or fretful, or

197

generally hateful. Everyone emits energy, and on one level or another, we respond to that.'

D.D. shrugged, 'Positive energies and negative energies equals positive people and negative people. What do you bring to the table, Mr. Lightfoot?'

'I have a variety of skills,' he offered.

'Dazzle me.'

'I am a fifth-generation healer, passed down through my paternal line.'

'Lightfoot?' She glanced dubiously at his sun-bleached hair. Not exactly a walking advertisement for Native American.

'I returned to using my great-great-grandfather's Indian name,' he explained. 'Seemed more appropriate for this line of work. Sadly, I can't do much about my fair features, a gift from my Irish mother.'

'How do you heal people?'

'It's a matter of becoming receptive to the energies. I put myself in a higher state, then I open myself up to the negativity. Illness or disease feels to me like slivers of ice, as if a glacier has taken root inside someone's center. I draw upon all the positive energy inside of me and from around me, and I channel it to my hands. Then I place my palms upon the person, and let the positive energy burn the negativity away. People tell me they can feel it. An intense warmth, starting at one point, then radiating throughout their body. Of course, I work with my clients to build their own positive energy as well. To shield themselves from negativity. To embrace the light all around them. Everyone, to a certain extent, can learn to heal themselves and keep themselves healthy. Some of us are simply more naturally adept.'

'You put your hands on a person,' D.D. said slowly, 'then declare him healed?'

'Told you you weren't the woo-woo type,' he said, smiling. Lightfoot tilted his head, regarding her thoughtfully for a minute. 'Let me guess. You're an accomplished detective. A work-hard, play-hard type of gal. You pride yourself on being tough, you always get your man. You would be the first to admit that you're in touch with your inner bitch.'

D.D. blinked, didn't say a word.

Lightfoot leaned forward, spoke in that same low, hypnotic tone. 'Maybe it's not about finding your inner bitch, Sergeant Warren. Maybe the key to happiness is finding your inner angel instead.'

He sat back and D.D. kept her eyes locked on his face, even as her hands clenched into fists. Nurse Danielle had been right. Arrogant son of a bitch. And yet . . . And yet.

'Would it surprise you to know that my father was in law enforcement?' Lightfoot offered abruptly. 'Not a big-city detective like you. Small-town cop. I, of course, was the ambitious son who couldn't wait to escape to the bright lights and big city. After my encounter with the fortune-teller, I called my father. He confirmed my shaman bloodlines, but was unwilling to give our heritage too much credit. So he had an instinctive ability to read people's true nature. He knew when someone was lying. He knew which men hit their wives and which women abused their children. And he knew when something bad was going to happen. He could feel it, the negativity building in the air like an electrical charge. He'd round up the usual suspects, in case that would make a difference.

'I don't think my father believed in his skills, as much as he puzzled over them. Because we lived in a peaceful community, did that mean he had few healing instincts? Or did we live in a peaceful community *because* he had such great healing instincts? Welcome to the nature of woo-woo.'

'Work much with kids?' D.D. asked abruptly.

'I work with all ages.'

'Let's talk kids,' D.D. insisted.

He spread his hands expansively. 'What would you like to know, Sergeant?'

'Does your healing extend beyond the physical to include mental illness? You know, troubled kids and all that?'

'I have worked with a number of kids others might classify as emotionally disturbed.'

'How would you classify them?'

'As old souls, as incredibly wise and sensitive beings who are being viciously attacked by other, more powerful negative forces. These negative energies are drawn to the light, particularly to old souls, and will stop at nothing to destroy them.'

D.D. had to think about this. 'We're back to the battle again? The war between light and dark? Kind of *Star Warsy*, don't you think?'

'Maybe *Lord of the Rings*,' Lightfoot said,

then grinned again. 'You're an old soul,' he said abruptly.

'It's the humidity.'

'You don't believe me.'

'Not for a second. Though I find it interesting that when someone like me meets someone like you, we're always someone important. An old soul. The former Queen of Sheba. The fortune-teller never says anyone was a peasant a thousand years ago, though most folks were. And apparently, a shaman never says you're just a flicker in the cosmos of life, though again, most folks are.'

'You must find the truth inside yourself.'

'As the saying goes, no shit, Sherlock.'

Lightfoot laughed, appearing delighted. D.D. glanced down at her half-filled coffee cup, fidgeted with her napkin. She could feel Alex watching her, seeing more than she wanted.

'Young kids, old souls,' she snapped. 'What are we talking about here?'

Lightfoot steepled his fingers again, back in lecture mode.

'Contrary to your statement, I don't believe in past lives. I believe all things are happening now, but on a limitless number of planes. Your soul visits this plane to experience this set of experiences. Joy, hurt, love, hate, etc., etc. Sometimes old souls come to this plane, but inside a baby's body. These old souls, which have so much power they emote across a multitude of planes, attract dark energies. All actions require a reaction. All positives call upon a negative.

'Unfortunately, young children don't have the

coping skills necessary to protect themselves against negative forces. Their oversensitivity means they're picking up on everything, from their mother's stress over not having enough money for groceries to the neighborhood kids' fear of being targeted by a bully. They're constantly battered by all of these conflicting energies, especially at night, when the negative forces gain power. These children appear fractured, impulsive, overstimulated. One day, Johnny is incredibly loving and charming, a personality ten times his or her size. The next day, Johnny is a monster, attacking everyone he sees, including his baby sister.

'Physically, these children run hot. They constantly shed clothing, coats, hats, mittens, shoes, and socks. Intellectually, they're bright, brilliant minds trapped inside a chaotic corporal cage. Emotionally, they operate at the nth degree of everything. They do not just love, they *love*. They do not just hate, they *hate*. Everything is more for these kids and nothing soothes them. Not therapy, not drugs, not the other five dozen things their parents have desperately tried before coming to me. The issue is not just physical, intellectual, or emotional. It is spiritual, and that's one plane today's experts deliberately overlook.'

'Are you talking exorcisms?' D.D. asked incredulously.

'Sergeant, I don't believe in God. Therefore, I can't believe in the Devil.'

'But you believe in light and dark.'

'Absolutely. That's where I begin with parents.

I start each family with basic rituals and skills. We work on meditation, spiritual cleansing, and protection exercises.'

'Exercises?'

'Would you like a handout?'

'Nothing would make me happier.'

'I will get you one before you leave. Or again, you can find the information at AndrewLightfoot.com . . . '

'You post the exercises? You give them away for free?'

'Remember, gifts are meant to be shared.'

'Right. But not negative energy.'

'Now you're getting it. These exercises are basic chants. I've written sample words for each exercise, as I find most traditional-minded people need help to get started. So I meet with the family in person, preferably in their home so I can get a sense of the energies present — '

'In the whole house?'

'Yes. These homes feel like an icebox. The negativity is everywhere. No wonder an old soul feels as if it's going insane.'

'So you're in the house . . . '

'I'll conduct a guided meditation, getting each family member to focus his or her light as much as possible. Once I have focused the group's love, I might attempt a protection exercise. I might also attempt a cleansing of select individuals, starting with the mother. A child's bonds with his or her mother are extremely powerful, so any negativity in the mother is being communicated to the child. As many physicians will tell you, mother the mother, mother the child.'

D.D. had heard that one before. 'So, you're doing chants, burning a feather, arranging crystals, what?'

He grinned. 'No burning feathers. I like crystals, but mostly because other people like crystals. Having a talisman gets them started. Me, I talk. I try to educate the families about energies and help them understand how their child is experiencing the world. I teach them to let go of their rage toward their child, to find tolerance and love once more. I try to help them feel the positive and resist the negative inside of themselves. If they can find their inner truth, then they can be effective parents again.

'These families are fractured. Marriages are strained. Parenting bonds are twisted. Sibling bonds are corrupted. The whole family requires healing, not just the 'problem child.' Another weakness, of course, of the modern medical system that studies only the weak link, but never the entire chain.'

'What about their doctors?' Alex interjected. 'Surely they have opinions about your work with their patients?'

Lightfoot shook his head. 'Very few. In my mind, the spiritual, physical, and mental are not mutually exclusive. All should be tended. My expertise is spiritual. I leave the doctors and therapists to the rest.'

'You just told us you help people choose not to be sick,' D.D. countered. 'That sounds like doctoring to me.'

'But these kiddos do not have a disease,'

Lightfoot retorted. 'They suffer from an onslaught of negativity that requires spiritual bolstering.'

'Or pharmaceuticals.'

'Most of the children I see have been prescribed plenty of those already.'

'Meaning you don't think they work.'

'I don't.'

'Do you tell the families that?'

'If they ask.'

'I'm gonna guess doctors don't take that well.'

'I'm gonna guess you're right.'

D.D. studied him. 'What else do you recommend? Beyond 'spiritual exercises'?'

'Detox. You're a detective; it might interest you to know that a study of prison inmates found they had significantly higher levels of heavy metals in their blood than the national average. High levels of mercury, in particular, have been known to exacerbate moodiness and increase rage. So I recommend a seven-day healthy-eating program to lower heavy metals and reduce inflammation. Feed the body, feed the soul.'

'Feed the body, feed the soul,' D.D. repeated. 'You're good with the one-liners.'

'I teach workshops, as well,' he replied without blinking. 'Again, AndrewLightfoot.com . . . '

D.D. glanced over at Alex. The dog was still asleep in his arms, but Alex had adopted the blank expression of a detective thinking many things at once.

'And the Harringtons,' D.D. asked finally, looking for a reaction on Lightfoot's face. 'What did you prescribe for them?'

'No,' Lightfoot said firmly. He didn't appear distressed or anxious. Just firm.

'No what?' D.D. asked carefully.

'I may not be a traditional medical practitioner, but I still respect the privacy of my clients. Anything you want to know about a specific patient, you must ask them.'

D.D. decided to go fishing. 'If I dialed Denise and Patrick Harrington right now, told them we were with you, and asked them to grant you permission, would you honor that?'

'I would need to call them myself,' Lightfoot said after a moment. 'To ensure it was the same Harringtons. But yes, if they say it's okay to speak with you, I'll honor that.'

'Call them,' D.D. said softly.

Lightfoot got up, crossed to an antique Chinese chest on the other side of the room, picked up a cordless phone, punched in numbers. D.D. glanced at Alex, who was stroking Tibbie's ears.

'He doesn't know,' Alex murmured.

'Or is a good actor.'

'He's very charming.'

'I'm sure it works for him.'

'Does it work for you?' Alex asked.

D.D. wouldn't dignify that with a response. Lightfoot returned, holding out the phone apologetically. 'Doesn't appear they're home,' he informed them.

'They're not,' D.D. agreed.

'You knew that?'

'Yep.'

Lightfoot wasn't smiling anymore. 'Sergeant, I believe I have had enough of this conversation. What is it you want to know?'

D.D. went with the obvious. 'Why you helped Ozzie Harrington kill his family.'

17

'Inner angel, my ass,' D.D. muttered twenty minutes later. They'd made it to the car, were pulling out of Lightfoot's driveway. It was after noon. Her blood pressure was too high, her blood sugar too low. She threw the car into gear and went grinding out into the summer traffic, heading for Rockport.

'Where are we going?' Alex asked. He had the window down, hand cupped over the top of the window frame for better leverage as she took the first corner a fraction too fast.

'Fudge shop,' she replied, accelerating steadily as she passed the first gawking driver, then the next. If people wanted to gaze at the ocean, they should park their cars and walk, for God's sake.

'Works for me,' Alex said.

It took her ten minutes to find the place she remembered vaguely from five years back, when she'd had a date in Rockport. Then she had to circle the crowded block half a dozen times before finding a parking spot almost exactly the same size as her car. Alex arched a brow. She considered it a matter of pride that she slid into the parking space parallel to the curb on the first try.

'Inner angel, my ass,' she gritted out again as she popped open her door, then stalked toward the fudge shop/deli. Inside, she ordered a grilled cheese, a Snapple iced tea, and four pounds of fudge. 'For the unit,' she said primly when Alex shook his head at the growing pile. 'Everyone's working hard.'

He ordered half a pound of white chocolate and praline fudge for himself, but no sandwich. Apparently, he only ate lunch once a day. Lightweight.

They commandeered the last available table, which was just large enough for two people to sit with their heads nearly touching. Alex unwrapped his fudge, eating it slowly and with a great deal of appreciation. That mollified D.D. The moment her shoulders came down and half her sandwich disappeared, however, he started.

'Shaman boy got to you.'

'Please. This from the man who French-kissed the dog goodbye.'

'She started it,' Alex said, but touched his mouth self-consciously. 'Besides, Tibbie isn't a potential murder suspect.'

'According to Lightfoot, neither is he.'

'And according to you?'

'Hate this fucking case,' D.D. growled, giving up on the grilled cheese, and opening the fudge instead. Chocolate with a thick ribbon of peanut butter. Better. 'Woo-woo, my ass.'

'Not into celestial planes?'

D.D. gave him a look. They'd shocked Lightfoot into discussing at least some details of the Harrington family. According to him, he'd started work with Ozzie nearly a year ago. After his initial visits with the family, he worked one-on-one with Ozzie to teach the boy basic meditation exercises, including how to focus on the light inside of himself, while constructing a shield against negative energies.

Lightfoot went on to explain, however, that his most effective work was done at night, in his own home, where he put himself into a meditative trance, and then, with the permission of Ozzie's parents, visited the entire family on the 'interplanes,' where he could work directly with their spirits. During the first of these trips, Lightfoot discovered that Ozzie was a product of rape. The boy carried much of his rage from his own inception, so Lightfoot arranged for spirit Ozzie to meet with his spirit rapist dad, in order for the 'healing process to begin.' Ozzie also carried the wound of his mother's death. Therefore, Lightfoot arranged for spirit Ozzie to meet his spirit mother, so he could hear directly from her that she'd never wanted to leave him and loved him very much.

Within four weeks, the nighttime work led to daytime progress, with Ozzie appearing calmer. Within two months, the boy had mastered the art of deep breathing, picturing seven angels giving him seven hugs. Within three months, he could produce his own protection barrier and his parents began weaning him off his medication, working with the consent of Ozzie's doctor, Lightfoot had assured them.

'Powerful, powerful soul,' Lightfoot had said with apparent awe. 'It is a beautiful thing to watch such a soul find itself again.'

D.D. had brought up the subject of Ozzie murdering neighborhood squirrels.

'A learning opportunity,' Lightfoot had informed

her. 'No one heals overnight. For every step forward, there are steps backwards.'

She decided the man loved his one-liners. And she decided that overwhelmed, stressed-out mothers must devour his words hook, line, and sinker. A televangelist for the alternative-medicine set.

'I think Lightfoot believes in what he does,' D.D. told Alex. 'And . . . I think his kind of charisma combined with his kind of looks is a pretty dangerous combo. Strong man. Weak parents. My bullshit meter hit an all-time high.'

Alex cut off another piece of fudge. 'Why?'

'Are you kidding me? Interplanes, spiritual healings, angel hugs. These kids have violent impulses. They bludgeon fathers, shoot mothers, stab siblings. I think they might need more than deep-breathing exercises.'

'What's the more?' Alex asked with a shrug. 'Remember nurse Danielle from the psych ward? Modern medicine doesn't know what to do with these kids either. Not enough available medicines, too many side effects. I don't know. I've never meditated a day in my life, but if I had a kid going crazy and the docs told me they were out of options . . . Sure, I'd give Lightfoot a call. Meditating isn't gonna *hurt* a child. Nor is vegetable broth or organic fruits or nighttime visits to the interplanes. You can't blame the parents for trying.'

'Exactly the danger,' D.D. said flatly.

Alex regarded her steadily. 'You don't buy any of it? What about his spiel on negative and positive personalities? I gotta say, my Aunt

211

Jeanine could drive the president of the Optimist Club to suicide. That woman's the walking, talking personification of a downer. I can believe she's sending negative energy out into the universe.'

'Big leap from naturally happy or sad people to nighttime surfing of the spiritual superhighway.'

'I think cops know woo-woo,' Alex continued. 'At least the good ones.'

'Instinct is instinct, not woo-woo,' D.D. said.

'Ah no. A lot of people would argue instinct is exactly woo-woo.'

'And they would be wrong. Instinct is evolutionary in nature. Darwinism one-oh-one. Those who can pick out the bad guys first live longer. And eventually produce generations of fine policing talent.'

Alex leaned forward, wiped a spot of peanut butter from the corner of her mouth with his fingertip. 'Shaman boy got to you,' he repeated.

'Oh, shut up,' D.D. snapped. But shaman boy *had* gotten to her. Because if getting in touch with one's inner love child was the secret to happiness, then she was well and truly screwed.

★ ★ ★

'Let's pretend to be cops,' she declared three minutes later. 'We have, oh' — she glanced at her watch, 'about four hours before the evening news broadcasts that a second family was murdered last night, making it two households in forty-eight hours. If we're lucky, given the differences in geography and socioeconomics, the reporters will assume it's a tragic coincidence, and run sidebars on getting better social services for stressed families during these tough economic times. If we're not lucky, some talking head will link the crimes, declare a serial killer loose in the greater Boston area, and there will be a run on handguns, possibly leading to a spike in accidental shootings of small children. Would you care to place your bet?'

'I think that's negative energy,' Alex told her.

'What can I tell you? I'm playing to my strengths.'

Alex opened his mouth, looked like he might refute that, but then closed it again. The moment came and went. D.D. wished she understood the interlude better, but she didn't.

'Opportunity,' Alex said tersely, and wrapped up his remaining fudge. 'Lightfoot worked with the Harrington family over the past year and was obviously trusted by them. If he knocked on the front door during dinner, they would've let him in.'

'But his work with them was mostly done. Ozzie had 'made great strides,' the whole family was 'making better choices,' succeeding in their 'learning opportunities,' and . . . what was that last thing?'

''Listening to their inner truths.''

'Exactly. Nothing says 'happy family' like listening to your inner truths.' D.D. paused, pushed away half a grilled cheese but didn't touch the fudge. 'We should download Lightfoot's photo from the Internet and take it to the neighbors. See if they agree he hadn't been around in a while. After all, can't forget AndrewLightfoot.com.'

'Can't forget,' Alex agreed. 'So he has opportunity. What about motivation?'

'Hell if I know. Pick your poison. Had an affair with the wife . . . '

'Can't picture him and Denise.'

'Had an affair with the daughter.'

'Interesting.'

'Parents found out. Seducing underaged girls definitely not good PR for an enlightened being. Lightfoot has to do something about it and, knowing Ozzie's history, goes with family annihilation.'

'Except he didn't frame Ozzie. He framed Patrick.'

'All right. Lightfoot's obviously a master manipulator . . . '

' 'Obviously'?'

D.D. ignored him. 'So he went to work on Patrick. Here's a father who's financially stressed and emotionally strained. Troubled kid is a lot of work. House is a lot of work. Now he finds out his 'good daughter' is dirty dancing with the local healer. Patrick confronts Andrew. Andrew twists it all around and convinces Patrick that all the 'negative energies' are winning, and Patrick should give up the fight.'

'Drives the man into killing his entire family?'

'Why not? We close the case, Lifetime makes the movie, I finally get sex.' D.D. stopped. Probably shouldn't have said that last part out loud.

'Does the sex part involve Lightfoot or me?' Alex asked.

'In that scenario, Lightfoot's gone to prison, so it doesn't involve him.'

'Perfect. Let's make the arrest.'

'Only after you solve the next problem: the Laraquette-Solis crime scene.'

Alex nodded, serious again. 'Lightfoot claimed not to know them, and I gotta say, I don't see them as the shaman type.'

'Though they do know their herbs.' D.D. shrugged, trying out different scenarios in her mind, not making much progress. She started to pack up her fudge. 'Grilled cheese?' she asked Alex, gesturing to the remaining half a sandwich. He considered the matter, then helped himself to a few bites. The gesture struck D.D. as intimate. Look at them, sitting forearm to forearm at this tiny little table in this cute little fudge shop in this gorgeous little town, sharing a sandwich.

She felt discomfited again. Torn between the life she had and the life she wished she had. Or, more accurately, torn between the person she was and the person she wished she could be.

'All set?' Alex asked after finishing the grilled cheese. D.D. nodded, and he graciously carried her tray to the trash. She replaced her fudge in the plastic bag, adding Alex's box on top. They waved goodbye to the proprietor, then stepped out onto the sun-drenched street, having to pick their way through the throng of summer tourists.

'Next stop?' Alex asked, angling automatically toward the ocean. At the end of the street, they could just make out a slice of blue water. It was

215

tempting to walk toward it.

'Don't know,' D.D. said, staring at the distant water, listening to the gulls.

'Dig deeper into Lightfoot?'

'Probably.' But her heart really wasn't in it.

'It might just be two coincidental crimes,' Alex said, as if sensing her apathy.

'I don't know that the crimes are linked,' she admitted. 'I feel it, but I don't know it.'

Beside her, Alex blinked. It took her another second to get it.

'Crap, I sound just like him!'

'Cops know woo-woo.'

'That's it, I want to go home and shower.'

'Works for me,' he said.

She shook her head and headed for the car. 'We're going to HQ.'

'No shower?'

'Nope. I'm getting out a whiteboard, we're poring through the reports, and we're gonna overanalyze every single detail of this case until we goddamn well know something. Screw woo-woo. You know what makes the world a better place? Good, old-fashioned hard work.'

18

DANIELLE

'So how are things at the PECB?' Dr. Frank asked.

He sat in a dark green wingback chair flecked with tiny gold stars. I sat across from him, not on the proverbial couch, but in a second star-dusted deep-green wingback. Between us was a cherry table with a tape recorder and two china cups: tea for him, coffee for me. We could be a set piece at a theater: prominent shrink interviewing prominent patient.

I picked up the fine rose-patterned china cup and took a sip before answering. Work was Dr. Frank's standard warm-up question. I only saw him a couple of times a year, so each occasion called for some sort of icebreaker, and he'd long ago realized I'd rather talk about other children's problems than my own.

'I have a new charge,' I said now, setting down the coffee. It was decaf, really terrible. I didn't know why I still accepted a cup, after all these years. You'd think I'd know better.

'Yes?' he said encouragingly, his gaze eternally patient.

'Her name's Lucy. She's a primal child. Fascinating, really. She soothes herself by taking on the persona of a house cat. Plays with her food, grooms herself, naps in sunbeams. As a cat, she's fairly workable. Lose the persona, however, she's aggressive, violent, wild . . . ' I lifted my hair to reveal a giant scratch alongside my neck, as well as an assortment of dark purple bruises. 'That was from an encounter last night.'

Dr. Frank didn't say anything. Talking is my half of the relationship.

'We'd assumed she was completely nonverbal,' I continued. 'But last night she spoke to me. Also, I've caught her listening a few times when the staff was speaking. The look in her eyes . . . I think there's a lot going on in her head we don't know about yet. In fact, I think she might be much more capable than we've assumed.'

'You said she's your charge?'

'Yeah. Well, I've been on the unit a lot these days, and if I'm on duty, I generally work with the nonverbals. My specialty.'

'I see.' Another standard Dr. Frank line. Sometimes, I felt like I could script these sessions before I ever arrived, which was probably why I didn't visit so much anymore. I'd quit altogether if not for Aunt Helen. She seemed to need for me to have a therapist, so Dr. Frank and I humored her.

Now Dr. Frank was eyeing me steadily. I knew what he was building toward, but I made him work for it. After all, asking was his half of the relationship.

'When did you get off work?' he questioned now.

'I got home around three in the morning.'

He glanced at his watch. It was ten a.m. Ten a.m. on a beautiful Saturday morning. I should

218

be hanging out in the parks along the Charles River, not sitting here.

'What time did you get up this morning?'

'What?'

'What time did you rise?'

My knee was starting to bounce. I forced it to stop. 'Don't know. Didn't pay attention.'

'Breakfast?'

'Sure.'

'What did you eat?'

'I don't know. Bagel. What does it matter?'

He eyed me, going in for the kill. 'You tell me, Danielle. Why does it matter?'

Both of my knees were jiggling now. Traitors. 'Fine,' I huffed out. 'So I'm not sleeping much. No surprise there, right? And okay, I skipped breakfast, and oh yeah, now that you mention it, dinner last night.' Not that it'll stop me from pounding a few drinks later on. No surprise there either.

I glared at him, daring him to tell me I don't have the right to self-destruct.

'Dreams?' he asked steadily.

'Same fucking ones.'

'Do you get out of your parents' house?'

'Nope. Nothing new there either.'

'Have you tried any sleep aids?'

'If you can believe such a thing, they make me crankier.'

'All right.' He picked up his own china cup, took a delicate sip of tea, then gently returned the cup to its saucer. 'So you have how many days to go?'

I continued to glare at him. He knew the

219

anniversary date as well as I did, the asshole.

He remained unflappable, blue eyes direct, white beard neatly trimmed, light gray suit dignified, so I finally bit out, 'Two.'

'Two days,' he repeated. 'And thus far, your coping strategy involves overworking, under-sleeping, overdrinking, and undereating. Does that about cover it?'

'Don't forget the annual pilgrimage to the graves with Aunt Helen. Can't forget that.'

'Do you want to go, Danielle?'

I didn't answer, so he pressed button number two: 'Do you want to get better? Do you wonder about your own capabilities, or does it remain easier to focus on one of your charges, such as Lucy?'

I refused to answer, so he went for the trifecta, lever number three: 'Let's talk about your love life.'

'Oh, shut up,' I said.

So he did. It was my session after all. I called the shots. I could lie as much as I wanted. I could deny as much as I wanted. I could hide as much as I wanted. Both of my knees were bouncing again and I wondered why I came. I should've stayed home. I should never leave my apartment again.

Because as of Monday it would be exactly twenty-five years. Twenty-five years to the day since my mother died, my siblings died, my father died, and I lived to tell the tale.

Except I had nothing to say. A quarter of a century later, I was not magically wiser. I didn't know why my mom and Natalie and Johnny had

220

to die. I didn't know why my first life had to end, and I didn't know why this second life was still so hard for me.

'Did you read about that case in the paper?' I heard myself ask. 'The family killed Thursday night in Dorchester?'

Dr. Frank nodded.

'Yesterday, two detectives came to our unit to ask questions about it. One of our kids was involved. His parents discharged him last year against our advice. Turns out we might have been right about that one.'

Dr. Frank was accustomed to my sarcasm.

I couldn't sit anymore. I was too edgy, agitated. I'd dreamed again last night. My fucking father standing outside my fucking room with a fucking handgun pointed at his fucking head. Fucking coward.

'This morning, they were talking about another family, too. In Jamaica Plains. Though maybe that was a drug deal gone bad. Nobody seems to know. Four kids, baby through teenager. Gone, just like that. If it was a rival drug dealer, why the infant? A baby can't be a witness, a baby can't rat anyone out. You'd think the shooter could've left the baby alone.

'Then again,' I heard myself ramble, 'maybe the baby didn't want to be left alone. Maybe the baby heard the shots and started to cry. Maybe the baby knew already that her mother and siblings were dead. Maybe the baby wanted to go with them.'

'What about the baby's father?'

'Fuck him.'

'The baby didn't miss her father?'

'Nope,' I answered, though his attempt to turn the baby into me is so Psych 101 I should laugh at Dr. Frank instead.

'There are no survivors,' I said. 'Do you think they're happier that way? Maybe there's a Heaven. Maybe the mother and her children get to be together there. And maybe, in Heaven, children don't have to listen to voices in their heads and parents don't have to scream to make themselves heard. Maybe, in Heaven, they can finally enjoy one another. I don't think it was fair of my father to deny me that.'

'Do you want to join your family?' Dr. Frank asked me steadily.

I couldn't look at him. 'No. I don't. And that sucks even more, because I hate my father for killing my family, then I have to turn around and be grateful to him for sparing me.'

'You don't have to be grateful,' Dr. Frank said.

'Yes I do.'

'You have a right to live, Danielle. You have a right to be happy and to fall in love and to find enjoyment in life. Your father didn't grant this to you and you don't owe him anything for it.'

'But he did.'

'Maybe your mother did,' Dr. Frank offered.

I scowled at him. 'My mother? What does she have to do with this?'

'Or maybe it was your brother,' Dr. Frank said.

I stared at him in confusion.

'Or maybe your sister, Natalie, or Sheriff Wayne, or your Aunt Helen.'

222

'What the hell are you talking about?'

'I'm just saying, there are many key people in your life, yet you hand all the power to your father. Why do you think you do that?'

'He took life. He granted life. He acted God-like, so I guess I make him God.'

'God doesn't drink a fifth of whiskey, Danielle. Least I hope not.'

I didn't have anything to add to that, so for a moment, we both fell silent. Dr. Frank sipped more tea. I prowled in front of his second-story window overlooking Beacon Street. It was busy outside. The streets swarmed with happy tourists buzzing about. Maybe they'd go for a walk through the gardens, indulge in a Swan Boat ride or a duck tour. So many things to do on a sunny August morning.

These families always seemed cheerful to me. I wondered if, twenty-five years ago, the neighbors thought the same about us.

'Do you think that if you're joyful, your father wins?' Dr. Frank asked now. 'You'll be indebted toward him?'

'I don't know,' I said. Which meant, of course, that I did.

'You want to know why your father didn't shoot you,' Dr. Frank said, steadily. 'Twenty-five years later, it still comes down to that. Why didn't your father kill you, too?'

'Yes.' I turned, less certain now, and stared at Dr. Frank. It wasn't like him to cut so quickly to the heart of my mixed-up, fucked-up life. I wasn't sure what to make of it.

'Maybe your mother called to him,' Dr. Frank

stated. 'Maybe she called out his name and that distracted him. Maybe she begged for your life.'

'Couldn't. She died instantly, single gunshot to the head.'

'Your sister, then; she was closer. Maybe she told him not to.'

'He shot her in the face, in the doorway of her bedroom. I don't think she could say much after that.'

'Your brother lived long enough to be rushed to the hospital.'

'Yeah, Johnny lived a good twenty minutes. Johnny also made like Superman and tried to fly down the stairs. His spine was shattered by a bullet, his neck fractured from the fall. Only thing he probably begged for was a second shot, for my father to finally get it right.'

'I see you've been reading the police reports again.'

I had them laminated in a scrapbook. Something Dr. Frank and Aunt Helen discovered years ago.

'Did your family love you?' Dr. Frank continued to press. He was relentless today. I was less certain of this Dr. Frank, and I started pacing again.

'I don't know.'

'You don't know, or you don't *want* to know?'

'I . . . I don't know.'

'Did you love them?'

'My mother and siblings,' I said instantly.

'Really?' He cocked his head to the side. The shrink's quintessential pose. 'Danielle, you have spent so much time and energy on their deaths.

If you truly love them, why not invest a little time and energy on their lives? That's what they'd want you to remember, don't you think?'

'But I loved *him*, too,' I heard myself whisper.

'I know.'

'I tried so hard to make him happy.'

'I know.'

'I thought, that night, if I did what he wanted, if I just made him happy, it would be okay.'

'What did he want you to do, Danielle? You are a grown woman now, a nurse with professional expertise. Don't you think you can finally say it out loud?'

But I couldn't. I wouldn't. There were things no child knew how to put in words. They didn't have the vocabulary to match the experience. A dime if you'll touch Daddy's penis. A quarter if you'll suck. What could a little girl say about that?

I worked now with two- and three-year olds who stuffed and regurgitated food in a desperate attempt to share. They didn't know the term 'oral sex'; they could only demonstrate the terrible violation, filling their cheeks with applesauce, then spitting it out while their mothers yelled at them for making such a mess. The children were honest in their desire to communicate. It was the adults who screwed everything up.

'She didn't save me,' I said tonelessly. 'But then, she didn't even save herself.'

'Who, Danielle?'

'My mother. She told me to go to my room. She told me it would be okay. She told me she would take care of everything.'

'What would she take care of, Danielle?'

'They started fighting. I could hear them yelling from my bedroom. He was drunk. You could tell he was drunk. He was always drunk.'

'And then?'

'I don't want to go to the cemetery this year. I don't see the point.'

'What happened that night, Danielle? You went to your bedroom. What happened next? Tell me what happened next.'

'He killed them,' I said bluntly. 'I tried to make him happy, but he killed them. Then he sang to me, so I would know it was all my fault.'

'You didn't kill your family, Danielle. A nine-year-old girl cannot stop a grown man. Surely at this stage of your life you realize that.'

I simply nodded, because even all these years later, I didn't feel like mentioning that at the start of that final evening, I was the one with my father's handgun.

★ ★ ★

Dr. Frank asked me more questions. I stuck with basic answers and we continued our dance. It occurred to me that, given the timeline, he and I were approaching our silver anniversary. I wondered if I should get him something. An engraved plate, maybe an heirloom-quality picture frame. Dr. Frank was one of the longest relationships I'd ever had. I wasn't sure what to make of that.

At the end of the hour, he surprised me again,

reverting to the direct probing from the beginning of our session. 'Do you feel your life is a success?' he asked me.

'Excuse me?'

'Do you feel your life is a success? Come, now, Danielle. You're a grown woman, well educated, with an admirable career. Do you feel your life is a success?'

I had to think about it. 'I think I've made a difference in many children's lives,' I said finally. 'I'm happy about that.'

'And these sessions? Our relationship? Has that made a difference in your life?'

'I am not sure I would've made it otherwise,' I said, which is probably true. At least close enough.

He nodded his head, seemed content. He shuffled some paper. 'You should know I'll be retiring at the end of the year.'

'Really?'

He smiled now, gesturing to his silver hair. 'I've long been driven by my profession. It's time to be driven by my hobbies instead. At least according to my wife.'

I tried to picture some Mrs. Dr. Frank, ordering him to hang up his hat, and that made me smile back. 'Well, congratulations.'

'You are always welcome to call,' he said gravely.

'Thank you.' We both knew I wouldn't. This relationship needed an end. His retirement provided a graceful exit for both of us.

'Danielle,' he said as I start to rise, 'I worry about you.'

The admission astonished me, and for an instant, I could tell it had shocked him. He recovered quickly. 'I believe we can agree there are aspects of your history you have yet to adequately acknowledge.'

I didn't say anything.

'I have a colleague I'd be happy to recommend. A woman. Perhaps you'd be more comfortable with a female doctor — '

'No, thank you.'

'These next few days will be hard.'

'I'll get through. I always do.'

'Have you considered staying with your aunt?'

'She has her own mourning to do.'

'You give each other strength.'

'Not this time of year.'

He sighed, appeared defeated. 'Please watch the drinking.'

'I will.' Tomorrow afternoon, I'd watch my arm come up, I'd watch the drink go down.

'And, Danielle, as I'm sure you must have already considered, perhaps this week is not the time to be watching the news. These other cases of family tragedy will only exacerbate what is already a difficult period for you. The Dorchester case in particular, which involves a child you once knew, is needless salt on the wound. Their tragedy is not your tragedy. That case has nothing to do with you.'

I took my leave without bothering to correct him. For every word spoken, so many more were left unsaid.

The story of my life.

19

The drug taskforce was good. D.D. returned to her desk to find an entire case file on Hermes Laraquette, aka The Rastaman. She thought any white guy who referred to himself as The Rastaman was probably doing something, and Hermes didn't disappoint. He had a long rap sheet of minor infractions, including burglary, theft, and possession of a controlled substance with intent to sell.

Fortunately for Hermes, the criminal justice system was overwhelmed, allowing his public defender to plead down half the charges, while getting the other half dismissed. Then Hermes made good on his vanishing act before Immigration caught up with him.

According to local intel, Hermes had hooked up with Audi Solis, a welfare mom already supporting three children by three different fathers. Nine months later, with Hermes's help, she was able to make that four kids by four fathers. Hermes was listed on the birth certificate of ViVi Bellasara Laraquette, born March 19.

At which time Audi applied for state aid for her youngest, while Hermes went back to doing what he did best, dealing pot.

The BPD drug taskforce believed Hermes was tapping Boston's growing immigrant population to help him import and export product. He moved bales at a time, but that still made him only a small fish in Boston's raging drug ocean. Given that he appeared to be using as well as dealing, Hermes wasn't likely to get ahead anytime soon.

So they had one petty drug dealer, shot on the sofa. One welfare mom stabbed in the kitchen. And four dead kids scattered across two bedrooms.

D.D. set down the drug taskforce's files and moved on to the rest of the reports, including interviews with the children's teachers and school administrators.

'Ishy or Rochelle?' she asked Alex, who'd taken the seat in the corner and was currently studying a sketch of the Laraquette crime scene as if reading tea leaves.

He set down the sketch. 'Ishy.'

D.D. handed him the preliminary victim report on seventeen-year-old Ishy Rivers, the oldest son, shot twice in the hallway. She took the report on eleven-year-old Rochelle LeBryant, who D.D. already knew liked pink paint and paperback novels. That left two pages on four-year-old Tika, who'd been shot on a dog bed, and one paragraph on five-month-old ViVi, who'd been suffocated in her crib. A life so brief the victim report didn't even fill a page.

They read in silence, sipping coffees, flipping pages. Alex finished first, then waited for D.D. to wrap up. When she set down the officer's report and picked up her coffee, he started talking.

'Ishy Rivers. No warrants, no arrests,' Alex rattled off crisply. 'Not in the juvy database and not in the DMV database, so a quiet life for a teenager. Two officers interviewed the neighbors, who 'don't know nothin' 'bout no one.''

'Funny, neighbors had the same thing to say about Ishy's younger sister.'

'Fortunately, the guidance counselor at the high school was more helpful — though, for the record, Ishy didn't spend much time at school.'

'Truant?'

'He attended a hundred and three days of his sophomore year, which is roughly half of the days he should've. They signed him up for summer school to make up the lost time, but he never showed.'

'They report him?' D.D. asked with a frown.

Alex shook his head. 'Sounds like the system gave up on Ishy about the same time Ishy gave up on the system. According to the guidance counselor, Ishy was coded early on with multiple learning disabilities. She described him as sweet, though his obsessive-compulsive behaviors made it difficult for him to integrate with his peers. He was fixated on credit cards, asking everyone he met what cards they had, what were the numbers on the front and back, and would frequently launch into a recitation of every known credit card ever made, including black, platinum, gold, and silver editions.'

'Identity theft?' D.D. spoke up.

'She was guessing Asperger's, which is often accompanied by OCD. Ishy was also deeply superstitious about stepping on cracks and could not enter the cafeteria or gym, as he was terrified the rafters would fall on him. A sweet kid, though.' Alex held up the report. 'The woman states it about eight or nine times. Sweet kid, struggling with school, and not getting the support on the home front to pull it all together. Guidance counselor's official opinion: She can't imagine Ishy committing murder, but does admit his obsessive behaviors could drive someone else to violence.'

'Interesting,' D.D. said. She held up her report, adding to the mix: 'Rochelle LeBryant. Eleven years old, due to start sixth grade next month. No arrests or warrants. Also not in the juvy or DMV database. If older brother, Ishy, couldn't wait to leave school, apparently younger sister Rochelle couldn't wait to get there. Her fifth-grade teacher reported that Rochelle had perfect attendance the previous year, and often arrived at school an hour before class started. The girl had sat quietly in the hall reading, until her teacher took pity on her and let her enter the classroom.

'Teacher describes Rochelle as quiet, serious, and very bright. The girl was anxious to help out, and couldn't stand making mistakes. Fortunately, she was smart enough — easily reading at a high school level, the teacher raved — that mistakes didn't happen often.

'Rochelle never spoke of her home life, but the girl's limited wardrobe, gaunt appearance, and lack of hygiene spoke for itself. In a fit of inspiration, Mrs. Groves stocked the bathroom with shampoos and Rochelle started washing her hair in the sink each morning before school started. Sometimes, Mrs. Groves would leave behind a few clean items of clothing, but Rochelle wouldn't take them. Rochelle seemed very prideful. Similar efforts to share food also failed, though the girl would accept books. She always returned them, but she couldn't say no to borrowing a novel.'

D.D. set down the report. 'Mrs. Groves can't imagine Rochelle harming anyone, though she had nothing good to say about the parents. 'Uninvolved,' 'uninterested,' and 'unloving' were just a few of her choice adjectives. She viewed Rochelle as essentially raising herself, and doing a decent job of it, all things considered.'

'Shit,' Alex said.

'Agreed.'

'What about the two youngest?'

'Not in school yet,' D.D. reported. 'Which leaves us with the statements from the neighbors — '

'Let me guess: They 'don't know nothin' 'bout no one.''

'How'd you know?'

'I think the neighborhood was Hermes's customer base, and most of them are pissed off they didn't get to that back shed before we did.'

'True. And now their bitterness makes it difficult for them to cooperate with the fine local cops who did get to the shed first. Jealousy, plain and simple.'

'The younger girl was covered in some pretty nasty cuts,' Alex said quietly. 'I saw scarring, too. Arms, legs, and around her face.'

'I'm assuming Phil will have some info from child services.' D.D. didn't like thinking of the four-year-old either. There was something too pitiful — that poor scarred body, curled up on a dog bed. It made her pinch the bridge of her nose, as if that would wipe the image away.

'Holding up?' Alex asked quietly.

'Always.'

'Not offending, just offering.'

D.D. looked at him. 'I'm good at my job.' It was important to her that he know that.

'I've noticed.'

'Don't need a man to fix me. Don't need a man to save me.'

'I've noticed.'

She grimaced. 'I hate my fucking pager.'

He smiled. 'I love working at the Academy.'

'Not gonna give it up for all this glamour?' She spread her hands over their piles of notes and reports.

'No. Visiting the field is good. Don't need to live here. 'Course, it helps me to be more understanding of a fellow investigator's crazy schedule.'

'Nothing regular about this job,' D.D. agreed.

'Plans get made and unmade. Dinners could be prepared that sadly grow cold.'

'Very sadly,' she assured him.

'I'm good at my job,' he said.

'I've noticed.'

'Don't need a woman to wait on me. Don't need a woman to stroke my ego.'

'I've noticed.' She paused, regarding him more seriously. 'So what do you want?'

'Let's start with dinner.'

'Really?' She didn't mean to sound disappointed.

'But I'm open to all possibilities,' he added hastily.

'Because I saw this ad — ' D.D. realized what she was about to say, and broke off, mortified.

Alex grinned. ''Cool chills, warm thrills'?'

She leaned closer. 'I'm dying to know,' she admitted.

He leaned closer. 'I'm dying to be of service.'

They both sighed. Heavily. Then leaned back, and returned to work.

'So,' D.D. said after a minute, clearing her throat, forcing herself to sound brisk. 'Where are we at? We got a drug dealer, a welfare mom, a truant teen, a brainy preteen, and two unknowns. High-risk lifestyle. Isolated mother and kids. What are the odds that Hermes smoked too much dope, tried a new product, and went postal on his own family?'

'Don't like the knife,' Alex remarked. 'If he starts with the knife, he should end with the knife.'

'Maybe stabbing Audi was the impulse part. They got into a fight in the kitchen, he took it too far. Ishy saw him, started to run, and Hermes realized he'd better do damage control real quick. Hermes gets out his handgun and goes to town.'

'Then, once he realizes what he's done . . . '

'Decides to finish it all. Suffocates his own baby, then lies down on the sofa and blows out his brains.'

'You're wrong.'

D.D. and Alex looked up sharply. Neil had appeared in the doorway, his pale face so lit up his freckles glowed. 'I got news, straight from the ME,' he burst out. 'Hermes wasn't shot. I mean, well, okay, he was shot. But it doesn't matter, because at the time he was shot, he was already dead. Whole sofa scene — totally staged.'

★ ★ ★

There were moments D.D. didn't like her job. The stress of working too many hours without a break. The tedium of poring over investigative reports. Her damn pager going off at precisely the wrong moment . . .

This moment, however, was not one of those moments. She, Alex, and Neil had taken over the conference room so they could spread out, and Neil was currently pacing up and down the length of the table, talking a mile a minute.

'Hermes Laraquette was hit with a Taser in the chest. Two jolts would be the ME's guess, to judge by the twin set of burns. Most men would've gone down, but recovered. Laraquette's lifestyle wasn't exactly heart-healthy, however, so he never got up again.'

'Taser killed him?' D.D. reiterated.

'Taser caused a massive coronary event, which dropped him deader than a stone.'

D.D. was standing at the whiteboard, dry-erase marker in hand. With Neil's affirmation of cause of death, she jotted down a fresh note. 'Hang on. If a Taser was used in the attack, where's the confetti?'

Tasers, which were illegal in Massachusetts, were supposed to discharge coded confetti with each stunning jolt. The code on the confetti could then be used to trace which Taser had been used in an attack — compensating for the fact that there was no bullet left behind for the police to trace. The confetti was a huge, fluttery mess, nearly impossible to clean up, especially given conditions at the Laraquette household.

'Don't know,' Neil said. 'But the ME is convinced it was a Taser. Has no doubts about the marks.'

D.D. frowned, decided to come back to the confetti. 'Okay. So that gives us four instruments for attack: Taser, handgun, knife, pillow. What else did the ME have?'

'Definitely stabbing as COD for the woman. Single fatal blow. No hesitation marks,' Neil reported, still pacing.

'Like the Harringtons,' D.D. said.

'Same size blade,' Neil reported. 'Meaning both households contained knife sets, and in both attacks perpetrator selected the same size blade.'

'The largest blade,' Alex said, his tone cautious. 'Which, if you think about it, is the most logical choice for murder.'

'True, true,' Neil mused, stopping his pacing long enough to stick his hands in his front pockets and jiggle the loose change.

'Can the ME check Patrick Harrington's body?' D.D. asked. 'See if he was tasered, too?'

'Already made the request.'

'Well?'

'Give him a couple of days. Between the two scenes, plus the rest of the city's normal mayhem, bodies are stacking up.'

'August,' D.D. muttered. 'Always a busy time of year. So what about the kids? The son was shot.'

'Yep. Same with the four-year-old and eleven-year-old girls,' Neil reported. 'Infant's gonna be tougher. Harder to rule on asphyxiation. More like nothing else seems to be physically wrong with the child, ergo it was probably suffocation. ME's sent the pillow out to be tested for DNA. Might be able to trace saliva on the pillow back to the infant, then it's a bit more conclusive.'

'How long?' D.D. was already bracing herself.

'Three to six months,' Neil said.

'Fuck.'

'Not right now, I'm already too excited.'

D.D. rolled her eyes at Neil. Sure, the lanky redhead talked a good game, but it wouldn't help her any. Alex, on the other hand, should look out.

'So what does this tell us?' she mused, riding the same adrenaline wave as Neil. She studied her whiteboard, then got busy with the marker: 'One, this takes Hermes out of the perpetrator column and moves him squarely into the victim category. After all, the man couldn't very well taser himself to death, then shoot himself to death.'

'Ambush,' Alex said.

She looked at him, nodded. 'That's what I'm thinking.'

'Stun Hermes, incapacitating him, then go after the rest of his family,' Alex continued.

238

'Why does Hermes have to be first?' Neil asked. 'Couldn't it be someone had attacked the family, then Hermes walked in on it?'

'If Hermes walks in, why taser him?' Alex pointed out. 'Someone walks in on a shooting, the perpetrator fires off an extra round. The perpetrator doesn't set down the gun and dig through his pockets for a new weapon.'

'True, true.'

'I think Hermes went first,' D.D. agreed. 'Perpetrator incapacitates the most obvious threat — the father — by stunning him multiple times.'

'Not exactly foolproof,' Alex commented. 'Especially a hard-core drug addict. I've seen guys stunned half a dozen times and they're still screaming bloody murder.'

D.D. chewed her lower lip. Considered it. 'Given that Tasers are illegal in Mass., maybe our perpetrator has a truly illegal, illegal Taser. Meaning, as long as he was acquiring a black market Taser, he got one with super-sized voltage. For the military, commercial grade, etc. Maybe custom cartridges, which would explain why no confetti was left behind. For a buck fifty, you can buy just about anything on the black market. Why not a super-volt Taser, guaranteed to silently incapacitate your problem, while leaving no evidence behind?'

The more D.D. thought about it, the more she liked it. 'Higher voltage might also explain Hermes's massive coronary event,' she continued. 'He wasn't just hit by a Taser, he was *hit by a Taser*.' She glanced at Neil. 'Any way the ME can study the burn patterns on Hermes's chest to estimate size of the hit?'

'I have no idea,' Neil said, 'but I can ask.'

'All right. Back to where we were. We know a Taser is being used, and it was strong enough to kill at least one man. So we'll assume that's part of the perpetrator's plan. Incapacitate the father figure with a Taser. Next up is the second adult — the mother. She's ambushed in the kitchen with a knife. Another silent weapon, maybe an attempt on the perpetrator's part to remain undetected for as long as possible. Once someone notices, however — '

'Ishy, in the hallway,' Alex said.

'Yeah. Now the subject has to move fast. Ishy's raising the alarm, there are two other kids capable of bolting for the neighbors'. The subject's gotta tamp down, or the whole scene will spiral out of control.'

'So the subject grabs a gun — '

'One he's taken off Hermes?' D.D. questioned.

'Unregistered, so no way to determine,' Alex said. 'But subject has a gun and now it's quick and dirty business. Fumbles the first shot with Ishy, but makes it right with the second. Then hits the girls' room. *Boom. Boom.* Kids are done. It's down the hall to the last member of the family.'

D.D. nodded. 'All right. But the last member of the Laraquette family is a five-month-old baby. Infants can't talk or bear witness. Why kill the baby?'

Neil and Alex were both silent for a minute, contemplating the matter.

240

'He has to kill the baby,' Alex said at last. 'Because it has to be the whole family. It's a script, remember? The family must be dead and the father must appear to have done it. So the baby must die. Then Hermes must be moved to the sofa and posed accordingly. It's what the killer does. What he needs.'

'Not a gangland hit,' D.D. said slowly. 'Because in a gangland hit, the shooter would want to take credit. He'd want it known that he'd eliminated his rival's entire family, to strike fear into the hearts of other up-and-coming drug dealers. Plus, he wouldn't mess around with four different weapons. Too much fuss. This isn't about revenge. This is something deeper, something more personal to the killer.'

'A reenactment,' Alex murmured.

D.D. frowned, uncomfortable, not sure why. 'Hermes's death screwed it up. He was supposed to be stunned unconscious. Then, when the rest of the family had been eliminated, the killer could return, move Hermes to the sofa, wrap Hermes's fingers around the gun, and complete the final act in the story. But Hermes had a heart attack, breaking with the script, and giving us our first clue.'

Alex said suddenly, 'Hermes had the gun on him.'

D.D. and Neil turned to him. 'How do you figure?'

'Because the gun has to come from inside the home. It's part of the pattern, and if you think about it, it works. At the Harrington residence, the subject eliminates Patrick first. Stuns him,

241

we'll assume for the sake of argument. Then the subject slips into the kitchen, grabs a knife, and goes to town. Finally, the staging takes place. Patrick gets moved, the subject locates the gun, performs the final act.'

'Patrick lived,' D.D. pointed out.

'The risk you take with a twenty-two,' Alex countered. 'But the gun was registered to Patrick, remember? That's all he owned, and I bet if we ask his neighbor Dexter, he'll agree that Patrick was conscientious about handgun safety in a household with three kids. I bet he kept the twenty-two in a lockbox. So the killer had to wait to access it and use it. Hermes, on the other hand — '

'Probably had it stuffed in the waistband of his jeans,' D.D. finished for him. 'Lucky he didn't blow off his nuts.'

'Lucky he ate so much fast food, and suffered a heart attack.'

'So now all we have to do is find some kind of link between the Harringtons and the Laraquette-Solis family,' D.D. said. 'And figure out why someone's idea of fun is murdering entire families. Then we catch him. Preferably in time for the five o'clock news. Ideas?'

She looked at Alex, he looked at Neil. Neil looked back at her.

'Trace evidence,' Neil said finally, with a small shrug. 'Hair, fiber, prints, some link between the two crime scenes.'

'Look for parking tickets,' Alex offered. 'Subject had to come and go, and let's face it, parking in the city is a bitch, especially during

242

the summer months.'

'Footprints outside the windows.' Neil again, getting into the spirit of things. 'Subject probably scoped out the place first.'

Alex's turn: 'Reinterview the neighbors. To pull off something this sophisticated, the perpetrator had to have reconned. Did any of them notice the same car driving around the block several times? Or a new face suddenly taking walks in the morning, only to disappear again? Guy had to get his intel somehow.'

D.D. wrote down the list, added two of her own: ballistics, in case the slugs bore any similar markings between the two scenes, and also the ME's report on Patrick Harrington. If he had Taser burns on his chest, the scenes were linked. No doubt in her mind.

'Neil,' she said, tapping that last item, 'get back to the ME for us, will you? Couple of days is too long to wait for Ben to reexamine Patrick. We need the ME's report tomorrow morning at the latest, even if it's only his preliminary opinion. But this matters. Matters a lot.'

Neil nodded, then there was a rap on the door. Phil stuck his head in.

'Miss me?' the third member of their squad asked. 'I've been looking all over the damn place for you. What's with the conference room?'

'More space,' D.D. said. 'Neil caught a break from the ME. Turns out Hermes Laraquette actually died from a Taser, and the whole suicide-on-the-sofa thing was staged. Now we just gotta link the Harrington scene to the Laraquette-Solis scene and we'll be able to prove we're looking for a single predator who likes to reenact family annihilations. Why? What'd you do with your afternoon?'

'Tell me you love me.'

'Is this more or less than I love a medium rare cheeseburger?'

'Definitely more. I've linked the Harringtons to the Laraquette-Solis family. Remember the Laraquettes' four-year-old girl with the cuts all over her limbs?'

D.D. nodded her head; not an easy thing to forget.

'Child services was called, and the girl was taken into temporary state care, and guess what? Mommy and Daddy aren't the ones who hurt her. She does it to herself. A form of self-mutilation that has something to do with compulsion, depression, anxiety, yada yada yada. To make a long story short, the girl can't stop slicing her own skin. Uses everything from sharpened twigs to paper clips to the tabs from Coke cans. Well, nine months ago, Tika got her hands on a disposable razor and starting working on her neck. By the time Mommy noticed, girl was covered in blood. Mom rushed her to the emergency room, where she was diagnosed as an immediate threat to herself and . . . ' Phil paused a beat, waited for the drum roll.

D.D. connected the dots, just as Phil spoke the words out loud.

'And four-year-old Tika was admitted to the Pediatric Evaluation Clinic of Boston. Otherwise known as Ozzie Harrington's former home-away-from-home.'

20

VICTORIA

Am I a good mother?

In the months prior to our marriage unraveling, Michael claimed that my personal failings were holding Evan back. I refused to view my son and his issues objectively. I refused to consider that someone else — or perhaps, more specifically, somewhere else — would be in my son's best interest.

By believing I was the only person who could help Evan, I was, in fact, guilty of the worst sort of hubris. I was arrogant, self-centered, and putting my needs as a mother above the needs of my son. I was also ignoring my husband and my daughter, fracturing the family I was supposed to nurture and protect.

To hear Michael describe it, Evan's temper tantrums, violent acts, and chronic insomnia were all my fault. If I could just be a better mom, Evan would be a better child. Preferably one who was locked up somewhere, where parents could visit at their convenience and a younger sibling could forget he ever existed.

Stop being such a martyr, Michael kept saying. *This isn't about you. It's about what's best for him. Dammit, we have resources,* he'd add, as if Evan were some sort of remodeling project that if we just threw enough money at would be done to our satisfaction.

For the record, it's not easy to institutionalize a child. There are very few long-term-care facilities. The good ones have waiting lists. The bad ones are a rung below the maximum security prison where many of the kids like Evan will eventually wind up. Evan's third doctor, after the crowbar episode, said he could work some magic on our behalf. That's pretty much what it takes for immediate placement. It's like a letter of recommendation from a wealthy alumnus to get your kid into the right prep school. Except it's a request from a prominent child psychiatrist to institutionalize your child.

The place he recommended had once served as a monastery. It was known for its stripped-down simplicity and structured approach to life. Unbeknownst to Michael, I toured it one afternoon. The rooms were small and guaranteed not to overstimulate. The walls were carved out of stone so thick, no amount of lighting would ever diminish the gloom.

The facility promoted self-discipline, hard work, and independence. I thought it smelled like an old folks' home, someplace you went to die. I couldn't picture a seven-year-old boy here. I couldn't imagine Evan, with his brilliant smile and infectious giggle, ever wandering these dreary halls.

So I kept him home with me. And my husband and daughter left instead.

I don't know if I am a good mom. Evan isn't the child I planned on having. This isn't the life I dreamed of living. I get up each morning and do the best I can. Some days, I give too much. Some days, I don't give nearly enough.

But I'm not a martyr.

I know, because at 2 p.m. I'm going to do something that's absolutely, positively not in Evan's best interest.

And I don't give a damn.

★　★　★

I start my preparations at noon. First, I make Evan a peanut butter and jelly sandwich with a crushed Valium tablet sprinkled in the middle. Don't ask me how I learned to do this. Don't ask me what kind of pressure drives a mother to spend her afternoons crushing up various medications and mixing them into various lunch options. For the record, you need something sweet, like jelly or honey, to hide the bitterness. Grilled cheese . . . it took hours to effectively clean the grease spot off my glass sliders.

I serve the sandwich with apple slices and a cup of milk on the coffee table. Evan perks up. Lunch in the family room means he gets to eat while watching TV. This is a rare treat, and he's already shaking off the residues of our morning playground drama.

Next, I turn on Evan's favorite channel — the History Channel. Evan can watch tales of historical events for hours, from stories of Pompeii, to the life-sized clay soldiers recovered from the Chinese emperor's tomb, to images of the *Titanic*. His favorite books are the Magic Tree House series, where Jack and Annie travel to various places in time. He loves nonfiction, as well. Biographies, coffee-table books, old lithographs — all of it fascinates him.

He gets this from his father, yet one more thing Michael will never know.

Currently, the History Channel is airing a show on digging the tunnel between Britain and France. There are images of heavy machinery and men in hard hats covered in mud. Evan picks up the first half of his sandwich and is transfixed.

I walk to the entryway, where I check the front door. Evan learned to work the bolt lock by age three, escaping at whim. He also mastered chain locks and the heavy glass sliders. As a result, my front door now features a key-in, key-out bolt lock. I also converted the glass sliders, meaning that every entry/exit in the house can only be accessed using the key I wear on a chain around my neck. If there's ever a fire, and I lose said key, Evan and I will burn alive.

But at least he can't escape while I'm showering.

Upstairs I strip in the master bath. I take a moment to look at my reflection in the mirror, though I know I shouldn't. I was a beautiful girl once. The kind of lithe, silvery-blonde beauty that turns heads. I understood my power early on, and used it wisely. I lived in a mobile home with newspaper stuffed in the cracks for insulation. I wanted out, and my looks were just the ticket.

I started on the pageant circle, winning modest amounts of money, which my jealous mother stole from my bank account. I kept going, eventually securing a scholarship to college. That's where I met Michael. I recognized him immediately as someone just like me. Attractive, driven, desperate. We'd been stomped on enough in life and we weren't going to take it anymore.

I lost my virginity to him when I was twenty years old, though my mother had been calling me a slut for at least the past six years.

I cried that night. Michael held me, and I felt genuinely special. The pageants were just titles. It was Michael who made me feel like a princess.

I don't look like a beauty queen anymore. My face is gaunt, my skin nearly translucent, stretched too thin across my bony ribs and jutting pelvis. There's a giant green-and-yellow stain on my left side — I think Evan had pushed me down the stairs. Fresher purple bruises run up my right leg. Red welts mark my forearm. I look old and beaten, and for a moment, I want to cry.

For the beauty that faded too fast. For the youth that disappeared too quickly. For the dreams I thought I would fulfill.

There are pieces of yourself that once you give away . . .

But I want them back. Dear God, there are moments when I just want them back.

Two o'clock. Everything will be better at two o'clock. I turn on the shower, step in the spray, and begin to shave my legs.

★ ★ ★

I return downstairs nearly an hour later, an eternity in my world. I've taken the time to smooth my favorite rose-scented lotion into my skin. I've buffed my nails, loofahed my feet, used a special conditioner on my hair. If not prettier, at least I'm shinier than I used to be. It's the best I can do.

Evan's slouched into the sofa. The History Channel is blaring, the station having segued from the English tunnel to Boston's Big Dig. The sandwich's gone. Evan appears glassy-eyed. First the morning's dose of Ativan, now this.

I sit next to Evan, feather back his blonde hair. He stirs enough to look at me.

'Pretty,' he says thickly, and it amazes me how I can smile and feel my heart break at the same time.

'I love you.'

'Tired,' he says.

'Would you like to rest?'

'TV!' he yells, not totally under the influence yet.

'After TV, then.'

He shifts away, his gaze riveted once more to the magic box. We sit side by side, my son sinking deeper into drugged oblivion, me fidgeting with my push-up bra.

The show breaks for a commercial. I glance at my watch. Ten minutes to go. Now or never. I pick up the remote, turn off the TV. I wait for Evan's squawk, but it never comes. He's slack-jawed, already two beats from unconsciousness.

He doesn't protest as I slip an arm around his

250

shoulders, guide him off the sofa and up the stairs. For an eight-year-old boy, he feels nearly weightless against me. The ADHD, we're told, his constant agitation. He could follow Michael Phelps's diet, and still lose weight.

In his room, I tuck him in bed fully clothed. It's his second nap of the day and I will pay for it later. A long, sleepless night where my son will work off the edgy aftereffects by trashing the house.

But it will be worth it, I think. As long as I can have two o'clock.

I glance at my watch. Three minutes and counting.

'Mommy,' my son mumbles.

'Yes, Evan?'

'Love you.'

'I love you, too, honey.'

'Sorry.'

'What's that, honey?'

'This morning. Didn't hurt him. Wouldn't hurt him. Just wanted . . . a friend. Nobody likes me. Not even Daddy.'

I don't say anything, just brush his cheek and watch his thick lashes flutter close. I want to tell him it'll be okay. I want to tell him we'll go to the park another day. I want to tell him he'll make new friends and that his father still loves him.

Instead, I slip into the hallway, and lock my son in his room.

Doorbell rings.

A last nervous sweep of my hand through my hair, then I head downstairs.

My lover waits on the doorstep. He's dressed casually, white T-shirt stretched over his toned chest. His hair curls damply against the back of his neck. He smells of soap and sunshine, and I want to take a moment to breathe him in. Youth, freedom, carefree days.

He smells of what I've lost, and some days I want him for that as much as anything.

'I have only an hour,' he announces. I'm not surprised. In the beginning, he lingered. We shared foreplay, pillow talk, post-coital glow. Then something shifted. He became less charming, more demanding, while our interludes became less romantic, more transactional.

I can feel the edginess in him now. He'll be rough again, even abusive. The woman I used to be would've sent him home.

Now I open my door wider and let him into my home.

'Evan?' he checks. Have to give him credit for that. We met because of Evan. One good thing to come from this mess, I used to think. I'm not as sure anymore.

'Asleep,' I say.

'Locked in?'

'We won't be interrupted.'

He gets a smile that I already feel between my legs. He leads me to the family room, his callused fingers wrapped tightly around my wrist.

At the last second, I balk. Looking for, wanting . . .

'What about my surprise?' I hear myself ask.

'It's not Monday,' he says, leading me toward the sofa.

'Two days. Close enough.'

'Impatient?' He slants me a look. It is both flirtatious and dangerous. There are shadows in his eyes. Why have I never noticed that before? His blue eyes, once so clear, are now as dark as midnight. The phantom, I think. The phantom just won't leave me the fuck alone.

Then I don't want to think anymore. I don't want to know.

He pulls me to the sofa, where minutes before my son slumped in a semi-catatonic state. Except now I'm the one bending over the arm of the sofa, while male hands raise my skirt, palm my ass, and lower a zipper behind me.

I smell the August sun radiating from his skin. It takes me to another place, where I'm still young and my husband still loves me and we're walking hand in hand in Mexico, watching the sun set and thinking this is only the beginning of the best days of our lives.

Another man's fingers working against me, stretching me, preparing me. My own back arching instinctively against him.

Then he's inside me. The first hard thrust. His grunt of satisfaction.

'You will do exactly as I say,' he orders.

I close my eyes and give myself away.

21

DANIELLE

'What are you doing here?'

'Working. What does it look like?' I shoved my bag in the locker.

'You're not on the schedule,' Karen, my boss, persisted.

'Last-second change,' I said neutrally. 'Genn wanted to attend some cookout with her kids, so I agreed to take her shift.'

Karen adjusted her wire-rimmed glasses. She crossed her arms over her chest, letting me know I was in for a fight.

'Have you looked in a mirror lately?' she demanded. 'Because if you have, I think we can both agree why you won't be working tonight.'

I returned her stare, chin up, shoulders square. I could be stubborn, too. Especially tonight.

I fell asleep on the sofa after my visit with Dr. Frank. I dreamed of my father again, except this time he wasn't standing in the doorway. This time, he was in my room. Dr. Frank was right: There were things I'd never dealt with, events I'd never disclosed. I held them at bay, stuffed into a small closet in the back of my mind, where I kept the door locked tight. Except once a year, they managed to escape. They crept under the door, wiggled through the lock, then stalked through the dark corridors of my memory.

'*Danny girl. It's happy time . . .* '

As a professional, I understood that the unconscious mind had a will of its own. As a person, however, I wondered if this is how it felt to go insane. My heart raced even when I was sitting still. My hands fought a tremor even in the August heat.

I couldn't go home tonight. I just couldn't, and this place was as close to family as I had left.

'I'll be okay,' I tried now, but Karen wasn't buying it.

'First off,' she stated crisply, 'you were involved in not one but two major incidents with the same patient.'

I looked at her blankly. Maybe I had gone crazy, because I didn't know what she was talking about.

'Lucy,' she supplied, reading my face. 'She escaped yesterday. In fifteen years I've never had a child disappear. The hospital is demanding a formal investigation, as well they should. It's unconscionable that a child can slip through two sets of locked doors and have not a single nurse or milieu counselor notice. For heaven's sake, we're lucky nothing worse happened.'

'But I found her!' I protested. 'I'm the one who figured out where she went and got her back.'

'You were the one who should've been watching her in the first place.'

I hung my head, suitably shamed.

'Then, last night, I understand you and Lucy went a few rounds in the ring. To look at your face, you didn't win.'

'I dealt with the situation — '

'You weren't even on the clock, Danielle. You were supposed to be on your way home, not rushing down the hall to tend a child!'

'Lucy started screaming hysterically. What was I supposed to do, sit around and watch? We needed to calm her and I had the best chance of getting it done.'

'Danielle, a child physically attacked you! Your face is covered with scratches; you have bruises on your neck. I'm not worried about Lucy — you *did* calm her. But it was at a huge price to yourself. We need to debrief as a unit. You need physical and emotional support as an individual. Instead, you're pretending it's business as usual. That's not healthy.'

'I'm fine — '

'You look like hell.'

'It's been twenty-five fucking years. Of course I look like hell!' Too late I caught the slip, tried to rein myself in. But I was breathing hard and my heart was racing. I wanted to run.

'Have you been drinking?' Karen asked me.

'No.' *Not yet.*

'Good. For your sake, I'm happy to hear it. But you still can't work tonight.'

'I *have* to work tonight. I can contain it. I can be professional. We both know I'm good at my job.'

'Danielle,' she said kindly, 'you're great at your job — when you're a hundred percent. You aren't a hundred percent right now, and these kids deserve nothing less.'

She was going to send me home. I couldn't believe it. Karen was going to let the unit operate short-staffed rather than accept me.

'I want you to go downstairs,' she said now, voice brisk. 'You need a medical evaluation, if not for your own sake, then for our insurance company. I'm giving you a five-day leave of absence. Rest. Talk to one of our counselors. Deal with yourself. Then you can return to dealing with these kids.'

I can't go home, I can't go home, I can't go home.

'I'll go downstairs,' I heard myself say. 'I'll get a physical exam. Then can I come back? If the doctor says so . . . '

'Danielle . . . '

'I'll help her.'

I looked up. Karen turned around. Greg was standing behind her. We hadn't heard him enter, but it was obvious from his expression that he'd been listening for a bit.

He looked good. Dark hair still slightly damp from a recent shower. Broad shoulders filling the narrow space, a black gym bag slung over his shoulder.

'She can work with me,' he said, looking at Karen. 'It'll be the buddy system. That way, we'll have someone on the floor to supervise meds, but you won't have to worry about Danielle going solo.'

I felt pathetically grateful. How many times had I rejected this man? And he was still the best friend I had.

Karen looked like she wanted to protest, but at

the last second, she hesitated. A soft heart beat beneath her stern exterior. God knows, once a year she cut me more slack than I deserved.

'Downstairs first,' Karen stated abruptly, staring at me. 'If an intern will clear you physically, and Greg still feels like babysitting . . .'

I winced at the dig. She was testing me, seeing how in control of my emotions I was. 'Exam first,' I agreed meekly. 'Then I'd love to work with Greg. We're a good team.'

I had shamelessly tossed him the bone. He smiled, briefly, but it didn't reflect in his eyes. Maybe he knew me better than I thought.

The matter resolved, Karen squeezed past Greg back to the main office. It was nearly midnight, and she still had her own paperwork to close out before heading home; a head nurse didn't get much sleep.

Alone with Greg, I felt awkward again. He opened a locker, stuffed in his bag. I stood there, watching him. He looked tired, I thought. A little worn around the edges. Or maybe that was me.

'Thank you,' I said at last.

He didn't look at me. 'Night's young,' he said finally. 'Don't thank me yet.'

* * *

The police arrived at the PECB shortly after 1:30 a.m. They buzzed at the front doors — one, two, three times. They could see us. We could see them. And they got to wait.

The unit was in bedlam. Jorge, who normally

shared a room with Benny, had woken up agitated shortly after twelve-thirty. Ed pulled Jorge aside to read a book. Jorge made it halfway through the story, then yanked the book out of Ed's hand and hurled it across the hall, where it hit Aimee in the head. She woke up screaming, and the rest of the kids were off and running from there.

Now Aimee was curled up under a table in the fetal position, Jimmy and Benny were running laps around the chairs, and nine-year-old Sampson was standing in front of the closed kitchenette, yelling shrilly for a snack.

I'd been cleared by an intern just in time to chase five-year-old Becca down the hall. Somehow, she'd gotten her hands on a folded game board and she was beating it against any person unfortunate enough to cross her path. Greg was trying to untangle Jorge from Ed, while Cecille was working containment in front of Lucy's room, because we absolutely, positively couldn't have Lucy adding to the mix.

Third time by the receptionist's desk, I managed to hit the buzzer for the cops. I got Candy Land away from Becca about the same time the police entered the unit. The curly blonde took the lead, three dark-suited officers fanning out behind her in the main hall.

'I have a warrant,' the lead detective started.

A book flew down the hall. To give the Boston police some credit, the detectives jumped pretty fast.

'What the hell . . .' the sergeant muttered, the scene finally registering.

'Whatever you want, it gets to wait,' I informed them crisply. 'Keep your back to the wall. Don't touch anything. Oh, and look out. I think Jorge just got away.'

Sure enough, the wiry six-year-old was bolting down the hall straight toward us, thin arms pumping, blue eyes bulging. He looked like he was racing away from every bad thing that had ever happened to him. I knew the feeling.

I got one arm around Jorge's waist as he went flying by, and converted his momentum into a graceful little twirl I practiced at least once a week. 'Hey, buddy, where's the fire?' I asked, as if we did this kind of thing every night at one a.m.

'Bad man, bad man, bad man, bad man, bad man!' Jorge yelled.

'Did you have a nightmare, *chiquito*? Sounds like a doozy. Why don't you come with me, and I'll see what I can do to make all those bad men disappear.'

'¡*Maldito, maldito, maldito!*' Jorge added, as I led him down the hall. Ed and Greg shot me grateful looks. Then they were in the common area, where Aimee needed rescuing, and Jimmy and Benny had to be unwound like clocks, and then there was the care and feeding of Sampson . . .

In Jorge's room, I turned on every light, then went through the motions of checking each nook and cranny. I even shook out his covers to prove no monsters were hiding in his bed. When he remained unconvinced, I went with plan B, moving a mat into the hall and preparing an emergency nest. We lay down, side by side, and I pointed at the silver half globes dotting the ceiling, explaining how their reflective surfaces would allow him to see any bad men coming. 'They're like a personal protection system,' I told him. 'They'll keep you safe.'

Jorge's shoulders finally relaxed. He snuggled closer to me and I picked up a Dora book. By the halfway mark, his eyes were drooping. The hallway had quieted, the milieu restored.

Just the detectives remained, conspicuous in their dark suits. Greg paused in front of them. They were speaking too low for me to hear. Greg frowned, shook his head, then frowned again. Finally, he pointed toward me and the blonde turned expectantly.

In full view of her gaze, I finished the first book. Then I set it down, picked up a second, and opened the cover.

Whatever she had to say could wait, mostly because I didn't want to hear it.

'*Danny girl*,' my father sang inside my head.

I know, I know, I know.

* ⋆ ⋆

'We have a warrant for all records pertaining to Oswald James Harrington,' Sergeant D. D. Warren explained ten minutes later, stony-faced. 'We also have a warrant for all information pertaining to Tika Rain Solis. Detective Phil LeBlanc will oversee the transfer of all information. The rest of us have questions for the staff.'

I stared at Sergeant Warren blankly. She was still holding out several official-looking documents. For lack of anything better to do, I took them from her. They definitely read like warrants.

'I'll . . . I'll have to call Karen Rober, the nurse manager,' I said at last.

'You do that.'

'Are you sure this isn't something that can wait till morning? We run a lean crew at night, and can't spare any staff.'

'I'm sure.' She didn't blink and it occurred to me that the sergeant had planned this one-thirty ambush. Nine-to-five hours would've meant dealing with management, not to mention the hospital's cadre of lawyers. Middle-of-the-night raids, on the other hand . . .

'You're going to have to be patient,' I said, feeling frazzled. I'd never been served with a warrant before. How much did one give a detective? The warrant said everything, but what did that mean? The staff wasn't equipped for this. *I* wasn't equipped for this.

I needed to visit Lucy. She'd made it through Jorge's meltdown. I wondered if that meant she was now curled up and sleeping in a moonbeam.

'We'll move into the conference room,' Sergeant Warren declared briskly.

'Conference room?'

'You know, the room we used last time.'

'You mean the classroom?'

'Whatever. Don't worry. We know our way there.' She started striding down the hall, two of the detectives peeling off to follow her. The

262

fourth cop remained standing in front of me. Mid-forties, a little doughy around the middle, he wore a sheepish smile. Good cop, I decided. Anyone who worked with Sergeant Warren would have to be.

'Detective Phil LeBlanc,' he introduced himself. 'If you show me where you keep your records, I can take it from there.'

Not that big a dope, I unlocked the door leading to the Admin area and dug through the filing cabinet for the two patients in question: Oswald James Harrington and Tika Rain Solis. I pulled the files, showed Detective LeBlanc the photocopier, then called Karen.

She was half-asleep, but woke up fast enough once she heard the news. 'I'll be right there,' she assured me, which, given where she lived, meant at least an hour.

'Do we need a lawyer? How does this work?'

'Don't answer any questions you don't want to answer, and advise the rest of the staff to do the same. Showing up at one-thirty in the morning. Assholes.'

'I think Sergeant Warren considers that a compliment,' I said. As if summoning the Devil, Warren appeared at the end of the hall.

'We'd like to start with you,' she said: a command, not a request.

'No shit,' I muttered.

I hung up the phone. As the most senior person on the floor, I would have to shoulder this load and play nice with the detectives. Lucky me.

'Fine,' I said.

'Good,' Warren returned.

'Just gotta grab a glass of water.'

'I'll wait.'

'Make yourself comfortable.'

I turned away from the detective and headed for the kitchenette. At the last minute, however, I continued down the hallway to Lucy's room. I peered in, expecting to see Lucy sleeping in a corner.

Instead, she was dancing.

She moved around the room in graceful circles, swooshing from one moonbeam to the next. The oversized surgical scrub shirt ballooned around her as she twirled, leaping across her mattress, then pirouetting in front of the windows.

She was a cat again, moving in the languid style of a feline. Maybe she was trying to catch moonbeams in her paws. Maybe she simply liked the way it felt to sway to and fro. She hit the windows, placed her hands open-palmed against the glass. Then she stilled, and I knew she saw my reflection.

Was she angry after our last confrontation? Fearful, defiant?

Lucy turned away from the glass. Slowly, she meandered and twirled her way toward me. At the last minute, as I felt myself tense, she held out her hand, pale fingers extended. She dangled a tiny ball of string, something she'd fashioned from rolling together loose carpet fibers. A homemade cat toy.

I hesitated. She jiggled it again.

I accepted her gift, closing my fist around it as

she swooped away, long pale limbs flashing silver in the moonbeams.

I tucked her peace offering into my pocket and returned to Sergeant Warren.

★ ★ ★

I'd just entered the classroom when I realized I had forgotten my water. I returned to the kitchenette to fetch a glass, and Greg found me. Benny and Jimmy still couldn't settle. I poured out doses of Benadryl for the two kids. Greg took the Benadryl, then I headed back to the classroom, where the look on Sergeant Warren's face told me I still didn't have water.

I returned to the kitchenette again, this time finding a glass and banging on the tap. The other detective, LeBlanc, poked his head out of the Admin area. Copier had run out of paper.

I reloaded the copier, glancing at the records he'd already duplicated. I offered to carry the copies to the classroom, but he refused. I shrugged, and since he appeared done with Tika's original file, I took that for myself to use as a reference.

I made it all the way to the classroom; then, right outside the door, I realized I'd left my water glass sitting next to the copier. Back to Admin I went, grabbing my water, and making it to the classroom with everything in hand.

Sergeant Warren glanced at her watch as I took a seat. She was flanked on either side by a detective.

'Always take you fifteen minutes to grab a

drink?' she asked me.

'Oh, sometimes it takes twenty. Tonight I was lucky; I only got interrupted four or five times. Don't worry, someone will need something shortly.'

'Crazy night,' the detective on her left commented. I recognized him from the first visit. George Clooney playing the role of a Boston cop.

'Birthday party,' I said. 'Does it every time.'

'Birthday party?' he asked.

'Priscilla turned ten. We had a celebration for her after dinner. The kids made cupcakes; we hung streamers, handed out party hats. The kids got very excited, which, for our crowd, has consequences.'

'Then why have the party?' Sergeant Warren asked, with a frown. I could see this woman running the Gestapo. She'd be good at it.

'Because most of these kids have never been to a birthday party,' I explained. 'They're either too poor or too emotionally disturbed or too unloved to ever be so lucky. They're still kids, though, and kids should get to have a party.'

'Now they'll be up all night, torturing you and one another?'

I regarded the cops steadily. 'Priscilla has brain damage from being shaken as a baby; it impairs her ability to process numbers. Tonight, however, she counted out ten candles and jammed them all onto one cupcake. Speaking for the staff, we don't care if the kids spend the rest of the night tearing this place apart. It's worth it for that moment.'

Sergeant Warren studied me. I couldn't tell if my words had affected her or not. Then again, this was a woman who spent her time rolling over dead bodies so she could note their faces. She probably could take me at poker.

'And Tika Solis? She have a party?'

'I don't know.' I started to open the file. Sergeant Warren reached across the table and slapped it shut.

'No. Off the top of your head. What do you remember about her?'

'I don't.'

'What do you mean *you don't*?'

I shrugged my shoulders. 'I don't. Name's not ringing any bells.'

'You remembered Ozzie Harrington,' she said crossly.

'I worked with Ozzie one-on-one over the course of many months. Of course I remember him.'

'But not Tika?'

'Can't even bring her face to mind.'

The sergeant continued to stare at me, as if I were holding something back. 'Girl liked to cut herself. That jog your memory?'

I shook my head. 'You'll have to be more specific.'

'Please, a little girl who self-mutilates? That doesn't stand out in your mind?'

'We have two of those cases right now, so no, it doesn't.'

'Two?'

I pulled the file out of her grasp. 'Children are direct, Sergeant. Sometimes, they can't verbalize their emotions, but that doesn't mean they're not attempting to communicate. A child who hates the world will act hateful. And a child who hurts inside will externalize that pain, cutting her arms, legs, wrists, in order to show you her ache.'

'Tika was three when she was admitted here. That's not exactly a teenager brooding over the poems of Sylvia Plath,' the sergeant countered skeptically.

'Three?' Three was young for slicing and dicing. Not unheard-of, but young. My turn to frown. 'When was she admitted?'

Sergeant stared at me. 'Around the same time as Ozzie Harrington.'

I searched my memory banks, trying to bring a whole cluster of kids into focus. The dynamics of the kids impacted the milieu as much as anything. Who were the kids we'd had with Ozzie? What was the dynamic? We'd been so busy for the past year. More and more kids, each with a case file more horrific than the last . . . 'Wait a second. Tiny little thing? From Mattapan?'

Sergeant Warren flicked a glance at the redhead sitting on her other side. 'They moved to Jamaica Plains from Mattapan,' he murmured. The sergeant nodded at me.

'Okay, I remember her,' I admitted. 'But I didn't work with her much. I was busy with Ozzie; besides, Tika didn't care for women. She responded better to the male MCs.'

'What do you mean, 'responded'?'

'Wanted a father figure, most likely.' I shrugged. 'Tika didn't have one at home, so she was anxious to find one elsewhere. If Greg or Ed asked her to do something, she did it. If Cecille or I spoke to her, it was all la, la, la, la, la, wind blowing through the trees. We're acute care — not our job to change that, just our job to work with it. So male counselors it was.'

'You're saying she worked most closely with the gym coach out there?'

'Gym coach . . . Greg? Yes. Here, may I?' I gestured to the file. The sergeant finally let me open it. I skimmed through the reports. Sure enough, most of them were written up by Greg, Ed, and Chester. Male MCs indeed. 'Greg and Ed are both here tonight,' I commented. 'They might be able to help you.'

'Did Tika and Ozzie interact?' the sergeant wanted to know.

'Probably. In the common area, during group, that sort of thing.' There was something obvious I should be understanding. Ozzie and Tika. Tika and Ozzie. Then it came to me. My hands stilled on the file. I stared at the three detectives, horrified.

'Are you saying . . . Tika's dead?' Then, a second later, 'Oh my God, Jamaica Plains. The family that was murdered last night in Jamaica Plains. That was *Tika's* family? Two kids from here, two families . . . '

I didn't want to compute the implications of such a connection. Then it came to me, the way the detectives were regarding me. Not as a nurse, supplying background on two patients, but as a suspect. The common denominator between two families that met equal tragedy.

My background. Did they know my background, because if they knew my background . . .

I couldn't breathe. White spots appeared in front of my eyes, and I heard my father's damn voice again: '*Danny girl. Oooooh, Danny girl.*'

Shut up, shut up, shut up.

A knock on the closed door. I forced myself to turn, stand up, function as a professional. Breathe in. Breathe out. Compartmentalize. Nurses were good at this sort of thing, and psych nurses were the best. I opened the door.

Greg stood on the other side, looking wild-eyed.

'Have you seen her?' he blurted out.

'Seen who?'

'Lucy. Dammit, we've been searching every-where. Lucy's vanished.'

22

LUCY

Hush, little baby, don't say a word. Mama's gonna buy you a mockingbird. And if that mockingbird won't sing, Mama's gonna buy you a diamond ring.

Shadows. Shadows breathe. Shadows move.

And if that diamond ring turns brass, Mama's gonna buy you a looking glass. And if that looking glass gets broke, Mama's gonna buy you a billy goat.

Shadows. Shadow says, Follow me. I do.

And if that billy goat won't pull, Mama's gonna buy you a cart and bull. And if that cart and bull turn over, Mama's gonna buy you a dog named Rover.

Shadows. Floating down the hall, slipping through the door. Follow me, follow me. I do.

And if that dog named Rover won't bark, Mama's gonna buy you a horse and cart. And if that horse and cart fall down, you'll still be the sweetest little baby in town.

Shadows. Pulling, tugging, yanking, wanting. I do, I do.

Hush, little baby, don't say a word. Hush, hush, hush . . .

★ ★ ★

D.D. watched Danielle with growing suspicion.

'Did you check the solarium?' the nurse was asking the gym coach MC. 'Behind the palm trees?'

'First stop we made.'

'And you've done the entire floor? Inside cabinets, behind wardrobes, beneath bathroom sinks?'

'Yes.'

'And how long has Lucy been missing?'

'Twenty minutes.'

'*Twenty minutes?* You kept this to yourself for twenty minutes?'

'Hey, you're sequestered with a bunch of detectives, and it's not like we haven't searched for a kid before. The staff's been on it. We've done this floor, the solarium, and a quick tour through the hospital halls. No dice. It's time to alert the medical center's security, so here I am, telling you what you need to know.'

'We'll help,' D.D. said.

Danielle and the gym coach turned to stare at her. If anything, they both grew more irritated.

'We can handle this,' Danielle said tightly.

'Really? Then where's the kid?'

Danielle thinned her lips and looked like she wanted to hit something. Preferably, D.D. D.D. spread her hands. 'Sounds like you need to launch a search — right? — while also managing the unit. You need bodies. Here's a news flash: We're four bodies who all have experience looking for missing people. Don't be an idiot. Let us help.'

'Well, since you asked so nicely,' Danielle muttered.

D.D. smiled. 'All right,' she announced briskly, taking control of the situation. Phil was walking down the hall, holding a stack of paperwork. She waved him over, and her squad clustered around the nurse and MC. 'Who are we looking for? Description?'

'Nine-year-old female,' Danielle supplied. 'Thin, with long dark hair matted around her face. Last seen wearing an oversized green surgical scrub top. She might be naked, however. She's clothing-challenged.'

D.D. arched a brow. 'You said the solarium. That mean she's gone AWOL before?'

The nurse nodded. 'Yesterday. Which is very unusual,' she added. 'We have two sets of locked doors. We can't remember a child ever getting off the floor of the PECB once, let alone twice in two days.'

'So she has some skill.'

'Apparently.' But Danielle was frowning again. She and the MC exchanged troubled looks, and D.D.'s cop radar flared. Something was definitely up with the unit. Given that the pediatric psych ward was now the common denominator between two heinous crimes, D.D. and her detectives planned on turning this place inside out, and searching for a missing kid was a great place to start. Gave them extenuating circumstances to poke their noses in every nook and cranny, and see what was to be seen. Save a kid, expose a psych ward. Night was looking up.

'We'll need to see your security video,' D.D. announced.

'We don't have cameras.'

'You don't have surveillance? A place like this, with these types of kids and God knows what type of parents? Please, surveillance cameras are for your own protection in this day and age of lunatic lawsuits.'

'We don't have cameras,' Danielle repeated. 'We have a checks system: a staff member assigned to write down the location and activity of every child every five minutes. One, that enables us to keep tabs on all the kids so, in theory, this kind of thing doesn't happen. Two, it provides a written record so that six months from now, when a child or parent suddenly alleges inappropriate behavior, we can verify that the child was indeed safe and accounted for during the alleged time. The system has worked well for us.'

'Until tonight.'

'Until Lucy,' the nurse murmured. She hesitated, then added, 'Lucy's a primal child. She has no social awareness, no sense of her own humanity. Since coming here, she's adopted the persona of a house cat. That seems to keep her calm. If that illusion gets shattered, however, she becomes violent and unpredictable.' The nurse raised her dark curtain of hair, revealing a string of fresh purple bruises on her neck. 'I would consider her a threat to herself and/or others.'

'Damn,' D.D. breathed. She felt some of her earlier euphoria dim.

'If you find her,' Danielle continued, letting

274

her hair fall back down, 'don't approach her. Dealing with her is our job, and trust me, you're not qualified. Do you understand?'

'We're not total idiots,' D.D. said, which was neither an affirmation nor a denial about approaching the child. 'All right, we'll split into pairs. We'll work each floor of the medical center, top to bottom, and ask hospital security to work bottom to top.'

'I'll be assisting,' Danielle said tightly.

'Me, too,' the gym coach chimed in. He glanced at Danielle, face grim. 'Buddies, remember?'

Another look exchanged between them. Personal relationship: D.D. would stake her job on it.

'Our nurse manager, Karen, will help, too. She should be here in' — Danielle glanced at her watch — 'another twenty minutes or so.'

D.D. nodded. 'Tell you what. You're the pros. So, Danielle, how about you partner with me. Gym Coach . . . er — '

'Greg,' he supplied.

'Greg, you're with Neil. Phil and Alex can be team number three. We can alert one another the second we find the girl. Any other advice?'

'Think like a cat,' Danielle said. 'Lucy's drawn to quiet places with natural light. Sunbeams, moonbeams, that sort of thing. Or she may curl up someplace cozy instead: inside a cabinet, under a desk. Like a cat.'

D.D. and Danielle would start with the psych ward, the top floor of the hospital. Greg and Neil would cover the seventh floor, while Alex and

Phil would take level six.

D.D. secured in a locker the records Phil had photocopied. Then she and Danielle hit the unit.

The nurse led D.D. down the hallway, where a huge window overlooked a dazzling city nightscape. They passed half a dozen kids tossing and turning restlessly on mats, with a lone staff member keeping watch. Danielle greeted the MC by name. Ed informed her that another MC, Cecille, was tending Aimee, while Tyrone had Jorge in the TV room.

D.D. got the impression that the unit remained a busy place, even though it was now nearly three in the morning.

At the end of the hallway, Danielle paused, gesturing to the first pair of dorm rooms. Danielle took the one to the right, D.D. the one to the left, and they blitzed their way down the corridor. From what D.D. could tell, each room was identical to the last, with the exception of one that contained only a bare mattress. Apparently, that room belonged to the missing child, who had a tendency to turn furniture into weapons.

They finished checking the sleeping quarters, then the bathrooms, the locked kitchenette, and the locked Admin area. D.D. looked under every desk, even found herself pulling out the paper tray for the copier.

'Think like a cat,' she muttered to herself. 'Think like a cat.'

D.D.'d never had a cat. Hell, she didn't trust herself with a goldfish. They made it through the Admin area, the common room, the classrooms, and the waiting room. From there, she and Danielle discussed more creative possibilities — accessing ductwork, climbing up into ceiling tiles, exiting through a window.

The windows didn't open, the nine-foot ceiling was too high for a child to reach, and the vents weren't big enough for crawling.

D.D. contacted Neil. He and Greg had finished the seventh floor and moved to the fifth. Phil confirmed he and Alex were still searching the sixth level, so D.D. and Danielle took the elevators to the fourth floor and resumed their hunt.

The nurse's movements were jerkier now, her face paler. The woman was definitely worried about the missing girl, and doing her best to hide it.

'So what happens to a kid like Lucy?' D.D. asked presently as they made their way to the nurses' station. Only two nurses were on duty this time of night, and neither had seen a stray child. They promised to keep an eye out, tending to their own duties as D.D. and Danielle started searching each patient room.

'You said she's primal,' D.D. continued. 'What does that mean? You give her enough meds, stick her in enough therapy, she transforms from wild cougar to tame pussycat?'

'Not exactly.' Danielle stuck her head into the medical supplies room. No nine-year-old child magically hiding here. They moved on, footsteps faster now, seeking the next target.

'Lucy's missed most of the key developmental stages,' Danielle explained. 'It's improbable for a nine-year-old to make up that kind of ground. We once worked with a primal child who was three. If he was hungry, he trashed the refrigerator. If he was thirsty, he drank out of the toilet. If he had to go potty, he found a corner. It took a year of intensive training to get him to recognize his own name, and another year for him to come when he was called. That was at three. Lucy's nine. These developmental stages aren't hurdles anymore, they're mountains, and there are dozens of them she needs to climb.'

'So she'll stay with you guys until she figures them out?' D.D. asked. They ventured into a darkened room where a heavyset man sprouting half a dozen wires and tubes snored in the middle of the bed. They worked by the glow of the monitor lights, peering under the bed, behind the chair, inside the shower.

Danielle shook her head. 'We're acute care, remember? Lucy will require lifelong assistance. Only place that can handle her is a hospital run by the Shriners. They do unbelievable work and have the waiting list to prove it.'

D.D. felt uncomfortable. She was better with felonious adults than broken children, though she supposed one became the other. They exited the snoring man's room, hit the next one. Danielle took the chair, while D.D. peered under the bed.

'Do all primal kids escape?' D.D. asked. 'Is it like . . . the call of the wild?'

'Oh, they're wilder, touch of Tarzan, yada yada. Still, never had a kid escape once, let alone twice.'

'What set Lucy off?'

'Don't know. We haven't had time yet to get a sense of how she experiences the world.'

They exited the patient room, hit a unisex bath.

''A sense of how she experiences the world'?' D.D. repeated.

'That's what it's about,' Danielle replied. She paused in the middle of the hallway, finally looking D.D. in the eye. 'Our jobs are the same. You think like a criminal in order to capture the criminal. I think like a nine-year-old primal child in order to reach the primal child. It's why the parents break. They're not trained to think like an autistic child or schizophrenic child, or an ADHD child. They don't realize Timmy is refusing to put on his coat, not because he's a little shit, but because the sound of the zipper makes his ears bleed. Loving a child isn't the same as understanding a child. And take it from a pediatric psych nurse, love is *not* all you really need.'

'Grim,' D.D. said.

'If I heal them now, you won't have to arrest them later.'

'Not so grim,' D.D. concurred. 'Now, where the fuck is Lucy?'

'Agreed,' Danielle said tiredly. 'Where the fuck is Lucy?'

Hush, little baby, don't say a word. Mama's gonna buy you a mockingbird. And if that mockingbird won't sing, Mama's gonna buy you a diamond ring.

'You will do as I say.'

And if that diamond ring turns brass, Mama's gonna buy you a looking glass. And if that looking glass gets broke, Mama's gonna buy you a billy goat.

'Take the rope.'

And if that billy goat won't pull, Mama's gonna buy you a cart and bull. And if that cart and bull turn over, Mama's gonna buy you a dog named Rover.

'Climb onto the chair.'

And if that dog named Rover won't bark, Mama's gonna buy you a horse and cart. And if that horse and cart fall down, you'll still be the sweetest little baby in town.

'Now show me how you can fly.'

Hush, little baby, don't say a word. Hush, hush, hush . . .

D.D.'s cell rang. She checked the number, flipped it open. 'What's up?'

'We got a sighting,' Phil said tersely. 'Girl was heading toward radiology. Apparently with a rope.'

'With a rope?'

'A rope.'

D.D. didn't like the sound of that. To judge by the stricken look on Danielle's face, neither did she. 'Radiology,' D.D. confirmed. 'We're on our way.'

She flipped the phone shut, then she and Danielle rushed down the hall. 'Elevators are too slow,' Danielle said. 'Stairwell. This way.'

The nurse shouldered through the door and they clattered down the steps, *rat-a-tat-tat-tat.*

D.D. stayed on Danielle's heels as the nurse rounded the landings. She muscled through the exit door once again, then they bolted down a dimly lit hall.

This part of Kirkland Medical Center appeared quiet. Empty chairs, vacant receptionist desks. Three in the morning. Appointments done, just the odd job here and there for the ER docs. Lots of long, empty corridors for a child to wander at will.

They broke into what appeared to be a waiting area. D.D. glanced around, seeing half a dozen closed doors and little else. She heard running footsteps, then Alex and Phil burst in the area.

'Which way? Where?' D.D. asked. She was on the balls of her feet, ready for action.

'Think like a cat, think like a cat,' Danielle was muttering. 'The imaging rooms! They're small and dark, and sometimes still warm from the machines.' She pointed to a handful of doors, each bearing a number. 'Go.'

D.D. grabbed the doorknob closest to herself as the others did the same. The first was locked; she went to the second. It opened and she dashed inside, to discover a dark cocoon. She flashed on the light, saw it was really two rooms. One with a table, and a smaller, glass-windowed chamber where no doubt a technician stood to man the imaging equipment. She checked both spaces. Nothing. She reappeared in the waiting area. Phil was exiting a room. Alex, too, then Danielle. Each was shaking his or her head.

More footsteps. Greg and Neil pounding down the corridor toward them.

'Other rooms?' D.D. asked Danielle.

'Sure,' the nurse said blankly. 'It's a whole level of rooms. I mean, janitorial closets, receptionist areas, offices. There are rooms and rooms and rooms.'

'All right. This is central station.' D.D. pointed where they stood. 'We work from this area out, likes spokes on a wheel. Everyone, grab a room.'

They moved urgently now. The rooms were small, easily cleared. It took twelve minutes, then they returned to central station, eyeing one another nervously. The floor was quiet, just the distant twitches and hums of a large building that grumbled in its sleep.

Phil spoke up first. 'Now what? I swear, we spoke to a janitor who saw her walking down this corridor. She had to be going somewhere.'

D.D. puzzled over that, chewing her bottom lip. This floor felt right. Dark, secluded, lots of little spaces. If you were going to hide in a hospital, this was the place to be.

And then . . .

She turned slowly, regarding the first room she had tried. The only locked door on an entire floor of unlocked rooms. And suddenly, just like that, she knew.

'Danielle,' she said quietly. 'We're going to need that key.'

★ ★ ★

The janitor supplied the master key. D.D. did the honors, already gloved, careful not to touch

282

anything more than she had to.

The heavy wooden door swung open. She stepped in slowly, snapped on the light.

The girl's body hung from the middle of the ceiling, rope secured to a hook, wheeled desk chair cast aside. The green surgical scrub shirt shrouded her skinny frame, and her body swayed lightly, as if teased in the wind.

'Get her down, get her down' came Danielle's voice, urgent behind her. 'Code, code, code! Dammit, Greg, call it in!'

But Greg wasn't moving. It was obvious to him, as to D.D., that the time for medical attention had come and gone. To be certain, D.D. took one step forward, wrapped her hand around the girl's ankle. Lucy's skin was cool to the touch, no pulse beating feebly at the base of the foot.

D.D. stepped back, turned to Neil. 'When you notify the ME, remind Ben we'll want the knot on the rope left intact.' She turned to Danielle and Greg. 'You two can return upstairs if you'd like. We'll take it from here.'

But neither of them took the hint. Greg's arm went around Danielle. She turned, ever so slightly, into him.

'We'll stay,' the nurse said, her voice flat. 'It's the duty of the lone survivor. We must bear witness. We must live to tell the tale.'

23

DANIELLE

Six months after the funeral, Aunt Helen took me to pick out tombstones for my siblings' graves. She'd already selected a rose-colored marble for my mother, inscribed with the standard name and timeline. But when the moment came to select a stone for Natalie and Johnny, Aunt Helen wasn't able to bear it. She walked away.

So my sister and brother lay in unmarked graves for the first six months, until Aunt Helen decided it was time to get the job done. I went with her. It was something to do.

The monument store was a funny place. You could pick out lawn ornaments, decorative fountains, or, of course, tombstones. The man in charge wore denim overalls and looked like he'd be more comfortable gardening than helping a black-suited woman and her hollow-eyed niece pick out grave markers for two kids.

'Boy like baseball?' he asked finally. 'I could engrave a bat and ball. Maybe something from the Red Sox. We do a lot of business with the Red Sox.'

Aunt Helen laughed a little. It wasn't a good sound.

She finally selected two small angels. I hated them. Angels? For my goofy siblings, who liked to stick out their tongues at me, and were always one whack ahead at punch buggy? I hated them.

But I wasn't talking in those days, so I let my aunt do as she wanted. My mother was marked in rose marble. My siblings became angels. Maybe there were trees in Heaven. Maybe Natalie was saving bunnies.

I didn't know. My parents never took me to church, and my corporate-lawyer aunt continued their agnostic ways.

We didn't bury my father. My aunt didn't want him anywhere near her sister. Since she was the one in charge of the arrangements, she had him cremated and stuck in a cardboard box. The box went in the storage unit in her condo building, where it stayed for the next twelve years.

I used to sneak the key from my aunt's purse and visit him from time to time. I liked the look of the box. Plain. Small. Manageable. Surprisingly heavy, so after the first visit, I didn't try to lift it anymore. I wanted to keep my father this way, remember him this way. No bigger than a stack of tissues, easy to tuck away.

I could loom over this box. I could hit it. Kick it. Scream at the top of my lungs at it.

A box could never, ever hurt me.

My twenty-first birthday, I got drunk, raided my aunt's storage unit, and, in a fit of rage, emptied the box into a sewer grate. I flushed my father down into the bowels of Boston, having to keep my mouth closed, but still inhaling bits of him up my nose.

Immediately afterward, I was sorry I'd done such a thing.

The cardboard box had contained my father, kept him small.

Now I knew he was somewhere out there, floating down various pipes and channels and water systems. Maybe the ash was soaking up the water, steadily expanding, enabling my father to grow again, to loom once more in the dark undergrowth of the city. Until one day, a white hand would shoot up, drag back a sewer grate, and my father would be free.

The cardboard box had contained him.

Now, for all the evil in the world, I had only myself to blame.

* * *

'I thought we'd agreed on the buddy system,' Karen was snapping at Greg. It was after four. We were all tired, pale-faced, shocked. Karen had arrived just in time to hear the news of Lucy's death. She'd stood with us while the ME gently lowered Lucy's green-shrouded frame onto the waiting gurney. Then the man took Lucy away.

A child is like a snowflake. First thing you learn in pediatric nursing. *A child is like a snowflake.* Each one unique and original from the one before. Lose one and you have lost too much, because there will never be another quite like her again.

I had my left hand in my pocket, my fingers wrapped around Lucy's final gift, rolling the little string ball between my fingers again and again.

'*Oh Danny girl. My pretty, pretty Danny girl . . .* '

'She was with the police,' Greg answered tightly. 'I thought that was buddy enough. 'Sides, unit was busy. We had a lot going on.'

'Apparently!'

'Dammit, Karen, you can't possibly think — '

'It doesn't matter what I think. In a situation like this, appearance matters as much as reality. Fact is, we had a staff member and a child off radar for at least fifteen minutes. You were in charge of checks, Greg. What the hell were you doing?'

'I checked! Cecille vouched for Lucy; we agreed on twenty-minute intervals for her, so I waited another twenty to check again. As for Danielle, she was with the police. Or so I thought.'

Now all eyes were on me. I didn't say anything, just rolled the string ball between my fingers.

'*Oh Danny girl. My pretty, pretty Danny girl . . .* '

'You said you went to fetch a glass of water,' Karen repeated directly to me. 'Did you see Lucy tonight? Visit her at all?'

'I saw Lucy. She was dancing in moonbeams. She was happy.'

'When?'

'Before I got water.'

'Danielle, start talking. The hospital will be launching an investigation. The state will be

287

launching an investigation. You need to tell us what happened.'

'I saw Lucy. I got a glass of water. I met with Greg about Jimmy and Benny. Reloaded the copy machine. Met with the detectives. That's everything I did. All that I did.'

'That doesn't take twenty minutes,' Sergeant Warren stated.

'But it did.' I finally looked at her. 'You were right before. It'd be better if we had security cameras.'

*   *   *

Sergeant Warren asked me to come with her for questioning. I refused. Karen informed me I was on paid leave, effective immediately, and I was not to come to work until the hospital granted permission. I refused.

Not that it mattered. Everyone was asking me questions, but no one was listening to my answers.

'She didn't kill herself.' I spoke up, my voice louder, edgier. 'Lucy wouldn't do that. She wouldn't.'

Greg and Karen shut up. Sergeant Warren regarded me with fresh interest. 'Why do you say that?'

'Because I saw her. She was happy. She was a cat. As long as she was a cat, she was okay.'

'Maybe someone burst her bubble. Or the delusion slipped away. You said she was volatile, dangerously unpredictable.'

'She'd never shown any signs of suicide before.'

288

'That's not true,' Karen protested. 'She'd already demonstrated a need for self-mutilation, as well as debasement.' She turned to Sergeant Warren. 'First day she was here, Lucy cut her arm and used the blood to draw patterns on the wall. The child did terrible things, because terrible things had been done to her. I don't think we can say with any degree of certainty what she was, or was not, capable of.'

'She didn't kill herself!' I insisted again, angry now and realizing how much I needed that rage. 'She wouldn't do that. Someone helped her get out. That's the only way you can explain her getting through two sets of locked doors. Someone helped her. First time was yesterday, maybe as a trial run, then again tonight. Face it, the unit was hopping, we were short-staffed, and then the police suddenly appeared. Plenty of distractions, providing the perfect opportunity for someone to harm her. That's what happened.'

'Someone,' Sergeant Warren drawled, looking right at me.

'I was only gone five to ten minutes — '

'Eighteen. I timed you.'

'I was with your own detective for part of that — '

'About two minutes, he says.'

'That's not enough time to smuggle a child out of the unit and get down to radiology and back.'

'But someone did. You just said so.'

'Not *me* — someone,' I snapped. 'Someone else, someone.'

'Really? Because I thought Lucy didn't trust anyone else but you. So who could that someone-else someone be?'

I opened my mouth. Closed it. Opened it again. Gave up. Fuck if I knew.

Lucy, dancing in the moonlight. Lucy, swinging from the ceiling.

Then, out of the blue: my mother, with a single bullet hole in the center of her forehead.

'I'll take care of this, Danny. Go to bed. I will take care of everything.'

'Oh Danny girl. My pretty, pretty Danny girl . . .'

'Do you need to sit down?' Karen asked me gently.

I shook my head.

'How about a glass of water? Greg, fetch Danielle a glass of water.' Karen found my right hand, cradling my fingers between her palms. But I snatched my hand back, held it against my chest. I didn't want to be touched right now. I wanted to feel the rage, let it flood me like a river.

'Tika and Ozzie,' I stated, looking at Karen. 'Ask Sergeant Warren about Tika and Ozzie.'

D.D. explained. Karen went chalky white.

'But . . . but . . . that doesn't make any sense,' she protested feebly. 'We can't be the common denominator between two murdered families. We don't make home visits. We work with the child, but hardly know anything about the family. Where they live, what they do . . . that's not us . . .'

'But you have that information,' Sergeant Warren said. A statement, not a question.

'In the files, yes.'

'And didn't I see some poster in the lobby about an open-door policy? Parents can visit the floor anytime they want?'

'Parents are invited to visit their child whenever they want. That still doesn't mean we *know* them. Their time on the floor is a small slice of their overall universe, assuming they visit at all. Most of them don't.'

'The Harringtons?' Sergeant Warren pressed.

Karen fidgeted with her glasses, adjusting and readjusting them on her face. 'Ozzie's parents, right? The mother, she came several times. Stayed over in the beginning, then came once or twice a week after that.'

'What about the rest of the family?'

'I have no memory of them. A shame, too. Parents seem to feel they'll traumatize their other children by bringing them to an acute-care unit, when really, it's good for all the children to see one another and reaffirm that each is doing okay.'

D.D.'s eyes narrowed. 'And Tika's family?'

Karen shook her head, bewildered. 'Greg?' she asked.

He'd just returned with a tray bearing four cups of water. He handed me one, then Karen, then offered one to Sergeant Warren, who passed.

'Tika?' he repeated. 'Little girl, 'bout a year ago? Cutter?'

'That's the one,' Warren assured him. 'I understand you worked with her.'

He nodded. 'Cute little thing. Had a wicked

sense of humor if you could get her to open up. But yeah, she had some self-esteem issues, depression, anxiety. Maybe even suffered sexual abuse, though she never disclosed.'

'What was her family like?' Sergeant Warren wanted to know.

'Never visited.'

'Never?'

'Never. Tika's file described the mother as 'disengaged.' We never experienced anything different.'

'And our records show them living in Mattapan,' I spoke up, remembering the exchange between Sergeant Warren and the George Clooney detective. 'We wouldn't know they'd moved; our involvement was over and done.'

'Not so hard to look up,' Sergeant Warren said with a shrug.

'But why? We're caretakers. We don't hurt children. We help them.'

'Tell that to Lucy.'

'*Fuck you!*' I exploded.

'Eighteen minutes,' the sergeant shot back. 'Gym Coach here just fetched four cups of water in a fraction of that time. Explain eighteen minutes.'

'Easy,' Karen interjected, ever the manager. 'Let's just take a deep breath here.'

'Lucy wouldn't just wander into a radiology room,' I insisted hotly. 'And where would she find the rope?'

'Like you said, someone must have helped her.'

'Lucy didn't trust anyone. Had limited social skills, limited speech skills. Hell, we don't even know that she had the dexterity required to tie knots. Whatever happened, it was done *to* her, not *by* her.'

'By someone she trusted,' the sergeant reiterated, staring at me, then the little string ball I held in my left hand.

'I wasn't gone that long!'

'Maybe hanging a troubled kid is quick work.'

'Sergeant!' Karen protested.

As I heard myself say: 'Dammit, I *loved* Lucy.'

'She attacked you.'

'It was nothing personal — '

'Looks like she tried to wring your neck.'

'It's part of the job!'

'Does the rest of the staff have any bruises?'

'You don't know what it's like here. We're the last line of defense these kids have. If we can't help them, nobody can.'

'Really?' The sergeant's voice turned thoughtful. 'I remember now. In your own words, not much hope for a child like Lucy. Missed too many development stages. Doomed to be institutionalized the rest of her life. Some might say she was better off dead.'

Karen gasped.

I heard myself scream: 'Shut up. Just *shut the fuck up!*'

Lucy, dancing in the moonlight. Lucy, swinging from the ceiling.

My mother with the single hole in the middle of her forehead.

'*I'll take care of this, Danny. Go to bed. I'll*

293

take care of everything.'

'*Oh Danny girl. My pretty, pretty Danny girl . . .* '

My knees gave way. The rage wasn't enough to stave off the pain after all. Lucy, who never got a chance. My mother, who I loved so much and who still didn't save me. Natalie and Johnny, stuck forever as stone angels.

Blood and cordite. Singing and screaming. Love and hate.

Vaguely, I was aware of Karen bending over me, ordering me to place my head between my knees. Then Karen's voice louder, directed at the sergeant.

'You shouldn't be pressuring her like this. Not so close to the anniversary of what happened to her family.'

'Her family?'

Greg's voice, angry, protective. 'Are you arresting her?'

'Do you think I should?'

'You need to leave now,' Karen was saying. 'You've done enough damage for one night.'

'Two families connected to this unit are dead and one of your patients was just found hanging from the ceiling. Frankly, I think the damage is just beginning.'

'We'll take care of it,' Greg snapped.

Greg and Karen closed in around me, a protective shield. My second family, the unit I'd probably fail just as badly as the first. I squeezed my eyes shut, wished it would all go away.

As if reading my mind, the sergeant

announced crisply, 'This time tomorrow, I'll know everything there is to know about every single one of you. So you might as well get used to my charm, people. From here on out, you belong to me.'

24

Despite D.D.'s big words, she and her team departed shortly after five a.m. The four of them had been up for thirty-six hours. Given the location of the crime scene and the sheer number of people to now question, they faced a grueling stretch of days. Might as well grab four or five hours of sleep before returning to the trenches.

As the crime-scene guru, Alex had spent the evening working in radiology. Unfortunately, the room had yielded scant physical evidence — no blood, no signs of struggle, no unexplained scuffs, dents, debris. They had the hangman's knot from the rope, and that was about it.

Neil, who'd taken a break from flirting with the ME in order to interview every janitor in the joint, reported similar results. Yes, a janitor had caught sight of a small figure in green surgical scrubs rounding a corner. Yes, the janitor happened to notice she was trailing a rope behind her. Yes, he happened to think that was odd. No, he didn't pursue the matter; he had other work to do.

Cameras would've been great, except, as Phil learned from security, the hospital used them mostly for the main-level entrances and exits, plus maternity. Radiology didn't make the cut.

Which left them with a crime scene that, four hours later, might or might not be a crime scene.

D.D. arranged for a fresh homicide squad to take over canvassing for witnesses. She also got the hospital to agree to a twenty-four-hour security guard for the psych ward. Then she made it down to the hospital lobby before her shoulders sagged and her steps faltered from fatigue.

She took a minute in the parking lot stairwell, pinching the bridge of her nose and waiting for the worst of it to pass. She didn't care what anyone said — the death of a kid never got any easier, and the second it did, she was quitting her job. Apparently, she didn't have to retire just yet.

The night had sucked. She wanted to go home, take a long hot shower, then pass out on top of her bed.

Instead, her pager went off. She checked the number. Couldn't place it. Then, given the early-morning hour and sheer curiosity, she entered the number on her cell phone and pressed Send.

'I'm worried about you.' A man's voice immediately filled her ear.

'Who is this?'

'Andrew Lightfoot.'

'How'd you get this number?'

'You gave it to me, on your card.'

D.D. paused, searched her mental banks, and remembered that at the end of the interview, she'd handed Andrew Lightfoot her business card. Routine protocol — she'd already forgotten all about it.

'Little early to be calling, don't you think?'

She leaned against the stairwell wall, giving the conversation her full attention.

'I knew you were up. I dreamed of you.'

Lotta things D.D. could say to that. Given her shitty night, and her instinctive distrust of anyone who called himself a spiritual guru, she didn't. 'Why're you calling, Lightfoot?'

'Please call me Andrew.'

'Please tell me why you're calling.'

Hesitation. She found that interesting.

'There's something wrong,' he said at last. 'I don't know how to explain it. At least not in terms you would understand.'

'A disturbance in the fabric of the cosmos?' she asked dryly.

'Exactly.'

I'll be damned. 'You talk,' D.D. decided. 'I'll listen.'

'The negative energies are building. When I visited the interplanes earlier tonight, I found entire pockets of dark, roiling rage. I could feel a hum, like a vibration of great evil. The light had fled. I've never seen so many shadows.'

'The negative forces are winning the war?'

'Tonight, I would say yes.'

'Has that happened before?'

'I've never encountered such a thing. Sometimes, when I'm leading group meditation, I'll stumble across a particularly malevolent force. But the collective strength of the group, the exponential power of the light, enables me to confront such negativity and force it back into its small and insignificant space. Tonight . . . it's as if the inverse has happened. Dark calling to dark. Feeding, growing, exploding. Alone and unprepared, there was nothing I could do.'

'You got your ass kicked on the spiritual superhighway?'

'I wouldn't laugh about this, D.D.'

'And I don't have jurisdiction over evil energies. What the hell do you want from me?'

Andrew's voice changed. 'You're tired. You've suffered tonight. I apologize.'

Instantly, she was on edge. 'What do you know of my suffering?'

'I'm a healer. I can feel it. Your aura, bright white when we first met, has turned to blue. You're not comfortable with blue. You do better with red, though I prefer white.'

D.D. pinched the bridge of her nose again. 'Why are you calling, Andrew?'

'Something is coming.'

'Evil wants to take over the universe.'

'Evil always wants to take over the universe. I'm telling you that this time, it's winning.'

'How?'

'It has a purpose, I think. The purpose has given it power.'

'What's its purpose?'

'It wants something.'

'All right,' she said wearily. 'What does it want?'

No immediate answer. Maybe Andrew had gone back to the interplanes. In the silence, it occurred to her to ask: 'How's Tika doing?'

'Tika?' Andrew echoed back. Good answer.

'Danielle Burton thought you knew her,' D.D.

fished again. 'You know, from the Boston psych ward.'

'She's angry with me.'

'Tika?'

'Danielle. I want her to heal more than she wants to heal. Forgiving is hard work. It's easier for her to hate me.'

'So you two know each other. Spend much time on the psych ward, Andrew?'

'Don't be angry with Danielle,' he continued. 'Without the children, she would be lost. Without their love, the darkness would consume her completely.'

'Why do you say that, Andrew?'

'Her story to tell.'

'But you want her to heal. Tell me, and I'll help.'

'Do you think I'm stupid?' he said abruptly, and there was an edge to his voice she hadn't heard before. 'I lived in your world, Sergeant Warren, playing hardball with the best of them. I know a skeptic when I meet her. And I recognize bullshit when it's shoveled at me. You're a cop. You have no interest in healing. Your job is to judge. And you are extremely good at your job.'

In spite of herself, D.D. felt her hackles rising. 'Hey, now — '

'She hurts,' he continued. 'I feel Danielle's pain and it calls to me, only because it's so unnecessary. But not everyone wants to heal. I accept her choice, just as I accept that you will never truly believe what I say until it's too late.'

'Too late?'

'Something's coming. It's powerful. It has purpose.'

'Tell me what you want, Andrew.'

'I want you to be careful, Sergeant Warren. Spirits don't want something. They always want *someone*.'

Andrew clicked off the phone. Apparently, she'd pissed him off enough. Which was just as well, given that he'd confused her enough.

Negative energies, forces of evil, dark tidings.

D.D. thought of tonight's scene, a nine-year-old girl's forlorn body, swaying from a noose. D.D. didn't need to be policing the spiritual interplanes. She had her hands full enough on this one.

She finally made it down the stairwell. She pushed open the heavy door, worked her away across the nearly empty space. She decided there was no sound quite as lonely as a single set of footsteps echoing through a vacant parking garage.

She was tired. She did hurt. Lightfoot had been right about some things.

She rounded a broad support pillar and discovered Alex Wilson waiting beside her vehicle. She stopped walking. They eyed each other. He had shadows under his eyes. Stubble across his cheeks. Wrinkles in his once crisp white dress shirt.

'Before . . . I was wrong,' D.D. said.

'Yeah?'

'Sometimes, I do need a man to take care of me.'

He nodded. 'That's okay; sometimes, I do

need a woman to stroke my ego.'

'You look like hell,' she told him.

'Compliment enough for me. Come on. I'll drive you home.'

She followed him to his car, leaving her vehicle to be retrieved later.

He drove the first five minutes in silence. It gave her a chance to lean her head against the warm window glass and close her eyes. Morning would be coming. Maybe it was already here. She could open her eyes and look for the sun, but she wasn't ready yet. She needed this moment, dark and contained, inside herself.

'Andrew Lightfoot called,' she said presently, eyes still shut.

'What did he want?'

'To warn me that something wicked this way comes.'

'Can it fashion a noose and does it have an address?'

D.D. opened her eyes, sat up. 'Excellent questions, if only I'd thought to ask them.' She sighed, rearranged herself in the seat. 'I dropped Tika Solis's name, but he didn't bite. He definitely knows nurse Danielle, however. He requested that we not be too hard on her. Healing's not for everyone.'

'Easy for a healer to say. Means he can charge twice his going rate.'

'Ah, but it's a *gift* . . . '

Alex finally smiled. He drove toward the North End. 'Homicide or suicide?' he asked at last.

'You're the expert; you tell me.'

302

'Lack of physical evidence,' he said.

'Yeah, I got that message. Crime scene has nothing, janitor saw nothing. Sucky all the way around.'

'No, I mean *lack* of physical evidence. As in no latent prints. As in door handle, office chair, light switch — none of them bore prints small enough to be a nine-year-old's. Tricky, if you think about it — a girl opening a door, turning on the light, setting up a chair, yet never leaving behind a single fingerprint.'

'Fuck,' D.D. said, a world of exhaustion behind that one word.

Alex reached over, squeezed her shoulder. 'Not what you were expecting this evening — from executing routine search warrants to processing a dead body.'

'Not what I was expecting,' D.D. agreed. Alex's hand returned to the steering wheel; she felt its loss. 'I don't . . . I mean . . . Hell. One moment I'm on a date, next I'm at a house with five dead bodies. And that leads to another house with six dead, which leads us to a psych ward where a nine-year-old child escapes and hangs herself while we're on the property. What are the odds of that?'

'A date?' Alex asked.

'Nothing serious. Never even made it through the entrée,' she assured him.

'You gonna try again?'

'Nah. Bachelor number one's kind of faded by the wayside.'

'Good to know. Please continue.'

'So we got five dead, plus six dead, plus one

hanged. They're connected somehow. Gotta be connected. Only thing that makes sense, except, of course, none of it makes sense. How do you go from two family annihilations to one hanged child?'

Alex didn't say anything, just touched her shoulder again.

'Fuck,' D.D. muttered, and turned to stare out the window, where the morning sun was staining the sky.

She'd have to start monitoring her squad for burnout, she thought. Especially Phil. She couldn't imagine going from scenes like the ones they had to tucking your kids into bed. Phil would stop talking, the first sign he was starting to fail.

And her? She wasn't sure of her signs. Seems like she never slept when she was working a hot case and she was cranky during the best of times. Maybe she'd secretly burned out years ago, and now it didn't matter anymore. God knows she went long periods of time without ever connecting with another human being. No hugs, no morning cuddles, no kisses on the cheek. She didn't own a dog to walk or have a cat to pet. She didn't even have a plant to soothe her with its pretty green leaves.

Get in touch with your inner angel, Andrew Lightfoot had said.

Asshole wouldn't last a day in homicide.

'I think Danielle Burton is the key,' D.D. murmured after a moment. 'The nurse had a little episode when I was questioning her, then her boss Karen and her boyfriend, Gym Coach

Greg, closed ranks. Karen let it drop that A Bad Thing had happened to Danielle's family and out of sheer compassion we should play nice with her. Then Andrew Lightfoot essentially said the same.'

'Gym Coach is her boyfriend?' Alex asked with interest.

'Almost positive. Definitely something above and beyond the call of duty.'

Alex smiled at her. 'I feel the exact same way about you.'

D.D. laughed, which finally made her feel a little lighter on the inside.

'I'm telling you, they're an item, and she has a secret,' D.D. said.

'And I'm telling you . . . I know her secret.'

'Say what?'

'Way back when, Danielle's father killed Danielle's mother and siblings. Little bit of unemployment, lot of whiskey, and he shot the entire family, except her.'

'How'd you learn this?'

'A milieu counselor named Ed told me everything. How sad it was for Danielle to have to deal with Lucy's tragedy, particularly so close to the anniversary of her family's death, yada yada yada.'

'Sure it was only a gun?' D.D. asked. 'What about a knife? Maybe her father also stabbed someone?'

'We'll have to look it up.'

'Oh, we'll definitely look it up.' D.D. leaned back in the passenger's seat. 'Interesting. Personal. Isn't that what you said after the

Laraquette scene? Whoever is doing this is following a script. The murder business is personal to him. Or her, as the case might be.'

'Danielle survived her father's massacre. If she's reenacting a past trauma, shouldn't the scene involve a lone survivor?'

D.D. shrugged. 'Hell, I'm a lowly sergeant, not a criminologist. Maybe she resents being the survivor. Maybe she's determined to get the deed done right. Maybe Danielle's actually a very strong man, which would explain her ability to take out Denise Harrington and Jacob Harrington, each with a single killing blow.'

'Makes perfect sense,' Alex agreed.

'One way or another, all roads lead back to the acute-care facility,' D.D. pressed. 'And inside the acute-care facility, all fingers point at Danielle Burton.'

'Bears consideration,' Alex granted.

They were almost in the North End now. He slowed the car and D.D. felt her earlier fatigue. Another lonely return to her one-bedroom wonderland. Another sleepless night, followed by another single-espresso morning. It really had been an atrociously long time since she'd had anything other than an Italian coffee machine to make her smile.

'You know who would be extremely good at taking out an entire family?' Alex was saying now. 'The kind of player who has height, strength, and fitness on his side?'

D.D. regarded him blankly. 'Who?'

'Couple of the MCs on the unit. Particularly, Gym Coach Greg.'

Alex double-parked outside her condo building, D.D, looked at the tall brick unit, tucked shoulder to shoulder with dozens of other two-hundred-year-old brick units. Then she looked back at Alex.

'Wanna come up?' she heard herself ask.

He hesitated. 'Yeah,' he answered. 'I do want to come up. But I think I'm going to pass. I think, if we're going to do this . . . '

'*When* we're going to do this?' she tried.

'Okay, *when* we're going to do this . . . I want to do it right. I'm thinking red sauce and homemade pasta and really terrific Chianti. I'm thinking eating and talking and laughing and then . . . then all of that, all over again. It's the advantage of being older and wiser. We know good things are worth the wait.'

'I've waited a long time,' D.D. said. 'You have no idea.'

He smiled. 'I've waited a long time, too.'

D.D. sighed, gazed back up at her building. 'What if I said no hanky-panky?'

'No hanky-panky?'

'Just two consenting adults, remaining fully dressed.'

'Different,' he said.

She blew out a puff of air. 'I don't want to be alone. Okay? Maybe you don't want to be alone either. So we go upstairs and we work on not being alone together. I'll leave my shirt on, you leave your shirt on, and we'll both go to bed.'

'Will there be spooning?' he asked.

'I hope so.'

'All right. I'm in.'

'Really?'

'Really,' Alex said, and pulled away from the curb in search of a parking place.

SUNDAY

25

VICTORIA

'Knock knock.'
  'Who's there?'
  'Interrupting cat.'
  'Interrupting cat — '
  'MEOW!'
I dutifully laugh as Evan cuts me off.
Interrupting cat is his favorite knock knock joke.
He's been telling it for three years now, and it
never grows old for him. I don't mind. I'd
expected a long night with Evan, one where he
worked out his agitation and frustration from
being overmedicated the day before. Instead, he
slept all the way till six this morning, one of his
longest stretches ever.

He woke up surprisingly happy. We went for a
bike ride around the neighborhood, then broke
out the sidewalk chalk and drew an elaborate
race car shooting flames on the driveway.

After a midmorning snack of raspberry fruit
smoothies, we're now relaxing in the shade of the
backyard, birds chirping, squirrels scampering,
and a neighborhood cat stalking both.

This is charming Evan, silly Evan, let's-goof-
off-and-hang-out Evan. This is the son I can't let
go.

'Your turn,' he says now.
I think about it for a second. 'Knock knock.'

311

'Who's there?'

'Iguana.'

'Iguana who?'

'Iguana give you a hug.' I lean across the grass and capture Evan in a giant bear hug. He bursts into a fit of giggles, squirming his way out my arms.

'Mommy germs!' he shrieks.

'Iguana kiss you, too!' I growl, crawling after him. The backyard is more dirt than grass these days, but I bravely stalk my eight-year-old across the patchy lawn. Evan scampers away just enough to pretend to resist.

We're no different from any other abusive relationship, I think as I chase my laughing son around the yard. After every episode of explosive violence comes the temporary euphoria of reconciliation. Evan's contrite for yesterday's incident in the park. I'm contrite for drugging my child so I could have sex with a man who wants me only for my body. Now Evan and I are both on our best behavior. We need these moments, or neither one of us would make it.

The phantom would win.

We run around for a bit. I declare defeat first, flushed and panting from the oppressive humidity. Evan appears equally overheated, so we retreat inside for a blast of AC. I set up Evan on the couch with water and *SpongeBob*, then I return to the deck, filling the kiddy pool. Today would be perfect for going to the beach. I'm not that brave, or maybe I just don't want to risk ruining the moment, so I work on the kiddy pool. Evan will add a fleet of fire engines and two Super Soaker guns. He'll splash and spray. I'll sit on a deck chair with my feet in the cool water, grateful for the relief.

I've just finished filling the pool when the doorbell rings. I pause, rooted to the spot in surprise. We don't exactly get a lot of visitors. And there aren't deliveries on Sundays.

Evan is still engrossed with whatever Sponge-Bob and Patrick are up to. Warily, I make my way to the front door and peer through the peephole.

Michael is standing there.

I have to concentrate to fit the key into the lock. I focus on my hands, willing them not to tremble as I crack open the front door, facing my ex-husband, but holding him at bay.

'Morning, Victoria,' he says stiffly. He's dressed in summer business casual. Brooks Brothers khaki shorts, a sharply pressed button-up shirt with little yellow and green stripes. He's like a picture from a men's magazine: fit high-finance at play.

'Is Chelsea all right?' It's the only thing I can think of to say.

He nods, then clears his throat, shifting from one brown leather boat shoe to the next. He's nervous. I remember my ex-husband well enough to recognize the signs. But why?

'I thought about what you said,' he states abruptly. 'About Evan and the wedding.'

'What did I say?' I ask stupidly.

'Chelsea misses Evan. She thinks it's unfair for her to be in the wedding but not him. In fact, she says she won't serve as flower girl if Evan's not included.'

Michael flushes charmingly, admitting with his expression that he knows he's being outmaneuvered by a six-year-old, and is already declaring defeat. I'm used to angry Michael. Cold Michael. Frustrated Michael. I don't know what to make of this man.

He spreads his hands. 'Can I come in, Victoria? See Evan? Maybe discuss?'

I still have my body in the doorway, blocking Michael's presence from our former home. Despite my pleas for him to see his son, now that he's here, I wish he weren't. His sudden appearance will agitate Evan, wreck our happy morning. I've enjoyed the past few hours. I don't want them to end.

Too late. I hear footsteps behind me, Evan's natural curiosity driving him toward the entryway. I know the moment he's spotted his father because Evan's footsteps still. I turn around, and will myself to handle whatever Evan does next.

'Daddy? Daddy. *Daddy!*'

Evan rockets across the foyer. He's through the door and hurtling into his father's arms with the speed of eight-year-old lightning. Michael staggers under the unexpected onslaught, but manages to keep his footing. Then Evan is holding his father's hands and dancing all around him, touching him, poking him, plucking at him, while saying over and over again: 'DaddyDaddyDaddyDaddyDaddyDaddyDaddy DaddyDaddy.'

Michael shoots me a look. I shrug. You don't surprise a kid like Evan. Michael knows that as well as anyone. At least he should.

To give Michael some credit, he doesn't say or do anything right away. He lets Evan bounce around on his tiptoes, circling, prodding, jumping, shrieking, blowing off steam. Then, when it appears the initial euphoria is subsiding, Michael pats Evan lightly on the shoulder, and says: 'Hey, you got tall.'

'I'm very tall. I'm HUGE.'

'Strong, too.'

'LOOK AT MY MUSCLES!' Evan screams, dropping into a body-builder's pose.

I wince. 'Evan,' I say, as calmly as I can, 'I just filled your pool. Why don't you show your father your new pool?'

Evan loves this idea. He bounds back into the house on his tippy toes — a sure sign of agitation — and goes running straight for the sliders. In his heightened state, however, he forgets to open the doors. Instead, he smashes into the glass, ricocheting onto the floor, nose exploding, blood spraying. Evan scrambles up, covers his bleeding nose with his right hand, and attempts to leap through solid glass a second time. This time, he stuns himself enough to stay down for the count.

'Jesus Christ,' Michael says. But he doesn't retreat down the drive. Instead, he enters the fray.

We fall into old patterns, rituals so deeply entrenched they come back naturally, without either of us ever saying a word. Me, the nurturer, crossing to Evan, taking his hand and murmuring words of comfort as I inspect the damage. Michael, the fixer, already in the kitchen, filling a washcloth with fresh ice, then returning to place it high on Evan's nose. I have a flashback, to the days when Michael stood shoulder to shoulder with me to handle Evan, to raise Chelsea, to fight the war. He simply grew tired. Who could blame him?

Evan's not crying. He's so revved up by his beloved father's unexpected return that he's beyond tears. His emotions are running about three planets beyond the moon, and there are no tears in outer space. Just black holes everywhere.

We need to get him to his pool, where he can splash and jump and scream out the tension wiring his bony frame. He'll come down from orbit without anyone getting hurt.

Michael seems to remember about water, too. After brushing back Evan's hair — another old pattern, a natural gesture of fatherly tenderness — he opens the unlocked sliders and gestures toward the pool.

'Doing okay, buddy?'

'Yeah,' Evan replies in a thick voice. He probably still has blood in his throat. Sure enough, he takes two steps out onto the deck, then turns and spits out a huge wad of gory red.

It doesn't faze me anymore. I've seen worse.

Michael leads him into the pool. Evan climbs into the shallow water. Michael takes back the ice-filled washcloth. He dabs under Evan's nose, doing a little cleanup. Evan will have a giant, swollen honker. But again, we've seen worse.

'Super Soaker!' Evan shouts. He picks up the first gun, fills it with pool water, and lines up his father in his sights. I wait for Michael to protest, to make some motion to protect his sharply pressed shirt. Instead, he grabs the second Super Soaker, and for the next ten minutes, father and son go at it while I retreat back inside the house to watch from behind the safety of the glass slider.

Maybe this is therapeutic. Maybe this is exactly what they need. Because Evan's coming down off his toes. And his shrieking slowly transitions from glass-shattering to little-boy fun. Maybe this will turn out okay after all. Maybe this will be my lucky day.

Michael's soaked. He's laughing, declaring defeat. 'You *have* gotten strong,' he tells Evan. 'Here, I'm gonna stand in a sunbeam and dry off.'

Evan hesitates, unsure if his father is leaving now, disappearing forever. But when Michael remains standing at the edge of the deck, eight feet away, Evan finally relaxes. He gets busy with his fire engines and I join Michael outside.

'He's calming down,' Michael says softly. 'Managing his emotions better than I thought.'

'Some days are like that,' I say.

'And other days?'

'I administered Ativan five times last week.'

Michael looks at me. For once, he doesn't seem distant or angry. He seems tired. Maybe he looks as tired as I feel. Or maybe that's only my wishful thinking. 'I didn't come here to fight,' he begins, so naturally, I brace myself. 'You're going to do what you're going to do. I've come to accept that, Victoria. Whether we're married or not you're Evan's mother and you're going to do what you think is best for him, regardless of my opinions on the subject.'

'What's best for him,' I repeat stubbornly.

'Sure. But, Victoria . . . ' He spreads his hands. 'For your own sake . . . how can you go on like this? For every good moment, there's gotta be half a dozen more when you're pulling out your hair. Every day is about trying to hold off the inevitable explosion, then picking up the pieces afterward. You don't get time for yourself. You don't get time with your daughter. Chelsea misses you, you know. One night a week isn't what a six-year-old needs from her mom.'

'You said you didn't come here to fight.'

Michael sighs, drops his hands. 'I'm trying to find some middle ground. For Chelsea's sake. For Evan's sake. For all of our sakes.'

'Such as?'

'Chelsea's therapist thinks — '

'Chelsea has a therapist?'

Michael appears bewildered. 'Of course she has a therapist. It was part of the terms of the divorce.'

'I didn't realize . . . I thought you had a different opinion on that subject.'

'Oh, for God's sake, Victoria, I'm not a total asshole.' His voice has grown hard. Evan immediately stares at us from the pool, body tensing, as if ready to join the battle. Which side would he take? His father's; no doubt in my mind.

Michael, however, waves him off. 'Sorry, buddy. Just telling some story from work. Hey, I see another fire engine over there on the deck.

Maybe that one can help the others with the rescue operation.'

Evan obediently trots out of the pool to fetch his smaller fire truck. Michael and I resume our conversation.

'The therapist, Dr. Curtin, would like you to bring in Evan a few times, just to get to know each other. Once Evan is comfortable with her and the surroundings, then Chelsea can show up, too. She and Evan can visit each other, in a controlled environment where both of them will hopefully feel safe.'

I don't know what to say. 'When? How . . . how often?'

Michael shrugs. 'It'd have to be weekends, given that Chelsea's school's about to start. I figured a couple of times a month? Say, every other weekend, an hour at a time, see how it goes.'

'And if it doesn't go well? If Evan has a bad episode?'

Michael shrugs, as if to say, what's he supposed to do?

'It would be unfair to string them along,' I say. 'To reintroduce Chelsea and Evan, only to halt the relationship again.'

'I agree. Hopefully, having a professional such as Dr. Curtin involved will help manage the downside. Then again, given Evan's volatility . . . We try it or we don't try it, Victoria. Those are the options.'

I have to think about it. He's right, of course. There are no guarantees with a child like Evan. We're supposed to set him up for success, but some days I don't know what that is.

'He misses his sister,' I say at last. 'He asks for Chelsea nearly every day.' I look at him, 'He misses you, too.'

Michael looks down now. He studies his leather shoes. 'I'll be there every other weekend, as well.'

'The History Channel is his favorite channel,' I hear myself say. 'He knows almost everything there is to know about the Romans. Dates, famous leaders, major battles. He's smart, Michael. He's unbelievably smart. And he's incredibly lonely.'

'I know.'

'How . . . how could you leave us? How could you give up on him like that?'

'Because Chelsea's lonely, too. And troubled and traumatized and scared to death that, one day, she's going to wake up as violent and angry as her brother. That's a lot for a little girl to deal with, Victoria, and as long as she lived here, it wasn't going to get dealt with. Every day would be about Evan. But Chelsea needs us, too.'

His words are matter-of-fact. Somehow, this makes them harder to take.

'What does Melinda think of this?' I ask pointedly.

At the mention of his fiancée, Michael stiffens, but doesn't retreat. 'My kids are her kids. She gets that.'

'So you'll start over. A new little family. Is she young? Does she want children? Does that scare the crap out of you?'

He regards me evenly. 'Yes, she wants kids.

And yeah, it scares the crap out of me.'

'It's not fair,' I whisper.

'No, Victoria, it's not.' He hesitates. For a second, I think he might say more, he might touch my cheek. Then the moment passes.

I can't look at him anymore. I stare down at the deck and will myself not to cry. This is not about me. This is about Evan. Getting to see his sister again. Getting to see his father again. Evan and his sister reclaiming part of their family.

'I'll bring him to the doctor's office,' I say. 'I'll work with Dr. Curtin. If this means Evan can see you and Chelsea, I'll do what I can.'

'Thank you.'

'Thank you,' I say, on behalf of Evan. Then I don't speak anymore because my throat is thick with tears and I don't want to say something stupid, such as *I'm lonely, too*. Or even worse, *I still love you*.

Michael crosses to Evan. He starts to say his goodbye. Evan doesn't take it well. Michael negotiates a compromise. One last round of Super Soaker warfare, then Evan can watch a show on the History Channel after Michael departs.

They return to their battle. I retreat inside the house to the upstairs master bath, where I splash water on my face and realize for the first time that my hair is snarled, my shirt is spattered with Evan's blood, and I have dirt on both my knees. Doesn't matter. Michael and Melinda, Melinda and Michael, two little lovebirds sitting in a tree. K-I-S-S-I-N-G.

Downstairs, Michael and Evan are entering

the family room, both pink-cheeked and water-soaked.

'What do you think?' Michael asks Evan. 'Can I visit you again?'

Evan regards Michael thoughtfully. 'You left me.'

'I was away longer than I thought I would be,' Michael says.

'You left.'

'I'm here now.'

'But you left.'

Michael finally concedes. 'Yeah, buddy, I left. And I missed you every day, and I hurt every day, and I don't want to hurt like that again. So here I am — '

'Leav-ing,' Evan singsongs.

'Returning,' Michael corrects. 'I don't live here anymore, Evan. I can't stay, but I can come back.' He looks at me for support.

I add, 'He can come back, Evan. You'll see.'

Evan doesn't look like he believes us, but he's also tired from the morning's events. He's prepared to be mollified with TV, so I turn on cable, then escort my ex-husband to the door.

Michael doesn't say goodbye, just turns and kisses me lightly on the cheek.

I stand there long after he's departed, my fingers touching the spot on my skin as if that will keep him with me.

★ ★ ★

I always thought when the moment came it would be in the middle of the night. Evan would be screaming and shrieking. I would be bolting down a hallway or up a flight of stairs. Maybe I'd trip, or maybe I'd just be one step too slow. I'd go down, and my frothing son would be upon me.

Instead, I sit next to Evan on the sofa. He keeps his eyes on the TV, slightly slack-jawed, deep in TV coma. I relax, feeling sleepy from so much time outdoors. Maybe I'll take us for ice cream after this. Maybe we can attempt a public outing.

I feel a prick. A pain in my side, I reach down to rub it away, and notice a knife handle sticking out from between my ribs. My son's hand is holding it. And my son, my beautiful son, is glaring at me.

'*Et tu, Brute?*' he snarls.

At that moment, staring into the black pools of his eyes, I get it. Why my son appears so calm: because there's no more turmoil inside him. Evan's surrendered to the phantom. He's let the phantom win.

I stare at the paring knife. I stare at my blood, dripping down the handle, across his pale thin fingers, into the tan sofa cushion. And I feel pain now, white-hot, dizzying. I feel other drippings, inside my body, from whatever vital organs have just been pierced.

I watch the day dim before my eyes, grow shadowy around the edges.

Such a pretty day, I think. *Such a happy day to end like this.*

I look at my son. And I do what any mom would do.

I wrap my fingers around his bloody hand, and I say, before the darkness takes me, 'It's okay, Evan. It's all going to be okay. I love you. I will always love you.'

26

DANIELLE

I was on paid administrative leave. No point to staying on the ward. I should return home, shower, eat, and sleep for the next forty-eight hours. Naturally, I lingered on the unit instead.

I hung out in the Admin area, tackling general paperwork, then, reluctantly, writing up the last few hours of Lucy's life. I made a minute-by-minute account of everything that happened during my shift, from my medical evaluation downstairs to Jorge's meltdown upstairs. The detectives' arrival. The execution of the warrant, the handing over of files, my solo outing for the infamous glass of water, as well as my brief visit to Lucy's room. I recorded Lucy's state of mind, her feline waltz through the moonbeams. Finally, I mentioned refilling the stupid copier, answering the detectives' questions, and then, after Greg's announcement, launching our desperate hunt through various hospital corridors. I went over it, again and again and again.

The repetition didn't make it any easier to take. I couldn't find the state of numbness that's supposed to follow such tragedies. We'd never lost a child before. We'd had some attempt suicide. We'd heard of others who met tragedy after leaving here. But we'd never had a kid die on our watch. I didn't know what to do to ease the tightness in my chest. I hadn't cried since that one week with my Aunt Helen, when I'd realized that tears were both too much and too little for mourning an entire family.

So I wrote my report. When I was done, I took the string ball Lucy made for me, and stapled it to the upper right-hand corner.

Eight a.m. The kids were up, the sun was shining through the windows, and the newly appointed security guard was standing outside the doors.

I headed for the hospital cafeteria and waited for Karen to find me there.

★ ★ ★

It was past nine when Karen finally showed. She entered the cafeteria and headed straight for me. Her wire-rimmed glasses were perched on the end of her nose, her ash-colored hair pinned back messily, an administrator who'd been roused from her bed and still hadn't had the chance to return there. Her footsteps were brisk. Her gaze level. She was all business, my boss. She'd been heading the unit for at least a dozen years now, and I couldn't think of anyone better for the job.

She pulled out the chair across from me, setting down her ubiquitous pile of papers, and pushing her glasses into place with one finger. She eyed my uneaten bagel, cup of coffee. 'Do you need a refill?' she asked, gesturing to my mug.

I shook my head. My stomach couldn't take

any more caffeine, let alone my nerves.

She headed for the food, loading up a tray, then returning to me. She had a banana, a muffin, and steaming mug of Lipton tea. This was kindness on her part. We had a kitchenette in the unit where she could eat the exact same meal for free. But there's something about meeting someone in a cafeteria. You must break bread together; it's part of the tradition.

She peeled her banana. I managed a bite of bagel. Then, because I just couldn't take it, I spoke first.

'You know I didn't hurt her, right?' I burst out. 'You know I would never do anything to harm Lucy, or any other child.'

'I don't know that,' Karen said, and I felt my stomach lurch. She continued, 'I believe that, however. If asked an opinion, I would say you would never intentionally harm a child.'

I nodded, pathetically grateful for her show of faith. 'I don't know what happened,' I whispered.

'I don't know either. In this matter, we're going to have to defer to the police.'

'Who will take care of her?' I asked, meaning Lucy's body.

'I don't know,' Karen said again. 'Abuse charges are pending against her foster parents; she went straight from their custody to ours. Does the state claim her body, make arrangements for her? This is my first time in a situation like this.'

'We should do it,' I said immediately. 'It'll give our kids a chance to say goodbye.'

'Danielle, Lucy only stayed with us a matter of

days. And she never mingled with the other kids. They still haven't figured out she's gone.'

'What will you tell them?'

'Given her limited impact on their lives, very little. We'll answer any questions they ask, of course, but I'm not convinced they'll ask many.'

The comment depressed me more. I sank lower in my chair. 'Doesn't seem right,' I murmured. 'She was a child, a nine-year-old girl, and now she's dead and no one misses her. That doesn't seem right.'

'I miss her,' Karen said steadily. 'You miss her, too.'

My eyes burned. I looked away, staring hard at the blue linoleum floor.

'Go home,' Karen said. 'Run or rest, scream or meditate, do whatever it is you need to do to heal. You're an exceptional nurse, Danielle. And a good person. This is going to pass. You're going to feel okay again,'

'I want to work,'

'Not an option.'

'I need the kids. Taking care of them *is* how I take care of myself.'

'Not an option.'

'I'll observe. Catch up on paperwork, Stay out of everyone's way. I promise.'

'Danielle, the police will be returning at any moment. You don't need to be on the unit. You need to be at home, phoning a good lawyer.'

'But I didn't — '

Karen held up a hand: 'Preaching to the choir. Take care of *you*, Danielle. You matter to the kids. You matter to all of us.'

I wished she wouldn't say stuff like that. I swiped at my eyes, stared harder at the cafeteria floor.

'There will be two staff debriefings,' Karen added finally. 'Two p.m. for the day shift; eleven p.m. for the night shift. If you want to attend, off the clock, you're welcome. We need to establish new procedures so this kind of thing never happens again. I'm also arranging for counseling for any who need it. Something else for you to consider.'

I nodded. She'd tossed me a bone. I accepted it.

Across the way, I noticed Greg now walking into the cafeteria, scanning each table. He headed toward me, then spotted Karen and hesitated. Karen, however, saw him, too. It was almost as if she'd been waiting for him.

She grabbed her paperwork, topped it with her uneaten muffin.

'You need to take care of you,' she repeated firmly, then she departed as Greg approached. He walked straight toward me. Made no move to grab breakfast, made no motion to pull out a chair. He halted before me.

'Come home,' he said.

'Can't stand the thought,' I told him honestly.

'Not your home, Danielle. Mine.'

So I did.

⋆　⋆　⋆

Turned out Greg shared a three-bedroom apartment with two other guys. Like many local apartments, it was carved out of a once grand home, with hardwood floors, nine-foot ceilings, and bull's-eye molding around the expansive bay windows. The place felt worn around the edges, an aging matriarch with good bones but tired skin. I commented on the crown molding. Greg shrugged. Apparently, he wasn't into architecture.

His roommates were gone. Probably down by the river, he mumbled. Perfect day for hanging out on the Charles. Hot, humid, hazy, Greg turned on the window AC units as he gave me the nickel tour. Still, we were both sweating by the time we reached the end of the hall.

He opened the last door, gestured inside. 'My pad,' he said simply.

It was neater than I expected. No towels or stray clothing strewn across the floor. The furniture was College Dorm 101. A double mattress, sans frame and headboard. An old maple dresser, slightly lopsided, missing one knob. An equally old maple desk, small for a guy Greg's size, and dwarfed by a black office chair.

No posters hanging up. No pictures adorning the dresser. The room featured cream-colored paint on the walls, dark green sheets on the bed, and tan blinds on the sunny windows. That was it. The room was a way station. A place for someone to crash, not for someone to live.

I looked at Greg, realizing for the first time how little I knew about him.

'No photo of the girlfriend on the nightstand?' I commented.

'No nightstand,' he said. 'No girlfriend,'

'Family?'

'Got a sister in Pennsylvania.'

'You never talk about her.'

'You never ask.'

He had me there. I rarely questioned him or anyone else. It was ironic, if you thought about it. My entire personal history entered the room way before I did; I could see it on people's faces when we were finally introduced. *Oh, so she's the one whose father shot everyone* . . . .Therefore, I didn't inquire about others. That would invite them to ask about me, and then I'd have to verify the rumors in their heads.

'Ever see her?' I asked now. 'Your sister?'

'Not lately.'

'Why not?'

He shrugged. 'Busy working, I guess.' He set his duffel bag down next to the wall. We both stared awkwardly at each other, too aware of the mattress in the corner.

'Not much artwork,' I commented at last.

'No.'

'Don't plan on staying for long?'

'Don't spend much time here,' he answered. 'I work two jobs, and save my pennies to buy a home someday. I want a fenced-in yard, a puppy, a wife, and two-point-two kids. That's where I'm going. This is just where I am now.'

I didn't say anything. It was a nice dream. Fit him. He wasn't screwing around. That kind of baggage . . . all mine, not his.

Greg cleared his throat. 'Thirsty?'

'Okay.'

We returned to the kitchen. Dishes crowded

the sink, the counter-top could use a scrubbing. Greg made a disparaging sound in the back of his throat, so I was guessing the roommates made the mess. He left it, however, opening the vintage fridge to retrieve one Gatorade and one Diet Coke. He handed me the Diet Coke, opened the Gatorade for himself.

'Got any rum?' I joked, taking the first cold sip.

He regarded me for a second, then reached above the fridge and pulled down a bottle of Captain Morgan. He handed it to me, like a dare. How badly did I want to self-destruct?

After a minute, I handed the bottle back, untouched. He replaced it on top of the fridge. I finished my Coke. He finished his Gatorade. Then we were back to our staring contest.

'I'll take the couch,' he said. 'You can have the bedroom. AC should've cooled it by now. I'll get you some clean sheets.'

'Brought me all the way here to sleep alone?' I asked.

He replied calmly, 'I'm not your father, Danielle. I won't fuck you.'

I hit him. Hard, before either of us expected it. He took the blow squarely in the jaw. I heard my knuckles crack. His head, on the other hand, barely wavered. So I hit him again, this time in the hard plank of his stomach. Not so much as an *oomph*, the fit bastard.

I went to town, slapping at him, pummeling desperately. I whacked his sides, his chest, his shoulders. I hit and hit and hit. And he stood there, as if he were a marble statue and I were a feral pigeon flapping around his feet.

'I hate you, I hate you, I hate you!' I heard myself scream.

I brought up my knee, going for the money shot. At the last second, he blocked the jab. Then his hands captured my wrists, and suddenly he had me backed up against the far wall. Now I was the one on the defensive, my small frame pinned by his larger build.

He leaned down, face so close I could count the beads of sweat dotting his upper lip. His eyes were a deep dark brown. Chocolate, with a ring of gold in the middle.

He was going to kiss me. In my agitated state, I couldn't decide if I would kiss him back, or bite him.

'I won't fuck you,' he said again.

'Bastard!'

'When I let you go, you'll stop hitting me. You'll go down the hall, get into bed, and get some goddamn sleep. Do you understand?'

'Asshole!'

'Feel better yet?'

I growled at him. He still didn't release my wrists. Then, abruptly, our bodies so close together, I felt the hard length of him against my hip. He wanted me. It gave me a sense of power I hadn't had in days. I moved against him, slightly dipped and swayed.

The gold ring around his pupils contracted. Another bead of sweat appeared on his upper lip.

I raised my right leg, hooking it around his hips and jerking his pelvis deeper into mine. I decided that fucking Gym Coach Greg might be the best way ever of escaping from my own mind.

His head lowered, his lips hovering just above mine. I worked my hips again, until I could feel his erection right where I wanted it. I started rubbing, slowly, lightly, picking up speed and pressure as I went along.

He was panting. So was I. Maybe we wouldn't move. Maybe we'd dry hump right here in the kitchen. After that, I'd take some rum. I'd chug it before walking out of this goddamn apartment and going home alone.

Then, God help me, I saw Lucy again, her small body hanging from the ceiling, and I broke. Tears welled up. I wanted to cry. I needed to cry. But it wouldn't be enough. Couldn't be enough. My mother, Natalie, Johnny. Lucy.

I hit Greg again. Weak, this time. Weary. Then I collapsed into the support pillar of his body, my face buried in the salty curve of his neck.

Greg scooped me up. He carried me down the hall. He tucked me into bed.

'Sleep.'

He closed the door, I was pitched into darkness, where I could once again smell cordite and blood. Except this time, I was the one holding the gun, standing beside my mother's bed.

'You said you'd help me. You said you'd make him stop.'

'Danielle . . .'

'You said you believed me.'

'Danielle — '

The front door slamming shut. My father's

334

drunken voice booming up the stairs, 'Honey, I'm home!'

Me raising the gun.

'Danielle!'

Cordite and blood. Singing and screaming. Love and hate.

The story of my life.

My eyes snapped open.

I lay on Geg's mattress, curled up in the cool darkness, and didn't sleep again.

★ ★ ★

Phone was ringing. The sound came from the living room and it finally roused me from my post-weeping lethargy. I rolled off the mattress, tested out my legs, and decided they'd hold.

I opened the bedroom door, hearing Greg's deep baritone in the living room.

'Yeah, I can come in. What time does the kid arrive? What are the protocols?'

There was silence as he listened to the answers. He was talking to Karen. A new child was arriving at the unit and, for some reason, Karen wanted Greg there for the show.

I walked into the living room, waited for him to see me. His dark hair was damp from a recent shower; he was wearing a navy blue towel around his waist and nothing else. I stared at his deeply tanned torso, ridged with muscle, and my mouth went dry.

I retreated to the single bathroom, where I splashed cold water on my face and tried to regain my bearings. Greg was Greg. Greg had always been Greg.

But I'd never realized before what Greg looked like naked.

I took another minute, then opened the bathroom door to find Greg in the hallway. He'd changed into gym shorts and a white polo shirt. It made it easier for both of us.

'That was Karen,' he announced. 'Listen, I gotta go to work. You can stay if you'd like. My roommates probably won't return until late.'

'What time is it?'

'Four p.m.'

I frowned, surprised by the time. Perhaps I'd dozed off after all.

'What's up?' I asked.

'New arrival,' he said, already walking down the hall to retrieve his gym bag. I trailed after him.

'Why you?'

'Kid has a history of violence. Karen would feel better with me there.'

'What'd he do?'

'Stabbed his mother.'

'When?'

'Sounds like this morning,'

'Mother okay?'

'Don't know.'

'How old's the kid?'

'Eight. Currently catatonic, according to the ER docs. Most likely shock.'

'And once that wears off . . . ' I agreed. The panic would set in, and the explosive child would explode.

'Looks like it'll be a night.' Greg slipped on a pair of nylon workout pants over his shorts. He slung his bag over his shoulder and, that quickly, he was good to go.

I stared at him. He stared at me. A faint bruise marred the line of his jaw. I took a step forward without thinking. I traced the bruise lightly with my fingertips, then, standing on my tiptoes, I gently kissed the mark I'd left on his skin.

'I'm sorry,' I said honestly.

'Danielle . . . ' he said thickly.

'What?'

'It's not always about you. Just remember that, okay? It's not always about you.'

'Okay.'

I kissed his jaw again. I inhaled the fragrance of his freshly showered skin, then I stepped back. He went to work.

I had other business to tend to.

27

D.D. got her taskforce. The linking of the Harringtons to the Laraquette-Solis family via the pediatric psych ward, plus the subsequent death of another child in the same unit, all served to catch the superintendent's attention. D.D. made a step up from being viewed as an extremely paranoid investigator to being one smart cookie. The fact that the media had latched on to the salacious news potential of two heinous mass murders in two days didn't hurt either. The press hadn't linked the family murders yet, but were granting enough coverage of the two tragedies that the superintendent saw the wisdom of quickly closing out both the Harrington and Laraquette-Solis cases. D.D. got ten detectives to throw at the hospital scene.

She also got to wake up in the arms of a handsome man.

Her damn pager was going off at the time, meaning they shared half a dozen glazed donuts instead of half a dozen bouts of steamy sex, but still, best morning she'd had in years.

She was smiling when Alex drove her back to the psych ward, perhaps even whistling as they walked through the lobby and rode the elevators to the eighth floor. They exited the elevators outside the secured glass doors of the pediatric unit, and discovered Andrew Lightfoot chatting up the security guard.

'What the hell are you doing here?' D.D. demanded.

'Working,' he said. 'Can't you feel it?' He held out his forearm, which was covered in goose bumps. 'Bad juju,' he murmured as they entered the unit. 'Better find your inner angel, Sergeant. Because, take it from me, your inner bitch's got nothing on whatever's going on in here.'

★ ★ ★

D.D. and her team set up in their favorite classroom. They were armed with search warrants and they knew how to use them. In the next twenty-four hours, D.D. planned on obtaining preliminary statements from every staff member working the unit. Back in HQ, Phil was running background reports on each employee, while Neil was formulating a list of other hospital workers — doctors, therapists, janitors, food service employees, local shamans, etc. — who routinely visited the floor. Two more detectives would be sent out to work the list, tracking down each person, securing an initial interview, and doing the background checks.

It was the classic machine-gun approach: fast and furious. D.D. didn't mind. She was on the hunt for big game, and jazzed about it.

The hospital, of course, had sent its lawyer to supervise the activities. Being that it was a gorgeous Sunday afternoon and most of the high-powered partners were out on their yachts, some young chick in a navy blue Ann Taylor pantsuit had drawn the short straw. The lawyer made a big show of inspecting each search warrant, slowly scrutinizing every word, before returning the documents with a crisp 'Fine.'

D.D. liked her already. The kind of looks-good-but-has-no-experience legal eagle a BPD sergeant could eat for lunch.

D.D.'s team got to it, setting up for interviews and preparing to copy more files. Satisfied with their progress, D.D. went in search of her first target of choice: Andrew Lightfoot.

She found him in the dead girl's room. The lone mattress remained in the middle of the floor. Andrew sat in front of it, cross-legged, feet bare, eyes closed, hands resting on his knees, palms up. His lips were moving, but no sound came out.

D.D. walked around until she stood in front of him. The minute her shadow touched his face, Lightfoot opened his eyes and stared at her. He didn't seem surprised by her sudden presence, and that pissed her off enough to attack first.

'Why didn't you tell us you worked here?' she demanded.

'I don't.'

D.D. arched a brow, waving her hand around the room. 'And yet, here you are.'

Lightfoot rose fluidly to standing. 'Karen asked me to come. The unit is acute, the energies imbalanced. She asked me to perform a cleansing exercise, and assist with her staff. So here I am.'

'Karen, the nurse manager? She hired you?'

'Not everyone is a skeptic.' He smiled patiently.

D.D. felt pissed off all over again. 'How long have you and Karen known each other?'

'Two years.'

'Personal or professional?'

'Professional.'

'How'd you meet?'

'Through a family. They asked that I assist with their child, who was admitted here. Karen became impressed by the child's progress. She asked me to work with her staff on basic meditation and energy-boosting exercises. From time to time, she also recommends my services to other families.'

'She likes you?'

'She believes in my work.'

'You're rich and good-looking. Bet that doesn't hurt.'

'You think I'm rich and good-looking?' Lightfoot smiled again.

'I think you're cocky and arrogant,' D.D. countered.

Lightfoot's smile grew broader. 'Leopard can't change all of his spots,' he agreed.

'You and Karen ever go out?'

'It is strictly a professional relationship, Sergeant. I assist her and her staff. She recommends my services.'

'Did she recommend you to the Harringtons?'

'That referral came from a different source.'

'When was the last time you saw Ozzie?'

'Three months ago.'

'And Tika?'

'I don't know that child.'

'Yet you know she's a child,' D.D. pounced.

341

Lightfoot regarded her evenly. 'We are talking about kids, thus it stands to reason that Tika is a kid. Sergeant, you seem angry. We should leave this room; it's not good for you.'

He didn't give her a chance to reply, but turned toward the doorway. It forced her to follow him, which, come to think of it, made her angrier.

'We'll go to the classroom — ' she started tightly.

'This is perfect,' Lightfoot said, as if she'd never spoken. He'd stopped in front of the huge window at the end of the hall. 'Here, in the sunbeam. You've been spending too much time under fluorescent bulbs, Sergeant. You need more vitamin D.'

D.D. stared at him wide-eyed.

'I'm a healer,' Lightfoot said quietly. 'Just because you don't believe doesn't mean I'm going to change who I am.'

'Have you ever worked with a child who was a cutter?' D.D. asked.

'Who self-mutilates, you mean? Not lately.'

'Karen refer you to such a family?'

'No.'

'What was the last family she referred you to?'

'I don't really remember, or keep track,' Lightfoot said vaguely. D.D. narrowed her eyes, studied him for a bit.

Up close and personal, she could make out deep shadows beneath Lightfoot's eyes, a pallor beneath his tanned skin. Apparently, she wasn't the only one not getting enough vitamin D.

'Up late last night?' she asked him.

He hesitated. 'I have been up late ever since you visited my home. I had planned to take a few more days off, but it is not to be.'

'Why?'

He turned toward the window, seemed to be studying the sun. D.D. was startled to realize that the healer was shivering slightly, his bare arms still covered with goose bumps.

'I have spent the past two evenings on the spiritual interplanes,' he said at last. 'As I tried to explain to you by phone, something is coming. I can feel it. Have you ever heard the expression 'a darkness deeper than night'?'

D.D. nodded, still studying him.

'I never knew what that meant, but now I do. There's something terrible out there. Or maybe, now it's in here,' Suddenly, Lightfoot reached out, touched her cheek.

In spite of herself, D.D. gasped. Lightfoot's fingers felt like dry ice against her skin. So cold they nearly burned. She took an instinctive step back.

The healer nodded. 'Negative energy feels like a deep chill. However, I'm an advanced and powerful healer. Meaning I should be able to fight that cold. I should be able to warm my hands. But since entering the unit, I can't do it. Something terrible holds sway here. It's rooted in Lucy's room, but is already expanding to the entire floor. A cold, malevolent force. A darkness deeper than night. Lucy couldn't survive it. And neither, I think, can we. It's why I asked you to leave that room and join me here in the sun.'

'Because some celestial Big Bad hurt Lucy?' asked D.D.

'I'm tired,' Lightfoot said, as if it were important for her to understand that. 'I've been expending vast amounts of energy on the interplanes each night. Then I've had healing exercises to tend to during the day. And now I'm trying to cleanse the taint that has corrupted this ward. I'm drained. Not at my best today. I'm sorry I can't do more to protect you.'

'What?' D.D. said, looking around.

'You're angry,' Lightfoot continued. 'You're hurt. Under better circumstances, I would help you center more, bolster your own defenses. But not this afternoon.'

'Okay.' D.D hesitated, trying to get the healer back on track. 'Tell me about Danielle Burton. You said her pain calls to you.'

'There's an old saying that doctors make the worst patients. Same with psych nurses. I have known Danielle since starting to work at the unit. I would like to help her. Unfortunately, her skepticism mirrors your own.'

'She won't work with you?'

He shrugged. 'It's why I am willing to speak with you. She's not a client and, in her own mind, not even a friend. But I worry about her.'

'Why?'

'She's an old soul,' Lightfoot said immediately, his expression more distant now, seeing something only he could see, 'For centuries she has returned to this plane, always seeking, never finding. She has honed her hatred, when only love can set her free.'

344

'Sounds like a song I once heard,' D.D. said. She couldn't help herself. 'Are you talking reincarnation?'

'I'm talking experiential lessons. Her soul is drawn to this plane to learn what it needs to learn. But she hasn't mastered the lesson. Until she does, she's doomed to repeat. Unfortunately, there are other souls also involved. Their experiences are intertwined with her own, her inability to move forward sentencing them all to a spin cycle of ever-repeating violence. I've tried to explain this to her, but . . . '

'Her father?' D.D. filled in.

'That would make sense,' Lightfoot said.

D.D. narrowed her eyes. Interesting answer, she thought, and she was beginning to realize that for all his woo-woo, Lightfoot was very careful with his replies.

She got it, suddenly: 'You mean Gym Coach Greg. You're worried about his and Danielle's relationship.'

'He asks. She refuses. He needs. She rejects. He still searches for love. She still chooses hate. And they spin and they spin and they spin.'

'Greg seems like a nice guy,' D.D. countered mildly.

'They spin and they spin and they spin,' Lightfoot repeated, sounding both tired and sorrowful.

D.D. regarded him for a bit. The healer made no attempt to break the silence, and after several minutes, she declared defeat.

'You ever miss it?' she asked finally.

'What?'

'The money, the fast car, the trappings of your former life?'

'Never.'

'Had to have been an adrenaline rush, picking up pretty women, making fistfuls of cash, screwing over your rivals. From all that, to this?'

'Wall Street is nothing but a playground. There are no meaningful rewards, there are no significant consequences. Whereas in there . . . ' Lightfoot pointed toward Lucy's open doorway. 'In there is where I fight to win.'

As if to prove his point, the healer marched back down the hall.

He paused outside Lucy's room. D.D. saw the man shiver before he headed in.

★   ★   ★

With Lightfoot back to the business of spiritual cleansing, D.D. wandered the unit until she found the nurse manager, Karen Rober, sitting in the common area with a little boy who was resiliently mashing fruit in a bowl. The boy looked up when D.D. approached and she recognized him from the first day. One of the three amigos into Matchbox cars and running laps. D.D. searched her mental files for a name but came up blank; she'd never been great with kids.

'Do you want a fruit smoothie?' the boy asked her, feet swinging, shoulders rocking. He stated in one breathless rush: 'I can do banana strawberry raspberry blueberry maybe grape but

346

not oranges they're too hard to mash.'

He went back to pounding fruit with his plastic spoon, rocking, rocking, rocking. D.D. started to cue in on a few things. First, while the boy remained seated at the table, he was agitated. Very agitated. A hand grenade, just waiting for someone to pull the pin.

Second, he wasn't the only one. Two kids were rollerblading down the hallway, pushing and shoving at each other as they went, while another kid sat under a table, banging his head against the wall.

What was it they called the environment of the unit — the 'milieu'? D.D. was no expert, but even to her, the milieu was wiggy today.

Karen had spotted the head-banger. 'Jamal,' she said sharply. 'Enough of that. Why don't you join Benny and me? Come on, Jamal. Benny will make you a fruit smoothie. What flavor would you like?'

'*Eat eat eat eat eat*,' Benny singsonged, holding out his first concoction for Karen.

The head nurse took it from him, smiling her thanks.

'*Eat eat eat eat eat.*'

D.D. watched in fascination as Karen swallowed an honest-to-God spoonful, smile never slipping from the nurse manager's face. Benny clapped his hands in glee. Jamal finally crawled out from beneath the other table to join the party.

In no time, Karen had him set up with his own fruit-smashing project. Then the nurse manager summoned another staff member to take over the table, freeing herself to join D.D. in the hallway.

'Whatever they're paying you, it's not enough,' D.D. told Karen.

The nurse smiled faintly. 'Trust me, I've been fed worse.'

'But you ate it. Can't you fake your way out of something like that?'

'Do you have kids, Sergeant?'

'No.'

'Well, someday, if you do, you'll understand.'

Dismissive and curt. D.D. warmed to the challenge. 'Your place or mine?' D.D. asked, gesturing to either the Admin area or down the hall, where D.D.'s team had set up shop. Karen arched a brow, no doubt tempted to remind D.D. that, technically, it was all Karen's. But finally, the administrator sighed, and pointed to her own office area. She located the key on the lanyard around her neck and opened the door. D.D. followed.

'How long have you known Lightfoot?' D.D. asked as they entered the cramped warren of rooms. Karen led her back to a tiny staff room, where they could both have a seat at a table.

'Two years.'

Consistent. 'How'd you meet him?'

'Parents of a child who came to stay. Their son liked to capture bullfrogs, stick firecrackers in their mouths, and light the fuses. He also enjoyed covering the walls of their home with pictures of his mother being killed in various manners. It was amazing the level of detail he could capture using only red crayons.'

Also consistent. 'How old was the child?' D.D. asked, curious.

'Ten.'

'Scary.'

Karen shrugged. 'I've seen worse. The boy, however, was not responding to medication and the parents were frantic. So they brought in Andrew. I was initially skeptical, but Andrew was calm and courteous, respectful of our staff and the other kids. And I have to say, within three weeks we noticed a marked improvement in the boy's behavior. Incidents that previously would've thrown him into a rage were greeted with more tolerance. We'd see the child tense up, but then he'd mumble, 'Find the light, seven hugs from seven angels.' He'd relax, a remarkable feat for a child with his level of psychosis. Naturally, I started to ask Andrew about his work. As did many of our doctors.'

'What do they think?' D.D. asked.

'Most of them have no issues with it. Medicine is already starting to note the role of love and laughter in the recovery process. It's not so much of a stretch to acknowledge that faith and spirituality can also make a difference.'

'Angels healed a troubled kid?'

Karen smiled. 'Do you know everything there is to know about the cosmos? Because if you do, you're a smarter woman than I, Sergeant.'

D.D. scowled at her. 'How many of your kids has Andrew worked with?'

'You'd have to ask him. I rarely refer his services; mostly, other parents do.'

'Sounds like he worked with the Harringtons.'

Karen didn't say anything.

'Danielle implied that he interfered with your care of their son, recommending that Ozzie be discharged before the docs thought he was ready.'

Karen shrugged. 'It was a gray area. Ozzie was definitely improved. I would've liked more time to ensure his recent changes in behavior stuck, but they felt it was more important to get him back to a home environment. There was logic to both sides of the argument. Now, for the record, Ozzie never bounced back here. So I have to believe that the Harringtons' approach worked for their son. Andrew worked for their son.'

'The Harringtons were murdered.'

'By the father, I thought.'

'We're not sure of that.'

Karen faltered for the first time, hands dropping to the table, blinking behind her wire-rimmed glasses. 'Are you saying . . . Ozzie?'

'It's possible.'

The head nurse didn't defend Ozzie. She sighed instead. 'It's hard to know with these kids. They're not out of control because they're weak or lazy. They suffer from physiological differences, issues with brain chemistry, hormones, DNA. And there's so little we can do for them. So few tools available to us.'

'Hence Lightfoot, a handsome white knight, promising to save lost children while reducing your pharmaceutical bill. Gotta like that.'

The nurse manager didn't say anything, so D.D. took it one step further. 'Are you sleeping with him?'

'My husband would object.'

'Maybe he doesn't know.'

'My conscience would object.' Karen shook her head. 'I understand you're skeptical of Andrew. In many ways, I also held his looks and background against him. But if you watch him with the kids ... He is genuinely tender, exceedingly patient. He doesn't just soothe them, he teaches them to soothe themselves. I never thought I'd be advocating energy cleansings in a clinical environment. And yet I'm respectful of the results.'

D.D. scowled, refusing to be convinced. 'What about other members of your staff. Say, Danielle? Andrew's good-looking. She's young and pretty.'

'You would have to ask Danielle.'

'She's a bit of a mess,' D.D. commented.

Karen didn't take the bait.

'I mean,' D.D. continued conversationally, 'her father slaughters her whole family except her. There's some baggage to carry. And now she works with a whole ward of violent kids. It's like she needs the drama.'

For a moment, Karen was silent. Then: 'In policing, don't you see officers who come from a long tradition of policing? Sons, daughters, nieces, nephews of other cops?'

'True.'

'Our line of work is like that, too. You want to dig, most of our staff has stories that will break your heart. They didn't grow up happy, driving them to preserve for others the childhood they never had. By that logic, Danielle isn't the

351

exception in our unit. More like the norm.'

'Really? What's Greg's story?'

'Greg?' The nurse manager seemed surprised by that name, of all names. 'I'm not sure Greg has a story. He's not one to talk about his personal life.'

'How long has he worked here?'

'Five years.'

'Any complaints? Issues?'

'Not one,' Karen answered firmly. 'He's quiet, conscientious, brilliant with the children. Both adults and kids like him, which is not something I can say for all of our staff.'

'Adults?' D.D. asked.

'The parents. Some of our people . . . ' Karen hesitated. 'Some of our staff are in this line of work because they have an immediate rapport with children. Unfortunately, that rapport doesn't always extend to adults.'

D.D. thought about it. Gym Coach Greg was a good-looking guy. Strong, fit. She'd bet some female adults did have an immediate rapport with him.

'What are the requirements for an MC?' she asked now, pulling out her spiral pad to make a note. 'Does he have a special license, or have to pass board certification?' What could D.D. have Phil look up as part of Greg's background report?

But the nurse manager was shaking her head. 'Our nurses have degrees and board certification, of course. The MCs are only required to have a high school education, and a lot of energy and creativity with kids.'

352

'You're kidding me. The majority of your staff are MCs, and you're telling me they have no special training?'

Karen looked at her. 'Sergeant, what classroom module could ever prepare someone for the kids we see here?'

Good point. 'Greg have a family?' D.D. asked with a frown.

'He doesn't talk about one.'

'Girlfriend?'

'I don't know.'

'So he has eyes only for Danielle,' D.D. supplied.

'I don't get involved in my staff's personal lives,' Karen answered coolly.

'Really? Because everyone's talking about it. Greg says yes. Danielle says no. Around and around they go. Sounds like a lot of flirtation on company time. You can't be happy about that.'

'I've never seen either one act anything other than professional.'

'Maybe you ought to get out of Admin more.'

The head nurse glared at her.

D.D. waited a moment, then decided she'd had enough of all the tap dancing. She cut to the heart of the matter: 'Don't you think it's odd that two families affiliated with this unit have been murdered, right around the anniversary date of one of your staff member's own family being killed?'

'It's odd — ' Karen started.

'Then,' D.D. cut in, 'a girl was hanged last night, who also happens to be working with the same staff member whose family was murdered almost exactly twenty-five years ago. Another coincidence?'

'These things happen.'

'Really? How many kids have you found hanging in the hospital? How many patients have you discharged who've wound up murdered?'

Karen didn't reply anymore. She looked as tired as Lightfoot. The head nurse sighed, then reached for a stack of paperwork on her desk. She pulled out a report, then looked back up at D.D.

'When were the Harringtons killed?' Karen asked. 'Wednesday? Thursday?'

'Thursday evening.'

The nurse glanced at the report. 'Danielle worked that night. In fact, she pulled a double, working night shift on Thursday and day shift on Friday.'

'What time is night shift?'

'Seven to seven.'

D.D. considered the matter. The Harringtons had presumably died around dinnertime. Considering how long it would take to subdue an entire family, clean up, make it from Dorchester to Cambridge . . . 'What time did she clock in?' D.D. asked.

'Danielle arrived at six-thirty and prepared for her shift.'

'And Friday night?'

Karen thinned her lips. 'Technically speaking, Danielle concluded her day shift at seven p.m. She remained on the unit, however, debriefing with me, then catching up on paperwork until after eleven. At which time she was involved in an altercation with Lucy, who had a violent episode.'

'The bruises on Danielle's neck,' D.D. said, remembering.

'Exactly. So while Danielle was not on the clock, she was here, and I have it documented, per hospital policy.'

D.D.'s turn to thin her lips. Meaning Danielle had alibis for both the Harrington and Laraquette-Solis murders.

'She was working last night when Lucy disappeared,' D.D. said.

'Correct.'

'Now, call me crazy, but you're saying she worked Thursday night, Friday day — lingering until after eleven p.m. — then was back-for Saturday night shift. That's a lot of hours in a short span of time.'

'Our staff tends to lump their shifts, pulling doubles in order to maximize their days off. Work-three-days, play-five kind of thing.'

D.D. stared at the nurse administrator.

'Danielle is also a workaholic,' Karen conceded. 'Particularly this time of year.'

'Who else knows her history?' D.D. asked.

'Everyone.'

'Everyone?'

'She's infamous, even by our drama-rich standards. Most of the parents hear about her past sooner or later, as well. Gossip, rumors. People are people.'

'What about Gym Coach Greg? Was he working Thursday night? Or Friday?'

A fresh perusal of the time sheet. 'Not

Thursday night. On Friday, he had the day shift. Seven a.m. to seven p.m. Of course, he was also working last night, when Lucy . . . ' The nurse's voice trailed off.

D.D. digested that. So Danielle had an alibi for the Harrington and Laraquette-Solis murders, but not Greg. Good to know. She adopted her conversational tone again. 'So who do you think'll be next?'

'Excuse me?'

D.D. shrugged. 'The Harringtons were murdered Thursday night. The Laraquette-Solis family was murdered Friday night. Lucy was hanged Saturday night.' D.D. glanced at her watch. 'It's now nearly five o'clock. I figure we got, what, one hour, two, three, then it's time for Sunday-night action. Another child here? Another family out there? Clock's ticking. Place your bets.'

Karen stared at her, wide-eyed.

'You think I'm messing around?' D.D. asked. 'You think I have nothing better to do than terrorize a bunch of hardworking professionals on a pediatric psych ward? Families are *dying*. Children are being *murdered*. Now, start telling me what the fuck is going on, so my squad can shut it down. Five o'clock, Karen. Don't ask me who'll be dead by six.'

Then, almost as if someone had heard her words, the first scream sounded from outside the Admin area. It was followed by a second, a third. High-pitched, frantic wails that swiftly disintegrated into a whole chorus of terrified shrieks.

'Common area,' Karen said immediately. She

was already out of her chair, grabbing the keys around her neck, running for the door.

D.D. was right on her heels. She could just make out words now. 'Devil!' the children were screaming. '*Diablo. Está aquí. Está aquí.* The Devil is here.'

28

VICTORIA

I dream of distant beaches. Of silky white sand that sinks beneath my feet. Of turquoise waves rocking against the shoreline. Of a deep-orange sun warming my upturned face.

I dream of walking with my husband, hand in hand.

Our children are running ahead, laughing together happily. Evan's golden curls stand out in the bright sunlight, Chelsea's darker-topped head bent near his. They dig a hole with a stick, just out of reach of the lapping ocean.

Then Evan reaches over and casually pushes his sister into the hole. The sand collapses, swallowing her in one greedy gulp. Laughing, Evan runs back toward us. Now I realize he doesn't hold a stick, but a long pointed blade. He aims it at his father, and picks up speed, the phantom dancing in his eyes as he races across the opalescent beach.

'You're mine,' he says to me as he runs his father through. 'You will always be mine.'

Then he advances with the bloody sword . . .

* * *

I wake up to a strange beeping sound. The high-pitched tone hurts my ears. I squeeze my eyes shut as if that will dull the sound. It doesn't, so I open them again, becoming aware of many things at once.

I'm in a hospital room. My side aches with a nearly impossible pain. Monitors surround me, with wires and lines sprouting from my left hand. I'm hot. I'm confused. I have no idea what has happened to me.

Then I discover belatedly that Michael's asleep in a chair next to my bed.

While I stare at him in bewilderment, he slowly rouses, glancing at me, then performing a double-take when he realizes I'm awake.

'Victoria?' he says in a raspy voice.

'Evan?' I ask in panic.

Immediately, Michael's face shudders. He climbs out of the chair, wearing the same khaki shorts and Brooks Brothers shirt he wore to my house. This confuses me more. What day is it? What's happened to me?

'How do you feel?' he asks, crossing to the bed, glancing at the monitors, as if they mean something to him.

I swallow once, twice, three, times. 'Th- thirsty.'

'I'll ring for a nurse.'

I nod. He pushes a button. 'Evan?' I try again.

'He's okay.'

'Chelsea?'

'She's at home. With Melinda. What do you remember?'

I shake my head. I don't remember. But then it comes back to me. Sitting down on the couch next to my sun-drunk child. Feeling a little sleepy. The sudden pain in my side . . .

My hand drops down to my ribs. Sure enough, my left side is covered in a swathe of gauze. I don't have to touch it to feel the pain, the red, swollen mess of it. My son stabbed me.

'The knife penetrated your liver,' Michael tells me, as if reading my thoughts. 'If the EMTs hadn't gotten you here in time for emergency surgery, you would've died.'

'Evan?' I ask for the third time.

'Do you understand me, Victoria? You would've *died.*'

A nurse appears. She bustles in, picking up my wrist, checking my pulse even though some cumbersome plastic object attached to my fingertip must be telling her the same thing. 'How do you feel?' she asks, studying the monitors.

'Thirsty.'

'I can bring you ice chips. If you hold those down, next we can attempt water. Sound like a plan?'

I nod. She exits, returning quickly with half a cup of ice chips. I take them sparingly, realizing the increasing discomfort in my abdomen. I've never been good with anesthesia. Ice chips probably are the best I can do.

'Doctor will be in to talk to you shortly,' she says. Then the nurse is gone and Michael and I are staring at each other again.

'Thank you for coming,' I manage. I don't know what else to say.

He shrugs. 'Someone had to come. It was either me or your mother.'

We both know what he means. My mother would've pulled the plug. I'm not a daughter to her. More like the competition. At least I used to be. It's been so long since she's visited me or her grandkids, she has no idea how far I've fallen.

'Evan?' I try yet again.

'Evan's okay.'

'He didn't mean to — ' I start.

Michael holds up a hand. His face is the angriest I've ever seen. 'You know why I left?' he said abruptly. 'You know why I took Chelsea and got the hell out of our home?'

I shake my head. His anger frightens me.

'Because I figured it was only a matter of time before I had to kill my son in order to protect my wife and daughter. And call me crazy, but I didn't want to kill Evan. Dammit, I love him, too, Victoria. I've *always* loved him, too.'

I don't know what to say.

'Do you know what you've done to him?' he continues, the force of his emotions causing his voice to tremble. 'He's eight, and he now has to deal with the knowledge that he stabbed his own mother. That he nearly killed you. He's just a kid, for Christ's sake. How's he supposed to handle that? With everything else going on in his fucked-up head, how the hell is he ever supposed to deal with *that*?'

I don't know what to say.

'I thought you'd died. I got the call, and the way the emergency room nurse was talking . . . I raced all the way here thinking you were dead. That Evan had murdered you. Then I run into the emergency room, and the police have a million questions and the doctors have a million questions. I can't even see you; you've already been whisked away to the operating room. And Evan's shackled to a hospital bed. They've got him cuffed and everything. My son. My little boy . . . '

Michael's voice breaks. He turns away from me, walks toward the wall, and stares at it for a bit.

'I had to call Darren,' he says at last, referring to an old college friend who'd become an attorney. 'I had to get legal advice for Evan. That's where we are with things, Victoria.'

'He didn't mean — ' I try again.

Michael whirls around. '*Shut up*. Just shut up. I don't care that you're hurt. I don't care that you almost died. I want to hurt you worse, Victoria. I want to slap you until you realize once and for all that your denial is destroying our son. Evan did mean to hurt you. He intentionally stole that goddamn knife out of the drying rack. He cleverly slipped it inside the fabric on the underside of the sofa, where you wouldn't find it. And he carefully retrieved it during an opportune moment, just so he could drive it through your ribs.'

'How do you know all that? How can you possibly know?'

'Because he told me.'

I stare at him, slack-jawed, disbelieving.

'He's broken. He answered my questions by rote. There's no light in his eyes. He stabbed you, but he broke himself. And I don't know if

362

we'll get him back. Sure this was better than an institution, Vic?'

The bitterness of his words hurts, just as he intends. I feel the full force of his helplessness. The buried rage from all the times I overrode him, shut him out of the parenting process because I didn't agree with his solutions, couldn't let go of my own notions of what was best for my child. I'm the nurturer. Michael, the fixer. We were doomed from the start.

'Did . . . did they arrest Evan?' I ask, shifting a little in the bed, trying to get comfortable. I feel queasy, but that might be from the conversation as much as the aftereffects of the anesthesia.

'I'm sure an arrest warrant is only a matter of time. At the moment, however, given his fragile mental state, he's been hospitalized.'

I stare at him in confusion. 'Where?'

'Upstairs. Turns out this medical center has a locked-down pediatric psych ward on the eighth floor. Evan's now a patient.'

My eyes widen. Once again Michael holds up a hand. 'I don't want to hear it. I had Darren pull our divorce decree. I still have custodial rights to Evan and, given your current physical and emotional state, I'll take you to court and demand full custody if I have to. Our son's experienced a psychotic break. He's upstairs and he's gonna stay there.'

'He's just a child — '

'Which is why it's a pediatric ward. And, since you asked so nicely, it's an excellent acute-care program. Highly recommended, considered very progressive in its approach to mentally ill kids.

You can visit anytime you want, assuming you get yourself healed enough to get out of bed.'

'Bastard.'

'I wish I'd become one sooner,' he says flatly. 'Maybe then we could've avoided this.'

'I'm not a bad mom,' I whisper after a moment. It seems a stupid thing to say, given that I've just been stabbed by my own child.

But Michael seems to understand. His face smooths, some of the tension seeps from his shoulders. He sighs, rubs his forehead. Sighs again. 'No, you're not a bad mom, Vic. And I'm not a bad dad, and Evan, when he's Evan, is not a bad kid. And yet, here we are.'

'What will happen next?'

'I don't know.'

'I won't press charges,' I state defiantly. 'They can't arrest him without me, right?' My stomach rolls. I am going to vomit.

Michael, however, shakes his head. 'Not that simple, Vic. He stabbed you, then confessed to the police. Those officers will prepare affidavits. Those affidavits can be used by the prosecutor to demand an arrest warrant. According to Darren, the court will probably be willing to accept Evan being held in a mental institution versus a juvenile center for the time being. So that's step one. Next, we let the legal process grind along while focusing on improving Evan's state of mind. If we can show he's more stable, the court may be more forgiving. Maybe. But it's going to take time, Vic. Time for him, time for you, time for the legal system. We're in it for a bit.'

I cringe at what that means. Evan staying in a

locked-down ward. My son, eight years old and institutionalized indefinitely.

My turn to look away, to study the white walls.

So many things I want to tell my son. That I love him. That I still believe in him. I'm not in denial. I've seen the darkness in his eyes. But I've seen the light, too. I've seen all the moments that Evan got to be Evan, and I wouldn't have missed those moments for anything.

Something occurs to me. I turn my head to peer at my husband. 'You said I was lucky the EMTs got me to the hospital in time. But how did they know? Who called them?'

Michael sticks his hands in his pockets. 'Evan,' he says at last. 'He dialed nine-one-one, told the operator he'd stabbed his mother. He said you were bleeding and needed help.'

'He tried to save me.'

'Maybe. Maybe not. The operator asked him what happened. You know what he said?'

I shook my head, bewildered.

'He said the Devil made him do it. And he said the ambulance had better come quick, because the Devil wasn't finished yet.'

29

DANIELLE

When Aunt Helen opened the door, first thing I noticed was her red-rimmed eyes. She tried to hide her tears. Brushed at her cheeks, ran her fingers through her short brown hair. Her cheeks remained wet, her face blotchy. She noticed that I noticed and, for both our sakes, gave up on pretense. She gestured for me to come in.

She'd moved out of her downtown condo years ago. Now she had a newer townhouse just outside the city limits. Lower maintenance as she approached the downsizing phase of life. She'd retired from her corporate-lawyer gig years ago. Instead, she worked thirty hours a week for a nonprofit that specialized in promoting better rights, funding, and legislation for abused and at-risk kids. She liked the work, she said, precisely because it was a one-eighty from her previous career. She'd gone from protecting the fat cats to fighting for children's rights.

You'd think this would give us more in common, easy conversation for the few nights a month we shared dinner. Instead, neither of us ever talked about work. Maybe we had those kinds of jobs; you had to leave them at the office, or you'd go nuts.

'Coffee?' she asked, leading me into the small but expensively appointed kitchen.

'Whiskey,' I replied.

Sadly, she thought I was joking. She poured us both glasses of water. I didn't think that was strong enough for what I needed to do next.

She carried the glasses to another small but beautifully decorated room. The sitting area featured gleaming hardwood floors, a white-painted fireplace mantel, and a vaulted ceiling. Off the family room was a screened-in porch that overlooked a stretch of wetlands. Earlier in the summer, we'd sat on that porch and watched for herons. This late in August, however, it was too hot and sticky.

We perched on the L-shaped sofa, I sipped my water and felt the ceiling fan brush freshly chilled air across my cheeks. Aunt Helen didn't speak right away. Her hands were trembling on her glass. She wouldn't meet my eyes, but gazed at the floor.

This time of year always hit her harder than it did me. Maybe because she gave herself the permission to grieve, to release the floodgates one week out of every year. She cried, raged, blew off steam. Then she picked up the pieces and returned to the business of living.

I couldn't do it. Never could. I didn't want to release the floodgates; I was afraid I'd never get them closed again. Plus, all these years later, I remained mostly angry. Deeply, deeply enraged. Which was why I rarely visited my aunt around the anniversary. It was too hard for me to watch her weep, when I wanted to shatter everything in her house.

My visit today had probably surprised her. She

367

twisted her water glass between her fingers, waiting for me to speak.

'Doing okay?' I asked at last. Stupid question.

'You know,' she replied with a small shrug. Better answer. I did know.

I cleared my throat, looked out the sunny bank of windows. Unexpectedly, my eyes stung and I fought through the choke hold of strangling emotion.

'Something's happened,' I managed at last.

She stopped fiddling with her water glass and studied me. And suddenly, I was staring at my mother's blue eyes. I was standing in the doorway of my mother's bedroom, holding my father's gun behind my back, while I tried to muster the courage for what I needed to say next.

'He hurt me,' I heard myself whisper.

'Danielle?' My aunt's voice, my mother's voice. They ran together, two women, both who'd claimed to love me.

I licked my lips, forced myself to keep talking, 'My father. On the nights when he drank a lot . . . sometimes he came to my room in the middle of the night.'

'Oh Danielle.'

'He said if I did what he wanted, he wouldn't have to drink so much. He'd be happy. Our family would be happy.'

'Oh Danielle.'

'I tried, in the beginning, I thought, if I just made him happy, I wouldn't have to hear my mom cry at night. Things would get better. Everything would be all right.'

My aunt didn't speak, just regarded me with my mother's sorrowful blue eyes.

'But it got worse. And he drank more, came in more often. I couldn't do it. Couldn't take it. I went to Mom's room that night. To tell her what he was doing. And I brought his gun with me.'

'You threatened Jenny?' my aunt asked in confusion. 'You were going to shoot your mother?'

'No, I threatened my father. I told my mom that if she didn't make him stop, I was going to shoot him. That was my plan. Not bad for a kid, huh?'

'Oh Danielle. What happened?'

'He came home while we were talking. He was drunk, calling our names. We listened to him come up the stairs. Mom demanded that I give her the gun. She said she'd take care of everything. She'd help me. She promised. I just had to give her the gun.'

'What did you do?'

'I handed her his gun. Then I bolted down the hall and hid under the covers in my bedroom. I didn't come out until . . . afterward.'

My aunt took a shaky breath, released it. She set her water glass on the coffee table, then stood, walking a few steps toward the window. My aunt wasn't a restless person. Her actions now distracted me, made me study her intently. She wouldn't look at me. She stared out at the sun-bleached wetlands, where the birds had to be more comforting than our current conversation.

'You think it's your fault, what your father

369

did,' she said, softly.

'I was a kid. Can't be my fault.'

She turned, smiling wanly at me. The first tear trickled down her cheek. She wiped it away, crossing her arms over her chest. 'Dr. Frank taught you well.'

'He should've; you paid him enough.'

'Do you hate me, too, Danielle? Are my sister's failings my own?'

'Did you *know*? You've been so adamant about therapy all these years. Did my Mom tell you what he was doing?'

Slowly, Aunt Helen shook her head. Then she caught herself, a second tear trickling down, a second tear wiped away. 'I didn't know about the abuse. I suspected. Dr. Frank suspected. But, Danielle, not everything going on in your family had something to do with you.'

'I told on him. I tried to make it stop and everyone died. My mom, Johnny, Natalie. If I hadn't said anything . . . if I'd just kept trying to make him happy . . . '

'Your father was a self-centered son of a bitch. No one could make him happy. Not Jenny, not his kids, not all the second chances Sheriff-Wayne gave him. Don't pin this on yourself.'

'It wasn't fair, especially for Natalie and Johnny. I can hate my mom. Some nights I do. She stayed with him. Worse, she took the gun from me. If she'd let me keep it and go with plan A . . . So during my bad moments, I tell myself mom got what she deserved. But Natalie and Johnny — ' My voice broke. I got up and paced. 'They died because they poked their heads out

370

of their rooms. And I lived because I was too scared to get out of bed. It's not fair, and no number of passing years changes that.'

'Danielle, I don't know exactly what happened that night. I can't tell you who did what to whom and I won't tell you any of it was fair. But you're wrong about your mother. She'd had enough. The day before your father . . . did what he did, Jenny called me. She wanted the name of a good divorce lawyer. She planned on kicking your father out. She'd had enough.'

'What?'

My aunt hesitated, then seemed to reach some kind of decision. 'She'd met someone. A good man, she told me. A good man who was willing to help her. She just needed to get her ducks in a row. Then she was going to ask your father for a divorce.'

I didn't say anything, just stared at my aunt, stunned.

'It might be,' she continued now, 'that your mother never confronted your father with your accusations. Maybe, after hearing what you had to say, she was angry enough to kick him out that night. Told him she wanted a divorce. And he . . .'

I could see it in my mind's eye. The gun, which I'd carried to the bedroom, now lying on my mother's nightstand. My mother, yelling at my drunken father to get the hell out. My father, caught off guard, enraged by my mother's sudden defiance, seeing his own handgun, reaching for it . . .

Natalie, wondering about the noise, Johnny,

371

curious about the loud pop down the hall.

I loved them. All these years later, I still loved them. If I'd known back then that I had to make the choice between my father's abuse and my family's love, I would've chosen my family. I would've chosen them.

'Danielle,' my aunt tried now, 'it's not your fault.'

'Oh, for fuck's sake. It's been twenty-five years, Will everyone stop telling me that?'

'Will you ever start believing it?'

'We were a family. Everyone's action is someone else's reaction. If he hadn't started drinking, if she hadn't tried to leave him, if I hadn't found his damn gun. We might as well have been a row of dominoes. I carried the gun to my parents' bedroom. I told my mom what he was doing. I tipped the first domino, then we all started to fall.'

'Your *father* is to blame!' my aunt said sharply.

'Because he killed your sister?' I retorted just as sharply. 'Or because he saddled you with his kid?'

My aunt crossed the tiny space in three strides and slapped me. The sting of the blow shocked me. I stared at her, startled by her fury.

'Don't you *dare* talk about yourself that way! Goddammit, Danielle. I have loved you since the day you were born. Just as I loved Jenny, and Natalie and Johnny. I would've taken you all in. I would've stuffed my silly condo to the ceiling with all of you if I'd been given the option. But Jenny had a plan. And being a good older sister, I listened to her

372

plan and trusted her to manage her own life. That's what family does. Her failings aren't my failings, nor are they your failings. Life sucks. Your father was a bastard. Now cry, dammit. Let yourself bawl it all out, Danielle. Then let yourself heal. Your mother would've wanted that. And Natalie and Johnny would've wanted it, too.'

Then, just as quickly as my aunt had slapped me, she wrapped her arms around me and hugged me tight. I didn't pull away. I could only surrender to her, my aunt, my mother. Things got so blurred with the passage of time.

'I love you,' my aunt whispered against my cheek. 'Dear God, Danielle, you are the best thing that ever happened to me, even when you break my heart.'

'I want them back.'

'I know, sweetheart.'

'I can't picture them anymore. I see only you.'

'You don't have to see them, Danielle. Just feel them in your heart.'

'I can't,' I protested. 'It hurts too much. Twenty-five years later, it *aches*.'

'Then feel the pain. No one ever said family didn't hurt.'

But I couldn't. Wouldn't. Instead I was in the bedroom again, handing the gun over to my mother. Trusting the woman with my aunt's eyes to make everything all right.

'*Go to bed, sweetheart*,' she'd whispered. '*Quick. Before he sees you. I'll take care of everything. I promise.*'

My mother taking the gun. My mother setting

it carefully on the nightstand. Where the clock read . . .

I froze. Caught the scene in my head, forced it to rewind. My mother, placing the gun in front of her digital clock, red numbers glowing 10:23 p.m. Myself, scurrying down the hall toward bed, where I pulled the covers over my head and blocked out the rest.

10:23 p.m. I'd talked to my mother at 10:23 p.m.

But according to the police report, my family didn't die until after one a.m., at least two and a half hours later.

I pulled away from my aunt. 'I need to go.'

'Danielle — '

'It's okay. I mean, it's not, but you're right. Someday, it will be. I love you, Aunt Helen. Even when I'm a bitch, I know how lucky I am to have you.'

'Tomorrow,' she said, still holding my hands, 'we'll go together.'

'Tomorrow,' I agreed. Now I pulled my hands free and made my way toward the door, frantic to get out of her house.

I hit the driveway, already punching numbers on my cell phone as I ran for my car. All these years later, I didn't know his number, so I did the sensible thing and dialed the sheriff's office. Then, the second I got someone on the phone: 'I'm looking for Sheriff Wayne. My name is Danielle Burton and I need to speak with him immediately.'

30

Blood. D.D. noticed it first in the common area. It splattered across one table, dotted a nearby wall, then trailed down the carpeted hall.

'Jesus Christ,' D.D. breathed. She'd been wrong. They didn't have until six p.m. The evildoer had already struck, while she'd been chattering away in Admin. Shit.

'The kids,' Karen exclaimed immediately. 'Where are the kids?'

Just then, another rage-filled scream, high and piercing from down the hall: 'No, no, no. Get away. I will kill you. I will EAT YOUR EYEBALLS!'

D.D. and Karen bolted toward the sound, making it partly down the hall before drawing up short. A bathroom loomed to the right. The door was open and an older girl with huge dark eyes and lank brown hair stood in front of the sink, holding a pair of scissors and dripping blood. Outside the bathroom, an older MC was positioned with his hands outstretched, as if to block the girl's escape.

'Don't fucking touch me! I'll punch you in the nuts. I'll rip off your penis!' The shrieks continued farther down the hall. D.D. shook her head in confusion. So far, she heard one extremely pissed-off young boy, and she saw one very bloody young girl. What the hell?

'Come on, Aimee,' the MC was crooning as

D.D. and Karen approached. 'Time to hand over the scissors. Everything's all right. Just take a deep breath and put the scissors down. Nothing we can't handle here, right? You and me, a few of your favorite coloring books — '

'*I WILL DRINK YOUR BLOOD!*' the distant boy roared.

Aimee held up her left arm and, deliberately, dragged the blade of the scissors down her forearm. A thin line of red bloomed across her skin. She stared at it with rapt fascination. More lines covered both arms, her cheeks, the exposed column of her throat. Her skin looked like a crazy quilt, seamed with stitches of blood.

A violent crash from the end of the hallway. Something heavy and wooden smashing against a wall. '*DON'T TOUCH ME DON'T TOUCH ME DON'T TOUCH ME.*'

Aimee jerked toward the sound, then promptly sliced open her collarbone.

'Jesus Christ, get the damn scissors,' D.D. commanded. 'What are you waiting for?'

Karen, however, placed a quieting hand on her shoulder.

'Ed?' the nurse manager asked softly.

'Aimee didn't start it,' the MC murmured back. 'Not sure what happened. New kid arrived. Greg was escorting him through the unit, when all of a sudden Benny bolted across the common area into a wall. That set off Jimmy, who started tossing chairs, and everything disintegrated from there. I was trying to get Jamal back to his room. Cecille had Jimmy in a bear hug, Greg was trying to get the new kid tucked away. Andrew came out to see what he could do, and Jorge socked him in the eye.'

'*NO NO NO NO NOOOOOOOO!*'

'Jorge?' Karen asked in shock. 'Hit *Andrew?*'

'Solid right hook. Who knew? Fortunately, Lightfoot is, as his name implies, light on his feet. He started working with Jorge. I returned from tending Jamal and, lo and behold, discovered that during the ruckus, our friend Aimee got her hands on a pair of scissors.'

'How? We keep the craft supplies locked up.'

Ed stopped staring at Aimee long enough to give his boss an exasperated stare. 'News flash, Karen, we're not exactly at the top of our game. Unit's a little funky, and that was *before* Benny tried to fly through Sheetrock.'

'BITCH BITCH BITCH, I WILL RIP OFF YOUR EARS. I WILL BEAT YOUR BRAINS. MASH THEM UP. BRAIN SMOOTHIE. ADD BANANAS. YUM YUM YUM.'

'Oh no.' D.D. finally figured out who was screaming. Benny. The small, dark-eyed boy who liked mashing fruit and playing with cars and making airplane noises. She could tell by Karen's resigned expression that the head nurse already knew, had figured it out way before D.D. A day in the life.

Ed returned his attention to Aimee, whose dark eyes glazed over as she ran the open scissors along a vein in her neck.

'Hey, Aimee,' Ed said, voice sharper now, commanding the girl's attention. 'I know your safety plan requests that you not be touched. You want to be talked through these episodes. But we're nearing the end of talking here. What are the rules of this unit? We treat ourselves and one another with respect. You're not showing yourself respect. You're hurting yourself, and you're ignoring my orders. You have until the count of ten, Aimee. Then I come in after you.'

More crashing. Fresh screams, not Benny's but another child's as the agitation spread from room to room. Aimee calmly lifted her left hand and sliced open her palm. She inspected the wound, then added a second.

'Take her out,' D.D. hissed in Karen's ear, practically dancing on the balls of her feet with the need for action. 'I'll grab her, you grab the scissors. Come on!'

Karen curled her fingers on D.D.'s forearm and didn't let go. 'The cuts are mostly shallow and will heal. Betray a child's trust, however, and we lose months of hard work . . . '

'She's filleting her own skin — '

'Five, six, seven . . . ' Ed intoned.

'No, no, no,' another child wailed down the hall. 'Won't do it! Can't make me, YOU FUCKING CUNT!'

'Shhh, shhh, shhh . . . '

'¡Diablo, Diablo, Diablo!'

D.D. didn't think she could take it. She needed to tackle Aimee and grab the scissors. She needed to dash down the hall and take down crazy Benny. So many places to be, so many things to do. More screaming. Fresh cries. A dark-eyed girl making happy with craft scissors . . .

'Eight, nine, ten,' Ed completed.

The MC squared his shoulders, took a determined step forward. Aimee raised the scissors. She held them aloft, right above her heart, and in that instant of time, D.D. knew exactly what the girl was going to do.

D.D. started to cry, '*Stop!*' Started to dash forward.

Aimee's white hand flashed down, bloody scissors slicing through the air —

'*I WILL GET YOU ALL. I WILL KILL EVERY LAST ONE OF YOU. JUST YOU WAIT JUST YOU WAIT JUST YOU WAIT. I WILL HAVE MY REVENGE —*'

Ed grabbed Aimee's wrist. The burly MC twisted the small girl's arm behind her back as quickly and effectively as any cop. The girl cried out once. The scissors clattered to the floor. Aimee slumped forward, all fight draining from her body.

'I'll grab bandages,' Karen said.

While down the hall came a fresh burst of screams.

★ ★ ★

It took an hour to restore the unit. Children were medicated; soothed with music; bribed with Game Boys; placated with small, quiet spaces; and read endless stories. D.D. paced. Banned from the action, treated as the inexperienced outsiders they were, she and her investigative team prowled the classroom end of the unit, trying to read files, but mostly twitching as various screams, crashes, and thuds echoed across the ward.

379

D.D. couldn't sit. Neither could Alex. They roamed the lower hallway, feeling as agitated as the kids.

'Negative energy,' Alex told her, hands deep in his front pockets, restlessly jiggling his loose change.

'Fuck you.'

'Just proved my point.'

'Still fuck you.'

'No inner angel?'

'I will strangle you with my bare hands.'

'Again, score one for the shaman. I haven't felt a vibe this bad since I visited Souza-Baranowski.' The Souza-Baranowski Correctional Center was Massachusetts's maximum security prison.

'This is what happens at institutions. One person goes crazy, everyone goes crazy.'

'From shared negative energy,' Alex chirped.

'Seriously, I will strangle you.'

'Or we could find a broom closet and have sex.'

D.D. drew up short. Blinked several times. Was genuinely shocked by how instantaneously she wanted to do exactly that. Rip off Alex's shirt. Dig her fingers into his shoulders. Ride him like a —

Her expression must've given her away, because his eyes darkened. 'As much as I'd like to take credit for the look on your face, I think it's score two for the shaman. In the midst of the negative, we are drawn to the positive. Each action calling for an equal level of reaction.'

'Every act of destruction calling for an equal act of creation?'

'Hell yeah. In a broom closet.'

'Deal.'

Or not. The unit doors opened and Danielle Burton strode into the common area. The nurse spotted the blood and stopped short, just as Andrew Lightfoot appeared in the hall.

D.D. motioned to Alex. They drew back quietly and got ready for the show.

★　★　★

'What happened?' Danielle demanded. 'Who's hurt? How bad?'

'Aimee got her hands on a pair of scissors,' Lightfoot provided, walking toward the dark-haired nurse. He came to a halt just a foot away from Danielle, taking a long drink from his water bottle. He studied her intently. She took a noticeable step back.

'Is Aimee okay?' Danielle asked, refusing to meet Lightfoot's gaze.

'Well enough,' the healer murmured, dropping his water bottle to his side. 'The milieu went acute, each child going off like firecrackers. I'd like to say there were many learning opportunities, but I'm not sure. The energy here . . . it is all wrong. Toxic. I've spent hours trying to cleanse the girl's room. I can't make headway, I'm too spent for this deep a taint.'

'You were working in Lucy's room?' Danielle asked sharply.

'At Karen's request.'

'You didn't know her.'

'I've met her soul on the interplanes. She said

to tell you thank you.'

'Stop.' Danielle walked away, setting her bag down on one of the tables. For the first time, she noticed D.D. and Alex, standing at the classroom end of the hallway, 'Don't you have work to do?' Danielle asked them pointedly.

'Doing it,' D.D. replied. She and Alex remained in place.

'How are you feeling, Danielle?' Lightfoot asked.

'Just fine,' she bit out.

'It's not polite to lie.'

'It's not polite to pretend you know me better than I do.'

'If you feel that I'm overstepping, then I apologize. It's never my intention to cause you discomfort.' Lightfoot positioned himself closer to Danielle, sticking one hand in the pocket of his white linen trousers, the other tapping his water bottle against his leg.

Despite his earlier assertion that his interest in Danielle was purely professional, D.D. decided his gaze looked awfully personal. As if he wanted to step closer to the young nurse, savor the scent of her skin.

Danielle, on the other hand, clearly didn't return the sentiment. She marched over to a set of cabinets, unlocked them, and started to pull out cleaning supplies. She snapped on plastic gloves, then grabbed a disinfectant spray.

'Clean or bounce,' she informed Lightfoot. 'Those are the choices.' She turned to D.D. and Alex. 'That goes for you two, as well. This is a working psych ward, not an after-dinner show.

Earn your keep, or get lost.'

D.D. looked at Alex. He shrugged his agreement, so they crossed the common area and helped themselves to cleaning supplies. A small price to pay.

Apparently, Andrew thought the same. He got his hands on a roll of paper towels. 'Your father *needs* to talk to you — ' he started, his attention back on Danielle.

'Not interested.'

'Hatred is a negative energy, Danielle. Denying him only hurts yourself.'

'Stop it. We've already had this conversation. Your mumbo jumbo is your business. I'm not going there. For God's sake, didn't you do enough damage with Ozzie?'

Lightfoot frowned. D.D. perked up.

'Ozzie made remarkable progress,' the healer told Danielle. 'His entire family was on the path to becoming more centered and loving — '

'His entire family is dead.'

'I don't know what happened, but I'm sure it wasn't Ozzie's fault.'

'You're sure? How? Ozzie's soul tell you that on the interplanes?'

Good question, D.D. thought.

'Unfortunately,' Lightfoot said, 'while souls enter this plane to experience the corporal world, once they leave they show little interest in the physical realities encountered here. Ozzie's soul is not fixated on corporal death. Instead, he's moved on to the next set of desired experiences. Which is how it should be.'

'Really?' Danielle mocked, starting to scrub

the nearest table. 'So Ozzie, a young boy who was brutally murdered, has already moved on, but my father, twenty-five years later, still wants to chat.'

Lightfoot shrugged. 'Your father's soul has unfinished business. The lesson has not been learned. The experience isn't completed.'

'And Lucy?'

'I dreamt of her last night,' Lightfoot said. 'She was dancing among the moonbeams of my mind. I knew immediately she was someone special, a being of incredible light and love. She told me she loves you. And she asked me to help you. She worries about you, senses the sadness in your heart.'

'Yeah? Did she tell you who killed her, too? Or is that too mundane a topic for your higher mind?'

D.D. looked expectantly at Lightfoot. Another excellent question.

'Death is merely a transition,' Lightfoot started, and across the table from D.D., Danielle rolled her eyes. D.D. found herself liking the nurse more than she should.

Lightfoot remained steadfast, 'The unit is acute. You must find your forgiveness, Danielle. You must open your heart to love. Let go of your past. If you don't, the dark forces will win.'

'And now a message from our sponsor,' Danielle said, 'Hello, One-Nine-Hundred Rent A Soul? My boyfriend has a thing for asps, so for next Friday night, can I borrow Cleopatra?'

'I'm not joking,' Andrew said stiffly.

'Neither am I.'

'He has unbelievable power, Danielle.'

'Who?'

'You tell me.'

Lightfoot stared at the nurse. The nurse stared back at him. Slowly but surely, Danielle set down her cleaning supplies.

'You want to help someone, Andrew, pick a room, any room. The kids need you. I don't.'

'It's bad and it's going to get worse.'

'Then go work a little voodoo. In your own words, life is about choice, and I don't choose you.'

Lightfoot thinned his lips. His eyes flashed darkly. Slowly but surely, he turned and stalked down the hall. Upon reaching Lucy's room, he glanced over his shoulder one last time at Danielle. Then he disappeared inside.

D.D. released a breath she hadn't realized she'd been holding.

'I take it you don't care for woo-woo,' D.D. said.

'No, I don't.' The nurse gathered her cleaning supplies. 'Unfortunately, Andrew's not wrong about everything.' She started scrubbing a bloody wall. 'Man, this place is fucked up.'

31

DANIELLE

'Did you come back just for me?' the sergeant asked a few minutes later. We'd finished cleaning and were now combining smaller tables to form a larger rectangle for the upcoming staff meeting. The other detective, the George Clooney look-alike, had taken over scrubbing the blood out of the carpet. Kept him busy, but also within earshot. D.D. continued, 'Because I'd love to speak with you.'

'I'm here for the debriefing,' I said stiffly, fitting in the final table. 'Karen said I could attend.'

'Gonna mention the anniversary, Danielle? You remember that twenty-five years ago your father gunned down your family?'

The sergeant was goading me. I understood that, and still had to work not to rise to the bait. I noticed some blood droplets on the far window, picked up the Windex, and got busy again.

For the past twenty-five years, I thought I'd done okay. I'd gotten myself through college. I'd landed a job that I loved, and three hundred and sixty days out of the year, I was pretty solid, I didn't replay the events of one night over and over again. I didn't dredge up old photos of my family. I didn't recall the stink of whiskey on my

386

father's breath and I didn't fixate on the weight of a nine-millimeter gun in a child's hands.

I worked with my kids. And I made it a point not to look back.

Until one goddamn week a year.

I felt inundated with my family these days. Scalded by memories I'd made it a point not to remember. And suddenly flush with new information. My mom had been leaving my dad? She'd found a 'good guy'? Maybe my father had slaughtered everyone over her affair, instead of my rebellion?

I didn't know, and for the first time, I was desperate to speak with someone about my past. I'd tried Sheriff Wayne, wanting to ask exactly what time he'd arrived at the house that night. Could it really have been two and half hours between my conversation with my mom and my father opening fire?

A police receptionist had informed me that Sheriff Wayne had passed away two years ago. Died in his sleep. I couldn't believe it. Sheriff Wayne was supposed to live forever. He owed it to me.

Now there was only Aunt Helen and myself who remembered my mother's smile, my sister's giggle, my brother's goofy grin. It wasn't enough. I needed more people. I needed more information.

'Tell us about Lightfoot,' D.D. prodded, behind me. 'Is it just me, or is he way into you?'

I stopped wiping windows, turning around enough to meet the detective's eye. 'Andrew and I are not, and never were, *an item*. We had one date, which he spent grilling me about my father. Call me old-fashioned, but I don't consider discussions of my homicidal parental unit to be a turn-on. That was the beginning and end of our *personal* relationship right there.'

'He's solely interested in your father?'

'From what I can tell, I represent some kind of celestial challenge. If Andrew can get me to forgive my father, to open my heart to the light, then, hey, he can convert anyone. Score one for the good guys.'

'But you don't want to forgive your father.'

'Nope. I'm comfortable hating him. No need for group hugs on the mumbo-jumbo superhighway.'

D.D. arched a brow. 'Is that what Lightfoot wants to do? Arrange a 'meeting' on the spiritual interplanes?'

'That's the drift. If you want the details, better ask him, not me. I'm not buying what he's selling.'

'Did Greg have any better luck?'

That detective's transition was so smooth, I almost spoke first and thought later. At the last second, I caught myself. 'Greg and I are friends.'

'Friends with privileges?'

'Hardly.'

'Friends who go to bars? Friends who bare their souls?'

'Friends who share an occasional pizza. This job wears you out. Not a lot left over for post-work rendezvous.'

'You left with Greg today,' the detective

replied evenly. 'Looked pretty comfortable doing it, too.'

The statement caught me off guard. But of course the cops were interviewing everyone in the hospital, and it wasn't like Greg and I crept away in the still of the night. Any number of people could've seen us leaving together and reported it.

'Greg walked me out,' I conceded. 'He's thoughtful that way.'

'And drove you home?'

'He drove me to his place.'

'That's sounding personal again.'

'We talked. He knows this time of year is rough for me.'

'I wouldn't mind crying on his shoulder,' the sergeant commented.

I couldn't help myself: 'He's a little young for you, don't you think?'

'Meee-oww,' the sergeant drawled, clearly amused by my cattiness. 'Word on the street is that Greg's been chasing you for years. He finally get to cross the finish line, Danielle?'

I wouldn't even dignify that with a response. Mostly because I didn't want to think of my morning with Greg. I had been rejecting him for years. Only to finally go to his place, and have him reject me.

'Look,' I said impatiently, 'I don't have relationships. I work with kids, and I leave the personal crap alone. End of story.'

'I don't think so.'

'What do you mean?'

D.D. tilted her head, regarding me curiously.

389

'Two families connected to this unit have been murdered, almost exactly twenty-five years after your family was shot to death. And last night, the child you were working most closely with was hanged. You still don't think that has anything to do with *you?*'

I felt my heart spike, then the blood drain from my face. 'But . . . My past is over. My family's gone. Who's left to hurt me?'

'Good question,' the sergeant mused. 'Who's left to hurt you?'

I didn't have an answer for her. This couldn't be about me. *I didn't have the gun this time*, I wanted to blurt out. *I swear, I didn't have the gun*.

'I need to review a report,' I mumbled, then I bolted from the common area. I couldn't be in front of the police anymore. I didn't want them to see the horror on my face. I didn't want them to misinterpret my regret.

* * *

Fifteen minutes later, staff members began to assemble in the common area. It was nearly eleven-thirty, everyone running late. Given earlier events, that was hardly a surprise. The unit still felt wonky. I couldn't remember a time when we'd had so many acute episodes back-to-back. I couldn't remember a time when all of us felt as jittery as the kids.

I remained in Admin, watching from the observation window. The cops had finally disappeared. I could join the MCs at the table, but suddenly I felt self-conscious. The sergeant had put thoughts in my head, like maybe this was all my fault, like maybe I was to blame for Lucy's death.

I was waiting for Greg, I realized. I was waiting for his presence to ground me.

When five more minutes passed without him appearing, I went looking for him.

I wandered down the hall, past children sleeping in various nooks and crannies, past doors of darkened rooms and past doors of hundred-watt brilliance. I didn't see Greg, but then I heard his unmistakable baritone coming from the last room on the right.

I peered in. Greg was sitting on the floor, his legs sprawled in front of him, his attention focused away from me, on a small boy with bright blonde hair who was curled into a ball. Greg was stroking the boy's head and talking lightly, trying to encourage the boy to uncoil. The boy wasn't buying it.

The new charge, I guessed. The one who'd stabbed his mother this morning. He was tucked in on himself, trying to block everything out. This couldn't be happening to him. This strange room, this strange place, these strange people talking at him over and over again.

'Mommy,' the boy whispered. 'I want my mommy.'

My heart contracted. First words spoken by so many children over so many years. Even from the kids whose mothers beat the shit out of them.

'I know,' Greg replied steadily.

'Take me home.'

'Can't do that, buddy.'

'You could stay with me. Like we've done before.'

I stilled. *Like they'd done before?* I eased back, out of sight of the open doorway.

'You get to stay here for a bit, buddy. We're going to work with you on calming down, on controlling that temper of yours, until you feel stronger, better about yourself. Don't worry. This is a nice place. We'll take good care of you.'

'Mommy,' the boy said again.

Greg didn't reply.

'I hurt her,' the boy murmured. 'Had the knife. Had to use it. Had to, had to.'

The boy sounded mournful. Greg continued his silence, letting the quiet do his work for him.

'I am a naughty, naughty boy,' the child whispered, so low I could barely hear him. 'Nobody loves a boy as naughty as me.'

'You called nine-one-one,' Greg told him. 'That was smart thinking, Evan. A good thing to do.'

'Blood is sticky. Warm. Didn't know she'd bleed like that. I think I ruined the sofa.' Suddenly, the boy started to cry. 'Greg, do you think Mommy will hate me? Call her, you must call her. Tell her I'm sorry. It was an accident. I didn't know she'd bleed like that. *I didn't know!*'

The boy's voice picked up dangerously, his agitation spiking. I strode into the room, just as Greg began, 'Evan, I want you to take a deep breath — '

'*I ruined the sofa!*'

'Evan — '

'*I want to go home, go home, go home. I'll be a good boy this time. I promise, I'll be a good boy. No more knives. Just let me go home home home home home.*'

The boy rolled away from Greg, dashing for the doorway. I blocked his way just in time, sticking out my arms. He bounced off me like a rubber ball, crashing into the neighboring wall. Rather than a second escape attempt, he slammed his head against the Sheetrock, a frustrated scream escaping him: '*Ahhhahhhahh-hhahhhhahhh . . .* '

Benadryl? I mouthed to Greg over the noise.

He shook his head. 'Paradoxical reaction. Grab Ativan.'

I rushed down the hall for the meds as Greg tried again in his firm baritone: 'Evan. Listen to me, buddy. Look at me, buddy. Evan . . . '

By the time I returned, Evan had blood running down his nose from a cut on his forehead and Greg was holding out his cell phone, trying to capture the boy's attention. 'Evan. Evan, look at me. We'll call your mom. We'll call her right now. Okay? Just look at me, Evan. Watch me.' Greg punched some numbers into the phone. Evan stopped banging his head long enough to watch, his body shuddering with the effort to stay still. The boy was gone, his blood-rimmed eyes glazed over, his cheeks pale, his hands clenched into rigid fists. Most kids took days to recover from the emotional overload of a psychotic break. Evan, on the other hand, looked ready for round two.

I could feel it again, a wafting chill, like a dark cloud drifting across the sun. I wished I hadn't come here tonight. Something was wrong. Even more wrong than last night, when we found Lucy's body, dangling from the ceiling . . .

A receptionist had picked up at the other end of Greg's cell phone. 'Victoria Oliver,' he requested.

Evan started to dance, blue eyes wild, the blood dripping off the end of his nose, staining his blue-striped shirt. 'Mommy, Mommy, Mommy, Mommy, Mommy.'

'Take your medicine,' Greg told Evan, just as a woman's voice sounded in his phone. 'Victoria?'

'Hello?'

'Meds, Evan.'

Evan whirled on me, nearly toppling me over. I surrendered the paper cup. He popped the Ativan, dancing again as he eyed Greg's phone.

'Victoria,' Greg said again, tucking the phone to his ear. 'This is Greg. I'm here with Evan. I thought . . . He needs to hear that you're all right. And I thought you'd like to know that he's all right. Everything's good here.'

I couldn't catch the reply. Evan was spinning around, a whirling dervish of blonde hair, blue shirt, and red blood.

A rush of frigid air, swirling up my spine, whispering down my arms . . .

'The pediatric psych ward's on the eighth floor,' Greg was saying. 'Yes, it's a lockdown unit. Acute care. We're a good facility, Vic; it'll be okay.'

Vic? How did Greg know where to call Evan's

394

mother? Or that she'd take his call? Trying to contact a parent whose child had stabbed her wasn't the smartest thing in the world. Unless you knew that the parent was open to such a call, and had the mental fortitude to handle it. Unless you knew the parent . . .

I was cold. Very cold. Shivering uncontrollably.

Greg, on the phone: 'Can you . . . are you game? Just for a second. I don't think he can take much . . . No, you need to take care of *you*. *We'll* take care of *him*. Victoria . . . Vic . . . Trust me on this one. Evan needs you healthy. That's what your son needs.'

'Mommy, Mommy, Mommy, Mommy,' Evan whined, still twirling.

Greg held out the phone. 'One sentence, Evan. Listen to your Mom's voice. Know she's all right. Tell her you're all right. Then we're done.'

Evan grabbed the phone. He pressed it to his ear. He smiled, one bright second of relief as he connected to his mother. His posture relaxed, he came down off his toes.

Then, before I could move, before Greg could snatch the phone back:

'I will get you next time, bitch,' Evan snarled into the receiver. 'Next time I will carve out your FUCKING HEART!'

The boy hurtled the phone to the floor, then flung himself at the wall, banging his head savagely.

'Oh Evan,' Greg said tiredly.

I rushed down the hall to get more Ativan.

32

VICTORIA

Knock knock.
  Who's there?
  Evan.
  Evan who?
  Evan, the little boy who loves you.
  Knock knock.
  Who's there?
  Evan.
  Evan who?
  Evan, the little boy who wants to kill you.
  Knock knock. Who's there? Michael, your husband who's going to marry another.
  Knock knock. Who's there? Chelsea, your daughter who thinks you don't love her anymore.
  Knock knock. Knock knock. Knock knock.
  I lie in my hospital bed, watching the green line on my heart monitor. Sounds echo down the crowded floor. Busy nurses, grumpy patients, chirping machines. I fixate on the stark white paint on the wall nearest me. The mirror-bright silver of the bed's guardrails. The heavy black phone, weighing down the blanket on my legs. Then I study the monitor again, amazed at how a heart can remain beating long after it's been broken.
  My side hurts. Red blood flecks the white bandage. A deeper burn stings somewhere on the

inside. Maybe an infection's already building. It'll taint my blood, shut down my vital organs. I'll die in this room, and never have to go home.

Knock knock.

Who's there?

Evan, the little boy who loves you.

Knock knock.

Who's there?

Evan, the little boy who wants to kill you.

Knock knock.

Then it comes to me. Fuzzy at first, but with growing certainty. I don't want to live like this. I don't want to be this person. I don't want to lead this life. I need a new approach, a new attitude. I need to move, even if it kills me, because God knows, I'm already dying on the inside.

I think of summer sand. I remember the first time I held both of my children. And I remember the look on Michael's face the day he left me.

So many dreams that never came true, So much love I gave away, that never returned to me.

Knock knock.

Who's there?

Victoria.

Victoria who?

Well, isn't that the million-dollar question? Victoria who?

I need to get out of here. Then, suddenly, absolutely, I know what I'm going to do.

33

Meditation turned out to be a complicated matter, which must explain why D.D. never did it. There was much settling of oneself into a comfortable position, most of the staff members opting to sit on the floor, the pros in fancy lotus positions, the less converted sprawling casually, their backs against a wall.

Space seemed to matter, people selecting spots where they could be on their own. Even Greg and Danielle, late arrivals to the party, didn't buddy up. Greg positioned himself partway down the hall, while Danielle sat not far from where D.D. was currently standing.

The young nurse glanced at her. Opened her mouth slightly as if to say something. Then her jaw snapped shut. She closed her eyes and tilted her face toward the middle of the common area, where Lightfoot directed efforts in a low, melodic tone.

The shaman sat on top of a table, a bottle of iced green tea positioned within easy reach, a wrist resting on each knee and his fingers pointing up.

He spoke firmly, with a strong cadence. D.D. still thought he looked tired. Then again, it was after midnight now. She and her crew were equally beat, which made this a fun diversion for the evening.

Karen, the nurse manager, sat closest to the

Admin offices. She'd removed her glasses for the occasion. A large bear of a man — Ed, D.D. thought was his name — sat not far from her. The younger MC with the short black hair — Sissy? Cecille? — sat to the left of him. Then came three more MCs and another nurse, Janet. The only person who didn't participate was Tyrone, who had checks duty: Every five minutes, he recorded the location of each child and staff member. Given the kids and staff were currently quiet, the duty had him standing in the middle of the hallway, across from D.D. She felt like they were bookends — the only two vertical people at a horizontal party.

Gang's all here, she thought, and was very curious about what would happen next.

'Slowly inhale,' Lightfoot intoned. 'Feel yourself drawing the breath deep into your lungs, pulling in the air from your toes, bringing it up your entire body, every cell contracting, every pore of your body inhaling a slow rush of fresh oxygen. Still inhaling, for a long count of one, two, three, four, five, six, seven. Now exhale. Push the air out for a shorter count of one, two, three, four, five . . . '

D.D., leaning against the wall with her arms across her chest, found her breathing pattern falling into Lightfoot's hypnotic rhythm. She caught herself, forced a short exhale, and felt light-headed.

Alex had gone to fetch pizza. The taskforce members still had a long night ahead of them; given the earlier disruption with the kids, and now the 'debriefing,' the detectives hadn't had a chance to interview the staff yet. Karen had promised to start sending them MCs, one by one, the moment Lightfoot's session was over. Assuming of course the unit remained under control. Given the fresh rounds of screaming and banging D.D. had heard just ten minutes ago, she wasn't overly optimistic.

Lightfoot needed to live up to his hype or she didn't see how the kids or the staff were getting through the night.

Lightfoot was sweating. D.D. could see beads of moisture forming on his upper lip. Despite his instructions for slow and steady breathing, his own chest moved shallowly, and one hand trembled on top of his knee.

The force of his efforts to stave off so much negative energy? To find the light amidst the dark?

Good Lord, now she was starting to sound like him.

'I want you to release your tension,' Lightfoot instructed, his voice strained. Across from him, Karen opened one eye, frowning at the healer.

'Focus on your toes. Feel the tension in the bottom of each foot. The tight little muscles along the arch of your foot, the tendons moving up your heel. The tiny muscles clenching each toe, digging them into the carpet. Now catch that tension. Relax it, push it out. Feel your toes uncurl, your feet relax comfortably against the carpet. Your heels are soft and pliant, each foot relaxed. You can feel the light, your foot warming, a white glow spreading across the bottom of your heel. Focus on it. Feel it expand, climbing to your ankles, your calves, the bend of your knees.'

The white light had a ways to go. Many muscles had to relax. Many body parts needed to glow. Around the room D.D. could see various staff members giving themselves over to the exercise. Even Danielle appeared fresher, the lines in her forehead smoothing out, her slender wrists resting loosely on her knees.

Lightfoot, on the other hand, looked like hell. He was sweating profusely, his pale yellow Armani shirt blossoming with dark stains. He used the small break between glowing muscle groups to take discreet swigs of iced tea. He had the group relaxing their stomachs now, and the iced tea bottle was nearly empty. D.D. didn't think the healer was going to make it. Did one call for a time-out, a brief intermission, in the midst of meditation? Or did that ruin the moment, like checking your police pager in the middle of sex?

Now, as she watched, he grimaced. Rubbed his chest. Grimaced again. A muscle in his left shoulder did a funny little dance, then relaxed again. Lightfoot took another drink, squeezed his eyes shut, and seemed to settle in.

'Focus on the light,' he intoned. 'The warm glow of light, of love. Feel it expand your rib cage, filling your lungs. Then push it up. Push it into the chambers of your heart. Love is in your heart. Love is pulsing through your veins, pushing out the negativity, filling your limbs with a great weightlessness. Light is love. Love is light. You are flooded with it. You feel it beating in your chest. You feel it pulsing beneath your skin. Your arms want to rise on their own. They are alight with love, weightless with joy.'

Sure enough, around the room, several pairs of arms began to rise up. Not Danielle's, D.D. noticed. And not Karen's. The nurse manager had abandoned the meditation. She was studying Lightfoot instead.

'Warmth,' he intoned. 'Love. Light. Heat. Joy. I release all judgments. I understand I am responsible for all corporal actions and I forgive myself for my sins. I forgive others. I am a being of light. I call upon that light. I call upon the love in this room — ' A sudden spasm crossed his face, peeling his lips back from his teeth. Lightfoot caught the grimace, soldiered on. 'I seek the love of my friends, companions, coworkers — ' His voice broke off again. Both shoulders twitched, his left arm bouncing up from his knee. Then his eyes popped up, and he winced sharply, abandoning all pretense as he brought up a hand to shield his face from the overhead lights.

The break in rhythm caught the attention of others. Danielle opened her eyes. Greg, too. They eyed Lightfoot uncertainly.

Karen was already on her feet, returning her wire-rimmed glasses to her face. 'Andrew?' she asked as a fresh spasm shook his body.

D.D. pushed away from the wall, starting to understand that this was no longer business as usual.

Lightfoot raised his head toward the ceiling, shut his eyes, and bore down, as if fighting some kind of internal war.

'I call upon the LIGHT!' he boomed. 'I am a being of LOVE. I am filled with JOY and PEACE and CONTENTMENT. I release negativity. I cast off all judgment. I feel the love of my friends and community. Their LOVE gives me the strength to PUSH the darkness from this building. There will be no NEGATIVITY. There will be no anger, no PAIN. We are united in the light, filling this space with LOVE, holding this space with LOVE. I call upon THE LIGHT, THE LIGHT, THE LIGH — '

His rising voice broke off. Both hands gripped his face. The next instant, the healer pitched forward, rolling off the edge of the table and flipping onto the floor, where his body convulsed wildly.

'*The light, the light!*' he screamed. '*It's burning my eyes, my eyes!*'

'Code blue!' Karen bellowed, sprinting toward the fallen man. 'Call downstairs. We need a crash cart, *stat!*'

She was already on her knees beside Lightfoot, trying to secure his head in her hands as his body flailed and he beat at her with his hands.

'Bite stick!' Karen demanded, working to peel open one eyelid, check his vitals.

'*Don't touch me don't touch me don't touch. It burns . . .*'

The staff sprang belatedly into action. The nurses, Danielle and Janet, made a beeline for medical supplies. Greg grabbed a phone, while the other MCs pushed back tables, cleared the area. Lightfoot's neck and back arched, muscles

403

coiling and uncoiling rigidly beneath the tan sheath of his skin. Karen finally got his eyelid open. His eye was not rolled back up in his head, as D.D. had expected. Instead, he peered directly at Karen, quite conscious.

'*The light*,' he moaned. She released his eyelid. He moaned again, this time in relief.

Danielle and Janet were back with supplies. Karen took a Popsicle stick and jammed it into Lightfoot's mouth. He immediately tried to spit it out. '*Don't touch me!*'

'Towel,' Karen ordered, rolling him onto his side. 'Quick, over his eyes. Cecille, kill the overhead lights. We can work by the glow of the hallway bulbs.'

Cecille obeyed, darkening the common area as Ed raced down the hallway to grab a towel. The second the overhead lights winked out, Lightfoot seemed to relax.

'*Hurts. Can't stop*,' he muttered. 'Inside me. Feel it. Cold, cold, cold. Bitter . . . burns. Must fight. White light, white light, white light. Tired. So tired . . . Must find . . . the light.'

Ed returned with a stack of towels. They folded one and placed it over the top part of Lightfoot's face, shielding his eyes, D.D. took a second towel and, with effort, managed to pry Lightfoot's fingers from Karen's wrist and wrest his hand onto a rolled towel.

'Talk to me, Andrew,' Karen demanded fondly. 'Stay with us. Where do you feel the pain?'

'Legs . . . arms . . . back . . . body . . . muscles, hurt, hurt, hurt.' His body thrashed against the

404

floor. 'Too loud. Too bright. Stop, stop, stop, stop, stop . . . '

'The light hurts you?' Karen prodded.

'Burns . . . my eyes.'

'And noise?' D.D. spoke up.

'Ahhhhahhh,' he moaned, bringing up one hand to block his ears.

The doors burst open. Two medics bustled into the area, led by the security guard. They took one look at Lightfoot's convulsing form and sprinted over to him.

'Condition?' the first man asked Karen.

'Started three minutes ago. Convulsions, light sensitivity, noise sensitivity,' Karen reported. 'But conscious. Aware of his condition.'

'Pulse?'

'Two ten.'

The medic arched a brow. D.D. didn't blame him. With that pulse rate, Lightfoot should be racing up Mount Everest.

'History of seizures?' the medic asked, trying to check vitals.

'Unknown,' Karen answered, just as Lightfoot said, 'No. Not seizures. Spasms. Muscle . . . spasms . . . '

The medic glanced at Lightfoot's towel-draped face, then back at Karen. She shrugged.

'The dark . . . ' Lightfoot groaned. 'I'm filled with the dark. So, so cold . . . it burns . . . '

'Hallucinating,' the medic muttered. He straightened, nodded to his partner. They grabbed a backboard and looked ready to get to work.

'Wait a minute,' D.D. called out. A case she'd

read once, Lightfoot's uncanny consciousness, even during what appeared to be a grand mal seizure. She strode over to Lightfoot's table and sniffed his bottle of iced tea. Nothing. She touched her fingertip to the top edge, where a drop of moisture rested. She brought it cautiously to her mouth and, with a bolstering grimace, stuck out her tongue. It tasted . . .

Teaish. Grassy. Lemony. Then, beneath it all, a slightly bitter aftertaste.

'You need to get this tested immediately,' she informed the medic. 'But I'm guessing strychnine.'

'Rat poison?' Greg spoke up from the hallway.

'In his drink?' Karen echoed, frowning. The staff looked at one another, then down at Lightfoot's churning body.

'Symptoms fit.' She looked at the medic. 'Hypersensitivity, muscle spasms, initial consciousness . . . '

'Yeah.' The medic nodded. 'Now that you mention it . . . Well, we gotta motor, then, 'cause next on that list is respiratory failure. Come on, buddy. Hang in there with us. If you're ever going to get poisoned, a hospital is the place to do it.'

With help from the MCs, they got Lightfoot's body onto the gurney. Then they raced out of the unit for the elevator banks.

The elevator arrived with a *ding*. The doors opened, and Alex strode out, bearing a steaming tower of boxed pizzas. He looked at the medics, Lightfoot's strapped-down body, and the shell-shocked staff, all staring at him.

406

'What happened to the healer?' he asked.

'That,' D.D. replied, 'is an excellent question.'

★ ★ ★

Karen and her crew might be crack medics, but there was still a reason they paid D.D. the big bucks.

'Where did Lightfoot get the tea?' she demanded, the second the medics disappeared into the elevator.

'I don't know. I think . . . I assume he brought it with him.' Karen looked at her staff. They milled about the half-lit common area, kicking at towels, staring at hastily rearranged furniture. Several were rubbing their arms, as if fighting a chill.

'Sure there's no iced tea in the kitchenette?'

'No. We don't stock it here.'

'Downstairs cafeteria?'

Karen shook her head uncertainly. Danielle piped up, 'Andrew's tea, the Koala brand, is one of those all-natural, all-organic, keep-the-planet-green products. I don't think you can buy it around here.'

'Thank heavens for small favors,' D.D. muttered, as shutting down a hospital cafeteria and calling poison control was not high on her list of things she wanted to do right now. 'Lightfoot arrive with any stuff, maybe a lunchbox, briefcase?' D.D, had a fleeting image of a brown leather strap over Lightfoot's shoulder when she and Alex had first spotted him by the elevators. 'Maybe a manbag,' she mused. 'I want it.'

Karen dutifully led D.D. into the Admin area, where Lightfoot had stowed a brown leather satchel. D.D. flipped it open to find a container of Greek yogurt and a bag of sunflower seeds. She took the food for testing, then returned to the common area, where she could see the staff eyeing one another nervously for imminent medical collapse.

'Anyone else have iced tea?' D.D. asked.

One by one, they shook their heads.

'Who's eaten here tonight?'

Four staff members slowly raised their arms. D.D. noted that Greg and Danielle were not among them.

'What time?'

The MCs had started at seven p.m., taking a snack break between nine and nine-thirty.

'Good news,' D.D. informed them. 'Strychnine is one of the fastest-acting poisons, with symptoms emerging within five minutes of ingestion, so if you're vertical now, you're probably going to be vertical later. Timeline fits what we saw tonight: Lightfoot opened his drink, took a few sips, started the meditation, drank a bit more, and I'd say about eight minutes into it . . . '

'Collapsed in full convulsion,' Karen filled in, her voice subdued. Everyone stared at the table that Lightfoot had been sitting on.

'Strychnine is odorless,' D.D. informed the anxious staff members, 'but has a bitter taste. So if you run across anything that tastes funky, set it aside immediately. I'll phone the lab, have them send someone over to test the water, as well as everything in the kitchen, but that'll take some time. When are the kids due to eat again?'

'Not until breakfast,' Karen supplied, 'though some of the kids need a middle-of-the-night snack.'

D.D. thought about it. 'Stick to food or drink items that come from sealed packages. Snack-sized cereals, that sort of thing. As long as the seal hasn't been broken, they should be okay. Make sense?'

Everyone nodded mutely.

'All right. Who saw Lightfoot with the iced tea?'

The one with the short-cropped hair raised her arm. Cecille. 'Um, I was one of the first people to take a seat. Andrew wasn't here yet, but the iced tea was already on the table, like he'd maybe just opened it, then went to get something. Or maybe he went to throw away the cap.'

'The cap!' D.D. agreed. She marched over to the trash can. Right on top, one white lid stamped Koala Iced Tea. D.D. snapped on gloves and fished it out. Metal, for sealing a glass bottle. Not the kind of container that could be easily tampered with — say, penetrated by a syringe. Nope. Cap came off. Poison went in.

Now, possibly, the product had been poisoned at the warehouse level, part of a massive terrorist act. Or possibly, Lightfoot's barky little dog had plotted revenge and spiked her master's tea on the home front.

But D.D. was willing to bet Lightfoot's distinctive beverage took the hit while sitting exposed in the common area.

'How long was Lightfoot gone?' she asked Cecille.

The MC shrugged. 'I'm not sure. Not long. A few minutes. Five minutes maybe. People were starting to gather; I wasn't really paying attention.'

D.D. looked around the room. One by one, everyone dropped their gazes.

'I was with a kid,' Greg volunteered softly. He glanced at Danielle. 'She was with me. We came late.'

Establishing alibis. D.D. liked it. And they thought the milieu of the unit had been compromised before.

'I don't understand,' Karen spoke up. 'Why would someone poison Andrew? I mean, this whole thing . . . This is crazy.'

'Good question.' D.D. considered it. 'Maybe because you brought him here to fix the unit. Calm it down. Following that logic, maybe someone doesn't want the unit calmed down. That person wants you all jumpy and edgy and chasing after exploding kids. Lightfoot's poisoned. You're all freaked-out as hell. Mission accomplished.'

Karen gaped at her. 'That's insane.'

'Twelve dead and one injured. All connected with this ward. You're right — can't get much more insane than that.'

'Stop it! We are not those kind of people — '

'What kind of people?' D.D. asked with interest.

'Murderers. Dr. Deaths or Angels of Doom.'

410

'Medical caretakers who convince themselves that their patients — i.e., their troubled young charges — would be better off dead?' D.D. volunteered helpfully.

Karen glared at her. 'Myself, my staff, we are committed to healing children. Not *hurting* them.'

'People change.'

'No!' Karen blazed. 'You don't get it. This is a pediatric psych ward. We work as tightly together as any trauma team. And we succeed precisely because we know one another that well, we believe in one another that much. I'd trust anyone here to hand me a drink right now and I would down it without hesitation.'

D.D. waited to see if anyone would take Karen up on that offer. No one moved.

'Maybe that just proves you're the guilty party,' D.D. said.

'I was the *first* to help him.'

'Maybe because you already knew something bad was going to happen.'

'How dare you! I'm a *nurse* — '

'Yeah, yeah, yeah,' D.D. interrupted. 'So you've said. Fact remains, someone drugged Lightfoot's iced tea, and I'm guessing that someone is standing right here, unless you believe the unit's negative energy suddenly grew a pair of hands.'

No one said a word, which D.D. took as a sign of agreement. She continued briskly: 'Now, seems to me, problems here are growing bigger, not smaller. Meaning, it's time for my team to take a crack at your team, and meaning no one's allowed off this floor until personally cleared by a member of my squad. No trips to the cafeteria. No five-minute break to catch a smoke. Are we clear? Let's get this party started. And candidate number one will be . . . ' D.D. glanced around the common area, spotting her target of choice: 'Gym Coach, follow me.'

34

Greg didn't look happy. The big guy trailed down the hallway toward the BPD's makeshift command center, his gaze glued to the carpet, his high-top sneakers dragging. It made D.D. feel warm and fuzzy all over. Always nice to know she wasn't losing her touch.

Inside the classroom, Alex had set up the pizzas across one table. The scent of melted cheese, fresh-baked dough, and spicy pepperoni made D.D.'s stomach growl. There was probably something ironic about stuffing one's face right after watching a grown man get poisoned, but D.D. was starving. Alex and several of the other guys had already dug in, munching away. They looked up with interest as D.D. closed the door behind her and Greg then headed straight for the pizza. She found the fully loaded pie and slid two cheesy slices onto a paper plate.

'Want some?' she asked Greg.

He shook his head.

'Soda, water, iced tea?'

He gave her a look. 'No. Thank you.'

'I bet the food's safer in here than out there,' she told him.

'I'm with Karen on this one,' he answered stiffly.

'Loyal to the Corps?'

'You wouldn't understand.'

''Course not. Cops. Hell, what could we

possibly know about the importance of team-work?'

The classroom door opened. Danielle walked in.

'Not your turn, chickadee,' D.D. informed her, through a mouthful of pizza. 'Go back and play with your other friends.'

'Can't,' Danielle said. 'I'm on leave, right? Can't stay out there, so Karen sent me in here.'

'Wanna talk? Fine. Alex will take you next door. Alex.' D.D. gestured to him, just as Danielle said:

'Nope.'

'Yes.'

'Nope.'

D.D. frowned, set down her paper plate, and strode over to Danielle. She stood right in the nurse's face. Heightwise, D.D. had only an inch on the woman, but she knew how to use it. 'This is a private party. Out.'

'No.'

'What the fuck is your problem?'

The nurse shifted edgily. 'You. Him.' Danielle jerked her head toward Greg. 'The whole fucking unit. You think you need answers? I need them even more. Meaning Greg has got to start talking.'

D.D. snapped around to glare at Greg. 'Do you know what she means?'

He shook his head.

'Yes you do,' Danielle said, eyes still on D.D. 'I heard you with the boy. You know Evan. From off the unit. How can that be, Greg? How do you know him, and why didn't you tell us?'

414

'Danielle — '

'For God's sake!' Danielle exploded. 'Two families are dead, Greg. And Lucy. Plus, now Lightfoot's hospitalized. How many more, Greg? Something's terribly wrong. Someone's hurting our kids. You need to start talking. How do you know Evan?'

D.D. stuck her hands on her hips. 'Might as well confess now, buddy boy. Because none of us are letting you out of this room until you do.'

Greg remained standing there, lips thinned, face unreadable. He stared at Danielle. She stared back at him.

'I knew the families,' Greg said abruptly. 'All of them. Outside of the unit. I'm the missing link.'

★   ★   ★

'I started respite work couple of years ago,' Greg was saying five minutes later. He was seated at the table, Danielle next to him, D.D. and Alex across from him. Despite his earlier refusal, he and Danielle were now both armed with cans of soda, which they had opened themselves and tasted carefully.

'At first, I worked for just one family. I'd met them here; their four-year-old daughter suffered from schizophrenia. They were talking about how hard it was to get a break, to have a date night, go for a walk, buy groceries. Neither of their families were equipped to handle Maria, and there was a waiting list for trained help. I felt bad, especially for the mom. You could tell she

415

was losing it. So I offered to watch Maria while the parents had a night out.

'I didn't accept money.' He said this more to Danielle than to D.D. and Alex. 'I did it as a favor. It seemed like the right thing to do.'

Danielle nodded, tensely, her expression still guarded.

'But then they called me up again. They could use more help and they were willing to pay. Thirty bucks an hour. That's more than I make here.'

'Thirty bucks an hour?' D.D. repeated.

'There's a shortage of respite workers,' Danielle said, looking at D.D. and not Greg. 'Not enough training available, not enough people suited for the work. Given that families with special-needs children can't exactly hire the teenager down the street, the families end up held hostage. They have the highest burn job on the planet and can never take a day off. Meaning the ones who have means . . . '

'Pay well,' D.D. filled in.

'Very well,' Greg supplied, a tad self-conscious this time. 'And they network with other families with special-needs kids, and once the word gets around . . . '

'You got a pretty good gig moonlighting as a respite worker.' D.D. frowned at him. 'Why the secrecy, though?'

'It's considered a breach of protocol. Like a conflict of interest. I'm already being paid to help with kids here. To set up a side deal with the parents . . . '

'Double-dipping?' D.D. asked.

'More like . . . I think in the past, there were situations where an individual MC might have seemed aggressive about it. Like he or she was preying on overwhelmed parents to get work. That led to some rules.'

'You're not supposed to work with the families outside of the unit,' D.D. translated.

'Exactly.'

'But you have been. For years.'

Greg flushed, looked down. 'I swear, I've never solicited the work. They call me, not the other way around. I wouldn't prey. I wouldn't do that.'

'So why are you breaking the rules?' D.D. asked. 'You claim you're a good guy, but clearly you're not coloring within the lines.'

'Money,' he said softly, not looking at Danielle. 'I need the money.'

'Need the money? Or *want* the money?' D.D. pressed.

'Need.'

'Why?'

'My sister.'

'Feel free to extrapolate.'

'She's institutionalized. Will be for life. And the hospital the state's willing to pay for is more like a prison than a mental health facility. She's my sister. I couldn't leave her there.'

'So you found her a new place?'

'Private institution. But that means more money. State pays some. I make up the difference. To the tune of twenty grand a year.'

'Twenty *grand*?' D.D. asked incredulously.

'Matter of economics. Supply versus demand. When it comes to mental health, we don't have

417

enough supply, and every year, we have more demand. Ask Karen about it sometime. We used to see a handful of genuinely psychotic children a year. Now we make those same numbers within a month. We don't know what the hell to do with these kids; how are the parents supposed to know?'

'What about your parents?' D.D. asked. 'Can't they help with your sister?'

'No.'

'Again, feel free to extrapolate.'

But Gym Coach Greg suffered from a sudden attack of muteness. He stared at the table, fidgeted with the beveled edge.

'Hey, Danielle,' D.D. said after another minute. 'Take a hike.'

'No,' Greg spoke up. 'She stays.'

'Then you talk.'

He sighed, seemed to be debating something inside himself. 'My parents are dead,' he said abruptly.

'When?'

'Eighteen years ago.'

D.D. did the math in her head. 'You'd be, what? Twelve?'

'Fourteen.'

'Okay. Parents die. It's fourteen-year-old you and your, what . . . mentally ill older/younger sister?'

'Older. Sixteen.'

'She take care of you?'

'Couldn't.'

'Because she was mentally ill.'

'No.' He looked up, sighed again, seemed to

finally reach some kind of decision. 'Because she was under arrest for my parents' murder. She'd poisoned them. With strychnine.'

* * *

'Look, I don't know all the details,' Greg told them. 'I was a kid and my sister . . . I don't know. I've heard a lot of different stories over the years. At her trial, her attorney argued self-defense. That my father had abused her, and my mother didn't intervene, so Sally killed them to escape. Then she suffered a breakdown. The experts diagnosed her with severe depression, as well as borderline personality disorder. My sister's attorney argued the borderline personality was a result of the abuse; it all got very complicated. Eventually, the state agreed to waive the charges as long as my sister was institutionalized. My grandparents were serving as our guardians at the time. They made my sister take the deal and that was that. My sister went bye-bye, and we all pretended it never happened.'

'Where was this?' D.D. asked, making notes.

'Pittsburgh.'

'How'd your sister get the strychnine?'

'Don't know.'

'How'd she administer it?'

'Don't know. I was at a Boy Scout camping weekend when it all went down.'

D.D. eyed him skeptically. 'I want dates, place, and at least two corroborating witnesses.'

Greg rattled off dates, place, and the name of

two former Boy Scout leaders. The guy had apparently been asked to supply that information a couple of times before.

'You believe your father was abusing your sister?'

'I never saw any signs of abuse.'

'So maybe your sister simply wanted to off your parents?'

'I never saw any signs of violence.'

'Well, which is it, Greg? A or B? Your whole family history comes down to two choices, an abusive father or a homicidal sister. You can't tell us you've never considered the matter.'

'Consider it all the time,' he said matter-of-factly. 'Still don't have an answer. Welcome to mental illness.'

'But you're breaking your back — not to mention a few rules — to fund better housing for your sister. That's gotta mean something.'

Greg fell silent. When he spoke again, he didn't look at D.D., but at Danielle. 'There are answers about my family I'll never have. But maybe it doesn't matter. My sister either killed my father because he was doing something terrible, or because she was suffering from something terrible. Either way, not her fault. Either way, she's the only family I have left.'

Danielle didn't say anything. Her expression remained shuttered, her body language tight. Apparently, the nurse wasn't the forgiving type.

'Your grandparents?' D.D. asked Greg.

'Died several years back. The murders, the trial, my sister's hospitalization . . . it took a lot out of them. They never recovered.'

'So you're on your own and working here. Then you decide to upgrade your sister's hospital, which means you need more money. A lot more money. Good news, the world is filled with desperate parents overwhelmed by their psycho kids, so revenue opportunities abound. You take the first respite job, then what?'

'They referred me to another family, then another. And sometimes, on the unit, maybe it would come up in conversation.'

'So maybe,' D.D. filled in for him, 'you did prey on vulnerable parents.'

'No.' Greg said it firmly. 'They might ask. It's a natural segue. Here I am, qualified to assist with their kid, and there they are, needing assistance. They ask, I answer.'

'They ask,' Danielle confirmed quietly. 'I've even heard parents pester Karen to make staff available to babysit. Parents are desperate for options.'

'How did it start with the Harringtons?' D.D. asked.

'I knew them from the unit. Ozzie was a very active kid and, you know' — Greg shrugged — 'I don't have a problem with that. We can wrestle and chase and I can keep a handle on things. That's my job. And Denise and Patrick Harrington wanted that. So we arranged that one morning each week — it depended on my schedule here — I'd come over and take Ozzie to play. We'd go to the park, maybe bike. Something physical. They'd get time to themselves, Ozzie could blow off steam. It worked for everyone.'

'When did it start, when did it end?'

421

Greg had to think about it. 'September last year. Couldn't give you an exact date. Soon after they discharged Ozzie. It lasted nine months, then Patrick lost his job, and respite wasn't an option anymore.'

'What did you do?'

'What do you mean?'

'They fired you,' D.D. stated impatiently. 'What'd you do?'

'Fired me? They ran out of money. Not their fault. Frankly, I felt bad for them. Life was already tough. But they were good people. And Ozzie was doing a lot better by then. I figured they'd be okay.'

'What do you mean, 'Ozzie was doing a lot better'?'

'You know, with Andrew.'

D.D. cocked her head to the side. Studied Danielle and Greg. 'That's right. The Harringtons were using services from both Gym Boy and Healer Boy. Any other additional services?' She stared at Danielle.

Danielle shook her head. 'I'm a nurse. Even to babysit, you couldn't afford me.'

Greg, however, had turned a deep, dark shade of red.

D.D. leaned forward, regarded him steadily. 'Come on, spit it out. Confession's good for the soul.'

'There, um, there might be a reason the Harringtons used both me and Andrew.'

'Really? Do tell.'

Danielle was staring at him, too, the expression on her face wide-eyed, the person standing on the tracks seeing the train coming.

'Andrew found out about my respite work. Coincidentally, a family who hired me also hired him. He put the pieces together.'

D.D. arched a brow. So Lightfoot had something on the good-looking MC. So much for Karen's little spiel about knowing everything about her staff.

'So, um . . . ' Greg closed his eyes, blew out a breath. 'Andrew suggested that when I worked with a family, particularly a wealthy family, I could recommend his services. If the family ended up hiring him, he'd then throw a little something my way. Like a finder's fee.'

'Cash, you mean. More money.'

'Generally fifty bucks.'

'My, my, my,' D.D. mused. She turned to Alex. 'And here Lightfoot told us he was giving his gift away.'

'Oh sure,' Greg said sarcastically. 'To the tune of a hundred an hour.'

'Anyone else in on this?' D.D. asked.

'What do you mean?'

'Other MCs moonlighting as respite workers? Other therapists asking you to refer their services?'

'None that I know of. But again, not exactly something anyone can talk about on the floor. Maybe other staff members work outside the unit. Maybe not. You'd have to ask them.'

Alex spoke up. 'Wait a minute. First the Harringtons are paying you thirty an hour to take Ozzie to the park. Then they're paying Lightfoot a hundred an hour for counseling.

They didn't have that kind of money.'

'They'd submit the bills to the state, which generally covers a couple of hours of respite care a month. So the state paid for half my time, with the Harringtons making up the difference. As for Andrew, I don't know, but I'm betting they put it under 'psychiatric services.' I saw paperwork once, on the kitchen table. It didn't look like an invoice from a spiritual healer, but more like a clinical doctor. Andrew had initials after his name and everything. I'm guessing that was his way of finessing the system for people like the Harringtons.'

'People like the Harringtons maybe,' Alex said, still not sounding convinced, 'but what about Tika's family? No way they could afford even a fraction of your bill.'

'No, they couldn't,' Greg agreed. 'And they didn't. I saw Tika four times. Same deal. Established a rapport with her here, got to feel like she was making progress. When she was discharged, the dad asked if I could stop by from time to time. The mother was about to have a baby, she could use the break, yada yada yada.

'So I stopped by. First time I entered the house, I about lost my lunch. The dad was passed out on the couch, obviously stoned, the mom's ankles were so swollen from the pregnancy, she couldn't get out of bed. I propped up her feet, got her some water, then I took all the kids to the park. Kept them for four hours. When I returned, the father seemed to have gotten himself together. He thanked me profusely and offered me a baggie for my troubles.'

'He paid you in *drugs?*' Danielle asked sharply.

Greg shot her a look. 'I turned him down.'

'Oh, well, so you do have standards after all.'

He flushed, squared his jaw, then returned his attention to the cops. 'I turned down the drugs,' he repeated stiffly. 'What's-his-name said he'd pay me next week. I almost refused, but then Tika ran over and gave me this great big hug, and . . . I don't know. That house. I knew I was screwed, but sometimes . . . It's tough to walk away.'

'So what'd you do?' D.D. pressed.

'Played sucker three more weeks. Showed up, took all the kids to the park, never got a dime. And just so you know, it's not all about the money. If I thought I could've helped Tika — hell, I would've continued. But man, that family . . . Her stepfather . . . They're the kind of people you learn quickly to avoid. They're not interested in getting better. They *want* you to take care of them. They *want* you to do all the heavy lifting. Meaning nothing you do is ever gonna be enough, and nothing you do is ever gonna make a difference. You have to walk away, or they'll bleed you dry. Plain and simple.'

'And Lightfoot? You recommend the family to him?'

'I recommended he stay clear,' Greg answered dryly.

'And did he?'

Greg hesitated. 'I don't think so.'

425

'What makes you say that?'

'He seemed . . . interested in them. I mean, the parents were a mess, but the kids . . . Ishy, the oldest, clearly had some kind of autism, but he was a sweet, sweet boy. Then there was Rochelle, who was positively brilliant. And Tika . . . Tika was . . . complicated. Very sensitive, almost intuitive. Andrew seemed fascinated by all of them, but Tika in particular. Four old souls, he told me one day. Four old souls stuck in a corporal abyss.'

'Four?' Alex asked.

'The baby,' Greg supplied. 'Apparently, Andrew had already met it on the spiritual superhighway.'

'Really?' D.D. said.

'Sure. He even knew it was going to be a girl. Don't know, man, but sometimes . . . Andrew knew stuff. And sometimes he did work for free; he could afford to. So if he wanted to deal with Tika's family . . . ' Greg shrugged.

'Did he?' D.D. pressed.

'Don't know. It's not like we hang out.'

D.D. exchanged a glance with Alex. She could tell what he was thinking. Lightfoot had lied to them about not knowing Tika Solis. He'd also failed to mention that he was engaged in some manner of health-care fraud, billing the state for professional services he wasn't qualified to render. Made D.D. wonder what other secrets the healer had been keeping.

D.D. turned back to Greg. 'Jealous? I mean, here you are, tragic past, mentally ill sister, having to work so hard to scrape by. And there's

Lightfoot. He's got the looks, the life, the house on the beach. How are you ever gonna compete with a guy like him?'

'Compete?' Greg asked.

'Sure. He tosses you fifty bucks to send him some work, but we all know he'd give you even more if you'd hand over your girlfriend.'

'*Excuse me?*' Danielle this time.

'Please. The way Lightfoot looks at you,' D.D. drawled. 'Like you're a dessert he wants to gobble up.'

'He only cares about my family history — '

'No he doesn't.' Greg this time, voice curt.

Danielle turned to him. 'What the hell?'

'He wants you. Always has. Anyone can tell by watching him watch you. What I don't understand is why you don't want him.'

'Because he's an asshole?' Danielle offered.

'An asshole with money.'

'You do have issues,' she informed him, eyes blazing.

'Don't we all.'

'Look, I had one dinner with Andrew, that was enough. Like I'm some commodity for guys to buy and sell.'

'You never had dinner with me,' Greg retorted. 'How many times have I asked? One dozen? Two? Three? In your own words, you gave more consideration to the 'asshole' than you did to me.'

Danielle flushed. She slunk down in her chair, looked away. 'Well, I honestly like you,' she muttered. 'That makes a difference.'

'Assholes get dinner. Likable guys get squat.'

'As you said, we've all got issues.'

'Well, now I'm an asshole who milks desperate parents for money. Does that mean I can buy you dinner?'

'*Excuse me*,' D.D. interjected. 'Hate to intrude, but forget dinner: Next place Gym Coach here is heading is jail. You knew all the families. You had opportunity to hang Lucy and poison Lightfoot. You're also obviously familiar with the more deadly uses of strychnine, plus have a history with family annihilations — '

'Technically, no.' Greg interrupted, 'I have a family history of patricide. My sister killed my parents. That's *not* family annihilation.'

'He's correct,' Alex spoke up.

D.D. glared at him.

'And I have an alibi,' Greg continued. 'Thursday night, the Harringtons, right? I was working, watching Evan Oliver, the boy who was brought in this afternoon.'

'Wait a minute.' Alex leaned forward. 'The boy who was admitted today. That's the one who stabbed his mother, right?'

'Evan Oliver, yes. I work for his mom once a week.'

'You met the family outside the unit?'

Greg nodded.

'What about Lightfoot? Did he work with the boy, too?'

'I might have referred him. He might have paid me fifty bucks.'

Alex leaned back. Looked at D.D. Looked at Greg. 'Experienced with firearms, Greg?'

'Hardly.'

428

'What about Tasers?'

'What? Come on, look at me: I don't have to resort to toys.'

'Not even a pillow, maybe to suffocate a baby?'

'What?' Greg appeared horrified.

D.D. turned back to Alex. 'You think?' she asked.

'I'd like to ask Healer Boy a few questions,' Alex agreed. 'Including why he lied about not knowing the Laraquette-Solis family, when he decided to start billing for his 'gift,' and what kind of alibi might he have for Thursday or Friday night.'

'Then it's a good thing we know where he's at.' D.D. pushed back her chair. Alex followed suit. 'You two,' she addressed Danielle and Greg, 'stay put. If you're lucky, when I return I'll decide *not* to arrest you. But I make no promises.'

She smiled at them wolfishly, Then she and Alex were on the hunt again.

MONDAY

35

VICTORIA

A rumbling sound from the hallway wakes me up. My eyes pop open. I feel a moment of intense, overwhelming nausea, and roll onto my right side to vomit.

Then the queasiness passes, and I'm left disoriented and shaken. Slowly, I return to my back. I stare at the blank ceiling of my hospital room and give myself a moment to adjust.

Playing with my son. Speaking with my ex-husband. And then . . . this.

Should I cry? I want to. I think if your child stabs you, crying is probably a logical thing to do. But I can't summon any tears. I feel stark, hollowed out. For years I've fought a war. Then, in thirty seconds, I lost it.

Now there's no going back. This is the new reality. My son is a violent offender and I'm his first victim.

At least it wasn't Chelsea, I think, and then I do cry, low, muffled sobs of relief, because Michael wasn't the only one who'd spent years terrified that one day he'd have to harm his son to save his daughter. At least it didn't come to that. At least not that.

Then I picture Evan again, his bright blue eyes and infectious giggle as we raced around the backyard, and I cry harder.

433

I will always look at Evan and know what he did. And he will always look at me and know what he did, too.

Can't go back. No going back.

It comes to me again. The burning, obsessive realization: I have to get out of here. I can't be this person anymore. I can't lead this life. It hurts too much.

I sit up. The movement sends a sharp, bolting pain through my left side. I gasp, falter, then catch myself. After everything I've been through, I refuse to be cowed by something as trivial as physical pain. I grit my teeth, and force my way to standing.

My legs wobble. I grab the metal bed-rail and hang on tight.

When I'm finally convinced I won't collapse, I turn my attention to the row of machines. I turn off the heart monitor first, unclipping the plastic lead from my finger. Next, I remove the tape holding the IV needle in the back of my hand, sliding the needle free. A single drop of blood appears against my pale skin. I wipe it away and will myself not to bleed again.

I walk gingerly, five steps across the room; I'm not going to make it. With each inhale, my insides feel like they're being flayed by shards of glass. I'm light-headed, achy. I need to lie down. I can try again tomorrow. But when I turn back to the bed, I can't do it. Maybe I'm crazy. Maybe Evan isn't the only one who broke this morning. But I can't go back. I won't.

Goddammit, after the past eight years, I'm entitled to at least one nervous breakdown.

Tighter binding, I decide. Something wrapped around my ribs to support my weakened side.

Good news: I've spent years quietly repairing the results of Evan's rampages. I've reset finger bones, superglued deep cuts (I saw it on the Discovery Channel), and taped fractured ribs. All I need is a few supplies, and I'm a surprisingly decent medic.

Well, I *am* in a hospital.

I shuffle slowly into the hallway, clutching the back of my hospital gown. The clock on the wall shows it's after midnight. Sunday is over. Monday has officially begun. I try to find strength in that. A brave new day. Mostly, standing in the middle of the overbright corridor, I feel lost and alone.

The ward is quiet, the nurses' station empty. I keep moving. Four doors down, tucked against a wall, I find a cart of first-aid supplies. I slip a roll of gauze and a box of butterfly clips into my hands, then shuffle back to my room, shutting the door behind me. I have to rest. My head is spinning. I chew some ice chips, then crawl into bed. My lips hurt. I chew more ice; then, despite my best intentions, I fall asleep.

When I wake up, the wall clock tells me two hours have passed. Someone has placed a blanket over me, and a small duffel bag rests on the chair. Michael, probably. I feel an ache in my chest, as if my ex-husband has left me all over again. Crazy. I'm going crazy.

I don't care.

I'm still clutching the first-aid supplies. That fortifies me, returns my sense of purpose. I climb out of bed; my legs feel stronger this time and my breathing remains even.

I peel off my flimsy hospital gown, inspecting the bandage on my side. Dark pinpricks of rust. Old blood. Not fresh, Good enough for me.

I work carefully, wrapping the gauze around my rib cage, pulling it tight with each pass, until the constriction forces me to elongate my back and breathe in shallow gasps. Finally, I secure the binding, stabilizing my ribs and easing the sharpest edge of my pain.

Next I explore the duffel bag. Michael has thrown together the basics: sweats, underwear, socks, flip-flops, toiletries. I have a sense of déjà vu, then it comes to me: The duffel bag holds the same items as the hospital bag I packed for Chelsea's birth, and the one I'd planned to pack for Evan's birth, had I not gone into premature labor.

I struggle again. Wanting to finger each item as if it's a talisman of the life I can't give up, of the woman I'd hoped to be. I'll sit here. Cry pathetically with my sweatpants on my lap.

The wash of self-pity disgusts me. I'm sick of crying. I'm sick of loving a man who left me. And I'm sick of nurturing a child who drove a knife between my ribs, then phoned to tell me he'd get it right next time.

The life I thought I was going to lead is over. It's time for a new beginning, a new woman. One who walks white sandy beaches in a long purple peasant skirt, with a salt-rimmed margarita in hand. Maybe I'll meet a young, handsome surfer dude. We'll have sex under the palm trees and get sand in interesting places. I'll watch the sun rise while listening to the call of the gulls. I'll think only of myself and what I want to do every minute of every day. And I'll like it.

I have lost my mind.

Fuck it. I get dressed.

It hurts like hell. I use the pain to stiffen my resolve. Underwear. Sweatpants. T-shirt. Flip-flops. I brush my teeth and comb my hair. World, look out.

I'm sweating. My side burns. I drink the water left in the cup by my melted ice.

I have no money, no passport, no sanity. Not exactly a recipe for success.

And I remember now that I've never really liked the sun. I burn too easily, especially the top of my head. I don't want a margarita. I don't even want a surfer dude.

Mostly, I want to see Evan again.

Eighth floor, they said. Maybe I could creep upstairs, gaze in on him sleeping . . .

I will tell him that I love him, whisper it in his ear, the way I used to do every night when he was a baby.

I'll touch a blonde curl, the stubborn cowlick above his right eye. I'll finger its softness, and that'll remind me of all the times Evan hugged me, Evan kissed me, Evan told me he loved me.

To the moon and the stars and back again . . .

I don't want to run away. I just want to hold my son. I want us to be all right again.

Eighth floor. Not so far. Not so hard. A short elevator ride to Evan.

I crack open my door, peer down the hall. Coast is clear. I make a break for it, hobbling my way to freedom.

I pass the nurses' station, getting halfway down the hall, then three-quarters of the way. Almost to the elevator banks. So close. Fifteen more feet. Ten. Five. Two more steps, I'll be able to reach out —

'Victoria?'

The voice behind me brings me up short. I turn reluctantly, feeling doomed. *I can't go back*, I think wildly. I need my son. I need my freedom. I need something other than this incredible ache in my chest.

'Victoria?' my lover says again. His face a picture of concern. 'What are you doing up? You shouldn't be out of bed.'

'I'm feeling much better, thank you.'

'Victoria, I think your side . . . '

I look down. What do you know? I'm bleeding. He holds out an arm. 'Come on, follow me.'

'No.'

'Victoria?'

'I have to go upstairs. Find Evan. Please. Please help me.'

I realize for the first time that he's holding a large black gadget between his hands. It looks like a gun, but not really. 'What's that?' I ask.

He looks around. Still no nurses in sight. 'Expediency,' he says.

He points it at me. I feel a sudden electric jolt, and then . . .

438

36

D.D. and Alex bypassed the elevators in favor of the stairs. They needed to stretch their legs, and the empty stairwell was excellent for talking.

'What d'you think?' she asked Alex the moment the heavy fire door closed behind them.

'About Gym Coach Greg?'

'About all of them. We have Nurse Danielle, whose family history dovetails with the crimes, as well as having a personal connection to both Lucy and Lightfoot.'

'Lightfoot?'

'He was into her, even if she wasn't into him.'

Alex considered this as they descended the first flight of stairs. 'Meaning, if someone were targeting Danielle, the methodology of the first two crimes and the targets of the second two crimes would make sense.'

'Which also points the finger at Gym Coach Greg, who has motive.'

'Unrequited love.'

'Exactly. Worships Danielle for years, can't even get dinner with her, though she accepts Lightfoot's invite. He has opportunity — knows the Harringtons, knows the Laraquette-Solis family. He was on duty the night Lucy disappeared, and working tonight when someone spiked Lightfoot's drink.'

'He claims to have an alibi for the Harringtons' murders.'

'An alibi not easy to verify, given that the mother has been stabbed and the child's psycho.'

'Attack gone awry?' Alex mused.

'What d'you mean?'

'The son stabbed the mother. Sounds a bit like our first two crime scenes.'

D.D. shook her head. 'Too small. This family is just a mother and child. No father figure, and in the first two attacks, the father figure mattered. That's who had to be posed just so. The crimes had to reflect on the fathers.'

'Dads are evil.'

'At least the ones who kill their families.'

Alex seemed to accept this. 'Problem is, Lightfoot knew the families, too. So now we have two suspects to consider. Both of whom have lied to us.'

'Lightfoot told us he didn't know Tika Solis, when he did.'

'And Greg said he'd never met Tika's family, when he had.'

'Actually,' D.D. pointed out, 'Greg never said he hadn't met the family. He just said they didn't visit the ward.'

Alex gave her a look. 'You're letting him off on a technicality? Remind me to wear more tight-fitting T-shirts and speak in a baritone.'

D.D. rolled her eyes. 'Don't get me wrong — Gym Coach still makes the most sense. After all, Lightfoot wasn't working the night Lucy was hanged. Plus, there's the matter of him being poisoned.'

Alex nodded. 'Kind of wonder,' he said as they rounded the fifth-floor landing. 'First we had no links between the families, now we have all kinds: the unit, an MC/respite worker, and the local spiritual healer. Begs the question, who else don't we know about? Mentally ill kids appears to be a small and incestuous world. So maybe there are other experts — a psychiatrist, a therapist, a respite worker, a nurse?'

'Meaning we should check in with Phil and Neil: Phil, who's running the background reports, and Neil, who's making the list of all the employees who regularly visit the unit. Put those two items together . . . '

'See who else shakes out.'

D.D. liked it. They had four more flights to go, so she worked her cell phone.

She got Phil on the first ring. He sounded tired and hungry. Apparently, back at the ranch, they hadn't gotten around to take-out pizza. Then again, HQ hadn't dealt with a bunch of kids threatening to gouge out eyeballs. Win some, lose some.

So far, Phil had covered the basics: DMV records, employment history, and various criminal databases. Running the list of employees that Karen had supplied, Phil could report that no one had any outstanding warrants or history of arrest. Ed, the burly MC, liked to speed, and Danielle needed to clean up a few parking tickets. Greg, on the other hand, was clean as a whistle. D.D. supplied the MC's sordid family history. Phil promised to dig deeper into Greg and his sister's past.

'Though, by the sound of it, Sally was a juvenile and it never went to trial, so not sure what I'll find in the system,' Phil warned.

'Let's start with verifying that Sally exists, that her parents were poisoned with strychnine, and that her current residence is costing Greg an extra twenty grand a year.'

'That I can do.' D.D. could practically hear Phil cracking his knuckles over the phone lines. He loved a good data search.

'Have you heard from Neil? How's he coming with the list of other hospital employees, contractors, etc.?' D.D. asked.

'He turned in a preliminary list of janitors, food service workers, deliverymen, and a few contractors an hour ago. Still working on those, though one name did jump out — the healer, Andrew Lightfoot. Guessing Lightfoot's not a real name, because it's not in the system.'

D.D. glanced at Alex, then remembered. 'He mentioned in the first interview that he reverted to an old family name. Sounded better for business.'

'Well, if you want the skinny, get me better info.'

'Deal.' D.D. snapped her phone shut, turned to Alex. 'More questions for Lightfoot,' she reported. 'Starting with his real last name.'

Which shouldn't have been too hard, except when they reached the main ward of the hospital, Lightfoot had disappeared.

37

DANIELLE

'Why didn't you tell me?' I asked Greg.

'Why didn't you ever ask?' he replied.

We were huddled at the interrogation table, confined to the classroom, under another detective's watchful eye. The nanny detective was on the other side of the room, eating pizza and reading files. That gave us the illusion of privacy, though he probably had crack hearing and was writing down every word we said.

'I would've understood,' I said. I sounded petulant, even to me. Greg's secrets angered me. I was the one with baggage. He was supposed to be an open book. Now I had to face the fact that Greg had his own tragic past, and was still a better-adjusted person than me.

Greg regarded me thoughtfully. 'Why?'

'How can you even ask? Your family history, my family history. You could have told me about your sister. I would've understood!'

'Why?' he asked again. 'For me to presume to know what you're feeling, for you to presume to know what I'm feeling . . . ' He shrugged. 'Isn't there some quote: 'All happy families are alike, but each unhappy family is unhappy in its own way'?'

'*Anna Karenina*. Only line of the book I read. But still . . . ' I sat back, hands tucked in my front pockets, still scowling. 'Most people know who their families were, or *what* their families were. But we don't. Our family history remains a question mark. Was your father that bad or was your sister that ill? Was my father that bad or did the drinking make him that ill? We don't know. We'll never know. And that kind of not knowing really sucks.'

'I miss my parents,' Greg said after a moment. 'My dad was a good dad to me. My mom was a good mom. I wish they could see me now. I wish they could know that at least one of their kids got it right.'

I nodded. I thought that, too, the few times I allowed myself to think of my family. Would my mom be proud of me? Would Natalie and Johnny appreciate my work with troubled kids? Maybe, when I'd graduated from the nursing program, they would've cheered for me. And maybe, when I saw success with my first disturbed child, they would've liked to hear my stories from work.

I should've gone to dinner with Greg. He was a good person. The decent guy who didn't get the girl, because most girls, including me, were stupid about things like that.

'I don't want you feeling sorry for me,' he was saying now, voice grim. 'I don't need your pity.'

'Not what I was thinking.'

'I mean, look at the kids here. Most of them don't have fathers. Most of them don't have involved caretakers of any kind. That's life. If we expect *them* to get over it, *we* can, too.'

'You should come to my place,' I said. 'In two weeks. I'll be saner then. The dust will have

444

settled on this mess. I'll fix you dinner.'

Greg blinked. Paused. Blinked again. 'Your place?'

'I don't have roommates. And we have unfinished business.'

His mouth formed a soundless *Oh*. It made me feel better about things. But then Greg narrowed his gaze, studying me intently.

'Think you'll really be saner?' he asked. 'Think the dust really will have settled?'

'Hope so.'

'Why don't you let go, Danielle? It's been decades for you and, speaking strictly as a friend, each anniversary you get worse, not better. Is it that you ask too many questions, or not enough?'

'I don't know. Maybe . . . ' I sighed. The nanny detective still seemed preoccupied. What the hell. I bent my head closer to Greg's and whispered: 'For the longest time, I didn't ask any questions. I was angry and content to stay that way. But this time around . . . I've starting thinking about that night. Remembering. I was the one who brought my father's gun to my parents' room. I was fed up. My dad was . . . doing things. I wanted it to stop. My mother forced me to give her the gun. She said she'd take care of things. She promised me.

'Next thing I remember is my father standing in the doorway, blowing out his brains. I always thought it was my fault. I had confessed to my mother. She had confronted my father. He had gone berserk. Had to be my fault, right? But now . . . I don't know. My aunt says there were problems in the marriage, things that had nothing to do with me. And I'd swear the clock read ten twenty-three when I left my parents' room. The police didn't arrive until one a.m. That's two and a half hours later. What happened? My parents fought? My mother confessed to an affair, tried to kick him out? Two and a half hours is a long time. Two and half hours . . . '

I shook my head, confused. 'I always thought the central question of my life was whether my father spared me because he loved me that much, or because he hated me that much. Now I wonder if my entire life doesn't boil down to two and a half hours when I was hiding under the covers of my bed.'

'Danielle — ' Greg began.

'Remember the deal: no pity.'

'And dinner in two weeks.'

'Yeah, dinner in two weeks. No roommates.'

He grinned. It eased the tightness in my chest, made me want to touch the bruise I'd left on his jaw.

'I'm not good girlfriend material,' I reminded him. I heard the edge in my voice. 'I'm gonna try. It's time to forgive. Time to forget. But this is new territory for me. I'm better at being angry.'

'Danielle — '

'My family's dead. I'm still alive. I need start doing something with that.'

'Are you done?'

'Okay.'

'Danielle, how long have we known each other?'

'Years.'

'Five, to be exact. I've only been asking you out for the past two. You can be angry, Danielle. It's nothing I haven't seen. And you can be sad, because it's nothing I won't understand. And if you want to learn to forgive and forget, I'm happy to help with that, too. Maybe I'll even learn something along the way. But you don't have to change, Danielle. Not for me.'

'You're a brave man.'

He smiled. 'Nah, but I'm solid. Just am. And solid's not glamorous and it's not for every girl. But I'm hoping it will be enough for you.'

'I've never done solid. For me, solid will be glamorous.'

'So two weeks — ' Greg began, then stopped. He sat up, sniffed the air. 'Do you smell smoke?'

I paused, sniffed. At first, I smelled only cheese and pepperoni, but then . . . 'Yeah, I do.'

Suddenly, the smoke alarm split the air. I covered my ears, pushing back the chair.

Greg was already climbing to his feet, the detective, as well.

'You two, stay put — ' the detective began.

Greg cut him off. 'Not a chance. After that episode earlier this evening, most of these kids are heavily medicated. They're not walking out of here. We'll have to carry them.'

Greg headed for the door, placing his hand against it. 'Cool to the touch,' he reported. He flung it open. Tendrils of smoke were wafting down the hall and we could hear the rapid patter of running feet.

Definitely not a drill. Greg and I looked at the cop. The cop looked back at us.

'First kid you see,' I informed the detective, 'grab him or her and get down the stairs. Fourteen kids to go, and we'll be right behind you.'

We got to work.

★ ★ ★

Karen led the charge. We found her positioned before the ward's front doors, checklist in hand, wire-rimmed glasses askew on the tip of her nose. I still couldn't see the cause of the smoke or feel any heat, but the hallway was noticeably hazy, smoke curling around Karen's feet as she read off each child's name in a firm, tight voice.

Ed stood nearby, preparing to take the first group of kids, a groggy trio Cecille was herding down the hall. She had them walking single file, their hand on the shoulder of the child in front of them, just as we'd practiced. The kids, still wearing pajamas, stumbled along, too tired to do anything other than what they were told.

Then a door flew open, and Jorge and Benny bolted out. They charged into the trio, knocking Aimee to the floor before leaping onto the sofas, hands clasped over their ears, each boy screeching louder than the alarm itself.

'You,' Karen ordered Greg. 'Round up Benny and Jorge. And you,' she glanced at me, 'you'll take — '

'Evan,' Greg interrupted. 'The new kid. We gave him a double dose of Ativan just two hours ago. Kid's zonked out of his head.'

'All right.' Karen marked Evan's name, turned

back to me. 'You get Evan. You' — she pointed at Greg — 'you're still on monkey duty.'

Greg headed for the leaping Benny and Jorge. I raced down the hall.

I passed by two open doors, small faces with large eyes peering out at me. I wanted to grab each child, carry them personally to safety. Not gonna work. Had to stick to the plan.

'Single file, into the hall. Ed will come get you,' I told them, keeping on mission.

The smoke was thicker at the end of the hall, making my eyes sting. I started coughing, holding one hand over my mouth as I entered Evan's room. Despite the noise, the boy was passed out cold, curled up in a ball, with a blanket over his head.

I grabbed his shoulder, shook him, hard. Nothing.

The smoke made me cough again. I yanked off the blanket, lightly slapping Evan's cheeks. Still nothing.

More smoke. My eyes burning. My chest, getting tight.

Fuck it. I dug my hand under his shoulders and propped him into a sitting position. Evan's head rolled back against my arm, his mouth slack-jawed. I braced my legs, counted to three, then heaved him up, like an overgrown baby.

I staggered back, gritting my teeth. Right before I toppled, I found my balance, getting my legs beneath me as I shifted Evan's dead-weight in my arms. The boy wasn't too heavy but a long, awkward shape, with his scrawny limbs flopping about.

Coughing harder, I put one arm around Evan's shoulders, the other around his hips, then stumbled into the hall.

The hall was growing darker, harder to see, harder to breathe.

I tripped, almost going down. At the last instant, I caught Evan by the waist of his pajamas, and forged ahead. Vacant rooms loomed on either side of me. One, two, three, four, five.

The team had done their job. I passed the common area and arrived in front of Karen.

'Evan,' she triumphantly checked off. 'That's a wrap. Into the stairwell, Danielle. I'll bring up the rear.'

The smoke alarm was still shrieking. Karen held open the door for me. The lobby area was clear of smoke, allowing me to draw a deeper breath as I made my way toward the emergency exit. Evan felt heavier now. My arms burned. Lower back, too. I needed to hit the gym. Lift weights. Something.

I got the fire door open. One flight at a time. Help awaited at the bottom of the stairs.

I rounded the seventh-floor landing with my shoulder leaning against the wall for support. Above me, I heard the fire door clang shut: Karen, beginning her own descent.

Eight-year-olds are heavy. Seventh floor down. Then the sixth. One foot, then the other.

I made it to the third-floor landing, paused to catch my breath, then the door burst open. I blinked against the sudden infusion of light.

Andrew Lightfoot strode into the stairwell.

'Perfect,' he said. 'And you brought Evan. Makes my life even easier.'

'Andrew? Shouldn't you be recovering — '

I never finished. Andrew stepped forward, two slender black wires flew through the air, and I felt a zap wallop my chest.

Evan dropped to the floor. I was right behind him.

38

By the time the fire engines roared up to the front entrance of the Kirkland Medical Center, D.D. and Alex had already spent fifteen minutes fighting their way through the growing throng of overworked staff and confused patients. There were nurses directing wheelchairs with attached oxygen tanks, interns guiding hospital beds bearing patients, and security guards trying to keep the exits clear. Glass doors opened. People poured out. Firefighters rushed in. Alarms continued to shriek.

The whole episode had D.D. troubled. First Andrew Lightfoot was poisoned. Then, according to one frazzled nurse, he hopped off the gurney and walked out of the emergency room. An hour later, the smoke alarms sounded, and now the entire hospital was being evacuated.

What were the odds?

Standing in the parking lot, peering up at the seven-story building with her hands clasped over her ears, D.D. couldn't make out any sign of flames. Smoke, however, drifted up from rooftop vents. A fire in the walls? Electrical issues?

She turned to Alex. 'Real or fake?' she asked him above the din.

'Smoke seems real enough.'

'And where there's smoke . . . ' Screw it, it *felt* wrong. D.D. went in search of a fireman.

First one she spotted was standing next to the

fire engine, chattering on his walkie-talkie. He didn't look happy to be interrupted by a civilian, but responded to her detective's shield.

'What's the situation?' she asked, shouting to be heard.

'Reports of smoke on the eighth floor. Seems to be coming from the ventilation system.'

'Fire?' she asked.

'No heat,' the fireman said with a frown. 'Generally means we got a sleeper fire somewhere in the walls. Gotta watch how we vent, or we can create one helluva backdraft. Crew is climbing all over the building now, still can't find the source.'

'Mechanical room?'

'Working on accessing.'

'Thanks. Keep us posted.'

D.D. turned away from the fireman, went back to Alex. 'My Spidey-sense is tingly,' she muttered.

'Mine, too.'

'Cops do know woo-woo. Fucking Lightfoot. It's about the psych ward. He rigged something, did something to force the evacuation. Question is, why, and did he get what he wanted?'

'Where are the kids?' Alex asked, peering around the crowded parking lot. Bedridden patients, standing patients, and wheelchair-bound patients. No kids.

A nurse raced by. D.D. grabbed the man's arm, forcing him to pause.

'Hey, Boston PD!' she yelled. 'I need to know: the kids on the eighth-floor assessment unit. Where do they exit for one of these drills?'

The nurse blinked at D.D., obviously caught between multiple tasks. Then he pointed to the side of the massive building, his words rushed as he bolted for his next patient. 'They evacuate over there, the playground.' He raced off.

She and Alex hustled their way through the dense crowd to the other side of the building.

'It's Lightfoot,' D.D. muttered, hands back over her ears. 'I know it. But why him? And how?'

'We need his name,' Alex said. 'That's the problem. We don't even know who the hell he is.'

'Someone does.'

'Gym Coach Greg,' Alex said.

'Actually, I was thinking Danielle.'

★   ★   ★

When D.D. and Alex made it around the building to a grassy clearing, they discovered fourteen huddled children and seven frayed adults. The noise from the fire alarms was quieter here. The noise from the howling children louder. D.D. headed for the nurse manager, Karen, but Greg got to them first.

'Where's Danielle?' he demanded, his face tight.

'Funny, that's what we were going to ask you.'

'Karen sent her to get Evan. I haven't seen her since.'

They turned to Karen, who was already frowning. 'But she got Evan. I checked them off; they headed down the stairwell, right before me.'

454

'You saw them enter the stairwell?' D.D. clarified.

'Yes. I grabbed a last few things, then headed down. I could hear them in front of me. At least, I assumed it was them.'

'Danielle and a kid?'

'The Oliver boy. Evan. He was admitted earlier today — '

'Wait.' D.D. whirled back to Greg. 'This is the Evan you know? You worked for his mom, who was stabbed this morning?'

Greg nodded.

'And Lightfoot knew them, too, right?'

'He paid me a finder's fee.'

'Excuse me?' Karen spoke up. 'You worked for a family? Finder's fee?'

Greg winced, stuck his hands in his pockets. 'Once things are calmer, I have some things I need to tell you.'

Karen opened her mouth as if to demand an explanation immediately, but D.D. was already waving her hand. 'Yeah, yeah, yeah, and confession's good for the soul. But first things first: I want Danielle. I want Evan. And I want Lightfoot. Anyone got a clue where the hell they are?'

She glared at the nurse administrator, then Greg, then the staff as a whole.

One by one, they all shook their heads.

'She's the target,' Alex murmured in D.D.'s ear. 'Lightfoot did this to get to her. But why? And where?'

D.D. looked at him grimly. 'And how much time does she have left?'

39

VICTORIA

I jerk awake with my mouth open as if to scream. For a second, I lie still, struggling to get my bearings. My heart's racing. My side aches. I feel dazed, as if roused from a terrible dream.

By degrees, I register that I'm in my own bed. The windows are dark, my bedside clock glows four-fifteen. I start to relax, then realize I can't feel my arms and legs.

In a fresh rush of panic, I try to sit up.

And immediately understand the problem. My arms are tied behind my back. My legs are tied at the ankles. I am trussed up, like a Thanksgiving turkey. But I'm in my own home, in my own bed . . .

It comes back to me. Waking up in the hospital. My determined desire to see Evan on the eighth-floor pediatric unit.

I'd made it to the elevator banks. I can remember my hand reaching for the button. I can remember thinking that I was going to make it.

Then Andrew appeared. His presence confused me. We didn't have that kind of relationship. He used my body for sex, and I let him. And, Saturday's interlude aside, he hadn't wanted to see me at all. He needed to prepare something, he'd told me. A Monday surprise.

456

It comes to me. Today is Monday.

And when I'd met Andrew at the elevator banks, he'd hit me with some kind of electrical charge. A bone-deep, searing pain. And then . . .

My lover deliberately incapacitated me, and now here I am, alone in the dark.

I hear a groan, coming from downstairs.

No, not alone.

Michael is here, too.

What in the world?

Suddenly, I remember two recent cases in the news: families, both with troubled kids, murdered in their own homes.

We're missing Evan, I understand now. Andrew will bring Evan. Then the killing will begin.

Furiously, I work my hands against my plastic bindings. No time for the pain in my side. No time for the pain in my head. Have to get out. Have to get us all out. Michael, Evan, I have made such a terrible, terrible mistake.

But before I have a chance to get started, it all ends. I hear the door open downstairs. I hear footsteps in the foyer.

'Honey,' Andrew's voice croons. 'I'm home.'

40

DANIELLE

My fucking head. That was my first thought. Next came awareness of shooting pains down my arms, muscles cramping in my right shoulder. I needed to move, stretch out, sit up . . .

I was tied up.

The realization stunned me. I froze, trying to figure out what the hell had happened. I'd been carrying Evan, working my way down the stairwell. A door opened. Andrew stepped out.

The bastard had tasered me. The realization was so shocking, I tried to sit up again, and promptly whacked my head against a hard metal surface. Sagging, I honed in on the sound of tires on pavement, the scent of exhaust fumes, the stifling heat of a closed-in space, and the next piece of the puzzle struck me.

The bastard had tasered me, then tossed me into the trunk of his car.

Son of a bitch. He must've faked the whole poisoning episode. Gotten himself a free pass out of the unit, into the main hospital, where he'd disappeared, then circled back around to . . . torch the hospital? Attack the ward?

Evan. Oh God. What had happened to Evan?

I struggled desperately, rolling helplessly from side to side in the darkness of the trunk. I encountered something that felt like a metal tool

458

chest, then a soft duffel bag. But no Evan.

Maybe he was okay. Karen had been behind me. She would've found him, carried him to safety.

The thought comforted me. I rested, wiggling my fingers and toes as I heard the hum of the pavement below, and felt the weight of the trunk door above. I wanted to throw up. Instead, I forced myself to take a deep breath, then marshaled my resources, and determined the best plan of attack.

I wasn't scared. Maybe I should've been. But mostly, I was very pissed off.

I'd hidden once in my life. I'd handed over my safety to another and I'd buried myself under the covers. And we all knew how well that had worked out.

This time, I vowed, I was gonna put up one helluva fight.

* * *

The car slowed. I felt the momentum grind to a halt. Seconds later, the engine cut out; we'd reached our destination. My head pounded harder. The exhaust fumes had made me nauseous, while my right shoulder had locked up painfully. Despite my best efforts, I'd lost all feeling in my fingers and toes at least five miles ago.

I tensed, bracing myself for God knows what. Andrew would come around the car. Pop open the trunk. And I'd . . . leap out at him? Scream bloody murder? I was bound and gagged.

Couldn't move. Couldn't scream. Didn't have a cell phone. Didn't have a weapon. I was doomed.

A car door opened. Slammed shut. Another door opened, maybe a passenger door. Andrew was getting something out.

My body screamed with tension. I squeezed my eyes shut, though I was already lost in the dark.

Footsteps, growing closer. I had to do something. *Think.*

There was nothing I could do. I was trapped, helpless.

I didn't feel brave anymore. I pictured my sister, gunned down in the hall. I remembered my brother and his desperate race for the stairs. And I wanted to cry for them. I wanted to cry for all of us, because after tonight, I was pretty sure there would be no survivors.

The footsteps faded away. Long seconds ticked by without anything happening. My body relaxed, degree by degree. *Think, think, think.*

Both D. D. Warren and Greg seemed to feel that Andrew had personal feelings for me. Could I use that? Could I convince him that I liked him, too? If I could just sweet-talk him into loosening the bindings, giving myself one shot at escape . . .

The footsteps were back, growing louder. Then, before I was ready, the trunk flew open. Andrew loomed above me, his body shrouded in night. I couldn't see his face, but felt his eyes upon me.

'Do you understand?' he asked me.

Bewildered, I shook my head, cotton gag chafing my lips.

'You will. It's time to face your past, Danielle. I've been trying to tell you that, but you ignored me. Drastic times call for drastic measures. So here we are. Twenty-five years later. Same day. Time for a new understanding.'

He reached down, grabbed my shoulders, and forced me up. I screamed against the gag as blood-starved nerve endings roared to life. The sound was muffled, the shriek rebounding into my throat, where it died a quick death. Andrew grunted in satisfaction.

'You must open your senses,' he intoned, hands under my arms, dragging my deadweight from the trunk. 'Remove your judgments. Listen with your heart, remember with your mind. He'll find you. He's been trying to contact you for years.'

He set me on the pavement. *Run*, my head commanded, even as my legs crumpled and I fell against my captor. Andrew was strong. I remembered his stories of running six miles in soft sand. Now he hefted me easily onto his back in a fireman's hold. I tried to kick out with my legs, but couldn't get any momentum.

With me in place, Andrew trudged toward a large house I didn't recognize. He pushed open the front door and strode into the darkened foyer.

'Honey, I'm home,' he called out.

Upstairs, I heard a woman begin to weep.

★ ★ ★

461

Memory is a funny thing. My entire life had been defined by one episode, that until today, I'd assumed lasted no more than forty minutes. In my memory, my father was holding the gun. In my memory, my father shot himself, instead of me. In my memory.

Andrew removed my gag. I opened my mouth to scream, and he pressed a finger over my lips.

'Shhh, don't forget about Evan and his mother and father. Surely you'd like to save one family.'

I closed my lips and stared at Andrew. We were upstairs, in a pink ruffled bedroom that clearly belonged to a young girl. I didn't see any sign of her, and the bed was made, so I was hoping that meant she was no longer around, or maybe this room had been staged for my benefit. I wasn't sure, and the not knowing kept me silent.

I studied Andrew, a mouse pinned by a cat, desperate for a glimmer of escape.

'What do you mean?' I asked. My mouth felt cottony from the gag. I couldn't get enough saliva to enunciate clearly. I licked my lips, but it didn't help.

Andrew set the flashlight between us. I'd grab it and bash it against the side of his skull, except my hands remained tied behind me. He'd released my ankles, allowing us both to sit cross-legged on the floor. I had my back against a wall of dark windows. He had himself situated between me and the bedroom door.

I didn't hear crying anymore. The house had gone eerily quiet, the silence freaking me out more than the noises had. Bad things happened in places that were this hushed.

'Evan is an old soul,' Andrew stated.

This sounded like the Andrew I knew, so I nodded.

'He feels too much, is saturated by the negativity of this world. Other, crueler souls haunt his dreams. They seep into his waking consciousness. They encourage him to do bad things, such as kill his own mother. It's a terrible way to live, such a young boy, fighting a war nobody else can see.'

I'd heard this spiel before, so I nodded again.

'He's not the only one, Danielle. There are other souls caught in a horrible abyss. They cannot return to this world for a fresh set of experiences, nor can they journey to any other plane. They are trapped in the black hole of unfinished business. This is the Hell writers such as Dante described for us. It is a horrible, horrible existence, Danielle, for it has no end. Old, sensitive souls trapped for eternity.'

I had no idea what he was talking about, but I nodded again. Gag was gone. Ankle bindings were gone. If he'd just release my hands, I might have a chance of winning this.

'People fear death. They're bound by primitive notions of Heaven and Hell. But that assumes we exist only in one dimension. Once you accept that souls are capable of moving among many spiritual planes, then you understand the greater truth of our existence. Physical death is nothing, merely a blip on a soul's radar screen. Ozzie and his parents — they're not gone; they've simply moved to the next set of experiences. Ishy, Rochelle, Tika, and baby Vivi. Again, not destroyed, just set free from an unfortunate corporal existence.'

'You killed the Harringtons and the Laraquettes?' I exclaimed in horror.

'I enabled them to move on to the next plane of existence,' Andrew corrected.

'Oh my God. And Lucy, too?'

'I've already explained to you that she's happier now. You know what happened to her here. Surely you can understand it's been better for her to journey on.'

'You *hanged* her?'

'She saw through me, straight into my heart. A powerful soul, that one. So I waited until it was late, and the unit lightly staffed. Then I simply led her out of the ward. She followed willingly. Again, she's much happier — '

'You sick son of a bitch!' I interrupted hotly. 'You had no right! Maybe Lucy followed you through the doors, but what about when you entered the radiology room? What about when you tied the knot in the rope? You murdered her. You violated the choice she made to exist on this plane of being. How could you!'

Andrew glared at me. 'You're not listening — '

'You weren't even poisoned, were you?' I interrupted again, pissed off to the point of recklessness. 'That was just a little charade to get you away from the unit. You're a fraud. I knew it!'

'Quiet!'

'Fuck you!'

Suddenly, Andrew wasn't sitting across from me. Suddenly, he loomed over me, his face inches from mine, the fury in his eyes threatening to drill me to the floor. I wanted him to be crazy. I wanted to see a rabid light shining in his gaze. Instead, the determination in his face frightened me to the core.

'You will believe. You will visit the interplanes, you will open your mind and open your heart. Or you and everyone in this house will die. Are you paying attention yet, Danielle? Are you *listening* to me?'

Wordlessly, I nodded. His blue eyes were burning, burning, burning. He was on fire with something. Faith, I thought. Mad faith.

When he spoke next, his words were clipped and direct. 'I've hidden a gun in this house. It contains four bullets. I know where it is, and the person who killed your family knows where it is. Now we're going to have a race. Whoever finds the gun first gets to use it. To be fair about it, I'll give you a ten-minute head start. You may waste time searching for a phone, if you'd like. The phone service has been disconnected, just as the electricity has been terminated. Also, this house was set up by Evan's mother to contain him twenty-four/seven. The locks are key-in, key-out, and there's only one key that works.' Andrew lifted a chain around his neck, to reveal the single key.

'Finally, before you resort to smashing windows or other such, nonsense, understand that you'll be deserting Evan; his mother, Victoria; and his father, Michael, who did me the favor of showing up at the hospital. When the ten minutes are up, I will shoot them. I doubt you can break a window, race to the neighbors', and summon help before ten minutes expire, particularly as your hands will be tied for the duration of our little race. Continue your policy of denial and people will die. Face your past, open your heart, and you have a fighting chance. You've driven me to this, Danielle. But I'm trying to be fair about things.'

'You want . . . you expect me to find my father's soul on the spiritual interplanes and ask him about the hidden gun? I'm supposed to . . . talk to him?'

Andrew tilted his head. 'What do you fear most, Danielle? That he won't offer to save you? Or that he will?'

'You're insane.'

'An explanation that enables you to continue your policy of denial. Let me give you a hint: Who saved you that night, Danielle?'

'Sheriff Wayne.'

'How did he get there? You never left your room and your house was located miles from the nearest neighbor. Who heard the gunfire? Who called nine-one-one?'

I stared at him blankly, not getting it.

Andrew sighed, shook his head at me, then rose to his feet. 'You focus too much on the corporal world, Danielle. You hate yourself for not saving your family's lives. I want you to fight for their souls. You don't know the truth of that night. You refuse to see what you can't accept. And in doing so, you've damned them all, especially my father.'

'*Your* father?' I asked incredulously.

466

'The respectable Sheriff Wayne. An old soul trapped in the abyss. That's the true hell, Danielle. That's what all of us should wisely fear.'

Andrew glanced at his watch. 'Ten minutes. You can confront your past, or you can lose your future. You can save my father's soul, or I will use all four bullets. I'll start with the mother. That's how these things are generally done. Then Evan. Then his father. I'll save you for last, the order you know best. Tell me, Danielle, how many families are you prepared to lose?'

Andrew disappeared into the gloom of the hallway. I sat frozen, too stunned to move. Then I heard a new sound, from the room next to mine.

'Mommy?' Evan whispered, his voice tinny with fear. '*Mommy?*'

Andrew was insane, I thought, and we were all going to die.

41

Phil was a brilliant man. Via cell phone, D.D. gave him the update on Andrew Lightfoot, who appeared to have abducted Danielle and Evan. They needed Andrew's last name and background info, fast.

Phil answered by cross-referencing Lightfoot's address with the state licensing board for financial traders. Given that Lightfoot used to be an investment banker, it stood to reason that he kept his license up, if only to manage his own assets.

Sure enough, the database spit back the name Andrew Ficke, son of Wayne and Sheila Ficke. Sheila had an address in Newburyport, not far from her son. Wayne, a former sheriff, had died two years ago.

D.D. called Sheila, told the bewildered woman that her son was currently assisting the BPD with an urgent investigation and they needed to locate him immediately. A list of known addresses, please?

Turned out Andrew owned a seaside home, a yacht, and a co-op in New York. If souls really got to choose their experiences, D.D. was coming back as a New Age healer.

She doubted Andrew would run all the way to New York with an abducted woman. Seaside home too obvious. Yacht more interesting; lots of privacy out at sea. D.D. would notify local uniforms to watch the docks, and the Coast Guard to monitor the harbor.

'Sorry to call so late,' D.D. told the woman, not wanting her to be alarmed and attempt to contact Andrew. 'We're all set now. Thanks again.'

'What's the case?' Sheila asked.

'Excuse me?'

'You said Andrew was assisting with a case. Which case? If you can talk about it, of course.'

D.D. almost said no. But then, at the last second: 'He's helping us investigate the murders of two families. Maybe you've seen the reports on the news.'

'Oh, that sounds like Andrew. He's been fascinated by such cases ever since his father's involvement, of course.'

'His father's involvement?'

'Way before your time, dear. Back in eighty-five, when Wayne was still sheriff, one of his former deputies got drunk and turned his gun on his family, then himself. Only the girl survived. Danielle Burton. Such a terrible night. Wayne put together an album of the event, filled with newspaper clippings and such. Right up until his death I'd find him searching through it. I think he kept looking for what he might have done differently, the warning he should've spotted, the action he could've taken, which would've spared that poor family.'

'Where's the album?' D.D. asked immediately.

'Andrew took it. My husband was the first on the scene, carrying the girl from the house. Many of the newspapers dubbed him a hero. I

469

don't know that Wayne agreed, but the articles are flattering and it's nice for a son to have such stories of his father.'

'Wayne ever talk about that night? The details of what happened?'

'No, he wasn't a talking sort of man. He put together the album. I think that was his therapy.'

'What about Andrew? Did he question your husband about the case?'

'Andrew asked Wayne questions every now and then. But once my husband retired, he left those days behind him and took up fishing. That seemed to work for him.'

D.D. ended the call, turned to Alex.

'Andrew Lightfoot's father was the sheriff who handled the shooting deaths of Danielle's family twenty-five years ago,' she reported excitedly. 'What are the odds of that being a coincidence?'

'His father was at the scene?'

'His father was considered a hero for entering the carnage and rescuing Danielle.'

Alex blinked, paused, got the same intense look that was on her face. 'So . . . we have Andrew Lightfoot, linked to Danielle's past, linked to Danielle's present. Has a family connection to a historic mass murder. Has a personal connection to two families who have presently been murdered. Shit. It's a reenactment!'

'Reenactment?'

'The Harringtons and Laraquette-Solis family. He's staged them to be similar to Danielle's family.'

'But why?' D.D. demanded, running an

impatient hand through her hair. 'Million-dollar question, and we still don't have a penny's worth of answer.'

'I have no idea.' Alex grabbed D.D.'s arm. 'Wait. We're being stupid about this. The boy, Evan. Wasn't his mother admitted to the hospital earlier today with a knife wound?'

'I think so.'

'Where is she now?'

'Somewhere in the parking lot with all the other patients, I presume.'

They both turned back to the hospital, The fire engines were still on-site, as well as numerous uniformed officers. Patients, staff, and curious onlookers were now corralled a safe distance from the building, where nothing much seemed to be happening. No smoke. No shooting flames. The fire, if there had been one, appeared under control.

'Let's not presume.' Alex released her arm. 'We need to find her and ask about Lightfoot.'

'We don't know what she looks like.'

'Greg does.'

The staff and kids from the psych unit remained huddled by a copse of trees, waiting for the signal to reenter the hospital. Most of the kids were awake now and getting into trouble.

Greg flashed Alex and D.D. a quick glance as they approached. Then he yelled at Jorge to get out of the tree, told Jimmy to drop the stick, and whirled to grab an escaping Benny by the shoulder.

'We need you to find Evan's mom,' Alex informed the MC tersely.

'Right now?' Greg raised one arm, Benny dangling from his biceps. Jorge and Jimmy came racing toward them, arms outstretched like airplanes.

'*Vroom, vroom, vroom!*' the boys cried.

'Right now,' Alex said over the noise. 'This is about families, right? Entire families. So if Evan's gone . . . '

'Where is his family?' Greg filled in.

'Exactly.'

Benny dropped off Greg's biceps, and joined his *vrooming* friends, weaving among the bushes. Greg looked from the kids to the detectives and back to the kids again. His dilemma was clear.

'Oh crap.' D.D. closed her eyes and bit the bullet. 'I'll take the kids,' she informed Greg. 'You go with Alex and locate Evan's mom.'

Greg arched a brow. 'You sure?'

'I'm sure.' D.D. eyed the racing kids dubiously. 'But hurry. I mean it. For all of our sakes, *run!*'

42

DANIELLE

How long was ten minutes? When you were a kid, ten minutes seemed like forever. Once you were in school, it became a fifth of a class. And when your hands were bound and you were stumbling around a darkened house . . .

I was in the hallway, waiting for my eyes to adjust to the gloom. The night had been an endless one, and the first tendrils of morning were starting to seep into the sky. In another thirty minutes, the house would be bright with the daylight. Assuming any of us were alive to see it.

Evan was in the room next to the girl's; I could hear him mumbling a stream of agitated gibberish. There appeared to be four bedrooms on this floor. Probably a girl's room, a boy's room, a guest room, and the master suite. The traditional Colonial setup.

I didn't know where Andrew was, so I flattened my back against the hall wall for protection, and slid my way toward the room I hoped would be the master suite. I needed to find Evan's parents. If they were conscious, maybe between the three of us . . .

How did Sheriff Wayne get to my house? I never asked him the night I had him in my apartment. He was the sheriff. Of course he showed up at a crime scene. It never occurred to me to question his presence.

But our house was isolated, miles away from the nearest neighbor, and I hadn't called 911.

My mother? My sister or brother?

There was a logical explanation. There was always a logical explanation.

I heard weeping. I turned into the next doorway, discovering a large, shadowed space dominated by huge pieces of furniture. I made out a king-size sleigh bed, then realized there was a woman on the bed and she was crying.

'Hello?' I whispered softly.

She shut up. 'Who's there?' Her voice was as hushed as mine, cautious.

'Are you Evan's mom?' I edged closer, my eyes darting around the space, noting the standing mirror, perfect for Andrew to hide behind. Or maybe he was tucked behind that decorative tree, or inside the master bath, the walk-in closet.

'Andrew's not here,' the woman whispered, as if reading my mind. 'I'm Victoria.'

'Danielle.'

I hurried closer to the bed and she rolled toward the edge. Quick inventory revealed her hands and feet were bound with zip ties. The plastic bindings were too thick for either of us to pull off the other. We needed something. Knife, scissors, key.

'What does he want with you?' I asked, trying to figure out what to do next.

'I'm not sure. I hired him to help Evan, then we became lovers. But it wasn't an intense affair.

I don't think he'd kidnap me over that.'

'He kidnapped you?'

'From the hospital.'

'Me, too.'

'You were his lover?' she asked.

'I didn't even get through dinner with him. Apparently, I'm the person who damned his father's soul to Hell. We need scissors,' I muttered.

'In the master bath. Top drawer, right of the sink.'

I was impressed. Victoria was good under pressure. Then again, given Evan's history, she'd had lots of practice.

'I'll be back,' I promised.

'Thank you,' she murmured, and her gratitude grounded me. I wasn't alone. She wasn't alone. Together we'd get Evan, escape from the house, and call the police.

I located the bathroom drawer, pulled it out, and awkwardly searched for scissors with two hands bound behind my back.

As a voice suddenly boomed through the house: '*Oh Danny girl. My pretty, pretty Danny girl!*'

I dropped the scissors, recoiling against the wall. The voice boomed again, loud enough to pound against my skull, echoing so that I couldn't pinpoint the source. Megaphone, I thought. Somewhere in the house, Andrew was using a megaphone and this was his sick idea of the ten-minute countdown cheer.

'*Oh Danny girl. My pretty, pretty Danny girl!*' he sang again. 'How do I know that song,

Danielle? How do I know those are the last words your father spoke to you?'

Because I'd told the police that, I thought resentfully, pushing myself away from the bathroom wall. I'd told Sheriff Wayne.

My mother had called him. The realization stopped me in my tracks. My mother had called Sheriff Wayne. I could hear her voice, a distant memory, talking on the phone:

'I need you, Wayne. I can't do this anymore. He's drunk, out of control. And Danielle came to my room tonight. You won't believe what my little girl told me. It has to be tonight. Please, Wayne. I love you. Please.'

How much time was left? Seven, eight minutes?

I returned to the drawer, finally locating the metal scissors when they pricked my finger. The pain felt good. It cleared the cobwebs from my mind, focused me on matters at hand.

I crept back to the bed.

'What's he talking about?' Victoria whispered.

'The night my parents died. My father shot everyone to death. Then Andrew's father, the sheriff, found me.'

'Your father shot everyone but you?'

'Story of my life,' I said, but Andrew did good work because I was already wondering. *Or is it?*

Victoria rolled onto her stomach, lifting her bound wrists. I wedged my numb fingers into the loops of the scissor handles.

'Andrew's hidden a gun,' I told Victoria as I tried to locate her wrists with my back to her and my own mobility limited. 'If I find the gun first, I win. If he finds it first, he's going to kill us. I'm supposed to visit my father's soul on the spiritual superhighway and ask him for the weapon. While I'm there, I need to save Sheriff Wayne's soul. Sadly, I don't believe in spiritual interplanes, though I'm pretty certain Andrew's mad as a hatter.'

I finally located Victoria's hands. I stabbed her twice, myself three or four times. My fingers grew slippery with blood. I heard Victoria whimper once in pain. Just when I thought I was going to scream in frustration, I felt the jaws of the scissors slide around the plastic tie. I squeezed the handles, sawing the blades back and forth, back and forth . . . The tie snapped. One of us was freed.

How much time left? Six minutes?

'*Oh Danny girl. My pretty, pretty Danny girl!*' Andrew sang again, megavoice warbling down the hall.

His voice was all wrong. Too gleeful. My father hadn't sung like that.

As he stood in the glow of the hallway light, his hand raising the gun. Pointing it at me, pointing it at *me* . . .

'*Oh Danny girl. My pretty, pretty Danny girl!*'

'*Put the gun down. Joe. Wayne. Stop it. Not like this. This isn't what I wanted.*'

My head hurt. I had that feeling again — like my family was standing right beside me. If I concentrated hard enough, I could see them, maybe even reach out and touch them.

I dropped the scissors on the bed. Victoria sat up, shaking out her hands. Then she cut my bindings, as well as the ones around her ankles.

We stood side by side, two women armed with one pair of scissors in a darkened master bedroom.

'Evan,' she said.

I heard him, still muttering gibberish down the hall. Then I glanced at the bedside clock. Three minutes left, give or take.

'Evan can't help us,' I told her.

'He can't help me,' Victoria agreed. Then, after a heartbeat of silence: 'But I think he can help you.'

43

VICTORIA

I remember a story Michael and I once saw on the news: Two men in ski masks had broken into an upscale Boston townhouse and killed the entire family before fleeing with a jewelry box. Evan was nine months old at the time. As a new mom, I was appalled by the violence, shaken by the ruthless unfairness of it.

Michael had turned to me during the commercial break. 'Anything happens in our house,' he said, 'you get Evan and get out. Don't worry about me. Save Evan.'

So here I am, under siege in my own home, and the stranger I just met is going to find my son, while I search for Michael.

Time is ticking, and I don't see where we have many options. Andrew wasn't lying to Danielle — my house is a fortress, every detail designed to contain a troubled child.

The phones are dead, the electricity out. I have no idea what happened to my cell phone, and my laptop is downstairs in the family room. We're isolated, and according to Danielle, Andrew has a gun.

He'll start shooting soon, I know that, and I can't leave Michael to be his first target. I need him. He may be a pretty suit these days, but Michael grew up hard. He can take a punch and deliver in kind. He might be a match for Andrew, at least more of a match than two women and an eight-year-old boy.

Danielle heads for Evan's room. I scoot toward the staircase, scissors clenched like a weapon in my fist.

I can't hear Andrew anymore. No voice booming down the hall. The silence is unnerving, What's Andrew doing? Where is he hiding? What's he plotting next?

My hands are trembling. I want to stop, huddle like a small animal caught in the open by a bird of prey.

I won't do it. My house, my child, my ex-husband. I started this mess. I'll finish it.

Here's the home court advantage — I have spent years learning how to navigate these stairs so that I won't wake Evan in the middle of the night. I know each squeaky step, each groaning floorboard. Unfortunately, my stab wound isn't doing so well. I'm pretty sure I'm bleeding, and beneath the ache I feel an itchy burn. Infection, most likely. I grit my teeth, picture my family, and push forward.

I hit the bottom step and pause to get my bearings. Daybreak lightens the glass panes beside the door, I can just make out each corner of the foyer, the empty space behind the ficus tree, the yawning archway leading toward the kitchen. No Andrew. I slip away from the stairs, hugging the wall for support, heartbeat quickening.

I hear a groan from the living room. *Michael*. I want to rush to his side. I force myself to take small, measured steps, listening carefully. The silence terrifies me.

Then I hear rustling from down the hall. Maybe from the downstairs lavette, maybe the front study. I dart into the family room, ducking beside the entertainment center. From here, I can see the sofa. Michael is sprawled on the floor in front of it. His wrists and ankles are bound. His head is moving fitfully, as if he's struggling to wake from a nightmare.

For one second, I'm tempted to leave him. He's better off unconscious, not knowing what's happening to his wife and child, never seeing the bullet coming.

A glow appears in the hallway. Flashlight, coming toward the living room, on course to pass directly by me.

I bolt, racing to the other side of the entertainment unit, where I cover myself with the curtains. One of Evan's favorite hiding spaces.

'*Danny boy,*' Andrew is crooning as he appears in the living room. '*Oh Danny boy.*'

He stops, studying Michael's prone body on the floor. When Michael doesn't move, Andrew continues on to the foyer. 'Time's up,' he calls out. 'Know where the gun is yet, Danielle? Because I do.'

Andrew starts to climb the stairs, carrying something down by his right leg. A knife, I realize. A very large butcher knife.

And he's heading straight for my child.

I rush into the living room, collapse on my knees beside my husband, and quickly cut the zip ties. He moans again. I kiss him once. A foolish notion from a foolish woman still learning to let go. Then I slap him, hard.

'Dammit, Michael, wake up. Our son *needs* you.'

44

'Victoria's not here,' Greg reported ten minutes later, gasping slightly from his run around the hospital. Alex was three beats behind the MC and breathing harder.

'Nurse says Victoria must have left her room shortly after midnight,' he filled in. 'They haven't seen her since.'

'A woman who was stabbed disappeared from her room and they did nothing about it?'

'The nurse found the hospital gown on a chair, and noticed that the fresh set of clothes brought by Victoria's ex-husband was gone. She assumed Victoria checked herself out against doctor's orders. They put in a call to her ex, who I guess was handling everything, but they haven't heard back from him yet.'

'Her ex was here?'

Alex nodded. 'Michael dropped off some stuff, spoke with the doctors, yeah.'

D.D. scowled, turned instinctively back to the nearest bush, which was now filled with five hyperactive boys. Another MC — Ed — had come over to assist. It was possible that D.D. wasn't prepared to handle three crazy boys. It was possible no one was prepared to handle these three boys.

'So Evan, his mother, Danielle, and Andrew have all disappeared from this hospital in the past two hours,' D.D. summarized. 'Did you speak to the attendants who took Andrew to the emergency room?'

'Victor and Noam,' Greg said. 'They said Lightfoot's condition appeared to stabilize in the elevator. They got him to the ER, left him for just a second to file paperwork. When the nurse appeared with the first dose of medication, Lightfoot was gone. Hospital security was notified, but hasn't spotted him.'

'Hospital security,' D.D. mused, then perked up. 'Security cameras. We're going to need access to them.'

Alex nodded, but glanced pointedly at his watch. Viewing security footage could be arranged, but would take hours to execute. And in the meantime . . .

'It's a reenactment,' Alex told them, 'Andrew's going family by family, following some agenda only he understands. Assuming he's abducted Evan and Evan's mother, he will look to staging next.'

'The boat?' D.D. wondered. 'Very private.'

'Not the right feel. It needs to be domestic.'

'His house?' That didn't sound right to her. Lightfoot's house was an architectural marvel, not a suburban daydream.

'Why not the Olivers' house?' Greg suggested. 'Evan and his mom live in Cambridge, no more than ten, fifteen minutes from here. Andrew would know where it is; he worked for them.'

'Shit. You and me,' D.D. said to Alex, 'to Evan's house. I'll call for backup along the way.'

She and Alex took a step forward. Greg caught her shoulder.

'I want to go,' he started, then waved to the screaming kids behind him. 'Obviously, I can't. But you'll find Danielle, right? You'll keep her safe. Return her to us. She's . . . she's special to me.'

'Give me an hour or two,' D.D. said with forced optimism, 'and hopefully you can tell her that yourself.'

45

DANIELLE

'It's dark.'

'The electricity's out. Evan, my name's Danielle, I met you earlier this evening. I'm a friend of Greg's.'

I eased into Evan's bedroom, mindful of shadowed corners and Andrew's unknown location. Victoria thought he was downstairs, but neither of us was certain. She was going to try to free Michael, one more foot soldier to join the war. I was supposed to ask Evan to surf the mumbo-jumbo superhighway on our behalf. Find an angel, locate a gun. What the hell.

'It's dark,' Evan said again, sounding more petulant than frightened. I made it to his bed, where I saw he was lying on his side, hands and ankles captured in zip ties.

'I can cut you loose,' I offered. 'Do you have scissors anywhere?'

'Not allowed sharp objects,' Evan said.

On second thought, that made sense. Not sure how to proceed, I sat gingerly on the edge of the bed, trying to find Evan's face in the early-morning gloom.

'It's dark,' he said for the third time.

'The sun will be up soon.'

Somberly, he shook his head. 'That won't help you.'

I wondered if Andrew had told him something. Warned him, or tried to win him over to his side. Maybe it was just as well that Evan was tied up. Clearly, he was a kid capable of doing damage.

'Your mom says you've been working with Andrew,' I started. 'She says he's been teaching you how to control the energies around you.'

'The dark,' the kid insisted again. 'You must learn to control the dark.'

'The dark? Is that how you refer to the negative energies?'

'They're all around you.'

'Yes, the power is out.'

'No,' he said, 'they're all around *you*.'

It took me a second, then I finally got it. Evan wasn't talking about the lack of overhead lighting. He was talking about *me*. Apparently, *I* was the source of negative energy, a walking, talking black hole.

Given how tired and scared I currently was, that made perfect sense.

'Evan, can you tell me how you fight the dark?'

'Call upon the angels,' he reported. 'Close your eyes. Picture a white light. Call it to you. Seven hugs from seven angels. They will help you.'

'Can you do that for me? Call the angels? Then, when you feel the light, can you ask the angels a question?'

In the gloom, Evan blinked at me, curiously.

'Andrew has hidden a gun,' I said quietly. 'The angels know where it is. We need to find that gun, Evan. Can you ask the angels to help us?'

'Guns are bad,' said Evan.

'So is Andrew. Help us, Evan. Your mommy and daddy need you.'

Evan's chin came up. He regarded at me solemnly. 'I will help you.'

★ ★ ★

I hid Evan, still bound, inside his closet, beneath a pile of pillows and clothes. Ten minutes had to be up. Andrew was coming. With the gun. Without the gun. I scoured Evan's room for possible weapons. Maybe a lamp, clock radio, or a framed picture. Victoria ran a tight ship. No feasible weapons in her violent child's room.

Think, think, think.

My heart was beating too hard. I felt a dull roaring in my ears, becoming hyperaware of too many things at once: Evan's low whisper, 'Breathe in, one, two, three, four, five, six, seven . . . Exhale, one, two, three, four, five . . . ' Myself, standing unarmed in the middle of his darkened bedroom.

Then another sound, farther down the hall. The creak of a floorboard.

Andrew, coming up the stairs.

My father, singing as he approached my room. My father, blood spattered across his cheeks — my mother's, my sister's, my brother's.

I wouldn't curl up under the covers this time. I wouldn't hide in a bedroom.

I wanted to fight.

I *needed* to fight.

If I just had the damn gun . . .

Then, in the next heartbeat, it came to me. I didn't need Evan. I didn't need to visit the celestial superhighway. This was all about my father, right?

I knew exactly where the gun was.

I'd dumped my father into the damn sewer system, and the son of a bitch had been trying to escape ever since.

★ ★ ★

When Andrew topped the stairs, I was waiting for him in the hallway. I sat cross-legged on the floor, hands quiet on my lap. I had my eyes closed, listening to the low murmur of Evan's voice from the neighboring bedroom. I could feel currents of air whispering against my cheeks. Cold and warm. Light and dark.

I felt different. Tingling. Flushed. Powerful. As if maybe I was in the company of angels. The memories, I realized. I'd finally opened my mind. Allowed myself to know everything that I knew, and now it was as if I were back in the house that night, except this time my mother and siblings were beside me. We were united. Four against one.

And the images that filled my mind were both violent and painful.

'You don't have the gun,' Andrew stated. 'You failed.'

He took the first step forward, and I finally opened my eyes.

'Sheriff Wayne saved me,' I said, my voice strong. 'My father didn't kill himself that night.

489

SheriffWayne killed him.'

'You . . . you spoke to him?' Andrew sounded bewildered. He paused, six steps away, knife pressed against his pant leg.

'My mother loved him. Have you seen her on the interplanes? Have you asked her about that? SheriffWayne was a good man, and she cherished him for that.'

Andrew became immediately agitated. It proved what I was beginning to suspect.

'She called the sheriff after I spoke to her, after my father came home. She wanted to kick my father out. But my father refused to go. So she called your father — her lover, SheriffWayne — to assist.'

'He shouldn't have left his family,' Andrew snapped.

'Even a good man can be tempted,' I answered. 'Even a good man can want something he shouldn't have. Wayne came over as a man, not an officer of the law. He hoped to reason with my father, convince him to leave the property. Bullies crack under pressure, right? And everyone knew my father was a first-class bully.'

More agitation. The *whap whap* of the blade against Andrew's pant leg.

'It didn't go the way anyone planned. My father refused to budge from the bedroom, so SheriffWayne went upstairs to fetch him. They started to yell. Then my father spotted his gun, resting on the nightstand. He grabbed it, pointed it at SheriffWayne, just as my mother got between them. She took the bullet meant for her lover, dead before she hit the floor.'

Pictures again, like an old home movie streaming through my head. Had I crept out of my room that night, seen more than I'd known I'd seen? Or were the images from something else? The warmth caressing my cheek. The feel again — my mother, Natalie, Johnny. Four against one. The way it should've been that night, twenty-five years ago.

'My dad hesitated,' I whispered now, 'shocked by my mother's death. It gave Sheriff Wayne the time he needed to bolt from the house to his car. Service firearm, locked in the glove compartment. He had to work the key, hands trembling. Get the door open. Retrieve the nine-millimeter. Check the chamber.'

More images. A fourth presence, joining me in the hall.

'While he was gone, Natalie stuck her head out of her room. Johnny made a mad dash for the stairs. And my father started walking down the hall toward my bedroom.'

The air currents again, shifting. Hot and cold. Light and dark. Swelling.

'Sheriff Wayne saved my life,' I said loudly. 'He shot my father. He carried me from the carnage. Then he called for backup, never telling anyone what really brought him to the house that night. No point in harming his family with his dirty secret, now that my family was dead. As the officer in charge, he controlled the crime scene. That made it easy for him to write it up as a one-man rampage — my father killing most of his family before turning his gun on himself.

'Sheriff Wayne carried his guilt to his deathbed, where he finally confessed to his son. Is that what brought you to find me? Is that what convinced you I had to face my past, Andrew?'

I wondered if I'd see a spark of recognition in his eyes, a reaction to his name. But the swirling darkness around him remained impenetrable.

Evan's voice crested inside the closet, summoning the final angel, calling for the light.

'You didn't have to kill anyone,' I told Andrew. 'Your father's soul was freed the moment he confessed. He wasn't trapped in the void between the interplanes. But *my* father was . . . '

Andrew snarled. Fresh rage as he understood what I'd finally figured out. He raised his knife.

And I curled my fingers around the handle of the gun I'd found in the master bath. From my father's ashes dumped down a sewer, to his old service weapon taped to a toilet. In these last few seconds, it all started to make sense.

Andrew stormed down the hall.

And I had seen my father staring from his eyes.

My mother always smelled of oranges and ginger. She would feed me strawberry Popsicles on hot days, and stay up with me when I was sick. She loved the Sunday comics and used to pore over *Vogue* magazine, debating which expensive outfit she would one day love to buy.

Natalie liked to snack on fresh lemon slices sprinkled with sugar. She'd eat out the pulp, then curl the yellow peel over her teeth and smile at everyone. That last summer, she'd started using lemon juice to bleach out the freckles spattering across her nose. Though I never told her, I secretly loved her freckles and hoped every day to see some on my own face.

Johnny's favorite game had been hide-and-seek. He could contort his body into the tiniest spaces, and we couldn't find him. One day, he wedged himself behind the water heater and couldn't get out. Natalie laughed, but I could tell he was scared. I held his hand while my mother doused him in vegetable oil. Later, after he'd taken a bath, he shared his favorite comic book with me just to say thanks.

Andrew, charging. Six yards away, five, four . . .

My father, a crush of darkness roaring down upon me like a freight train.

. . . three, two . . .

'Evan!' a man cried behind Andrew. Michael Oliver, cresting the stairs.

'Michael, Michael, the police. They're here, they're here!' Victoria screamed from downstairs.

'Mommy!' Evan yelled from the bedroom closet. 'Mommy, Daddy!'

And then Andrew was upon me.

'Look out!' Michael roared.

A crash of breaking glass from the entryway.

'Daddy, Daddy, Daddy!'

Love and light. Light and love. A family's last stand.

'*Die!*' Andrew howled into my face, knife arcing down.

I thought of my mother's love, I remembered

my siblings' goofy grins. And this time I didn't hide.

I pulled the trigger.

* * *

The recoil snapped my arms up. The gun connected with Andrew's chin, knocking him backwards. Did I hit him? Was he bleeding? I couldn't tell. My ears were ringing, my eyes tearing from pain. My right hand throbbed, burnt from the ejecting brass.

Evan still screaming. Footsteps pounding up the stairs.

'Police, police! Drop your weapons!'

Andrew picking himself off the floor, shaking his head.

I noticed two things at once. His right side was bleeding, and he still held the knife.

He looked down at me and started to grin, just as Michael Oliver tackled him from behind.

'Son of a bitch. How dare you hurt my family. Son of a bitch!'

'Drop your weapon! For God's sake, drop it!'

Sergeant D. D. Warren had topped the stairs, blonde curls flying. She had her drawn weapon pointed at me, and her gaze locked on the tangle of grown men. Her partner, and Victoria, poured into the hall behind her.

'The police, Michael,' Victoria was trying to say. 'The *police*.'

'Mommy?' Evan cried from the closet.

'Drop your weapon!' D.D. screamed again.

I put down the gun, my gaze still on Andrew.

'Kick it away. Behind you,' D.D. ordered.

I did as I was told. Michael was on top of Andrew now, bashing Andrew's forehead into the floor.

'Stop it!' D.D. yelled angrily. 'Police! Get up, get away. *Now!*'

Her voice must have finally penetrated. Michael slowly released Andrew's hair. He rose shakily, breath shallow, expression wild. D.D.'s partner stepped forward to assist.

'Evan's in his closet,' I spoke up. 'He needs help. Please?'

Those words seemed to finally rouse Michael. He stepped back from Andrew. Victoria was already scurrying by the detectives into her son's room. She returned a minute later, Evan in her arms.

She looked at her husband. He looked at her. The next instant, they were together, parents, holding tight, their child cradled between them.

And I felt an ache, deep and endless inside my chest. My mother, Natalie, Johnny.

I love you. I love you. I love you. And I miss you so much.

A brush against my cheek. A flutter, like butterfly wings against my right temple. I wanted to hold on, hold close.

I love you, I thought again. Then I let go, as I should've done years ago.

The other detective was beside Andrew's prone form. He reached down to feel for a pulse while D.D. covered him with her gun.

The detective frowned, looked back at D.D., made a small shake of his head.

I realized then what we'd all missed before: the pool of blood slowly growing beneath Andrew's body. When Michael tackled him, Andrew had still been holding the knife. Apparently, it had finally found a target.

'Everyone out,' D.D. ordered flatly.

We moved to the driveway, where the sun was coming up. Michael and Victoria remained huddled close, Evan nestled between them, refusing to let their son go. I stood off to the side, turning my face toward the light.

Epilogue

VICTORIA

We've found a school for Evan. It's full-time care in a family-friendly environment in southern New Hampshire. The kids live in actual homes, with trained caretakers serving as surrogate parents. The campus includes a lake, huge gardens, and neighboring woods. The curriculum combines a structured schedule with plenty of outdoor time, where kids get to breathe fresh air, learn to garden, and benefit from the healing powers of nature.

The school even utilizes meditative training to help agitated children improve their self-soothing skills.

Evan's nervous, but not morally opposed. We can visit on weekends. If his behavior improves, he can come home for the holidays. It's beginning to feel manageable. Yes, he's on medication. Yes, he'll be going away. Yes, we have many 'learning opportunities' ahead.

But the school is beautiful. Evan's calmer. And our family is healing again.

The DA decided not to press charges against Evan. Our lawyer argued Evan had been unduly influenced by Andrew Lightfoot's now obviously violent tendencies. Prosecuting a child who'd just been kidnapped by his spiritual healer didn't make for great headlines, so the matter was quietly dismissed. After another week at the acute

497

care unit, a bit of tweaking with Evan's medication, and the development of a long-term plan, Evan was allowed to come home to finish out the summer before heading to his new school.

It gave me time to heal and go back-to-school shopping with my daughter.

Last week, Chelsea visited Evan and me twice, Michael acting as chaperone. Evan became over-excited, slamming his fingers in the front door, then tripping over his own feet and knocking his sister into the TV. But Chelsea hung in there, I hung in there, Michael hung in there. The calmer we remained, the calmer Evan became. By the end of the second evening, we even managed a family game of charades. Chelsea won. When I gave her a congratulatory hug, she clung to me and cried. So I cried with her.

Sometimes, that's just what you need to do.

The wedding has been postponed. More pressing matters to tend to, Michael told me, and I thought I saw some of the old familiar heat in his gaze. I know I felt it in mine.

I'm thinking of returning to interior decorating. I'm thinking of prizing every single second I have with my children. I'm thinking of being me again, independent, beautiful, and strong.

And I think if I do that, Michael doesn't stand a chance.

D.D.

D.D. loved it when a case came together. Andrew Ficke, aka Andrew Lightfoot, died at the scene, bleeding out after severing his femoral artery. Evidence, however, had a life of its own, and they found plenty of it.

A military-grade Taser was found on the front seat of Lightfoot's car. Tests determined it met the voltage requirements of the Taser used to attack Patrick Harrington, Hermes Laraquette, Danielle Burton, and Victoria Oliver. The Taser also contained custom cartridges, apparently available on the black market, that powered the device's twin wires without leaving behind any traceable confetti.

A search of Andrew's Rockport home also revealed a package of zip ties, same size, color, and durability as the ties used to subdue Danielle Burton and the Oliver family. Then there was the duffel bag in his car trunk, which lit up like the Fourth of July when tested for bodily fluids. The bag revealed three different blood types, most likely cross-contamination from once containing clothing stained with the blood of multiple murder victims.

Andrew Lightfoot was a known associate of all the victims. The police found no alibis for him on the nights of the murders, and security cameras showed him entering the hospital the evening Lucy was hanged. Fire investigators recovered fifteen smoke bombs in the ventilation system; latent prints recovered Andrew's prints from several of the devices, tying him explicitly to the emergency evacuation.

As far as D.D. was concerned, that was a wrap. Andrew had taken his world of spiritual interplanes a bit too seriously, convincing himself that the fate of his father's soul was more important than the continued corporal existence of various individuals. He had murdered A, believing he was saving B. Or more likely, he had just wanted to terrorize Danielle Burton after she rejected him.

Naturally, Alex argued with her. 'He was a spiritual healer. Man did good work, according to his clients — '

'Converts.'

'Clients. You don't go from being a respected shaman to a mass murderer overnight.'

'He was obsessed with Danielle. She wanted nothing to do with him. How much rejection can one man take?'

'According to her testimony, he wanted her to save his father's soul. How does killing two entire families accomplish that?'

'It didn't accomplish that,' D.D. pointed out with a shrug. 'Poor problem-solving skills. Definition of a murderer right there. Some guy wants a divorce, but doesn't want to lose half of his assets, so he kills his wife instead. Did he have to kill her? Were there other options that might have ended his marriage while preserving his bank account? Of course. But murderers don't see other options. That's why they're murderers.'

They were sitting in D.D.'s office. The other taskforce members had left. Case was closed, not to mention they'd heard this same conversation a couple of times before. That didn't stop D.D. and Alex.

'Yeah?' Alex continued now. 'And where in

business school and shaman studies did he cover how to slaughter an entire family? Single killing blow to a grown woman, as well as an athletic teenage boy? Not to mention how stone cold you gotta be to chase a screaming girl down the hall, then drag her back to her death. Or shoot a young girl in a dog bed. Or suffocate a baby in a cradle.'

'Merely proves how compartmentalized he was. Think about it: The man had two lives — Ficke the investment pro, Lightfoot the soul saver. Ficke was definitely not nice; he fucked women and screwed friends, all in the name of high finance. Then one day, Ficke up and reinvented himself as the kinder gentler Light-foot. Maybe in the beginning he honestly believed he saved his friend's life. Maybe, given some of the accounts of his work, he lived the life of woo-woo. But think about it: Healing is its own power trip. Next thing you know, the New Age adrenaline rush triggered his old predatory instincts. Andrew begins defrauding the state, taking advantage of overwhelmed mothers, and feeding his inner ego. Lightfoot returns to being Ficke, this time armed with a bunch of spiritual mumbo jumbo for manipulating the masses.'

'He wanted Danielle,' Alex said.

'Absolutely. All comes back to Danielle. The girl his father had once saved. The woman who still wouldn't do what Andrew said. Andrew *wanted* her, and Andrew always got what he wanted. Or no one else did.'

'Meaning one stubborn woman can drive a man over the edge.'

'It's a gift,' D.D. said modestly. 'Now case is closed. Perpetrator is dead. It's seven p.m. I haven't slept in four days. Why the hell are we still at work?'

'Because you haven't said yes.'

'To what?'

'To the chicken marsala I'm planning on making you. With a side of Italian bread, and a bottle of Chianti.'

'Is there tiramisu for dessert?' D.D. asked.

'Vanilla bean gelato.'

D.D. looked at him. Alex looked at her.

She sighed, took off her pager, set it carefully on her desk.

'Alex, take me home.'

DANIELLE

According to the police's final report, Andrew Lightfoot allegedly went crazy and murdered twelve people in his quest to gain my attention and save his father's soul. They used the term 'allegedly' because murdering twelve people is a complicated way of saving someone's soul. Or perhaps that's why they ruled him crazy.

I didn't contradict anything they said, though I had my own opinion on the subject. Nothing I could prove. Frankly, until a month ago, not even something I believed. But I work with children, and children are a powerful litmus test of human nature. At one time, kids loved Andrew. They responded to him. Even if I didn't consider myself a mumbo-jumbo sort of gal, I'd seen some of his results.

I don't think a madman could've helped those kids, particularly the hypersensitive ones, who would've perceived the taint. I think Andrew used to be Andrew. And I think, somewhere in his exploration of the celestial superhighway, he encountered a negative energy beyond his control. He met my father's corrupt soul, hoping to use him to learn more about his own father. Unfortunately, my father's spirit used Andrew to hunt me down in order to finish what he'd started twenty-five years ago.

There are things I'll never know. When carrying me into Evan's house, Andrew urged me to open my heart, to find the light. Was that the real Andrew pushing through, trying to help me survive? Or did my father simply assume that if he could get me to visit the land of interplanes, he could hurt me, too?

Don't know.

Is my father back in the abyss, even now waiting for the next corporal existence? I know I saw him that night, his eyes shining from Andrew's face. And I know I felt my mother, Natalie, Johnny, even Sheriff Wayne. Or maybe I just wanted to feel them. Maybe it was the illusion of seeing them that gave me strength. Then again, I found the gun. Surely that argues for my father's involvement, or I had a way-lucky guess.

I go back and forth, a thirty-four-year-old skeptic, discovering late in life that some part of her wants to believe.

I feel different these days. I remember my

family more often, and with less pain. I've lost my mother and siblings, and yet they're still with me.

Maybe there really are angels? Or maybe I've finally completed the five stages of grief?

Don't know.

What about Andrew? Assuming his soul was hijacked by my father's, did the end of corporal existence finally set him free? I asked Evan one day. He told me Andrew is an angel, and he talked to him just last night. Evan seemed relaxed about it, so I let it go. Evan's word is good enough for me.

The state buried Lucy. We took up a collection to pay for the marker. I ordered it shaped in the form of a sleeping cat, though the granite guy thought I was nuts. After her funeral, a giant rainbow appeared on the horizon. Strictly speaking, rainbows are a matter of light hitting water particles. I decided to view it as Lucy's spirit, granting us one last smile.

Maybe I do know.

I have a date.

He's handsome, solid, and currently unemployed. Karen fired Greg four weeks ago, saying his violation of unit policy left her no choice. Greg's thinking of either returning to school to become a psych nurse like me, or establishing a full-time respite-care business. In the meantime, he's busy assisting various families and soon, of course, he'll be even busier having sex with me.

I have moments when I'm still angry. I hate how easy it is for a parent to destroy the life of a child. I still see cases that break my heart. And I still make sure I walk way around any sewer grates.

But I get up each morning. And I find myself making the same vow each night.

I'm going to live with more light in my heart. I'm going to continue my work with troubled kids. And I'm going to fall in love with a really good man.

I'm the lone survivor, and this is what I've lived to tell.

Author's Note and Acknowledgments

When you hear of a first-grader being expelled for violence, you have a tendency to think of a kid with *those* parents. You know, the parents who don't care, aren't engaged, are perhaps violent themselves. So I was shocked two years ago when the troubled kid wasn't a stranger, but the son of a good friend. As parents went, she and her husband were caring, resourceful, and involved. And they still felt they were losing the war to save their child.

I'm indebted to this family for sharing their experiences with me. Their sessions with various specialists. Their multiple stays in a locked-down pediatric psych ward. And yes, their interaction with a spiritual healer who they believe has done the most to reach their child. They shared their story in hopes of garnering more understanding for mentally ill children and their often overwhelmed caretakers.

They'd like you to know that not all kids who can't sit still are brats. Not all kids who refuse to sleep are troublemakers. And not all kids who scream at the top of their lungs are disobedient.

They're kids, And they're trying. And so are their parents.

My deepest appreciation to Kathy Regan and

her staff at the Child Assessment Unit in Cambridge, Massachusetts. They tirelessly answered my questions, while allowing me to spend time on a real psychiatric ward. I could not have created my fictional psychiatric children's ward, PECB of the Kirkland Medical Center, without the benefit of learning about their experiences and approaches. While I allowed the fictional PECB to use a progressive approach inspired by CAU's impressive work, the center itself, its staff, and their actions are purely products of my (highly disturbed) imagination and bear no resemblance to the first-class operation run by Kathy and her staff at CAU.

For anyone who'd like more information on the CAU's progressive approach, I recommend *Opening Our Arms: Helping Troubled Kids Do Well*, by Kathy Regan. I also recommend *The Explosive Child*, by Dr. Ross W. Greene, for a detailed look at the collaborative problem-solving (CPS) approach.

On the more mundane side of research, a happy shout-out to my favorite pharmacist, Margaret Charpentier, who once again helped me pick the perfect poison. It's been a while since we've gotten to collaborate. I think the results are fun, as always.

Kill a Friend, Maim a Buddy: Congratulations to Audi Solis for being chosen as the sixth annual Lucky Stiff. I hope you enjoy your grand end. Sharing the fun across the Atlantic, Jo Rhodes won the Kill a Friend, Maim a Mate. According to Eleane Rhodes, it was the least I could do.

For anyone else who wants in on the action, the next sweepstakes should be up and running by September. Visit www.LisaGardner.com for more info.

Under 'Care and Feeding of Authors,' thank you to Michael Carr, whose pen functions more like a scalpel when editing a manuscript. I cried only for a little bit, and the book is better for it. My appreciation to my first readers, Kathleen, Barbara, and Diana, for doing an excellent job, as always, with the page proofs. And finally, the big guns — I couldn't do this without Meg, Kate, and the support of my entire publishing team. Thank you for making the magic happen.

On the home front, my love to my patient husband and my not very patient but always adorable child.

Finally, this book is in memory of Michael Clemons, a good man, gone too soon. We miss you.

We do hope that you have enjoyed reading this large print book.

Did you know that all of our titles are available for purchase?

We publish a wide range of high quality large print books including:
Romances, Mysteries, Classics
General Fiction
Non Fiction and Westerns

Special interest titles available in large print are:
The Little Oxford Dictionary
Music Book
Song Book
Hymn Book
Service Book

Also available from us courtesy of Oxford University Press:
Young Readers' Dictionary
(large print edition)
Young Readers' Thesaurus
(large print edition)

For further information or a free brochure, please contact us at:
Ulverscroft Large Print Books Ltd.,
The Green, Bradgate Road, Anstey,
Leicester, LE7 7FU, England.
Tel: (00 44) 0116 236 4325
Fax: (00 44) 0116 234 0205

Other titles published by
The House of Ulverscroft:

THE NEIGHBOUR

Lisa Gardner

It was a case guaranteed to spark a media feeding frenzy — a pretty young mother disappears without trace from her South Boston home. Her four-year-old daughter, the only witness — her handsome, secretive husband the prime suspect. But in the Jones's snug little bungalow, Detective Sergeant D.D. Warren suspects the picture of wholesome normality the couple has created. Jason and Sandra Jones seem like most hardworking couples raising a child. But under the surface things grow murkier. With the clock ticking on the life of a missing woman, the media firestorm is building and Jason Jones seems more intent on destroying evidence and isolating his daughter than on searching for his 'beloved' wife. Is the perfect husband trying to hide his guilt — or just trying to hide?

SAY GOODBYE

Lisa Gardner

Young women are disappearing . . . girls who
no one will notice have gone: prostitutes,
runaways, high-risk teens. One night they
exist, next morning they've vanished. But FBI
Special Agent Kimberly Quincy, five months
pregnant, has noticed. And when eighteen-
year-old Delilah Rose claims to have inside
information on the case, she will only talk to
Kimberly. After all, they both have something
in common: Delilah's pregnant too. Their
only lead — a man who gets his kicks in the
creepiest of ways. A twisted sadist with a
brutal past, Kimberly soon realises she must
become the prey if anyone else is to
survive . . .

HIDE

Lisa Gardner

The case had always haunted Bobby Dodge and now, in an underground chamber, the gruesome discovery of six mummified corpses resurrects his nightmare: the return of a killer he thought dead and buried. Bobby's only clue is a locket discovered with one of the dead — engraved with a name . . . Annabelle Granger has always been hiding, never knowing what her family was running from. When the body bearing her locket is unearthed, the danger is inescapable — but this time she won't run. Could it be the dead psychopath's copycat, his protégé — or something more terrifying? Dodge must solve the mystery of Annabelle Granger by teaming up with a woman who may be as dangerous as the new killer — a survivor-turned-avenger, with an eerie link to Annabelle . . .

GONE

Lisa Gardner

For ex-FBI profiler Pierce Quincy, it's his worst nightmare: a car abandoned on the Oregon highway, and his estranged wife, Rainie Conner, gone . . . Did a ghost from her past catch up with her? Or was it the result of one of the cases they were working on? With his daughter, FBI agent Kimberly Quincy, Pierce frantically searches for answers. Meanwhile, a man, adopting the alias of a killer from eighty years ago, has given the press his terms: he wants money, he wants power, he wants celebrity — or Rainie will be gone for good. As the deadline races ever nearer, Pierce plunges headlong into the search for a killer, and for the love of his life who may forever be . . . gone.

ALONE

Lisa Gardner

Massachusetts State Trooper Bobby Dodge watches a tense hostage stand-off unfold through the scope of his sniper rifle. Across the street, an armed man has barricaded himself in with his wife and child. The man's finger tightens on the trigger and Dodge has only a split second to react . . . Twenty-five years ago, the beautiful and dangerously sexy Catherine Rose Gagnon was buried underground during a month-long nightmare of abduction and abuse. Now, her husband has just been killed . . . What brings Bobby and Catherine together is a moment of violence — but what connects them is a passion far deeper and much more dangerous. For a killer is loose, and no one will see death coming until it has them cornered, helpless and alone . . .